H. P. LOVECRAFT'S
BOOK OF THE SUPERNATURAL

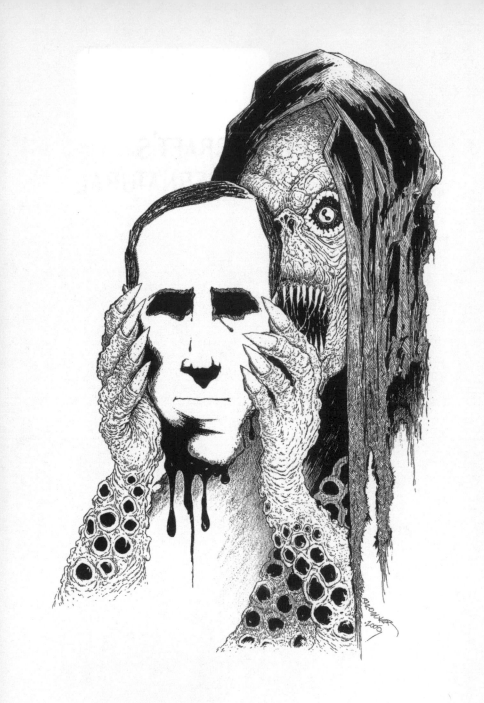

H. P. LOVECRAFT'S
BOOK OF THE SUPERNATURAL

20 Classics of the Macabre,
Chosen by the Master of Horror Himself

Edited by Stephen Jones

Illustrated by Randy Broecker

PEGASUS BOOKS
NEW YORK

H. P. LOVECRAFT'S BOOK OF THE SUPERNATURAL

Pegasus Books LLC
80 Broad Street, 5th Floor
New York, NY 10004

First Pegasus Books edition 2006
Fourth printing 2013

Library of Congress Cataloging-in-Publication Data is available.

ISBN: 1-933648-01-5

Interior design by Maria Fernandez

Printed in the United States of America
Distributed by W. W. Norton & Company, Inc.

For
Del and Sue,
who know what
Delicacies the Dark holds . . .

CONTENTS

ACKNOWLEDGMENTS

Special thanks to Claiborne Hancock, Randy and Sara Broecker, Hugh Lamb and Dorothy Lumley for all their help and support.

"Introduction: Supernatural Horror in Literature" copyright © Stephen Jones 2006

"Notes on Writing Weird Fiction" copyright © Arkham House Publishers, Inc. Originally published in *Amateur Correspondent* No. 1, May–June 1937 and *Supramundane Stories* No. 2, Spring 1938. Reprinted by permission of Arkham House Publishers, Inc.

"The Red Lodge" copyright © The Estate of H.R. Wakefield 1928. Originally published in They Return at Evening. Reprinted by permission of the author's agent, Curtis Brown Ltd.

"The Villa Désirée" copyright © The Estate of May Sinclair 1927. Originally published in *The Ghost-Book: Sixteen New Stories of the Uncanny*. Reprinted by permission of the author's agent, Curtis Brown Ltd.

"Novel of the White Powder" copyright © The Estate of Arthur Machen 1895. Originally published in *The Three Imposters*. Reprinted by permission of the author's agent, A.M. Heath & Company Ltd.

Editor's Note

Every effort has been made to trace the owners of the copyright material in this book. It is the Editor's belief that the necessary permissions from publishers, authors and authorized agents have been obtained, but in the case of any question arising as to the use of any material, the Editor, while expressing regret for any errors, will be pleased to make the necessary corrections in future editions of the book.

"Lovecraft opened the way for me, as he had done for others before me—Robert Bloch, Fritz Leiber, and Ray Bradbury among them. The reader would do well to remember that it is his shadow, so long and gaunt, and his eyes, so dark and puritanical, which overlie almost all of the important horror fiction that has come since."

—Stephen King

INTRODUCTION
Supernatural Horror in Literature

"The oldest and strongest emotion of mankind is fear."

—*H.P. Lovecraft*

I N NOVEMBER 1925, while he was briefly living in New York, H.P. Lovecraft was asked by his friend and fellow member of the United Amateur Press Association, W. Paul Cook, to write a study of supernatural fiction for Cook's early fanzine, *The Recluse*.

Howard Philips Lovecraft was already establishing his credentials as one of the most imaginative and influential authors of supernatural fiction of the twentieth century, with most of his tales appearing in the amateur press or the pulp magazine *Weird Tales*.

The 30,000-word piece, entitled "Supernatural Horror in Literature," was written in late 1925 or early 1926. It finally appeared in the first and only issue of Cook's magazine (alongside poetry by Lovecraft's friends Clark Ashton Smith and Frank Belknap Long, plus fiction by H. Warner Munn and Donald Wandrei), which was published in the middle of 1927.

Lovecraft's essay is now widely regarded as one of the earliest and most scholarly studies of horror fiction and its practitioners ever written. Opening with the observation, "The oldest and strongest emotion of mankind is fear," the author goes on to define the horror story by stating that, "a certain atmosphere of breathless and unexplainable dread of outer, unknown forces must be present."

After a general introduction, the article ranged over such topics as the early Gothic novel, European authors, Edgar Allan Poe (the only writer honored with his own chapter), the weird traditions in America and Britain, and such then-"modern" masters as Arthur Machen, Algernon Blackwood, Lord Dunsany and M.R. James.

The listing also exhibits an obvious bias towards what he terms the "literature of cosmic fear." This is a thematic concept that formed the central core of much of Lovecraft's own fiction—particularly a number of loosely connected stories about a banished alien race which once ruled the Earth and strive to return. These have subsequently become identified as "The Cthulhu Mythos."

Following the appearance of "Supernatural Horror in Literature" in *The Recluse,* Lovecraft almost immediately began making notes to update his essay, and a lightly revised version was serialized in Charles D. Hornig's *The Fantasy Fan* over seventeen installments between October 1933 and February 1935. However, the article was left incomplete when the magazine ceased publication.

Lovecraft apparently put the essay aside when *The Fantasy Fan* folded. Although he intended to work on it again at a later date, it was left unfinished at the time of his premature death in 1937.

It was this final—yet not completely revised—version of "Supernatural Horror in Literature" which Lovecraft's disciples August Derleth and Donald Wandrei included in their first collection of their mentor's best short stories, *The Outsider and Others* (1939), the first book published under their Arkham

House imprint (named after a fictitious New England town Lovecraft created).

Since then, Arkham has brought most of the author's work— stories, essays, verse and several volumes of correspondence— back into print, and "Supernatural Horror in Literature" has been widely reissued in collections and also as a single volume.

In the mid-1940s, the American critic Edmund Wilson (who was not a fan of Lovecraft's fiction) wrote: "Lovecraft himself, however, is a little more interesting than his stories. . . . His long essay on the fiction of supernatural horror is a really able piece of work. He shows his lack of sound literary taste in his enthusiasm for Machen and Dunsany, whom he more or less acknowledged as models, but he had read comprehensively in this field—he was strong on the Gothic novelists—and writes about it with much intelligence."

In 1993, Dave Carson and myself used the recommendations made by Lovecraft in his seminal essay as the basis for the anthology *H.P. Lovecraft's Book of Horror*, which also included the original article in its entirety.

This present volume is once again inspired by Lovecraft's recommendations and includes twenty entirely new selections and a number of different authors, each preceded by an appropriate excerpt from the essay.

It is a testament to the breadth of Lovecraft's knowledge and taste that yet another anthology of classic tales can be assembled from his insightful study of supernatural fiction, written eighty years ago but as relevant today as it was all that time ago.

And the concept is by no means exhausted yet . . .

—Stephen Jones
London, England
June 2005

FOREWORD
Notes on Writing Weird Fiction
H.P. Lovecraft

[1890–1937]

M Y REASON FOR WRITING stories is to give myself the satisfaction of visualising more clearly and detailedly and stably the vague, elusive, fragmentary impressions of wonder, beauty, and adventurous expectancy which are conveyed to me by certain sights (scenic, architectural, atmospheric, etc.), ideas, occurrences, and images encountered in art and literature. I choose weird stories because they suit my inclination best—one of my strongest and most persistent wishes being to achieve, momentarily, the illusion of some strange suspension or violation of the galling limitations of time, space, and natural law which forever imprison us and frustrate our curiosity about the infinite cosmic spaces beyond the radius of our sight and analysis. These stories frequently emphasise the element of horror because fear is our deepest and strongest emotion, and the one which best lends itself to the creation of Nature-defying illusions. Horror and the unknown or the strange are always closely connected, so that it is hard to create a convincing picture of shattered natural law or cosmic alienage or "outsideness" without laying stress on the emotion of fear. The reason why time plays a great part in so many of my tales is that this element looms up in my mind as the most profoundly dramatic and grimly terrible thing in the universe. *Conflict with time* seems to me the most potent and fruitful theme in all human expression.

While my chosen form of story-writing is obviously a special and perhaps a narrow one, it is none the less a persistent and permanent type of expression, as old as literature itself. There will always be a certain small percentage of persons who feel a burning curiosity about unknown outer space, and a burning desire to escape from the prison-house of the known and the real into those enchanted lands of incredible adventure and infinite possibilities which dreams open up to us, and which things like deep woods, fantastic urban towers, and flaming sunsets momentarily suggest. These persons include great authors as well as insignificant amateurs like myself—Dunsany, Poe, Arthur Machen, M. R. James, Algernon Blackwood, and Walter de la Mare being typical masters in this field.

As to how I write a story—there is no one way. Each one of my tales has a different history. Once or twice I have literally written out a dream; but usually I start with a mood or idea or image which I wish to express, and revolve it in my mind until I can think of a good way of embodying it in some chain of dramatic occurrences capable of being recorded in concrete terms. I tend to run through a mental list of the basic conditions or situations best adapted to such a mood or idea or image, and then begin to speculate on logical and naturally motivated explanations of the given mood or idea or image in terms of the basic condition or situation chosen.

The actual process of writing is of course as varied as the choice of theme and initial conception; but if the history of all my tales were analysed, it is just possible that the following set of rules might be deduced from the *average* procedure:

(1) Prepare a synopsis or scenario of events in the order of their absolute *occurrence*—not the order of their narration. Describe with enough fulness to cover all vital points and motivate all incidents planned. Details, comments, and estimates of consequences are sometimes desirable in this temporary framework.

(2) Prepare a second synopsis or scenario of events—this one in order of *narration* (not actual occurrence), with ample fulness and detail, and with notes as to changing perspective, stresses, and climax. Change the original synopsis to fit if such a change will increase the dramatic force or general effectiveness of the story. Interpolate or delete incidents at will—never being bound by the original conception even if the ultimate result be a tale wholly different from that first planned. Let additions and alterations be made whenever suggested by anything in the formulating process.

(3) Write out the story—rapidly, fluently, and not too critically —following the *second* or narrative-order synopsis. Change incidents and plot whenever the developing process seems to suggest such change, never being bound by any previous design. If the development suddenly reveals new opportunities for dramatic effect or vivid storytelling, add whatever is thought advantageous —going back and reconciling the early parts to the new plan. Insert and delete whole sections if necessary or desirable, trying different beginnings and endings until the best arrangement is found. But be sure that all references throughout the story are thoroughly reconciled with the final design. Remove all possible superfluities—words, sentences, paragraphs, or whole episodes or elements—observing the usual precautions about the reconciling of all references.

(4) Revise the entire text, paying attention to vocabulary, syntax, rhythm of prose, proportioning of parts, niceties of tone, grace and convincingness of transitions (scene to scene, slow and detailed action to rapid and sketchy time-covering action and vice versa . . . etc., etc., etc.), effectiveness of beginning, ending, climaxes, etc., dramatic suspense and interest, plausibility and atmosphere, and various other elements.

(5) Prepare a neatly typed copy—not hesitating to add final revisory touches where they seem in order.

The first of these stages is often purely a mental one—a set of conditions and happenings being worked out in my head, and never set down until I am ready to prepare a detailed synopsis of events in order of narration. Then, too, I sometimes begin even the actual writing before I know how I shall develop the idea—this beginning forming a problem to be motivated and exploited.

There are, I think, four distinct types of weird story; one expressing a *mood or feeling,* another expressing a *pictorial conception,* a third expressing a *general situation, condition, legend, or intellectual conception,* and a fourth explaining a *definite tableau or specific dramatic situation or climax.* In another way, weird tales may be grouped into two rough categories—those in which the marvel or horror concerns some *condition* or *phenomenon,* and those in which it concerns some *action of persons* in connexion with a bizarre condition or phenomenon.

Each weird story—to speak more particularly of the horror type—seems to involve five definite elements: (a) some basic, underlying horror or abnormality—condition, entity, etc.—, (b) the general effects or bearings of the horror, (c) the mode of manifestation—object embodying the horror and phenomena observed—, (d) the types of fear-reaction pertaining to the horror, and (e) the specific effects of the horror in relation to the given set of conditions.

In writing a weird story I always try very carefully to achieve the right mood and atmosphere, and place the emphasis where it belongs. One cannot, except in immature pulp charlatan-fiction, present an account of impossible, improbable, or inconceivable phenomena as a commonplace narrative of objective acts and conventional emotions. Inconceivable events and conditions have a special handicap to overcome, and this can be accomplished only through the maintenance of a careful realism in every phase of the story *except* that touching on the one given marvel. This marvel must be treated very impressively and deliberately—with a careful emotional "build-up"—else it will seem flat and unconvincing. Being the principal thing in the story, its mere existence should overshadow the characters and events. But the characters and events must be consistent and natural except where they touch the single marvel. In relation to the central wonder, the characters should shew the same overwhelming emotion which similar characters would shew toward such a wonder in real life. Never have a wonder taken for granted. Even when the characters are supposed to be accustomed to the wonder I try to weave an air of awe and impressiveness corresponding to what the reader should feel. A casual style ruins any serious fantasy.

Atmosphere, not action, is the great desideratum of weird fiction. Indeed, all that a wonder story can ever be is *a vivid picture of a certain type of human mood.* The moment it tries to be anything else it becomes cheap, puerile, and unconvincing. Prime emphasis should be given to *subtle suggestion*—imperceptible hints and touches of selective associative detail which express shadings of moods and build up a vague illusion of the strange reality of the unreal. Avoid bald catalogues of incredible happenings which can have no substance or meaning apart from a sustaining cloud of colour and symbolism.

These are the rules or standards which I have followed—consciously or unconsciously—ever since I first attempted the serious writing of fantasy. That my results are successful may well be disputed—but I feel at least sure that, had I ignored the considerations mentioned in the last few paragraphs, they would have been much worse than they are.

H. P. Lovecraft's
Book of the Supernatural

THE TALE OF THE GERMAN STUDENT
Washington Irving

[1783–1859]

"Washington Irving is another famous figure not unconnected with the weird; for though most of his ghosts are too whimsical and humorous to form genuinely spectral literature, a distinct inclination in this direction is to be noted in many of his productions. The *German Student* in *Tales of a Traveller* (1824) is a slyly concise and effective presentation of the old legends of the dead bride."

—*H.P. Lovecraft*

O N A STORMY NIGHT, in the tempestuous times of the French Revolution, a young German was returning to his lodgings, at a late hour, across the old part of Paris. The lightning gleamed, and the loud claps of thunder prattled through the lofty narrow streets—but I should first tell you something about this young German.

Gottfried Wolfgang was a young man of good family. He had studied for some time at Gottingen, but being of a visionary and enthusiastic character, he had wandered into those wild and speculative doctrines which have so often bewildered German students. His secluded life, his intense application, and the singular nature of his studies, had an effect on both mind and body. His health was impaired; his imagination diseased. He had been indulging in fanciful speculations on spiritual essences, until, like Swedenborg, he had an ideal world of his own around him. He took up a notion, I do not know from what cause, that there was an evil influence hanging over him; an evil genius or spirit seeking to ensnare him and insure his perdition. Such an idea working on his melancholy temperament produced the most gloomy effects. He became haggard and desponding. His friends discovered the mental malady preying upon him, and determined that the best cure was a change of scene; he was sent, therefore, to finish his studies amidst the splendors and gayeties of Paris.

Wolfgang arrived in Paris at the breaking out of the Revolution. The popular delirium at first caught his enthusiastic mind, and he was captivated by the political and philosophical theories of the day, but the scenes of blood which followed shocked his sensitive nature, disgusted him with society and the world, and made him more than ever a recluse. He shut himself up in a solitary apartment in the Pays Latin, the quarter of students. There, in a gloomy street not far from the monastic walls of the Sorbonne, he pursued his favorite speculations. Sometimes he spent hours in the great libraries of Paris, those catacombs of departed authors, rummaging among their hoards of dusty and obsolete works in quest of food for his unhealthy appetite. He was, in a manner, a literary ghoul, feeding in the charnel-house of decayed literature.

Wolfgang, though solitary and recluse, was of an ardent temperament, but for a time it operated merely upon his imagination. He was too shy and ignorant of the world to make any advances to the fair, but he was a passionate admirer of female beauty, and in his lonely chamber would often lose himself in reveries on forms and faces which he had seen, and his fancy would deck out images of loveliness far surpassing the reality.

While his mind was in this excited and sublimated state, a dream produced an extraordinary effect upon him. It was of a female face of transcendent beauty. So strong was the impression made, that he dreamed of it again and again. It haunted his thoughts by day, his slumbers by night; in fine, he became passionately enamored of his shadow of a dream. This lasted so long that it became one of those fixed ideas which haunt the minds of melancholy men, and are at times mistaken for madness.

Such was Gottfried Wolfgang, and such his situation at the time I mentioned. He was returning home late one stormy night, through some of the old and gloomy streets of the Marais, the ancient part of Paris. The loud claps of thunder rattled among the high houses of the narrow streets. He came to the Place de la Greve, the square where public executions are performed. The lightning quivered about the pinnacles of the ancient Hotel de Ville, and shed flickering gleams over the open space in front. As Wolfgang was crossing the square, he shrank back with horror at finding himself close by the guillotine. It was the height of the Reign of Terror (when this dreadful instrument of death stood ever ready, and its scaffold was continually running with the blood of the virtuous and the brave. It had that very day been actively employed in the work of carnage, and there it stood in grim array, amidst a silent and sleeping city, waiting for fresh victims.

Wolfgang's heart sickened within him, and he was turning shuddering from the horrible engine, when he beheld a shadowy form, cowering as it were at the foot of the steps which led up to the scaffold. A succession of vivid flashes of lightning revealed it more distinctly. It was a female figure, dressed in black. She was seated on one of the lower steps of the scaffold, leaning forward, her face hid in her lap; and her long disheveled tresses hanging to the ground, streaming with the rain which fell in torrents. Wolfgang paused. There was something awful in this solitary monument of woe. The female had the appearance of being above the common order. He knew the times to be full of vicissitude, and that many a fair head, which had been pillowed on down, now wandered houseless. Perhaps this was some poor mourner whom the dreadful ax had rendered desolate, and who sat here heartbroken on the strand of existence, from which all that was dear to her had been launched into eternity.

He approached, and addressed her in the accents of sympathy. She raised her head and gazed wildly at him. What was his astonishment at beholding, by the bright glare of the lightning, the very face which had haunted him in his dreams. It was pale and disconsolate, but ravishingly beautiful.

Trembling with violent and conflicting emotions, Wolfgang again accosted her. He spoke something of her being exposed at such an hour of the night, and to the fury of such a storm, and offered to conduct her to her friends. She pointed to the guillotine with a gesture of dreadful signification.

"I have no friend on earth," said she.

"But you have a home," said Wolfgang.

"Yes—in the grave!"

The heart of the student melted at the words.

"If a stranger dare make an offer," said he, "without danger of being misunderstood, I would offer my humble dwelling as a shelter; myself as a devoted friend. I am friendless myself in Paris, and a stranger in the land; but if my life could be of service, it is

at your disposal, and should be sacrificed before harm or indignity should come to you."

There was an honest earnestness in the young man's manner that had its effect. His foreign accent, too, was in his favor; it showed him not to be a hackneyed inhabitant of Paris. Indeed, there is an eloquence in true enthusiasm that is not to be doubted. The homeless stranger confided herself implicitly to the protection of the student.

He supported her faltering steps across the Pont Neuf, and by the place where the statue of Henry the Fourth had been overthrown by the populace. The storm had abated, and the thunder rumbled at a distance. All Paris was quiet; that great volcano of human passion slumbered for a while, to gather fresh strength for the next day's eruption. The student conducted his charge through the ancient streets of the Pays Latin, and by the dusky walls of the Sorbonne, to the great dingy hotel which he inhabited. The old portress who admitted them stared with surprise at the unusual sight of the melancholy Wolfgang with a female companion.

On entering his apartment, the student, for the first time, blushed at the scantiness and indifference of his dwelling. He had but one chamber—an old-fashioned salon—heavily carved, and fantastically furnished with the remains of former magnificence, for it was of those hotels in the quarter of the Luxembourg Palace which had once belonged to nobility. It was lumbered with books and papers, and all the usual apparatus of a student, and his bed stood in a recess at one end.

When lights were brought, and Wolfgang had a better opportunity of contemplating the stranger, he was more than ever intoxicated by her beauty. Her face was pale, but of a dazzling fairness, set off by a profusion of raven hair that hung clustering about it. Her eyes were large and brilliant, with a singular expression approaching almost to wildness. As far as her black dress permitted her shape to be seen, it was of perfect symmetry. Her whole appearance was highly striking, though she was dressed in the simplest style. The only thing approaching to an ornament which she wore, was a broad black band round her neck, clasped by diamonds.

The perplexity now commenced with the student how to dispose of the helpless being thus thrown upon his protection. He thought of abandoning his chamber to her, and seeking shelter for himself elsewhere. Still he was so fascinated by her charms, there seemed to be such a spell upon his thoughts and senses, that he could not tear himself from her presence. Her manner, too, was singular and unaccountable. She spoke no more of the guillotine. Her grief had abated. The attentions of the student had first won her confidence, and then, apparently, her heart. She was evidently an enthusiast like himself, and enthusiasts soon understand each other.

In the infatuation of the moment, Wolfgang avowed his passion for her. He told her the story of his mysterious dream, and how she had possessed his heart before he had even seen her. She was strangely affected by his recital, and acknowledged to have felt an impulse toward him equally unaccountable. It was the time for wild theory and wild actions. Old prejudices and superstitions were done away; everything was under the sway of the "Goddess of Reason." Among other rubbish of the old times, the forms and ceremonies of marriage began to be considered superfluous bonds for honorable minds. Social compacts were the vogue. Wolfgang was too much of a theorist not to be tainted by the liberal doctrines of the day.

"Why should we separate?" said he. "Our hearts are united; in the eye of reason and honor we are as one. What need is there of sordid forms to bind high souls together?"

The stranger listened with emotion; she had evidently received illumination at the same school.

"You have no home nor family," continued he; "let me be everything to you, or rather let us be everything to one another. If form is necessary, form shall be observed—there is my hand. I pledge myself to you forever."

"Forever?" said the stranger, solemnly.

"Forever!" repeated Wolfgang.

The stranger clasped the hand extended to her. "Then I am yours," murmured she, and sank upon his bosom.

The next morning the student left his bride sleeping, and sallied forth at an early hour to seek more spacious apartments, suitable to the change in his situation. When he returned, he found the stranger lying with her head hanging over the bed, and one arm thrown over it. He spoke to her, but received no reply. He advanced to awaken her from her uneasy posture. On taking her hand, it was cold—there was no pulsation—her face was pallid and ghastly—in a word, she was a corpse.

Horrified and frantic, he alarmed the house. A scene of confusion ensued. The police were summoned.

As the officer of police entered the room, he started back on beholding the corpse.

"Great heaven!" cried he; "how did this woman come here?"

"Do you know anything about her?" said Wolfgang eagerly.

"Do I?" exclaimed the police officer; "she was guillotined yesterday."

He stepped forward, undid the black collar round the neck of the corpse, and the head rolled on the floor!

The student burst into a frenzy. "The fiend! The fiend has gained possession of me!" shrieked he; "I am lost forever."

They tried to soothe him, but in vain. He was possessed with the frightful belief that an evil spirit had reanimated the dead body to ensnare him. He went distracted, and died in a madhouse.

MARKHEIM

Robert Louis Stevenson

[1850–1894]

"The romantic, semi-Gothic, quasi-moral tradition here represented was carried far down the nineteenth century by such authors as Joseph Sheridan LeFanu, Wilkie Collins, the late Sir H. Rider Haggard (whose *She* is really remarkably good), Sir Arthur Conan Doyle, H.G. Wells, and Robert Louis Stevenson—the latter of whom, despite an atrocious tendency toward jaunty mannerisms, created permanent classics in *Markheim, The Body Snatcher*, and *Dr. Jekyll and Mr. Hyde*."

—*H.P. Lovecraft*

Y ES," SAID THE DEALER, "our windfalls are of various kinds. Some customers are ignorant, and then I touch a dividend on my superior knowledge. Some are dishonest," and here he held up the candle, so that the light fell strongly on his visitor, "and in that case," he continued, "I profit by my virtue."

Markheim had but just entered from the daylight streets, and his eyes had not yet grown familiar with the mingled shine and darkness in the shop. At these pointed words, and before the near presence of the flame, he blinked painfully and looked aside.

The dealer chuckled. "You come to me on Christmas Day," he resumed, "when you know that I am alone in my house, put up my shutters, and make a point of refusing business. Well, you will have to pay for that; you will have to pay for my loss of time, when I should be balancing my books; you will have to pay, besides, for a kind of manner that I remark in you to-day very strongly: I am the essence of discretion, and ask no awkward questions; but when a customer cannot look me in the eye, he has to pay for it." The dealer once more chuckled; and then, changing to his usual business voice, though still with a note of irony, "You can give, as usual, a clear account of how you came into the possession of the object?" he continued. "Still your uncle's cabinet? A remarkable collector, sir!"

And the little pale, round-shouldered dealer stood almost on tip-toe, looking over the top of his gold spectacles, and nodding his head with every mark of disbelief. Markheim returned his gaze with one of infinite pity, and a touch of horror.

"This time," said he, "you are in error. I have not come to sell, but to buy. I have no curios to dispose of; my uncle's cabinet is bare to the wainscot; even were it still intact, I have done well on the Stock Exchange, and should more likely add to it than otherwise, and my errand to-day is simplicity itself. I seek a Christmas present for a lady," he continued, waxing more fluent as he struck into the speech he had prepared; "and certainly I owe you every excuse for thus disturbing you upon so small a matter. But the thing was neglected yesterday; I must produce my little compliment at dinner; and, as you very well know, a rich marriage is not a thing to be neglected."

There followed a pause, during which the dealer seemed to weigh this statement incredulously. The ticking of many clocks among the curious lumber of the shop, and the faint rushing of the cabs in a near thoroughfare, filled up the interval of silence.

"Well, sir," said the dealer, "be it so. You are an old customer after all; and if, as you say, you have the chance of a good marriage, far be it from me to be an obstacle. Here is a nice thing for a lady now," he went on, "this hand glass—fifteenth century, warranted; comes from a good collection, too; but I reserve the name, in the interests of my customer, who was just like yourself, my dear sir, the nephew and sole heir of a remarkable collector."

The dealer, while he thus ran on in his dry and biting voice, had stooped to take the object from its place; and, as he had done so, a shock had passed through Markheim, a start both of hand and foot, a sudden leap of many tumultuous passions to the face. It passed as swiftly as it came, and left no trace beyond a certain trembling of the hand that now received the glass.

"A glass," he said hoarsely, and then paused, and repeated it more clearly. "A glass? For Christmas? Surely not?"

"And why not?" cried the dealer. "Why not a glass?"

Markheim was looking upon him with an indefinable expression. "You ask me why not?" he said. "Why, look here—look in it—look at yourself! Do you like to see it? No! nor I—nor any man."

The little man had jumped back when Markheim had so suddenly confronted him with the mirror; but now, perceiving there was nothing worse on hand, he chuckled.

"Your future lady, sir, must be pretty hard favoured," said he.

"I ask you," said Markheim, "for a Christmas present, and you give me this—this damned reminder of years, and sins and follies—this hand-conscience! Did you mean it? Had you a thought in your mind? Tell me. It will be better for you if you do. Come, tell me about yourself. I hazard a guess now, that you are in secret a very charitable man?"

The dealer looked closely at his companion. It was very odd, Markheim did not appear to be laughing; there was something in his face like an eager sparkle of hope, nothing of mirth.

"What are you driving at?" the dealer asked.

"Not charitable?" returned the other, gloomily. "Not charitable; not pious; not scrupulous; unloving, unbeloved; a hand to get money, a safe to keep it. Is that all? Dear God, man, is that all?"

"I will tell you what it is," began the dealer, with some sharpness, and then broke off again into a chuckle. "But I see this is a love match of yours, and you have been drinking the lady's health."

"Ah!" cried Markheim, with a strange curiosity. "Ah, have you been in love? Tell me about that."

"I," cried the dealer. "I in love! I never had the time, nor have I the time to-day for all this nonsense. Will you take the glass?"

"Where is the hurry?" returned Markheim. "It is very pleasant to stand here talking; and life is so short and insecure that I would not hurry away from any pleasure—no, not even from so mild a one as this. We should rather cling, cling to what little we can get, like a man at a cliff's edge. Every second is a cliff, if you think upon it—a cliff a mile high—high enough, if we fall, to dash us out of every feature of humanity. Hence it is best to talk pleasantly. Let us talk of each other; why should we wear this mask? Let us be confidential. Who knows, we might become friends?"

"I have just one word to say to you," said the dealer. "Either make your purchase, or walk out of my shop."

"True, true," said Markheim. "Enough fooling. To business. Show me something else."

The dealer stooped once more, this time to replace the glass upon the shelf, his thin blond hair falling over his eyes as he did so. Markheim moved a little nearer, with one hand in the pocket of his greatcoat; he drew himself up and filled his lungs; at the same time many different emotions were depicted together on his face—

terror, horror, and resolve, fascination and a physical repulsion; and through a haggard lift of his upper lip, his teeth looked out.

"This perhaps, may suit," observed the dealer; and then, as he began to re-arise, Markheim bounded from behind upon his victim. The long, skewerlike dagger flashed and fell. The dealer struggled like a hen, striking his temple on the shelf, and then tumbled on the floor in a heap.

Time had some score of small voices in that shop, some stately and slow as was becoming to their great age; others garrulous and hurried. All these told out the seconds in an intricate chorus of tickings. Then the passage of a lad's feet, heavily running on the pavement, broke in upon these smaller voices and startled Markheim into the consciousness of his surroundings. He looked about him awfully. The candle stood on the counter, its flame solemnly wagging in a draught; and by that inconsiderable movement, the whole room was filled with noiseless bustle and kept heaving like a sea: the tall shadows nodding, the gross blots of darkness swelling and dwindling as with respiration, the faces of the portraits and the china gods changing and wavering like images in water. The inner door stood ajar, and peered into that leaguer of shadows with a long slit of daylight like a pointing finger.

From these fear-stricken rovings, Markheim's eyes returned to the body of his victim, where it lay both humped and sprawling, incredibly small and strangely meaner than in life. In these poor, miserly clothes, in that ungainly attitude, the dealer lay like so much sawdust. Markheim had feared to see it, and, lo! it was nothing. And yet, as he gazed, this bundle of old clothes and pool of blood began to find eloquent voices. There it must lie; there was none to work the cunning hinges or direct the miracle of locomotion—there it must lie till it was found. Found! ay, and then? Then would this dead flesh lift up a cry that would ring over England, and fill the world with the echoes of pursuit. Ay, dead or not, this was still the enemy. "Time was that when the brains were out," he thought; and the first word struck into his mind. Time, now that the deed was accomplished—time, which had closed for the victim, had become instant and momentous for the slayer.

The thought was yet in his mind, when, first one and then another, with every variety of pace and voice—one deep as the bell from a cathedral turret, another ringing on its treble notes the prelude of a waltz—the clocks began to strike the hour of three in the afternoon.

The sudden outbreak of so many tongues in that dumb chamber staggered him. He began to bestir himself, going to and fro with the candle, beleaguered by moving shadows, and startled to the soul by chance reflections. In many rich mirrors, some of home designs, some from Venice or Amsterdam, he saw his face repeated and repeated, as it were an army of spies; his own eyes met and detected him; and the sound of his own steps, lightly as they fell, vexed the surrounding quiet. And still as he continued to fill his pockets, his mind accused him, with a sickening iteration, of the thousand faults of his design. He should have chosen a more quiet hour; he should have prepared an alibi; he should not have used a knife; he should have been more cautious, and only bound and gagged the dealer, and not killed him; he should have been more bold, and killed the servant also; he should have done all things otherwise; poignant regrets, weary, incessant toiling of the mind to change what was unchangeable, to plan what was now useless, to be the architect of the irrevocable past. Meanwhile, and behind all this activity, brute terrors, like the scurrying of rats in a deserted attic, filled the more remote chambers of his brain with riot; the hand of the constable would fall heavy on his shoulder, and his nerves would jerk like a hooked fish; or he beheld, in galloping defile, the dock, the prison, the gallows, and the black coffin.

Terror of the people in the street sat down before his mind like a besieging army. It was impossible, he thought, but that some rumour of the struggle must have reached their ears and set on edge their curiosity; and now, in all the neighbouring houses, he divined them sitting motionless and with uplifted ear—solitary people, condemned to spend Christmas dwelling alone on memories of the past, and now startingly recalled from that tender exercise; happy family parties, struck into silence round the table, the mother still with raised finger: every degree and age and humour, but all, by their own hearths, prying and hearkening and weaving the rope that was to hang him. Sometimes it seemed to him he could not move too softly; the clink of the tall Bohemian goblets rang out loudly like a bell; and alarmed by the bigness of the ticking, he was tempted to stop the clocks. And then, again, with a swift transition of his terrors, the very silence of the place appeared a source of peril, and a thing to strike and freeze the passer-by; and he would step more boldly, and bustle aloud among the contents of the shop, and imitate, with elaborate bravado, the movements of a busy man at ease in his own house.

But he was now so pulled about by different alarms that, while one portion of his mind was still alert and cunning, another trembled on the brink of lunacy. One hallucination in particular took a strong hold on his credulity. The neighbour hearkening with white face beside his window, the passer-by arrested by a horrible surmise on the pavement—these could at worst suspect, they could not know; through the brick walls and shuttered windows only sounds could penetrate. But here, within the house, was he alone? He knew he was; he had watched the servant set forth sweethearting, in her poor best, "out for the day" written in every ribbon and smile. Yes, he was alone, of course; and yet, in the bulk of empty house above him, he could surely hear a stir of delicate footing—he was surely conscious, inexplicably conscious of some presence. Ay, surely; to every room and corner of the house his imagination followed it; and now it was a faceless thing, and yet had eyes to see with; and again it was a shadow of himself; and yet again behold the image of the dead dealer, reinspired with cunning and hatred.

At times, with a strong effort, he would glance at the open door which still seemed to repel his eyes. The house was tall, the skylight small and dirty, the day blind with fog; and the light that filtered down to the ground story was exceedingly faint, and showed dimly on the threshold of the shop. And yet, in that strip of doubtful brightness, did there not hang wavering a shadow?

Suddenly, from the street outside, a very jovial gentleman began to beat with a staff on the shop-door, accompanying his blows with shouts and railleries in which the dealer was continually called upon by name. Markheim, smitten into ice glanced at the dead man. But no! he lay quite still; he was fled away far beyond earshot of these blows and shoutings; he was sunk beneath seas of silence; and his name, which would once have caught his notice above the howling of a storm, had become an empty sound. And presently the jovial gentleman desisted from his knocking and departed.

Here was a broad hint to hurry what remained to be done, to get forth from this accusing neighbourhood, to plunge into a bath of London multitudes, and to reach, on the other side of day, that haven of safety and apparent innocence—his bed. One visitor had come: at any moment another might follow and be more obstinate. To have done the deed, and yet not to reap the profit, would be too abhorrent a failure. The money, that was now Markheim's concern; and as a means to that, the keys.

He glanced over his shoulder at the open door, where the shadow was still lingering and shivering; and with no conscious repugnance of the mind, yet with a tremor of the belly, he drew near the body of his victim. The human character had quite departed. Like a suit half-stuffed with bran, the limbs lay scattered, the trunk doubled, on the floor; and yet the thing repelled him. Although so dingy and inconsiderable to the eye, he feared it might have more significance to the touch. He took the body by the shoulders, and turned it on its back. It was strangely light and supple, and the limbs, as if they had been broken, fell into the oddest postures. The face was robbed of all expression; but it was as pale as wax, and shockingly smeared with blood about one temple. That was, for Markheim, the one displeasing circumstance. It carried him back, upon the instant, to a certain fair day in a fishers' village: a gray day, a piping wind, a crowd upon the street, the blare of brasses, the booming of drums, the nasal voice of a ballad singer; and a boy going to and fro, buried over head in the crowd and divided between interest and fear, until, coming out upon the chief place of concourse, he beheld a booth and a great screen with pictures, dismally designed, garishly coloured: Brownrigg with her apprentice; the Mannings with their murdered guest; Weare in the death-grip of Thurtell; and a score besides of famous crimes. The thing was as clear as an illusion; he was once again that little boy; he was looking once again, and with the same sense of physical revolt, at these vile pictures; he was still stunned by the thumping of the drums. A bar of that day's music returned upon his memory; and at that, for the first time, a qualm came over him, a breath of nausea, a sudden weakness of the joints, which he must instantly resist and conquer.

He judged it more prudent to confront than to flee from these considerations; looking the more hardily in the dead face, bending his mind to realise the nature and greatness of his crime. So little a while ago that face had moved with every change of sentiment, that pale mouth had spoken, the body had been all on fire with governable energies; and now, and by his act, that piece of life had been arrested, as the horologist, with interjected finger, arrests the beating of the clock. So he reasoned in vain; he could rise to no more remorseful consciousness; the same heart which had shuddered before the painted effigies of crime, looked on its reality unmoved. At best, he felt a gleam of pity for one who had been endowed in vain with all those faculties that can make the world a garden of enchantment, one who had never lived and who was now dead. But of penitence, no, not a tremor.

With that, shaking himself clear of these considerations, he found the keys and advanced towards the open door of the shop. Outside, it had begun to rain smartly; and the sound of the shower upon the roof had banished silence. Like some dripping cavern, the chambers of the house were haunted by an incessant echoing, which filled the ear and mingled with the ticking of the clocks. And, as Markheim approached the door, he seemed to hear, in answer to his own cautious tread, the steps of another foot withdrawing up the stair. The shadow still palpitated loosely on the threshold. He threw a ton's weight of resolve upon his muscles, and drew back the door.

The faint, foggy daylight glimmered dimly on the bare floor and stairs; on the bright suit of armour posted, halbert in hand, upon the landing; and on the dark wood-carvings, and framed pictures that hung against the yellow panels of the wainscot. So loud was the beating of the rain through all the house that, in Markheim's ears, it began to be distinguished into many different sounds. Footsteps and sighs, the tread of regiments marching in the distance, the chink of money in the counting, and the creaking of doors held stealthily ajar, appeared to mingle with the patter of the drops upon the cupola and the gushing of the water in the pipes. The sense that he was not alone grew upon him to the verge of madness. On every side he was haunted and begirt by presences. He heard them moving in the upper chambers; from the shop, he heard the dead man getting to his legs; and as he began with a great effort to mount the stairs, feet fled quietly before him and followed stealthily behind. If he were but deaf, he thought, how tranquilly he would possess his soul! And then again, and hearkening with ever fresh attention, he blessed himself for that unresting sense which held the outposts and stood a trusty sentinel upon his life. His head turned continually on his neck; his eyes, which seemed starting from their orbits, scouted on every side, and on every side were half-rewarded as with the tail of something nameless vanishing. The four-and-twenty steps to the first floor were four-and-twenty agonies.

On that first storey, the doors stood ajar, three of them like three ambushes, shaking his nerves like the throats of cannon. He could never again, he felt, be sufficiently immured and fortified from men's observing eyes; he longed to be home, girt in by walls, buried among bedclothes, and invisible to all but God. And at that thought he wondered a little, recollecting tales of other murderers and the fear they were said to entertain of heavenly avengers. It was not so, at least, with him. He feared the laws of nature, lest, in their callous and immutable procedure, they should preserve some damning evidence of his crime. He feared tenfold more, with a slavish, superstitious terror, some scission in the continuity of man's experience, some wilful illegality of nature. He played a game of skill, depending on the rules, calculating consequence from cause; and what if nature, as the defeated tyrant overthrew the chess-board, should break the mould of their succession? The like had befallen Napoleon (so writers said) when the winter changed the time of its appearance. The like might befall Markheim: the solid walls might become transparent and reveal his doings like those of bees in a glass hive; the stout planks might yield under his foot like quicksands and detain him in their clutch; ay, and there were soberer accidents that might destroy him: if, for instance, the house should fall and imprison him beside the body of his victim; or the house next door should fly on fire, and the firemen invade him from all sides. These things he feared; and, in a sense, these things might be called the hands of God reached forth against sin. But about God himself he was at ease; his act was doubtless exceptional, but so were his excuses, which God knew; it was there, and not among men, that he felt sure of justice.

When he had got safe into the drawing-room, and shut the door behind him, he was aware of a respite from alarms. The room was quite dismantled, uncarpeted besides, and strewn with packing cases and incongruous furniture; several great pier-glasses, in which he beheld himself at various angles, like an actor on a stage; many pictures, framed and unframed, standing, with their faces to the wall; a fine Sheraton sideboard, a cabinet of marquetry, and a great old bed, with tapestry hangings. The windows opened to the floor; but by great good fortune the lower part of the shutters had been closed, and this concealed him from the neighbours. Here, then, Markheim drew in a packing case before the cabinet, and began to search among the keys. It was a long business, for there were many; and it was irksome, besides; for, after all, there might be nothing in the cabinet, and time was on the wing. But the closeness of the occupation sobered him. With the tail of his eye he saw the door—even glanced at it from time to time directly, like a besieged commander pleased to verify the good estate of his defences. But in truth he was at peace. The rain falling in the street sounded natural and pleasant. Presently, on the other side, the notes of a piano were wakened to the music of a hymn, and the voices of many children took up the air and words. How stately, how comfortable was the melody! How fresh the youthful voices! Markheim gave ear to it smilingly, as he sorted out the keys; and his mind was thronged with answerable ideas and images; church-going children and the pealing of the high organ; children afield, bathers by the brookside, ramblers on the brambly common, kite-flyers in the windy and cloud-navigated sky; and then, at another cadence of the hymn, back again to church, and the somnolence of summer Sundays, and the high genteel voice of the parson (which he smiled a little to recall) and the painted Jacobean tombs, and the dim lettering of the Ten Commandments in the chancel.

And as he sat thus, at once busy and absent, he was startled to his feet. A flash of ice, a flash of fire, a bursting gush of blood, went over him, and then he stood transfixed and thrilling. A step mounted the stair slowly and steadily, and presently a hand was laid upon the knob, and the lock clicked, and the door opened.

Fear held Markheim in a vice. What to expect he knew not, whether the dead man walking, or the official ministers of human justice, or some chance witness blindly stumbling in to consign him to the gallows. But when a face was thrust into the aperture, glanced round the room, looked at him, nodded and smiled as if in friendly recognition, and then withdrew again, and the door closed behind it, his fear broke loose from his control in a hoarse cry. At the sound of this the visitant returned.

"Did you call me?" he asked, pleasantly, and with that he entered the room and closed the door behind him.

Markheim stood and gazed at him with all his eyes. Perhaps there was a film upon his sight, but the outlines of the newcomer seemed to change and waver like those of the idols in the wavering candle-light of the shop; and at times he thought he knew him; and at times he thought he bore a likeness to himself; and always, like a lump of living terror, there lay in his bosom the conviction that this thing was not of the earth and not of God.

And yet the creature had a strange air of the commonplace, as he stood looking on Markheim with a smile; and when he added: "You are looking for the money, I believe?" it was in the tones of everyday politeness.

Markheim made no answer.

"I should warn you," resumed the other, "that the maid has left her sweetheart earlier than usual and will soon be here. If Mr. Markheim be found in this house, I need not describe to him the consequences."

"You know me?" cried the murderer.

The visitor smiled. "You have long been a favorite of mine," he said; "and I have long observed and often sought to help you."

"What are you?" cried Markheim: "the devil?"

"What I may be," returned the other, "cannot affect the service I propose to render you."

"It can," cried Markheim; "it does! Be helped by you? No, never; not by you! You do not know me yet; thank God, you do not know me!"

"I know you," replied the visitant, with a sort of kind severity or rather firmness. "I know you to the soul."

"Know me!" cried Markheim. "Who can do so? My life is but a travesty and slander on myself. I have lived to belie my nature. All men do; all men are better than this disguise that grows about and stifles them. You see each dragged away by life, like one whom bravos have seized and muffled in a cloak. If they had their own control—if you could see their faces, they would be altogether different, they would shine out for heroes and saints! I am worse than most; myself is more overlaid; my excuse is known to me and God. But, had I the time, I could disclose myself."

"To me?" inquired the visitant.

"To you before all," returned the murderer. "I supposed you were intelligent. I thought—since you exist—you would prove a reader of the heart. And yet you would propose to judge me by my acts! Think of it; my acts! I was born and I have lived in a land of giants; giants have dragged me by the wrists since I was born out of my mother—the giants of circumstance. And you would judge me by my acts! But can you not look within? Can you not understand that evil is hateful to me? Can you not see within me the clear writing of conscience, never blurred by any wilful sophistry, although too often disregarded? Can you not read me for a thing that surely must be common as humanity—the unwilling sinner?"

"All this is very feelingly expressed," was the reply, "but it regards me not. These points of consistency are beyond my province, and I care not in the least by what compulsion you may have been dragged away, so as you are but carried in the right direction. But time flies; the servant delays, looking in the faces of the crowd and at the pictures on the hoardings, but still she keeps moving nearer; and remember, it is as if the gallows itself was striding towards you through the Christmas streets! Shall I help you; I, who know all? Shall I tell you where to find the money?"

"For what price?" asked Markheim.

"I offer you the service for a Christmas gift," returned the other.

Markheim could not refrain from smiling with a kind of bitter triumph. "No," said he, "I will take nothing at your hands; if I were dying of thirst, and it was your hand that put the pitcher to my lips, I should find the courage to refuse. It may be credulous, but I will do nothing to commit myself to evil."

"I have no objection to a death-bed repentance," observed the visitant.

"Because you disbelieve their efficacy!" Markheim cried.

"I do not say so," returned the other; "but I look on these things from a different side, and when the life is done my interest falls. The man has lived to serve me, to spread black looks under colour of religion, or to sow tares in the wheat-field, as you do, in a course of weak compliance with desire. Now that he draws so near to his deliverance, he can add but one act of service—to repent, to die smiling, and thus to build up in confidence and hope the more timorous of my surviving followers. I am not so hard a master. Try me. Accept my help. Please yourself in life as you have done hitherto; please yourself more amply, spread your elbows at the board; and when the night begins to fall and the curtains to be drawn, I tell you, for your greater comfort, that you will find it even easy to compound your quarrel with your conscience, and to make a truckling peace with God. I came but now from such a deathbed, and the room was full of sincere mourners, listening to the man's last words: and when I looked into that face, which had been set as a flint against mercy, I found it smiling with hope."

"And do you, then, suppose me such a creature?" asked Markheim. "Do you think I have no more generous aspirations than to sin, and sin, and sin, and, at last, sneak into heaven? My heart rises at the thought. Is this, then, your experience of mankind? or is it because you find me with red hands that you presume such baseness? and is this crime of murder indeed so impious as to dry up the very springs of good?"

"Murder is to me no special category," replied the other. "All sins are murder, even as all life is war. I behold your race, like starving mariners on a raft, plucking crusts out of the hands of famine and feeding on each other's lives. I follow sins beyond the moment of their acting; I find in all that the last consequence is death; and to my eyes, the pretty maid who thwarts her mother with such taking graces on a question of a ball, drips no less visibly with human gore than such a murderer as yourself. Do I say that I follow sins? I follow virtues also; they differ not by the thickness of a nail, they are both scythes for the reaping angel of Death. Evil, for which I live, consists not in action but in character. The bad man is dear to me; not the bad act, whose fruits, if we could follow them far enough down the hurtling cataract of the ages, might yet be found more blessed than those of the rarest virtues. And it is not because you have killed a dealer, but because you are Markheim, that I offered to forward your escape."

"I will lay my heart open to you," answered Markheim. "This crime on which you find me is my last. On my way to it I have learned many lessons; itself is a lesson, a momentous lesson. Hitherto I have been driven with revolt to what I would not; I was a bondslave to poverty, driven and scourged. There are robust virtues that can stand in these temptations; mine was not so: I had a thirst of pleasure. But to-day, and out of this deed, I pluck both warning and riches—both the power and a fresh resolve to be myself. I become in all things a free actor in the world; I begin to see myself all changed, these hands the agents of good, this heart at peace. Something comes over me out of the past; something of what I have dreamed on Sabbath evenings to the sound of the church organ, of what I forecast when I shed tears over noble books, or talked, an innocent child, with my mother. There lies my life; I have wandered a few years, but now I see once more my city of destination."

"You are to use this money on the Stock Exchange, I think?" remarked the visitor; "and there, if I mistake not, you have already lost some thousands?"

"Ah," said Markheim, "but this time I have a sure thing."

"This time, again, you will lose," replied the visitor quietly.

"Ah, but I keep back the half!" cried Markheim.

"That also you will lose," said the other.

The sweat started upon Markheim's brow. "Well, then, what matter?" he exclaimed. "Say it be lost, say I am plunged again in poverty, shall one part of me, and that the worse, continue until the end to override the better? Evil and good run strong in me, haling me both ways. I do not love the one thing, I love all. I can conceive great deeds, renunciations, martyrdoms; and though I be fallen to such a crime as murder, pity is no stranger to my thoughts. I pity the poor; who knows their trials better than myself? I pity and help them; I prize love, I love honest laughter; there is no good thing nor true thing on earth but I love it from my heart. And are my vices only to direct my life, and my virtues to lie without effect, like some passive lumber of the mind? Not so; good, also, is a spring of acts."

But the visitant raised his finger. "For six-and-thirty years that you have been in this world," said he, "through many changes of fortune and varieties of humour, I have watched you steadily fall. Fifteen years ago you would have started at a theft. Three years back you would have blenched at the name of murder. Is there any crime, is there any cruelty or meanness, from which you still recoil?—five years from now I shall detect you in the fact! Downward, downward, lies your way; nor can anything but death avail to stop you."

"It is true," Markheim said huskily, "I have in some degree complied with evil. But it is so with all: the very saints, in the mere exercise of living, grow less dainty, and take on the tone of their surroundings."

"I will propound to you one simple question," said the other; "and as you answer, I shall read to you your moral horoscope. You have grown in many things more lax; possibly you do right to be so; and at any account, it is the same with all men. But granting that, are you in any one particular, however trifling, more difficult to please with your own conduct, or do you go in all things with a looser rein?"

"In any one?" repeated Markheim, with an anguish of consideration. "No," he added, with despair, "in none! I have gone down in all."

"Then," said the visitor, "content yourself with what you are, for you will never change; and the words of your part on this stage are irrevocably written down."

Markheim stood for a long while silent, and indeed it was the visitor who first broke the silence. "That being so," he said, "shall I show you the money?"

"And grace?" cried Markheim.

"Have you not tried it?" returned the other. "Two or three years ago, did I not see you on the platform of revival meetings, and was not your voice the loudest in the hymn?"

"It is true," said Markheim; "and I see clearly what remains for me by way of duty. I thank you for these lessons from my soul; my eyes are opened, and I behold myself at last for what I am."

At this moment, the sharp note of the door-bell rang through the house; and the visitant, as though this were some concerted signal for which he had been waiting, changed at once in his demeanour.

"The maid!" he cried. "She has returned, as I forewarned you, and there is now before you one more difficult passage. Her master, you must say, is ill; you must let her in, with an assured but rather serious countenance—no smiles, no overacting, and I promise you success! Once the girl within, and the door closed, the same dexterity that has already rid you of the dealer will relieve you of this last danger in your path. Thenceforward you have the whole evening—the whole night, if needful—to ransack the treasures of the house and to make good your safety. This is help that comes to you with the mask of danger. Up!" he cried: "up, friend; your life hangs trembling in the scales; up, and act!"

Markheim steadily regarded his counsellor. "If I be condemned to evil acts," he said, "there is still one door of freedom open—I can cease from action. If my life be an ill thing, I can lay it down. Though

I be, as you say truly, at the beck of every small temptation, I can yet, by one decisive gesture, place myself beyond the reach of all. My love of good is damned to barrenness; it may, and let it be! But I have still my hatred of evil; and from that, to your galling disappointment, you shall see that I can draw both energy and courage."

The features of the visitor began to undergo a wonderful and lovely change: they brightened and softened with a tender triumph; and, even as they brightened, faded and dislimned. But Markheim did not pause to watch or understand the transformation. He opened the door and went downstairs very slowly, thinking to himself. His past went soberly before him; he beheld it as it was, ugly and strenuous like a dream, random as chance-medley—a scene of defeat. Life, as he thus reviewed it, tempted him no longer; but on the further side he perceived a quiet haven for his bark. He paused in the passage, and looked into the shop, where the candle still burned by the dead body. It was strangely silent. Thoughts of the dealer swarmed into his mind, as he stood gazing. And then the bell once more broke out into impatient clamour.

He confronted the maid upon the threshold with something like a smile.

"You had better go for the police," said he: "I have killed your master."

WHO KNOWS?

Guy de Maupassant

[1850–1893]

"The horror-tales of the powerful and cynical Guy de Maupassant, written as his final madness gradually overtook him, present individualities of their own; being rather the morbid outpourings of a realistic mind in a pathological state than the healthy imaginative products of a vision naturally disposed toward phantasy and sensitive to the normal illusions of the unseen. Nevertheless they are of the keenest interest and poignancy; suggesting with marvelous force the imminence of nameless terrors, and the relentless dogging of an ill-starred individual by hideous and menacing representatives of the outer blackness. Of these stories *The Horla* is generally regarded as the masterpiece. . . . Other potently dark creations of de Maupassant are *Who Knows?, The Spectre, He, The Diary of a Madman, The White Wolf, On the River*, and the grisly verse entitled *Horror*."

—*H.P. Lovecraft*

I

MERCIFUL HEAVEN! At last I've made up my mind to put on record what I've been through! But shall I ever be able to do it, shall I have the courage? It's all so mysterious, so inexplicable, so unintelligible, so crazy!

If I were not sure of what I've seen, certain that there has been no flaw in my reasoning, no mistake in my facts, no gap in the strict sequence of my observations, I should consider myself merely the victim of a hallucination, the sport of some strange optical delusion.

After all, who knows?

To-day I am in a Mental Home, but I went there of my own free will, as a precaution, because I was afraid. Only one man knows my story, the House Doctor. Now I'm going to put it on paper, I really don't quite know why. Perhaps in order to shake off the obsession, which haunts me like some ghastly nightmare.

Anyhow, here it is:

I have always been a lonely man, a dreamer, a kind of solitary: good-natured, easily satisfied, harbouring no bitterness against mankind and no grudge against Heaven. I have always lived alone, because of a sort of uneasiness, which the presence of others sets up in me. How can I explain it? I can't. It's not that I shun society; I enjoy conversation, and dining with my friends, but when I am conscious of them near me, even the most inti-mate, for any length of time, I feel tired, exhausted, on edge, and I am aware of a growing and distressing desire to see them go away or to go away myself and be alone.

This desire is more than a mere craving, it is an imperative necessity. And if I had to remain in their company, if I had to go on, I do not say listening to, but merely hearing their conversa-tion, I am sure something dreadful would happen. What? Who knows? Possibly, yes, probably, I should simply collapse.

I am so fond of being alone that I cannot even endure the proximity of other human beings sleeping under the same roof; I cannot live in Paris; it is a long-drawn-out fight for life to me. It is spiritual death: this huge, swarming crowd living all round me, even in its sleep, causes me physical and nervous torture. Indeed other people's sleep is even more painful to me than their conversation. And I can never rest, when I know or feel that there are living beings, on the other side of the wall, suffering this nightly suspension of consciousness.

Why do I feel like this? Who knows? Perhaps the reason is quite simple: I get tired very quickly of anything outside myself. And there are many people like me.

There are two kinds of human beings. Those who need others, who are distracted, amused, soothed by company, while loneliness, such as the ascent of some forbidding glacier or the crossing of a desert, worries them, exhausts them, wears them out: and those whom, on the contrary, the society of their fellows wearies, bores, irritates, cramps, while solitude gives them peace and rest in the unshackled world of their phantasy.

It is, in fact, a recognized psychological phenomenon. The former are equipped to lead the life of the extrovert, the latter that of the introvert. In my own case my ability to concentrate on things outside myself is limited and quickly exhausted, and as soon as this limit is reached I am conscious of unbearable physical and mental discomfort. The result of this has been that I am, or rather I was, very much attached to inanimate objects, which take on for me the importance of human beings, and that my house has, or rather had, become a world in which I led a lonely but purposeful life, surrounded by things, pieces of furniture and ornaments that I knew and loved like friends. I had gradually filled my home and decorated it with them, and in it I felt at peace, contented, completely happy as in the arms of a loving wife, the familiar touch of whose caressing hand has become a comforting, restful necessity.

I had had this house built in a beautiful garden, standing back from the road, not far from a town, where I could enjoy the social amenities, of which I felt the need from time to time. All my servants slept in a building at the far end of a walled kitchen-garden. In the silence of my home, deep hidden from sight beneath the foliage of tall trees, the enveloping darkness of the nights was so restful and so welcome that every evening I put off going to bed for several hours in order to prolong my enjoyment of it.

That evening there had been a performance of *Sigurd* at the local theatre. It was the first time I had heard this beautiful fairy play with music and I had thoroughly enjoyed it.

I was walking home briskly, with scraps of melody running in my head and the entrancing scenes still vivid in my memory. It was dark, pitch dark, and when I say that, I mean I could hardly see the road, and several times I nearly fell headlong into the ditch. From the toll-gate to my house is a little more than half a mile, or about twenty minutes' slow walking. It was one o'clock in the morning, one o'clock or half-past one; suddenly the sky showed slightly luminous in front of me, and the crescent moon rose, the melancholy crescent of the waning moon. The moon in its first quarter, when it rises at four or five o'clock in the evening, is bright, cheerful, silvery; but in the last quarter, when it rises after midnight, it is copper-coloured, gloomy and foreboding, a real Witches' Sabbath moon. Anyone given to going out much at night must have noticed this. The first quarter's crescent, even when slender as a thread, sheds a faint but cheering gleam, at which the heart lifts, and throws clearly defined shadows on the ground: the last quarter's crescent gives a feeble, fitful light, so dim that it casts almost no shadow.

The dark outline of my garden loomed ahead, and for some reason I felt an odd disinclination to go in. I slackened my pace. The night was very mild. The great mass of trees looked like a tomb, in which my house lay buried.

I opened the garden gate and entered the long sycamore drive leading to the house with the trees meeting overhead; it stretched before me like a lofty tunnel through the black mass of the trees and past lawns, on which the flower-beds showed up in the less intense darkness as oval patches of no particular colour.

As I approached the house an unaccountable uneasiness gripped me. I paused. There was not a sound, not a breath of air stirring in the leaves. "What has come over me?" I thought. For ten years I had been coming home like this without the least feeling of nervousness. I was not afraid. I have never been afraid in the dark. The sight of a man, a thief or a burglar, would merely have thrown me into a rage, and I should have closed with him, unhesitatingly. Moreover, I was armed; I had my revolver. But I did not put my hand on it, for I wanted to resist this feeling of fear stirring within me.

What was it? A presentiment? That unaccountable presentiment which grips a man's mind at the approach of the supernatural? Perhaps. Who knows?

As I went on, I felt shivers running down my spine, and when I was close to the wall of my great shuttered house, I felt I must pause for a few moments before opening the door and going in. Then I sat down on a garden seat under my drawing-room windows. I stayed there, my heart thumping, leaning my head against the wall, staring into the blackness of the foliage. For the first few minutes I noticed nothing unusual. I *was* aware of a kind of rumbling in my ears, but that often happens to me. I sometimes think I can hear trains passing, bells ringing, or the tramp of a crowd.

But soon the rumbling became more distinct, more definite, more unmistakable. I had been wrong. It was not the normal throbbing of my arteries which was causing this buzzing in my ears, but a quite definite, though confused, noise, coming, without any question, from inside my house. I could hear it through the wall, a continuous noise, a rustling rather than a noise, a faint stirring, as of many objects being moved about, as if someone were shifting all my furniture from its usual place and dragging it about gently.

Naturally, for some time I did not trust my hearing. But after putting my ear close to the shutters in order to hear the strange noises in the house more clearly, I remained quite firmly convinced that something abnormal and inexplicable was going on inside. I was not afraid, but—how can I express it?—startled by the sheer surprise of the thing. I did not slip the safety-catch of my revolver, somehow feeling certain it would be of no use. I waited.

I waited a long while, unable to come to any decision, with my mind perfectly clear but deeply disturbed. I waited motionless, listening all the time to the growing noise, which swelled at times to a violent crescendo, and then seemed to turn to an impatient, angry rumble, which made one feel that some outburst might follow at any minute.

Then, suddenly, ashamed of my cowardice, I seized my bunch of keys, picked out the one I wanted, thrust it into the lock, turned it twice, and pushing the door with all my force, hurled it back against the inside wall.

The bang echoed like a gunshot, and immediately the crash was answered by a terrific uproar from cellar to attic. It was so sudden, so terrifying, so deafening, that I stepped back a few paces and, though I realized it was useless, I drew my revolver from its holster.

I waited again, but not for long. I could now distinguish an extraordinary sound of trampling on the stairs, parquet floors and carpets, a trampling, not of human feet or boot soles, but of crutches, wooden crutches and iron crutches, that rang with the metallic insistence of cymbals. And then, suddenly, on the threshold of the front door, I saw an armchair, my big reading chair, come waddling out; it moved off down the drive. It was followed by others from the drawing-room, then came the sofas, low on the ground and crawling along like crocodiles on their stumpy legs, then all the rest of my chairs, leaping like goats, and the little stools loping along like rabbits.

Imagine my feelings! I slipped into a clump of shrubs, where I crouched, my eyes glued all the time to the procession of my furniture, for it was all on the way out, one piece after the other, quickly or slowly, according to its shape and weight. My piano, my concert grand, galloped past like a runaway horse, with a faint jangle of wires inside; the smaller objects, brushes, cut-glass and goblets, slid over the gravel like ants, gleaming like glow-worms in the moonlight. The carpets and hangings crawled away, sprawling pools of living matter, for all the world like devil-fish. I saw my writing-desk appear, a rare eighteenth-century collector's piece, containing all my letters, the whole record of anguished passion long since spent. And in it were also my photographs.

Suddenly all fear left me; I threw myself upon it, and grappled with it, as one grapples with a burglar; but it went on its way irresistibly, and, in spite of my furious efforts, I could not even slow it up. As I wrestled like a madman against this terrible strength, I fell to the ground in the struggle. Then it rolled me over and over, and dragged me along the gravel, and already the pieces of furniture behind were beginning to tread on me, trampling and bruising my legs; then, when I let go, the others swept over me, like a cavalry charge over an unhorsed soldier.

At last, mad with terror, I managed to drag myself off the main drive and hide again among the trees, watching the disappearance of the smallest, tiniest, humblest pieces that I had ever owned, whose very existence I had forgotten.

Then I heard, in the distance, inside the house, which was full of echoes like an empty building, a terrific din of doors being shut. They banged from attic to basement, and last of all the hall door slammed, which I had foolishly opened myself to allow the exodus.

Then I fled, and ran towards the town, and I didn't recover myself till I got to the streets, and met people going home late. I went and rang at the door of a hotel where I was known. I had beaten my clothes with my hands to shake the dust out of them, and I made up a story that I had lost my bunch of keys with the key of the kitchen-garden, where my servants slept in a house by itself, behind the garden wall which protected my fruit and vegetables from thieves.

I pulled the bed-clothes up to my eyes in the bed they gave me; but I couldn't sleep, and I waited for dawn, listening to the violent beating of my heart. I had given orders for my servants to be informed as soon as it was light, and my valet knocked at my door at seven o'clock in the morning. His face showed how upset he was.

"An awful thing has happened during the night, sir," he said.

"What is it?"

"All your furniture has been stolen, sir, absolutely everything, down to the smallest objects."

Somehow I was relieved to hear this. Why? I don't know. I had complete control of myself; I knew I could conceal my feelings, tell no-one what I had seen, hide it, bury it in my breast like some ghastly secret. I replied:

"Then they are the same people who stole my keys. The police must be informed at once. I'm getting up, and I'll be with you in a few minutes at the police station."

The enquiry lasted five months. Nothing was brought to light.

Neither the smallest of my ornaments nor the slightest trace of the thieves was ever found. Good Heavens! If I had told them what I knew. . . . If I had told . . . they would have shut up, not the thieves, but me, the man who could have seen such a thing.

Of course, I knew how to keep my mouth shut. But I never furnished my house again. It was no good. The same thing would have happened. I never wanted to go back to it again. I never did go back. I never saw it again. I went to a hotel in Paris, and consulted doctors about the state of my nerves, which had been causing me considerable anxiety since that dreadful night.

They prescribed travel and I took their advice.

II

I began with a trip to Italy. The sun did me good. For six months I wandered from Genoa to Venice, from Venice to Florence, from Florence to Rome, from Rome to Naples. Then I toured Sicily, an attractive country, from the point of view of both scenery and monuments, the remains left by the Greeks and the Normans. I crossed to Africa, and travelled at my leisure through the great sandy, peaceful desert, where camels, gazelles and nomad Arabs roam, and where, in the clear, dry air, no obsession can persist either by day or by night.

I returned to France via Marseilles, and, in spite of the Provençal gaiety, the diminished intensity of the sunlight depressed me. On my return to Europe I had the odd feeling of a patient who thinks he is cured, but is suddenly warned, by a dull pain, that the seat of the trouble is still active.

Then I went back to Paris. After a month I got bored. It was autumn, and I decided to take a trip, before the winter, through Normandy, which was new ground to me.

I began with Rouen, of course, and for a week I wandered about, intrigued, charmed, thrilled, in this mediaeval town, this amazing museum of rare specimens of Gothic art.

Then one evening, about four o'clock, as I was entering a street that seemed too good to be true, along which flows an inky-black stream called the Eau de Robec, my attention, previously centred on the unusual, old-fashioned aspect of the houses, was suddenly arrested by a number of second-hand furniture shops next door to one another.

They had, indeed, chosen their haunt well, these seedy junk dealers, in this fantastic alley along this sinister stream, under pointed roofs of tile or slate, on which the weather-vanes of a vanished age still creaked.

Stacked in the depths of the cavernous shops could be seen carved chests, china from Rouen, Nevers and Moustiers, statues, some painted, some in plain oak, crucifixes, Madonnas, Saints, church ornaments, chasubles, copes, even chalices, and an old tabernacle of gilded wood, now vacated by its Almighty tenant. What astonishing caverns there were in these great, lofty houses, packed from cellar to attic with pieces of every kind, whose usefulness seemed finished, and which had outlived their natural owners, their century, their period, their fashion, to be bought as curios by later generations!

My passion for old things was reviving in this collector's paradise. I went from shop to shop, crossing in two strides the bridges made of four rotten planks thrown over the stinking water of the Eau de Robec. And then—Mother of God! My heart leapt to my mouth. I caught sight of one of my finest cabinets at the edge of a vault crammed with junk, that looked like the entrance to the catacombs of some cemetery of old furniture. I went towards it trembling all over, trembling to such an extent that I did not dare touch it. I stretched out my hand, then I hesitated. It *was* mine, there was no question about it, a unique Louis XIII cabinet, unmistakable to anyone who had ever seen it. Suddenly, peering farther into the sombre depths of this gallery, I noticed three of my arm-chairs covered with "petit point" embroidery, then farther off my two Henry II tables, which were so rare that people came specially from Paris to see them.

Imagine, just imagine my feelings!

Then I went forward, dazed and faint with excitement, but I went in, for I am no coward, I went in like a knight in the dark ages entering a witches' kitchen. As I advanced, I found all my belongings, my chandeliers, my books, my pictures, my hangings and carpets, my weapons, everything except the writing-desk containing my letters, which I could not discover anywhere.

I went on, downstairs, along dark passages, and then up again to the floors above. I was alone. I called, but there was no answer. I was quite alone; there was no-one in this huge, winding labyrinth of a house.

Night came on, and I had to sit down in the dark on one of my own chairs, for I wouldn't go away. At intervals I shouted: "Hullo! Hullo! Anybody there?"

I had been there, I am sure, more than an hour, when I heard footsteps, light, slow steps: I could not tell where they came from. I nearly ran away, but, bracing myself, I called again, and I saw a light in the next room.

"Who's there?" said a voice.

I answered:

"A customer."

The answer came:

"It's very late, we're really closed."

I retorted:

"I've been waiting for you an hour."

"You could have come back to-morrow."

"To-morrow I shall have left Rouen."

I did not dare to move, and he did not come to me. All this time I saw the reflection of his light shining on a tapestry, in which two angels were flying above the dead on a battlefield. That, too, belonged to me.

I said:

"Well, are you coming?"

He replied:

"I'm waiting for you."

I got up and went towards him.

In the centre of a large room stood a very short man, very short and very fat, like the fat man at a show, and hideous into the bargain. He had a sparse, straggling, ill-kept, dirty-yellow beard, and not a hair on his head, not a single one. As he held his candle raised at arm's length in order to see me, the dome of his bald head looked like a miniature moon in this huge room stacked with old furniture. His face was wrinkled and bloated, his eyes mere slits.

After some bargaining I bought three chairs that were really mine, and paid a large sum in cash, merely giving the number of my room at the hotel. They were to be delivered next morning before nine o'clock. Then I left the shop. He showed me to the door most politely. I went straight to the Head Police Station, where I told the story of the theft of my furniture and the discovery I had just made.

The Inspector telegraphed, on the spot, for instructions, to the Public Prosecutor's Office, where the investigation into the theft had been held, asking me to wait for the answer. An hour later it was received, completely confirming my story.

"I'll have this man arrested and questioned at once," he said, "for he may have become suspicious, and he might move your belongings. I suggest you go and dine, and come back in two hours' time: I'll have him here, and I'll put him through a second examination in your presence."

"Excellent, Inspector! I'm more than grateful to you."

I went and dined at my hotel, and my appetite was better than I should have thought possible. But I was pretty well satisfied. They had got him.

Two hours later I was back at the Police Station, where the officer was waiting for me.

"Well, sir," he said, when he saw me, "we haven't got your friend. My men haven't been able to lay hands on him."

"Do you mean . . . ?"

A feeling of faintness came over me.

"But . . . you *have* found the house?" I asked.

"Oh yes! And it will, of course, be watched and guarded till he comes back. But he has disappeared."

"Disappeared?"

"Yes, disappeared. He usually spends the evening with his next-door neighbour, a queer old hag, a widow called Mrs. Bidoin, a second-hand dealer like himself. She hasn't seen him this evening and can't give any information about him. We shall have to wait till to-morrow."

I went away. The streets of Rouen now seemed sinister, disturbing, haunted.

I slept badly, with nightmares every time I dropped off. As I didn't want to seem unduly anxious, or in too much of a hurry, I waited next morning till ten o'clock before going round to the Police Station.

The dealer had not reappeared: his shop was still closed.

The Inspector said to me:

"I've taken all the necessary steps. The Public Prosecutor's Department has been informed; we'll go together to the shop and have it opened: you can show me what belongs to you."

We drove to the place. Policemen were on duty, with a locksmith, in front of the door, which had been opened.

When I went in, I saw neither my cabinet nor my armchairs, nor my tables, not a single one of all the contents of my house, though the evening before I could not take a step without running into something of mine.

The Chief Inspector, in surprise, at first looked at me suspiciously.

"Well, I must say, Inspector, the disappearance of this furniture coincides oddly with that of the dealer," I said.

He smiled:

"You're right! You made a mistake buying and paying for your pieces yesterday. It was that gave him the tip."

I replied:

"What I can't understand is that all the space occupied by my furniture is now filled with other pieces."

"Oh well," answered the Inspector, "he had the whole night before him, and accomplices, too, no doubt. There are sure to be means of communication with the houses on either side. Don't be alarmed, sir, I shall leave no stone unturned. The thief won't evade us for long, now we've got his hide-out."

My heart was beating so violently that I thought it would burst.

I stayed on in Rouen for a fortnight. The man did not come back. God knows, nobody could outwit or trap a man like that.

Then on the following morning I got this strange letter from my gardener, who was acting as caretaker of my house, which had been left unoccupied since the robbery:

Dear Sir,

I beg to inform you that something happened last night, which we can't explain, nor the Police neither. All the furniture has come back, absolutely everything, down to the smallest bits. The house is now just as it was the evening before the burglary. It's fit to send you off your head. It all happened on the night between Friday and Saturday. The paths are cut up, as if everything had been dragged from the garden gate to the front door. It was just the same the day it all disappeared.

I await your return and remain,

Yours respectfully,
PHILIP RAUDIN.

No! No! No! I will *not* return there!

I took the letter to the Chief Inspector of Rouen.

"It's a very neat restitution," he said. "We'll lie doggo, and we'll nab the fellow one of these days."

But he has not been nabbed. No! They've never got him, and now I'm afraid of him, as if a wild animal were loose on my track.

He can't be found! He'll never be found, this monster with the bald head like a full moon. They'll never catch him. He'll never go back to his shop. Why should he? Nobody but me can meet him, and I won't. I won't! I won't! I won't!

And if he does go back, if he returns to his shop, who will

be able to prove that my furniture was ever there? There's only my evidence, and I've a feeling that that is becoming suspect.

No! My life was getting impossible. And I couldn't keep the secret of what I had seen. I couldn't go on living like everyone else, with the fear that this sort of thing might begin again at any moment.

I went and consulted the doctor who keeps this Mental Home, and told him the whole story.

After putting me through a lengthy examination, he said:

"My dear sir, would you be willing to stay here for a time?"

"I should be very glad to."

"You're not short of money?"

"No, Doctor."

"Would you like a bungalow to yourself?"

"Yes, I should."

"Would you like your friends to come and see you?"

"No, Doctor, no-one. The man from Rouen might venture to follow me here to get even with me."

And I have been here alone for three months, absolutely alone. I have practically no anxieties. I am only afraid of one thing. . . . Supposing the second-hand dealer went mad . . . and suppose he was brought to this Home . . . ? Even prisons are not absolutely safe. . . .

THE INVISIBLE EYE
Erckmann-Chatrian
[1822–1899] [1826–1890]

"The collaborators Erckmann-Chatrian enriched French literature with many spectral fancies like *The Man-Wolf*, in which a transmitted curse works toward its end in a traditional Gothic-castle setting. Their power of creating a shuddering midnight atmosphere was tremendous despite a tendency toward natural explanations and scientific wonders; and few short tales contain greater horror than *The Invisible Eye*, where a malignant old hag weaves nocturnal hypnotic spells which induce the successive occupants of a certain in chamber to hang themselves on a cross-beam."

—*H.P. Lovecraft*

WHEN I FIRST STARTED MY CAREER as an artist, I took a room in the roof-loft of an old house in the Rue des Minnesängers, at Nuremberg.

I had made my nest in an angle of the roof. The slates served me for walls, and the roof-tree for a ceiling: I had to walk over my straw mattress to reach the window; but this window commanded a magnificent view, for it overlooked both city and country beyond.

The old second-hand dealer, Toubec, knew the road up to my little den as well as I knew it myself, and was not afraid of climbing the ladder. Every week his goat's head, surmounted by a rusty wig, pushed up the trap-door, his fingers clutched the edge of the floor, and in a noisy tone he cried: "Well, well, Master Christian, have we anything new?"

To which I answered: "Come in: why the deuce don't you come in? I'm just finishing a little landscape, and want to have your opinion of it."

Then his long thin spine lengthened itself out, until his head touched the roof; and the old fellow laughed silently.

I must do justice to Toubec: he never bargained with me. He bought all my pictures at fifteen florins apiece, one with the other, and sold them again at forty. He was an honest Jew.

This kind of existence was beginning to please me, and I was every day finding in it some new charm, when the city of Nuremberg was agitated by a strange and mysterious event.

Not far from my garret-window, a little to the left, rose the *auberge* of the Boeuf-gras, an old inn much frequented by the country-people. The gable of this *auberge* was conspicuous for the peculiarity of its form: it was very narrow, sharply pointed, and its edges were cut like the teeth of a saw; grotesque carvings ornamented the cornices and framework of its windows. But what was most remarkable was that the house which faced it reproduced exactly the same carvings and ornaments; every detail had been minutely copied, even to the support of the signboard, with its iron volutes and spirals.

It might have been said that these two ancient buildings reflected one another; only that behind the inn grew a tall oak, the dark foliage of which served to bring into bold relief the forms of the roof, while the opposite house stood bare against the sky. For the rest, the inn was as noisy and animated as the other house was silent. On the one side was to be seen, going in and coming out, an endless crowd of drinkers, singing, stumbling, cracking their whips; over the other, solitude reigned.

Once or twice a day the heavy door of the silent house opened to give egress to a little old woman, her back bent into a half-circle, her chin long and pointed, her dress clinging to her limbs, an enormous basket under her arm, and one hand tightly clutched upon her chest.

This old woman's appearance had struck me more than once; her little green eyes, her skinny, pinched-up nose, her shawl, dating back a hundred years at least, the smile that wrinkled her cheeks, and the lace of her cap hanging down upon her eyebrows—all this appeared strange, interested me, and made me strongly desire to learn who this old woman was, and what she did in her great lonely house.

I imagined her as passing there an existence devoted to good works and pious meditation. But one day, when I had stopped in the street to look at her, she turned sharply round and darted at me a look the horrible expression of which I know not how to describe, and made three or four hideous grimaces at me; then dropping again her doddering head, she drew her large shawl about her, the ends of which trailed after her on the ground, and slowly entered her heavy door.

"That's an old mad-woman," I said to myself; "a malicious, cunning old mad-woman! I ought not to have allowed myself to be so interested in her. But I'll try and recall her abominable grimace— Toubec will give me fifteen florins for it willingly."

This way of treating the matter was far from satisfying my mind, however. The old woman's horrible glance pursued me everywhere; and more than once, while scaling the perpendicular ladder of my lodging-hole, feeling my clothes caught in a nail, I trembled from head to foot, believing that the old woman had seized me by the tails of my coat for the purpose of pulling me down backwards.

Toubec, to whom I related the story, far from laughing at it, received it with a serious air.

"Master Christian," he said, "if the old woman means you harm, take care; her teeth are small, sharp-pointed, and wonderfully white, which is not natural at her age. She has the Evil Eye! Children run away at her approach, and the people of Nuremberg call her Fledermausse!"

I admired the Jew's clear-sightedness, and what he had told me made me reflect a good deal; but at the end of a few weeks, having often met Fledermausse without harmful consequences, my fears died away and I thought no more of her.

One night, when I was lying sound asleep, I was awoken by a strange harmony. It was a kind of vibration, so soft, so melodious, that the murmur of a light breeze through foliage can convey but a feeble idea of its gentle nature. For a long time I listened to it, my eyes wide open, and holding my breath the better to hear it.

At length, looking towards the window, I saw two wings beating against the glass. I thought, at first, that it was a bat imprisoned in my chamber; but the moon was shining clearly, and showed the wings of a magnificent night-moth, transparent as lace. At times their vibrations were so rapid as to hide them from my view; then for a while they would lie in repose, extended on the glass pane, their delicate articulations made visible anew.

This vaporous apparition in the midst of the universal silence opened my heart to the tenderest emotions; it seemed to me that a sylphid, pitying my solitude, had come to see me; and this idea brought the tears to my eyes.

"Have no fear, gentle captive—have no fear!" I said to it; "your confidence shall not be betrayed. I will not retain you against your wishes; return to heaven—to liberty!"

And I opened the window.

The night was calm. Thousands of stars glittered in space. For a moment I contemplated this sublime spectacle, and the words of prayer rose naturally to my lips. But then, looking down, I saw a man hanging from the iron stanchion which supported the sign of the Boeuf-gras; the hair in disorder, the arms stiff, the legs straightened to a point, and throwing their gigantic shadow the whole length of the street.

The immobility of this figure, in the moonlight, had something frightful in it. I felt my tongue grow icy cold, and my teeth chattered. I was about to utter a cry; but by what mysterious attraction I know not, my eyes were drawn towards the opposite house, and there I dimly distinguished the old woman, in the midst of the heavy shadow, squatting at her window and contemplating the hanging body with diabolical satisfaction.

I became giddy with terror; my strength deserted me, and I fell down in a heap insensible.

I do not know how long I lay unconscious. On coming to myself I found it was broad day. Mingled and confused noises rose from the street below. I looked out from my window.

The burgomaster and his secretary were standing at the door of the Boeuf-gras; they remained there a long time. People came and went, stopped to look, then passed on their way. At length a stretcher, on which lay a body-covered with a woollen cloth, was brought out and carried away by two men.

Then everyone else disappeared.

The window in front of the house remained open still; a

fragment of rope dangled from the iron support of the signboard. I had not dreamed—I had really seen the night-moth on my window-pane—then the suspended body—then the old woman!

In the course of that day Toubec paid me his weekly visit. "Anything to sell, Master Christian?" he cried.

I did not hear him. I was seated on my only chair, my hands upon my knees, my eyes fixed on vacancy before me. Toubec, surprised at my immobility, repeated in a louder tone, "Master Christian!—Master Christian!" then, stepping up to me, tapped me smartly on the shoulder.

"What's the matter?—what's the matter? Are you ill?" he asked.

"No—I was thinking."

"What the deuce about?"

"The man who was hung——"

"Aha!" cried the old broker; "you saw the poor fellow, then? What a strange affair! The third in the same place!"

"The third?"

"Yes, the third. I ought to have told you about it before; but there's still time—for there's sure to be a fourth, following the example of the others, the first step only making the difficulty."

This said, Toubec seated himself on a box and lit his pipe with a thoughtful air.

"I'm not timid," said he, "but if anyone were to ask me to sleep in that room, I'd rather go and hang myself somewhere else! Nine or ten months back," he continued, "a wholesale furrier, from Tubingen, put up at the Boeuf-gras. He called for supper; ate well, drank well, and was shown up to bed in the room on the third floor which they call the 'green chamber.' The next day they found him hanging from the stanchion of the sign.

"So much for number one, about which there was nothing to be said. A proper report of the affair was drawn up, and the body of the stranger buried at the bottom of the garden. But about six weeks afterwards came a soldier from Neustadt; he had his discharge, and was congratulating himself on his return to his village. All the evening he did nothing but empty mugs of wine and talk of his cousin, who was waiting his return to marry him. At last they put him to bed in the green chamber, and the same night the watchman passing along the Rue des Minnesängers noticed something hanging from the signboard-stanchion. He raised his lantern; it was the soldier, with his discharge-papers in a tin box hanging on his left thigh, and his hands planted smoothly on the outer seams of his trousers, as if he had been on parade!

"It was certainly an extraordinary affair! The burgomaster declared it was the work of the devil. The chamber was examined; they replastered its walls. A notice of the death was sent to Neustadt, on the margin of which the clerk wrote—'Died suddenly of apoplexy.'

"All Nuremberg was indignant against the landlord of the Boeuf-gras, and wished to compel him to take down the iron stanchion of his signboard, on the pretext that it put dangerous ideas in people's heads. But you may easily imagine that old Nikel Schmidt didn't listen with the ear on that side of his head.

" 'That stanchion was put there by my grandfather,' he said; 'the sign of the Boeuf-gras has hung on it from father to son, for a hundred and fifty years; it does nobody any harm, it's more than thirty feet up; those who don't like it have only to look another way.'

"People's excitement gradually cooled down, and for several months nothing happened. Unfortunately, a student from

Heidelberg, on his way to the University, came to the Boeuf-gras and asked for a bed. He was the son of a pastor.

"Who would suppose that the son of a pastor would take into his head the idea of hanging himself to the stanchion of a public-house sign, because a furrier and a soldier had hung themselves there before him? It must be confessed, Master Christian, that the thing was not very probable—it would not have appeared more likely to you than it did to me. Well——"

"Enough! Enough!" I cried; "it is a horrible affair. I feel sure there is some frightful mystery at the bottom of it. It is neither the stanchion nor the chamber——"

"You don't mean that you suspect the landlord?—as honest a man as there is in the world, and belonging to one of the oldest families in Nuremberg?"

"No, no! Heaven keep me from forming unjust suspicions of anyone; but there are abysses into the depths of which one dares not look."

"You are right," said Toubec, astonished at my excited manner; "and we had much better talk of something else. By-the-way, Master Christian, what about our landscape, the view of Sainte-Odile?"

The question brought me back to actualities. I showed the broker the picture I had just finished. The business was soon settled between us, and Toubec, thoroughly satisfied, went down the ladder, advising me to think no more of the student of Heidelberg.

I would very willingly have followed the old broker's advice, but when the devil mixes himself up with our affairs he is not easily shaken off.

II

In solitude, all these events came back to my mind with frightful distinctness.

The old woman, I said to myself, is the cause of all this; she alone has planned these crimes, she alone has carried them into execution; but by what means? Has she had recourse to cunning only or really to the intervention of the invisible powers?

I paced my garret, a voice within me crying, "It is not without purpose that Heaven has permitted you to see Fledermausse watching the agony of her victim; it was not without design that the poor young man's soul came to wake you in the form of a night-moth! No! all this has not been without purpose. Christian, Heaven imposes on you a terrible mission; if you fail to accomplish it, fear that you yourself may fall into the toils of the old woman! Perhaps at this moment she is laying her snares for you in the darkness!"

During several days these frightful images pursued me without cessation. I could not sleep; I found it impossible to work; the brush fell from my hand, and shocking to confess, I detected myself at times complacently contemplating the dreadful stanchion. At last, one evening, unable any longer to bear this state of mind, I flew down the ladder four steps at a time, and went and hid myself beside Fledermausse's door, for the purpose of discovering her fatal secret.

From that time there was never a day that I was not on the watch, following the old woman like her shadow, never losing sight of her; but she was so cunning, she had so keen a scent that without even turning her head she discovered that I was behind her, and knew that I was on her track. But nevertheless, she pretended not to see me—went to the market, to the butcher's, like a simple housewife; only she quickened her pace and muttered to herself as she went.

At the end of a month I saw that it would be impossible for me to achieve my purpose by these means, and this conviction filled me with an inexpressible sadness.

"What can I do?" I asked myself. "The old woman has discovered my intentions, and is thoroughly on her guard. I am helpless. The old wretch already thinks she sees me at the end of the cord!"

At length, from repeating to myself again and again the question, "What can I do?" a luminous idea presented itself to my mind.

My chamber overlooked the house of Fledermausse, but it had no dormer window on that side. I carefully raised one of the slates of my roof, and the delight I felt on discovering that by this means I could command a view of the entire antique building can hardly be imagined.

"At last I've got you!" I cried to myself; "you cannot escape me now! From here I shall see everything. You will not suspect this invisible eye—this eye that will surprise the crime at the moment of its inception! Oh, Justice! It moves slowly, but it comes!"

Nothing more sinister than this den could be imagined—a large yard, paved with moss-grown flagstones; a well in one corner, the stagnant water of which was frightful to behold; a wooden staircase leading up to a railed gallery, to the left, on the first floor, a drain-stone indicated the kitchen; to the right, the upper windows of the house looked into the street. All was dark, decaying, and dank-looking.

The sun penetrated only for an hour or two during the day the depths of this dismal sty; then the shadows again spread over it—the light fell in lozenge shapes upon the crumbling walls, on the mouldy balcony, on the dull windows.

Oh, the whole place was worthy of its mistress!

I had hardly made these reflections when the old woman entered the yard on her return from market. First, I heard her heavy door grate on its hinges, then Fledermausse, with her basket, appeared. She seemed fatigued—out of breath. The border of her cap hung down upon her nose, as, clutching the wooden rail with one hand, she mounted the stairs.

The heat was suffocating. It was exactly one of those days when insects of every kind—crickets, spiders, mosquitoes—fill old buildings with their grating noises and subterranean borings.

Fledermausse crossed the gallery slowly, like a ferret that feels itself at home. For more than a quarter of an hour she remained in the kitchen, then came out and swept the stones a little, on which a few straws had been scattered; at last she raised her head, and with her green eyes carefully scrutinised every portion of the roof from which I was observing her.

By what strange intuition did she suspect anything? I know not; but I gently lowered the uplifted slate into its place, and gave over watching for the rest of that day.

The day following Fledermausse appeared to be reassured. A jagged ray of light fell into the gallery; passing this, she caught a fly, and delicately presented it to a spider established in an angle of the roof.

The spider was so large, that, in spite of the distance, I saw it descend then, gliding along one thread, like a drop of venom, seize its prey from the fingers of the dreadful old woman, and remount rapidly. Fledermausse watched it attentively; then her eyes half-closed, she sneezed, and cried to herself in a jocular tone: "Bless you, beauty!—bless you!"

For six weeks I could discover nothing as to the power of

Fledermausse: sometimes I saw her peeling potatoes, sometimes spreading her linen on the balustrade. Sometimes I saw her spin; but she never sang, as old women usually do, their quivering voices going so well with the humming of the spinning-wheel. Silence reigned about her. She had no cat—the favourite company of old maids; not a sparrow ever flew down to her yard, in passing over which the pigeons seemed to hurry their flight. It seemed as if everything were afraid of her look.

The spider alone took pleasure in her society.

I now look back with wonder at my patience during those long hours of observation; nothing escaped my attention, nothing was indifferent to me; at the least sound I lifted my slate. Mine was a boundless curiosity stimulated by an indefinable fear.

Toubec complained.

"What the devil are you doing with your time, Master Christian?" he would say to me. "Formerly, you had something ready for me every week; now, hardly once a month. Oh, you painters! As soon as they have a few kreutzer before them, they put their hands in their pockets and go to sleep!"

I myself was beginning to lose courage. With all my watching and spying, I had discovered nothing extraordinary. I was inclining to think that the old woman might not be so dangerous after all—that I had been wrong, perhaps, to suspect her. In short, I tried to find excuses for her. But one fine evening, while, with my eye to the opening in the roof, I was giving myself up to these charitable reflections, the scene abruptly changed.

Fledermausse passed along her gallery with the swiftness of a flash of light. She was no longer herself: she was erect, her jaws knit, her look fixed, her neck extended; she moved with long strides, her grey hair streaming behind her.

"Oh, oh!" I said to myself, "something is going on!"

But the shadows of night descended on the big house, the noises of the town died out, and all became silent. I was about to seek my bed, when, happening to look out of my skylight, I saw a light in the window of the green chamber of the Boeuf-gras—a traveller was occupying that terrible room!

All my fears were instantly revived. The old woman's excitement explained itself—she scented another victim!

I could not sleep at all that night. The rustling of the straw of my mattress, the nibbling of a mouse under the floor, sent a chill through me. I rose and looked out of my window—I listened. The light I had seen was no longer visible in the green chamber.

During one of these moments of poignant anxiety—whether the result of illusion or reality—I fancied I could discern the figure of the old witch, likewise watching and listening.

The night passed, the dawn showed grey against my window-panes, and, slowly increasing, the sounds and movements of the re-awakened town arose. Harassed with fatigue and emotion, I at last fell asleep; but my repose was of short duration, and by eight o'clock I was again at my post of observation.

It appeared that Fledermausse had passed a night no less stormy than mine had been; for, when she opened the door of the gallery, I saw that a livid pallor was upon her cheeks and skinny neck. She had nothing on but her chemise and a flannel petticoat; a few locks of rusty grey hair fell upon her shoulders. She looked up musingly towards my garret; but she saw nothing—she was thinking of something else.

Suddenly she descended into the yard; leaving her shoes at the top of the stairs. Doubtless her object was to assure herself that the outer door was securely fastened. She then hurried up the stairs, three or four at a time. It was frightful to see! She rushed into one of the side rooms, and I heard the sound of a heavy box-lid fall. Then Fledermausse reappeared in the gallery, dragging with her a life-size dummy—and this figure was dressed like the unfortunate student of Heidelberg!

With surprising dexterity the old woman suspended this hideous object to a beam of the over-hanging roof, then went down into the yard to contemplate it from that point of view. A peal of grating laughter broke from her lips—she hurried up the stairs, and rushed down again, like a maniac; and every time she did this she burst into fresh fits of laughter.

A sound was heard outside the street door; the old woman sprang to the dummy, snatched it from its fastening, and carried it into the house; then she reappeared and leaned over the balcony, with outstretched neck, glittering eyes, and eagerly listening ears. The sound passed away—the muscles of her face relaxed, she drew a long breath. The passing of a vehicle had alarmed the old witch.

She then, once more, went back into her chamber, and I heard the lid of the box close heavily.

This strange scene utterly confounded all my ideas. What could that dummy mean?

I became more watchful and attentive than ever. Fledermausse went out with her basket, and I watched her to the top of the street; she had resumed her air of tottering age, walking with short steps, and from time to time half-turning her head, so as to enable herself to look behind out of the corners of her eyes. For five long hours she remained abroad, while I went and came from my spying-place incessantly, meditating all the while—the sun heating the slates above my head till my brain was almost scorched.

I saw at his window the traveller who occupied the green

chamber at the Boeuf-gras; he was a peasant of Nassau, wearing a three-cornered hat, a scarlet waistcoat, and having a broad laughing countenance. He was tranquilly smoking his pipe, unsuspicious of anything wrong.

About two o'clock Fledermausse came back. The sound of her door opening echoed to the end of the passage. Presently she appeared alone, quite alone in the yard, and seated herself on the lowest step of the gallery-stairs. She placed her basket at her feet and drew from it, first several bunches of herbs, then some vegetables—then a three-cornered hat, a scarlet velvet waistcoat, a pair of plush breeches, and a pair of thick worsted stockings—the complete costume of a peasant of Nassau!

I reeled with giddiness—flames passed before my eyes.

I remembered those precipices that drew one towards them with irresistible power—wells that have had to be filled up because of persons throwing themselves into them—trees that have had to be cut down because of people hanging themselves upon them—the contagion of suicide and theft and murder, which at various times has taken possession of people's minds, by means well understood; that strange inducement, which makes people kill themselves because others kill themselves. My hair rose upon my head with horror!

But how could this Fledermausse—a creature so mean and wretched—have made discovery of so profound a law of nature? How had she found the means of turning it to the use of her sanguinary instincts? This I could neither understand nor imagine. Without more reflection, however, I resolved to turn the fatal law against her, and by its power to drag her into her own snare. So many innocent victims called for vengeance!

I hurried to all the old clothes-dealers in Nuremberg; and by the evening I arrived at the Boeuf-gras, with an enormous parcel under my arm.

Nikel Schmidt had long known me. I had painted the portrait of his wife, a fat and comely dame.

"Master Christian!" he cried, shaking me by the hand, "to what happy circumstance do I owe the pleasure of this visit?"

"My dear Mr. Schmidt, I feel a very strong desire to pass the night in that room of yours up yonder."

We were on the doorstep of the inn, and I pointed up to the green chamber. The good fellow looked suspiciously at me.

"Oh! don't be afraid," I said, "I've no desire to hang myself."

"I'm glad of it! I'm glad of it! for frankly, I should be sorry—an artist of your talent. When do you want the room, Master Christian?"

"Tonight."

"That's impossible—it's occupied."

"The gentleman can have it at once, if he likes," said a voice behind us; "I shan't stay in it."

We turned in surprise. It was the peasant of Nassau; his large three-cornered hat pressed down upon the back of his neck, and his bundle at the end of his travelling-stick. He had learned the story of the three travellers who had hung themselves.

"Such chambers!" he cried, stammering with terror, "it's—it's murdering people to put them into such!—you—you deserve to be sent to the gallows!"

"Come, come calm yourself," said the landlord; "you slept there comfortably enough last night."

"Thank Heaven! I said my prayers before going to rest, or where should I be now?"

And he hurried away, raising his hands to heaven.

"Well," said Master Schmidt, stupefied, "the chamber is empty, but don't go into it to do me an ill turn."

"I might be doing myself a much worse one," I replied.

Giving my parcel to the servant-girl, I went and seated myself among the guests who were drinking and smoking.

For a long time I had not felt more calm, more happy to be in the world. After so much anxiety, I saw approaching my end— the horizon seemed to grow lighter. I know not by what formidable power I was being led on. I lit my pipe, and with my elbow on the table and a jug of wine before me, and sometimes rousing myself to look at the woman's house, I seriously asked myself whether all that had happened to me was more than a dream. But when the watchman came, to request us to vacate the room, graver thoughts took possession of my mind, and I followed, in meditative mood, the little servant-girl who preceded me with a candle in her hand.

III

We mounted the window flight of stairs to the third storey; arrived there, she placed the candle in my hand, and pointed to a door.

"That's it," she said, and hurried back down the stairs as fast as she could go.

I opened the door. The green chamber was like all other inn bedchambers; the ceiling was low, the bed was high. After casting a glance round the room, I stepped across to the window.

Nothing was yet noticeable in Fledermausse's house, with the exception of a light, which shone at the back of a deep obscure bedchamber—a nightlight, doubtless.

"So much the better," I said to myself, as I re-closed the window-curtains; "I shall have plenty of time."

I opened my parcel, and from its contents put on a woman's cap with a broad frilled border; then, with a piece of pointed charcoal, in front of the glass, I marked my forehead with a number of wrinkles. This took me a full hour to do; but after I had put on a gown and a large shawl, I was afraid of myself; Fledermausse herself was looking at me from the depths of the glass!

At that moment the watchman announced the hour of eleven. I rapidly dressed the dummy I had brought with me like the one prepared by the old witch. I then drew apart the window-curtains.

Certainly, after all I had seen of the old woman—her infernal cunning, her prudence, and her address—nothing ought to have surprised even me; yet I was positively terrified.

The light, which I had observed at the back of her room, now cast its yellow rays on her dummy, dressed like the peasant of Nassau, which sat huddled up on the side of the bed, its head dropped upon its chest, the large three-cornered hat drawn down over its features, its arms pendant by its sides, and its whole attitude that of a person plunged in despair.

Managed with diabolical art, the shadow permitted only a general view of the figure, the red waistcoat and its six rounded buttons alone caught the light; but the silence of night, the complete immobility of the figure, and its air of terrible dejection, all served to impress the beholder with irresistible force; even I myself, though not in the least taken by surprise, felt chilled to the marrow of my bones. How, then, would a poor countryman taken completely off his guard have felt? He would have been utterly overthrown; he would have lost all control of will, and the spirit of imitation would have done the rest.

Scarcely had I drawn aside the curtains than I discovered Fledermausse on the watch behind her window-panes.

She could not see me. I opened the window softly, the window over the way softly opened too; then the dummy appeared to rise slowly and advance towards me; I did the same, and seizing my candle with one hand, with the other threw the casement wide open.

The old woman and I were face to face; for, overwhelmed with astonishment, she had let the dummy fall from her hands. Our two looks crossed with an equal terror.

She stretched forth a finger, I did the same; her lips moved, I moved mine; she heaved a deep sigh and leant upon an elbow. I rested in the same way.

How frightful the enacting of this scene was I cannot describe; it was made up of delirium, bewilderment, madness. It was a struggle between two wills, two intelligences, two souls, one of which sought to crush the other; and in this struggle I had the advantage. The dead were on my side.

After having for some seconds imitated all the movements of Fledermausse, I drew a cord from the folds of my petticoat and tied it to the iron stanchion of the signboard.

The old woman watched me with open mouth. I passed the cord round my neck. Her tawny eyeballs glittered; her features became convulsed.

"No, no!" she cried, in a hissing tone; "no!"

I proceeded with the impassibility of a hangman.

Then Fledermausse was seized with rage.

"You're mad! you're mad!" she cried, springing up and clutching wildly at the sill of the window; "you're mad!"

I gave her no time to continue. Suddenly blowing out my light, I stooped like a man preparing to make a vigorous spring, then seizing my dummy slipped the cord about its neck and hurled it into the air.

A terrible shriek resounded through the street; then all was silent again.

Perspiration bathed my forehead. I listened a long time. At the end of an hour I heard far off—very far off—the cry of the watchman, announcing that midnight had struck.

"Justice is at last done," I murmured to myself; "the three victims are avenged. Heaven forgive me!"

I saw the old witch, drawn by the likeness of herself, a cord about her neck, hanging from the iron stanchion projecting from her house. I saw the thrill of death run through her limbs and the moon, calm and silent, rose above the edge of the roof, and shed its cold pale rays upon her dishevelled head.

As I had seen the poor young student of Heidelberg, I now saw Fledermausse.

The next day all Nuremberg knew that "the Bat" had hung herself. It was the last event of the kind in the Rue des Minnesängers.

THE TORTURE BY HOPE
Villiers de l'Isle Adam
[1838–1889]

"Villiers de l'Isle Adam likewise followed the macabre school; his *Torture by Hope*, the tale of a stake-condemned prisoner permitted to escape in order to feel the pangs of recapture, being held by some to constitute the most harrowing short story in literature. This type, however, is less a part of the weird tradition than a class peculiar to itself—the so-called conte cruel, in which the wrenching of the emotions is accomplished through dramatic tantalizations, frustrations, and gruesome physical horrors.'

—H.P. Lovecraft

MANY YEARS AGO, as evening was closing in, the venerable Pedro Arbuez d'Espila, sixth prior of the Dominicans of Segovia, and third Grand Inquisitor of Spain, followed by a *fra redemptor*, and preceded by two familiars of the Holy Office, the latter carrying lanterns, made their way to a subterranean dungeon. The bolt of a massive door creaked, and they entered a mephitic *in-pace*, where the dim light revealed between rings fastened to the wall a bloodstained rack, a brazier, and a jug. On a pile of straw, loaded with fetters and his neck encircled by an iron carcan, sat a haggard man, of uncertain age, clothed in rags.

This prisoner was no other than Rabbi Aser Abarbanel, a Jew

of Arragon, who—accused of usury and pitiless scorn for the poor—had been daily subjected to torture for more than a year. Yet "his blindness was as dense as his hide," and he had refused to abjure his faith.

Proud of a filiation dating back thousands of years, proud of his ancestors—for all Jews worthy of the name are vain of their blood—he descended Talmudically from Othoniel and consequently from Ipsiboa, the wife of the last judge of Israel, a circumstance which had sustained his courage amid incessant torture. With tears in his eyes at the thought of this resolute soul rejecting salvation, the venerable Pedro Arbuez d'Espila, approaching the shuddering rabbi, addressed him as follows:

"My son, rejoice: your trials here below are about to end. If in the presence of such obstinacy I was forced to permit, with deep regret, the use of great severity, my task of fraternal correction has its limits. You are the fig tree which, having failed so many times to bear fruit, at last withered, but God alone can judge your soul. Perhaps Infinite Mercy will shine upon you at the last moment! We must hope so. There are examples. So sleep in peace tonight. Tomorrow you will be included in the *auto da fé*: that is, you will be exposed to the *quémadero*, the symbolical flames of the Everlasting Fire: it burns, as you know, only at a distance, my son; and Death is at least two hours (often three) in coming, on account of the wet, iced bandages, with which we protect the heads and hearts of the condemned. There will be forty-three of you. Placed in the last row, you will have time to invoke God and offer to Him this baptism of fire, which is of the Holy Spirit. Hope in the Light, and rest."

With these words, having signed to his companions to unchain the prisoner, the prior tenderly embraced him. Then came the turn of the *fra redemptor*, who, in a low tone, entreated the Jew's forgiveness for what he had made him suffer for the purpose of redeeming him; then the two familiars silently kissed him. This ceremony over, the captive was left, solitary and bewildered, in the darkness.

Rabbi Aser Abarbanel, with parched lips and visage worn by suffering, at first gazed at the closed door with vacant eyes. Closed? The word unconsciously roused a vague fancy in his mind, the fancy that he had seen for an instant the light of the lanterns through a chink between the door and the wall. A morbid idea of hope, due to the weakness of his brain, stirred his whole being. He dragged himself toward the strange *appearance*. Then, very gently and cautiously, slipping one finger into the crevice, he drew the door toward him. Marvelous! By an extraordinary accident the familiar who closed it had turned the huge key an instant before it struck the stone casing, so that the rusty bolt not having entered the hole, the door again rolled on its hinges.

The rabbi ventured to glance outside. By the aid of a sort of luminous dusk he distinguished at first a semicircle of walls indented by winding stairs; and opposite to him, at the top of five or six stone steps, a sort of black portal, opening into an immense corridor, whose first arches only were visible from below.

Stretching himself flat he crept to the threshold. Yes, it was really a corridor, but endless in length. A wan light illumined it: lamps suspended from the vaulted ceiling lightened at intervals the dull hue of the atmosphere—the distance was veiled in shadow. Not a single door appeared in the whole extent! Only on one side, the left, heavily grated loopholes, sunk in the walls, admitted a light which must be that of evening, for crimson bars at intervals rested on the flags of the pavement. What a terrible silence! Yet, yonder, at the far end of that passage there might be a doorway of escape! The Jew's vacillating hope was tenacious, for it was *the last.*

Without hesitating, he ventured on the flags, keeping close under the loopholes, trying to make himself part of the blackness of the long walls. He advanced slowly, dragging himself along on his breast, forcing back the cry of pain when some raw wound sent a keen pang through his whole body.

Suddenly the sound of a sandaled foot approaching reached his ears. He trembled violently, fear stifled him, his sight grew dim. Well, it was over, no doubt. He pressed himself into a niche and, half lifeless with terror, waited.

It was a familiar hurrying along. He passed swiftly by, holding in his clenched hand an instrument of torture—a frightful figure—and vanished. The suspense which the rabbi had endured seemed to have suspended the functions of life, and he lay nearly an hour unable to move. Fearing an increase of tortures if he were captured, he thought of returning to his dungeon. But the old hope whispered in his soul that divine *perhaps,* which comforts us in our sorest trials. A miracle had happened. He could doubt no longer. He began to crawl toward the chance of escape. Exhausted by suffering and hunger, trembling with pain, he pressed onward. The sepulchral corridor seemed to lengthen mysteriously, while he, still advancing, gazed into the gloom where there *must* be some avenue of escape.

Oh! oh! He again heard footsteps, but this time they were slower, more heavy. The white and black forms of two inquisitors appeared, emerging from the obscurity beyond. They were conversing in low tones, and seemed to be discussing some important subject, for they were gesticulating vehemently.

At this spectacle Rabbi Aser Abarbanel closed his eyes: his heart beat so violently that it almost suffocated him; his rags were damp with the cold sweat of agony; he lay motionless by the wall, his mouth wide open, under the rays of a lamp, praying to the God of David.

Just opposite to him the two inquisitors paused under the light of the lamp—doubtless owing to some accident due to the course of their argument. One, while listening to his companion, gazed at the rabbi! And, beneath the look—whose absence of expression the hapless man did not at first notice—he fancied he again felt the burning pincers scorch his flesh, he was to be once more a living wound. Fainting, breathless, with fluttering eyelids, he shivered at the touch of the monk's floating robe. But—strange yet natural fact—the inquisitor's gaze was evidently that of a man deeply absorbed in his intended reply, engrossed by what he was hearing; his eyes were fixed—and seemed to look at the Jew *without seeing him.*

In fact, after the lapse of a few minutes, the two gloomy figures slowly pursued their way, still conversing in low tones, toward the place whence the prisoner had come; HE HAD NOT BEEN SEEN! Amid the horrible confusion of the rabbi's thoughts, the idea darted through his brain: "Can I be already dead that they did not see me?" A hideous impression roused him from his lethargy: in looking at the wall against which his face was pressed, he imagined he beheld two fierce eyes watching him! He flung his head back in a sudden frenzy of fright, his hair fairly bristling! Yet, no! No. His hand groped over the stones: it was the *reflection* of the inquisitor's eyes, still retained in his own, which had been refracted from two spots on the wall.

Forward! He must hasten toward that goal which he fancied

(absurdly, no doubt) to be deliverance, toward the darkness from which he was now barely thirty paces distant. He pressed forward faster on his knees, his hands, at full length, dragging himself painfully along, and soon entered the dark portion of this terrible and appalling corridor.

Suddenly the poor wretch felt a gust of cold air on the hands resting upon the flags; it came from under the little door to which the two walls led.

Oh, Heaven, if that door should open outward! Every nerve in the miserable fugitive's body thrilled with hope. He examined it from top to bottom, though scarcely able to distinguish its outlines in the surrounding darkness. He passed his hand over it: no bolt, no lock! A latch! He started up, the latch yielded to the pressure of his thumb: the door silently swung open before him.

"HALLELUIA!" murmured the rabbi in a transport of gratitude as, standing on the threshold, he beheld the scene before him.

The door had opened into the gardens, above which arched a starlit sky, into spring, liberty, life! It revealed the neighboring fields, stretching toward the sierras, whose sinuous blue lines were relieved against the horizon. Yonder lay freedom! Oh, to escape! He would journey all night through the lemon groves, whose fragrance reached him. Once in the mountains and he was safe! He inhaled the delicious air; the breeze revived him, his lungs expanded! He felt in his swelling heart the *Veni foràs* of Lazarus! And to thank once more the God who had bestowed this mercy upon him, he extended his arms, raising his eyes toward Heaven. It was an ecstasy of joy!

Then he fancied he saw the shadow of his arms approach him—fancied that he felt these shadowy arms enclose, embrace him—and that he was pressed tenderly to some one's breast. A tall figure actually did stand directly before him. He lowered his eyes—and remained motionless, gasping for breath, dazed, with fixed eyes, fairly driveling with terror.

Horror! He was in the clasp of the Grand Inquisitor himself, the venerable Pedro Arbuez d'Espila, who gazed at him with tearful eyes, like a good shepherd who had found his stray lamb.

The dark-robed priest pressed the hapless Jew to his heart with so fervent an outburst of love, that the edges of the monochal haircloth rubbed the Dominican's breast. And while Aser Abarbanel with portruding eyes gasped in agony in the ascetic's embrace, vaguely comprehending that *all the phases of this fatal evening were only a prearranged torture, that of* HOPE, the Grand Inquisitor, with an accent of touching reproach and a look of consternation, murmured in his ear, his breath parched and burning from long fasting:

"What, my son! On the eve, perchance, of salvation—you wished to leave us?"

Ms. Found in a Bottle
Edgar Allan Poe
[1809–1849]

"Poe's tales, of course, fall into several classes; some of which contain a purer essence of spiritual horror than others. The tales of logic and ratiocination, forerunners of the modern detective story, are not to be included at all in weird literature; whilst certain others, probably influenced considerably by Hoffman, possess an extravagance which relegates them to the borderline of the grotesque. Still a third group deal with abnormal psychology and monomania in such a way as to express terror but not weirdness. A substantial residuum, however, represent the literature of supernatural horror in its acutest form; and give their author a permanent and unassailable place as deity and fountain-head of all modern diabolic fiction. Who can forget the terrible swollen ship poised on the billow-chasm's edge in *Ms. Found in a Bottle*—the dark intimations of her unhallowed age and monstrous growth, her sinister crew of unseeing greybeards, and her frightful southward rush under full sail through the ice of the Antarctic night, sucked onward by some resistless devil-current toward a vortex of eldritch enlightenment which must end in destruction?"

—*H.P. Lovecraft*

Qui n'a plus qu'un moment à vivre
N'a plus rien à dissimuler.

—Quinault

O F MY COUNTRY AND OF MY FAMILY I have little to say. Ill usage and length of years have driven me from the one, and estranged me from the other. Hereditary wealth afforded me an education of no common order, and a contemplative turn of mind enabled me to methodize the stories which early study diligently garnered up. Beyond all things, the works of the German moralists gave me great delight; not from my ill-advised admiration of their eloquent madness, but from the ease with which my habits of rigid thought enabled me to detect their falsities. I have often been reproached with the aridity of my genius; a deficiency of imagination has been imputed to me as a crime; and the Pyrrhonism of my opinions has at all times rendered me notorious. Indeed, a strong relish for physical philosophy has, I fear, tinctured my mind with a very common error of this age—I mean the habit of referring occurrences, even the least susceptible of such reference, to the principles of that science. Upon the whole, no person could be less liable than myself to be led away from the severe precincts of truth by the *ignes fatui* of superstition. I have thought proper to premise thus much, lest the incredible tale I have to tell should be considered rather the raving of a crude imagination, than the positive experience of a mind to which the reveries of fancy have been a dead letter and a nullity.

After many years spent in foreign travel, I sailed in the year 18—, from the port of Batavia, in the rich and populous island of Java, on a voyage to the Archipelago Islands. I went as passenger —having no other inducement than a kind of nervous restlessness which haunted me as a fiend.

Our vessel was a beautiful ship of about four hundred tons, copper-fastened, and built at Bombay of Malabar teak. She was freighted with cotton-wool and oil, from the Lachadive Islands.

We had also on board coir, jaggeree, ghee, cocoanuts, and a few cases of opium. The stowage was clumsily done, and the vessel consequently crank.

We got under way with a mere breath of wind, and for many days stood along the eastern coast of Java, without any other incident to beguile the monotony of our course than the occasional meeting with some of the small grabs of the Archipelago to which we were bound.

One evening, leaning over the taffrail, I observed a very singular isolated cloud, to the N.W. It was remarkable, as well from its color as from its being the first we had seen since our departure from Batavia. I watched it attentively until sunset, when it spread all at once to the eastward and westward, girting in the horizon with a narrow strip of vapor, and looking like a long line of low beach. My notice was soon afterward attracted by the dusky-red appearance of the moon, and the peculiar character of the sea. The latter was undergoing a rapid change, and the water seemed more than usually transparent. Although I could distinctly see the bottom, yet, heaving the lead, I found the ship in fifteen fathoms. The air now became intolerably hot, and was loaded with spiral exhalations similar to those arising from heated iron. As night came on, every breath of wind died away, and a more entire calm it is impossible to conceive. The flame of a candle burned upon the poop without the least perceptible motion, and a long hair, held between the finger and thumb, hung without the possibility of detecting a vibration. However, as the captain said he could perceive no indication of danger, and as we were drifting in bodily to shore, he ordered the sails to be furled, and the anchor let go. No watch was set, and the crew, consisting principally of Malays, stretched themselves deliberately upon deck. I went below—not without a full presentiment of evil. Indeed, every appearance warranted me in apprehending a simoom. I told the captain of my fears; but he paid no attention to what I said, and left me without deigning to give a reply. My uneasiness, however, prevented me from sleeping, and about midnight I went upon deck. As I placed my foot upon the upper step of the companion-ladder, I was startled by a loud, humming noise, like that occasioned by the rapid revolution of a mill-wheel, and before I could ascertain its meaning, I found the ship quivering to its centre. In the next instant a wilderness of foam hurled us upon our beam-ends, and, rushing over us fore and aft, swept the entire decks from stem to stern.

The extreme fury of the blast proved, in a great measure, the salvation of the ship. Although completely water-logged, yet, as her masts had gone by the board, she rose, after a minute, heavily from the sea, and, staggering awhile beneath the immense pressure of the tempest, finally righted.

By what miracle I escaped destruction, it is impossible to say. Stunned by the shock of the water, I found myself, upon recovery, jammed in between the stern-post and rudder. With great difficulty I regained my feet, and looking dizzily around, was at first struck with the idea of our being among breakers; so terrific, beyond the wildest imagination, was the whirlpool of mountainous and foaming ocean within which we were engulfed. After a while I heard the voice of an old Swede, who had shipped with us at the moment of leaving port. I hallooed to him with all my strength, and presently he came reeling aft. We soon discovered that we were the sole survivors of the accident. All on deck, with the exception of ourselves, had been swept overboard; the captain and mates must have perished while they slept, for the cabins were deluged with water. Without assistance we could expect to do little for the security of the ship, and our exertions were at first paralyzed by the momentary expectation of going down. Our cable had, of course, parted like pack-thread, at the first breath of the hurricane, or we should have been instantaneously overwhelmed. We scudded with frightful velocity before the sea, and the water made clear breaches over us. The framework of our stern was shattered excessively, and, in almost every respect, we had received considerable injury; but to our extreme joy we found the pumps unchoked, and that we had made no great shifting of our ballast. The main fury of the blast had already blown over, and we apprehended little danger from the violence of the wind; but we looked forward to its total cessation with dismay, well believing that, in our shattered condition, we should inevitably perish in the tremendous swell which would ensue. But this very just apprehension seemed by no means likely to be soon verified. For five entire days and nights—during which our only subsistence was a small quantity of jaggeree, procured with great difficulty from the forecastle—the hulk flew at a rate defying computation, before rapidly succeeding flaws of wind, which, without equalling the first violence of the simoom, were still more terrific than any tempest I had before encountered. Our course for the first four days was, with trifling variations, S.E. and by S.; and we must have run down the coast of New Holland. In the fifth day the cold became extreme, although the wind had hauled round a point more to the northward. The sun arose with a sickly yellow lustre, and clambered a very few degrees above the horizon—emitting no decisive light. There were no clouds apparent, yet the wind was upon the increase, and blew with a fitful and unsteady fury. About noon, as nearly as we could guess, our attention was again arrested by the appearance of the sun. It gave out no light, properly so called, but a dull and sullen glow without reflection, as if all its rays were polarized. Just before sinking within the turgid sea, its central fires suddenly went out, as if hurriedly extinguished by some unaccountable power. It was a dim, silver-like rim, alone, as it rushed down the unfathomable ocean.

We waited in vain for the arrival of the sixth day—that day to me has not yet arrived—to the Swede never did arrive. Thenceforward we were enshrouded in pitchy darkness, so that we could not have seen an object at twenty paces from the ship. Eternal night continued to envelop us, all unrelieved by the phosphoric sea-brilliancy to which we had been accustomed in the tropics. We observed, too, that, although the tempest continued to rage with unabated violence, there was no longer to be discovered the usual appearance of surf, or foam, which had hitherto attended us. All around were horror, and thick gloom, and a black sweltering desert of ebony. Superstitious terror crept by degrees into the spirit of the old Swede, and my own soul was wrapt in silent wonder. We neglected all care of the ship, as worse than useless, and securing ourselves as well as possible, to the stump of the mizzen-mast, looked out bitterly into the world of ocean. We had no means of calculating time, nor could we form any guess of our situation. We were, however, well aware of having made farther to the southward than any previous navigators, and felt great amazement at not meeting with the usual impediments of ice. In the meantime every moment threatened to be our last—every mountainous billow hurried to overwhelm us. The swell surpassed anything I had imagined possible, and that we were not instantly buried is a miracle. My companion spoke of the lightness of our cargo, and reminded me of the excellent qualities of our ship; but

I could not help feeling the utter hopelessness of hope itself, and prepared myself gloomily for that death which I thought nothing could defer beyond an hour, as, with every knot of way the ship made, the swelling of the black stupendous seas became more dismally appalling. At times we gasped for breath at an elevation beyond the albatross—at times became dizzy with the velocity of our descent into some watery hell, where the air grew stagnant, and no sound disturbed the slumbers of the kraken.

We were at the bottom of one of these abysses, when a quick scream from my companion broke fearfully upon the night "See! see!" cried he, shrieking in my ears, "Almighty God! see! see!" As he spoke I became aware of a dull sullen glare of red light which streamed down the sides of the vast chasm where we lay, and threw a fitful brilliancy upon our deck. Casting my eyes upwards, I beheld a spectacle which froze the current of my blood. At a terrific height directly above us, and upon the very verge of the precipitous descent, hovered a gigantic ship of perhaps four thousand tons. Although upreared upon the summit of a wave more than a hundred times her own altitude, her apparent size still exceeded that of any ship of the line or East Indiaman in existence. Her huge hull was of a deep dingy black, unrelieved by any of the customary carvings of a ship. A single row of brass cannon protruded from her open ports, and dashed from the polished surfaces the fires of innumerable battle-lanterns which swung to and fro about her rigging. But what mainly inspired us with horror and astonishment, was that she bore up under a press of sail in the very teeth of that supernatural sea, and of that ungovernable hurricane. When we first discovered her, her bows were alone to be seen, as she rose slowly from the dim and horrible gulf beyond her. For a moment of intense terror she paused upon the giddy pinnacle as if in contemplation of her own sublimity, then trembled, and tottered, and—came down.

At this instant, I know not what sudden self-possession came over my spirit. Staggering as far aft as I could, I awaited fearlessly the ruin that was to overwhelm. Our own vessel was at length ceasing from her struggles, and sinking with her head to the sea. The shock of the descending mass struck her, consequently, in that portion of her frame which was nearly under water, and the inevitable result was to hurl me, with irresistible violence, upon the rigging of the stranger.

As I fell, the ship hove in stays, and went about; and to the confusion ensuing I attributed my escape from the notice of the crew. With little difficulty I made my way, unperceived, to the main hatchway, which was partially open, and soon found an opportunity of secreting myself in the hold. Why I did so I can hardly tell. An indefinite sense of awe, which at first sight of the navigators of the ship had taken hold of my mind, was perhaps the principle of my concealment. I was unwilling to trust myself with a race of people who had offered, to the cursory glance I had taken, so many points of vague novelty, doubt, and apprehension. I therefore thought proper to contrive a hiding-place in the hold. This I did by removing a small portion of the shifting-boards, in such a manner as to afford me a convenient retreat between the huge timbers of the ship.

I had scarcely completed my work, when a footstep in the hold forced me to make use of it. A man passed by my place of concealment with a feeble and unsteady gait. I could not see his face, but had an opportunity of observing his general appearance. There was about it an evidence of great age and infirmity. His knees tottered beneath a load of years, and his entire frame quivered under the burthen. He muttered to himself, in a low broken tone, some words of a language which I could not understand, and groped in a corner among a pile of singular-looking instruments, and decayed charts of navigation. His manner was a wild mixture of the peevishness of second childhood, and the solemn dignity of a God. He at length went on deck, and I saw him no more.

A feeling, for which I have no name, has taken possession of my soul—a sensation which will admit of no analysis, to which the lessons of bygone time are inadequate, and for which I fear futurity itself will offer me no key. To a mind constituted like my own, the latter consideration is an evil. I shall never—I know that I shall never—be satisfied with regard to the nature of my conceptions. Yet it is not wonderful that these conceptions are indefinite, since they have their origin in sources so utterly novel. A new sense—a new entity is added to my soul.

It is long since I first trod the deck of this terrible ship, and the rays of my destiny are, I think, gathering to a focus. Incomprehensible men! Wrapped up in meditations of a kind which I cannot divine, they pass me by unnoticed. Concealment is utter folly on my part, for the people *will not* see. It is but just now that I passed directly before the eyes of the mate; it was no long while ago that I ventured into the captain's own private cabin, and took thence the materials with which I write, and have written. I shall from time to time continue this journal. It is true that I may not find an opportunity of transmitting it to the world, but I will not fail to make the endeavor. At the last moment I will enclose the MS. in a bottle, and cast it within the sea.

An incident has occurred which has given me new room for

meditation. Are such things the operation of ungoverned chance? I had ventured upon deck and thrown myself down, without attracting any notice, among a pile of ratlin-stuff and old sails, in the bottom of the yawl. While musing upon the singularity of my fate, I unwittingly daubed with a tar-brush the edges of a neatly-folded studding-sail which lay near me on a barrel. The studding-sail is now bent upon the ship, and the thoughtless touches of the brush are spread out into the word DISCOVERY.

I have made my observations lately upon the structure of the vessel. Although well armed, she is not, I think, a ship of war. Her rigging, build, and general equipment, all negative a supposition of this kind. What she *is not,* I can easily perceive; what she *is,* I fear it is impossible to say. I know not how it is, but in sctutinizing her strange model and singular cast of spars, her huge size and overgrown suits of canvas, her severely simple bow and antiquated stern, there will occasionally flash across my mind a sensation of familiar things, and there is always mixed up with such indistinct shadows of recollection, an unaccountable memory of old foreign chronicles and ages long ago.

I have been looking at the timbers of the ship. She is built of a material to which I am a stranger. There is a peculiar character about the wood which strikes me as rendering it unfit for the purpose to which it has been applied. I mean its extreme *porousness,* considered independently of the worm-eaten condition which is a consequence of navigation in these seas, and apart from the rottenness attendant upon age. It will appear perhaps an observation somewhat overcurious, but this would have every characteristic of Spanish oak, if Spanish oak were distended by any unnatural means.

In reading the above sentence, a curious apothegm of an old

weather-beaten Dutch navigator comes full upon my recollection. "It is as sure," he was wont to say, when any doubt was entertained of his veracity, "as sure as there is a sea where the ship itself will grow in bulk like the living body of the seaman."

About an hour ago, I made bold to trust myself among a group of the crew. They paid me no manner of attention, and, although I stood in the very midst of them all, seemed utterly unconscious of my presence. Like the one I had at first seen in the hold, they all bore about them the marks of a hoary old age. Their knees trembled with infirmity; their shoulders were bent double with decrepitude; their shrivelled skins rattled in the wind; their voices were low, tremulous, and broken; their eyes glistened with the rheum of years; and their gray hairs streamed terribly in the tempest. Around them, on every part of the deck, lay scattered mathematical instruments of the most quaint and obsolete construction.

I mentioned, some time ago, the bending of a studding-sail. From that period, the ship, being thrown dead off the wind, has continued her terrific course due south, with every rag of canvas packed upon her, from her truck to her lower studding-sail booms, and rolling every moment her top-gallant yard-arms into the most appalling hell of water which it can enter into the mind of man to imagine. I have just left the deck, where I find it impossible to maintain a footing, although the crew seem to experience little inconvenience. It appears to me a miracle of miracles that our enormous bulk is not swallowed up at once and forever. We are surely doomed to hover continually upon the brink of eternity, without taking a final plunge into the abyss. From billows a thousand times more stupendous than any I have ever seen, we glide away with the facility of the arrowy sea-gull; and the colossal waters rear their heads above us like demons of the deep, but like demons confined to simple threats, and forbidden to destroy. I am led to attribute these frequent escapes to the only natural cause which can account for such effect. I must suppose the ship to be within the influence of some strong current, or impetuous undertow.

I have seen the captain face to face, and in his own cabin—but, as I expected, he paid me no attention. Although in his appearance there is, to a casual observer, nothing which might bespeak him more or less than man, still, a feeling of irrepressible reverence and awe mingled with the sensation of wonder with which I regarded him. In stature, he is nearly my own height; that is, about five feet eight inches. He is of a well-knit and compact frame of body, neither robust nor remarkable otherwise. But it is the singularity of the expression which reigns upon the face—it is the intense, the wonderful, the thrilling evidence of old age so utter, so extreme, which excites within my spirit a sense—a sentiment ineffable. His forehead, although little wrinkled, seems to bear upon it the stamp of a myriad of years. His gray hairs are records of the past, and his grayer eyes are sybils of the future. The cabin floor was thickly strewn with strange, iron-clasped folios, and mouldering instruments of science, and obsolete long-forgotten charts. His head was bowed down upon his hands, and he pored, with a fiery, unquiet eye, over a paper which I took to be a commission, and which, at all events, bore the signature of a monarch. He murmured to himself—as did the first seaman whom I saw in the hold—some low peevish syllables of a foreign tongue; and although the speaker was close at my elbow, his voice seemed to reach my ears from the distance of a mile.

The ship and all in it are imbued with the spirit of Eld. The crew glide to and fro like the ghosts of buried centuries; their eyes have an eager and uneasy meaning; and when their fingers fall athwart my path in the wild glare of the battle-lanterns, I feel as I have never felt before, although I have been all my life a dealer in antiquities, and have imbibed the shadows of fallen columns at Balbec, and Tadmor, and Persepolis, until my very soul has become a ruin.

When I look around me, I feel ashamed of my former apprehension. If I trembled at the blast which has hitherto attended us, shall I not stand aghast at a warring of wind and ocean, to convey any idea of which, the words tornado and simoom are trivial and ineffective? All in the immediate vicinity of the ship is the blackness of eternal night, and a chaos of foamless water; but, about a league on either side of us, may be seen, indistinctly and at intervals, stupendous ramparts of ice, towering away into the desolate sky, and looking like the walls of the universe.

As I imagined, the ship proves to be in a current—if that appellation can properly be given to a tide, which, howling and shrieking by the white ice, thunders onto the southward with a velocity like the headlong dashing of a cataract.

To conceive the horror of my sensations is, I presume, utterly impossible; yet a curiosity to penetrate the mysteries of these awful regions predominates even over my despair, and will reconcile me to the most hideous aspect of death. It is evident that we are hurrying onward to some exciting knowledge—some never-to-be-imparted secret, whose attainment is destruction. Perhaps this current leads us to the southern pole itself. It must be confessed that a supposition apparently so wild has every probability in its favor.

The crew pace the deck with unquiet and tremulous step; but there is upon their countenance an expression more of the eagerness of hope than of the apathy of despair.

In the meantime the wind is still in our poop, and, as we carry a crowd of canvas, the ship is at times lifted bodily from out of the sea! Oh, horror upon horror!—the ice opens suddenly to the right, and to the left, and we are whirling dizzily, in immense concentric circles, round and round the borders of a gigantic amphitheatre, the summit of whose walls is lost in the darkness and the distance. But little time will be left me to ponder upon my destiny! The circles rapidly grow small—we are plunging madly within the grasp of the whirlpool—and amid a roaring, and bellowing, and thundering of ocean and tempest, the ship is quivering—oh God! and—going down!

WHAT WAS IT?

Fitz James O'Brien

[1828–1862]

"Among the earliest of Poe's disciples may be reckoned the brilliant young Irishman Fitz James O'Brien, who became naturalised as an American and perished honourably in the Civil War. It is he who gave us *What Was It?*, the first well-shaped short story of a tangible but invisible being, and the prototype of de Maupassant's *Horla*. . . . O'Brien's early death undoubtedly deprived us of some masterful tales of strangeness and terror, though his genius was not, properly speaking, of the same titan quality which characterised Poe and Hawthorne."

—*H.P. Lovecraft*

I
T IS, I CONFESS, with considerable diffidence that I approach the strange narrative which I am about to relate. The events which I purpose detailing are of so extraordinary and unheard-of a character that I am quite prepared to meet with an unusual amount of incredulity and scorn. I accept all such beforehand. I have, I trust, the literary courage to face unbelief. I have, after mature consideration, resolved to narrate, in as simple and straight-forward a manner as I can compass, some facts that passed under my observation in the month of July last, and which, in the annals of the mysteries of physical science, are wholly unparalleled.

I live at No.—Twenty-sixth Street, in this city. The house is in some respects a curious one. It has enjoyed for the last two years the reputation of being haunted. It is a large and stately residence, surrounded by what was once a garden, but which is now only a green inclosure used for bleaching clothes. The dry basin of what has been a fountain, and a few fruit-trees, ragged and unpruned, indicate that this spot, in past days, was a pleasant, shady retreat, filled with fruits and flowers and the sweet murmur of waters.

The house is very spacious. A hall of noble size leads to a vast spiral staircase winding through its centre; while the various apartments are of imposing dimensions. It was built some fifteen or twenty years since by Mr. A—, the well-known New York merchant, who five years ago threw the commercial world into convulsions by a stupendous bank fraud. Mr. A—, as everyone knows, escaped to Europe, and died not long after of a broken heart. Almost immediately after the news of his decease reached this country, and was verified, the report spread in Twenty-sixth Street that No.—was haunted. Legal measures had dispossessed the widow of its former owner, and it was inhabited merely by a care-taker and his wife, placed there by the house-agent into whose hands it had passed for purposes of renting or sale. These people declared that they were troubled with unnatural noises. Doors were opened without any visible agency. The remnants of furniture scattered through the various rooms were, during the night, piled one upon the other by unknown hands. Invisible feet passed up and down the stairs in broad daylight, accompanied by the rustle of unseen silk dresses and the gliding of viewless hands along the massive balusters. The care-taker and his wife declared that they would live there no longer. The house-agent laughed, dismissed them and put others in their place. The noises and supernatural manifestations continued. The neighborhood caught up the story, and the house remained untenanted for three years. Several parties negotiated for it; but somehow, always before the bargain was closed, they heard the unpleasant rumors, and declined to treat any further.

It was in this state of things that my landlady—who at that time kept a boarding-house in Bleecker Street, and who wished to move farther up town—conceived the bold idea of renting No.— Twenty-sixth Street. Happening to have in her house rather a plucky and philosophical set of boarders, she laid her scheme before us, stating candidly everything she had heard respecting the ghostly qualities of the establishment to which she wished to remove us. With the exception of one or two timid persons—a sea-captain and a returned Californian, who immediately gave notice that they would leave—every one of Mrs. Moffat's guests declared that they would accompany her in her chivalric incursion into the abode of spirits.

Our removal was effected in the month of May, and we were all charmed with our new residence. The portion of Twenty-sixth Street where our house is situated—between Seventh and Eighth Avenues—is one of the pleasantest localities in New York. The gardens back of the houses, running down nearly to the Hudson, form, in the summer time, a perfect avenue of verdure. The air is pure and invigorating, sweeping, as it does, straight across the river from the Weehawken heights, and even the ragged garden which surrounded the house on two sides, although displaying on washing-days rather too much clothes-line, still gave us a piece of green sward to look at, and a cool retreat in the summer evenings, where we smoked our cigars in the dusk, and watched the fire-flies flashing their dark-lanterns in the long grass.

Of course we had no sooner established ourselves at No.— than we began to expect the ghosts. We absolutely awaited their advent with eagerness. Our dinner conversation was supernatural. One of the boarders, who had purchased Mrs. Crowe's "Night Side of Nature" for his own private delectation, was regarded as a public enemy by the entire household for not having bought twenty copies. The man led a life of supreme wretchedness while he was perusing the volume. A system of espionage was established, of which he was the victim. If he incautiously laid the book down for an instant and left the room, it was immediately seized and read aloud in secret places to a select few. I found myself a person of immense importance, it having leaked out that I was tolerably well versed in the history of supernaturalism, and had once written a story, entitled "The Pot of Tulips," for *Harper's Monthly,* the foundation of which was a ghost. If a table or a wainscot panel happened to warp when we were assembled in the large drawing-room, there was an instant silence, and every one was prepared for an immediate clanking of chains and a spectral form.

After a month of psychological excitement, it was with the utmost dissatisfaction that we were forced to acknowledge that nothing in the remotest degree approaching the supernatural had manifested itself. Once the black butler asseverated that his candle had been blown out by some invisible agency while in the act of undressing himself for the night; but as I had more than once discovered this colored gentleman in a condition when one candle must have appeared to him like two, I thought it possible that, by going a step farther in his potations, he might have reversed this phenomenon, and seen no candle at all where he ought to have beheld one.

Things were in this state when an incident took place so

awful and inexplicable in its character that my reason fairly reels at the bare memory of the occurrence. It was the tenth of July. After dinner was over I repaired, with my friend Dr. Hammond, to the garden to smoke my evening pipe. Independent of certain mental sympathies which existed between the Doctor and myself, we were linked together by a secret vice. We both smoked opium. We knew each other's secret, and respected it. We enjoyed together that wonderful expansion of thought; that marvelous intensifying of the perceptive faculties; that boundless feeling of existence when we seem to have points of contact with the whole universe; in short, that unimaginable spiritual bliss, which I would not surrender for a throne, and which I hope you, reader, will never—never taste.

Those hours of opium happiness which the Doctor and I spent together in secret were regulated with a scientific accuracy. We did not blindly smoke the drug of Paradise, and leave our dreams to chance. While smoking we carefully steered our conversation through the brightest and calmest channels of thought. We talked of the East, and endeavored to recall the magical panorama of its glowing scenery. We criticised the most sensuous poets, those who painted life ruddy with health, brimming with passion, happy in the possession of youth, and strength, and beauty. If we talked of Shakespeare's "Midsummer Night's Dream," we lingered over Ariel and avoided Caliban. Like the Gebers, we turned our faces to the East, and saw only the sunny side of the world.

This skillful coloring of our train of thought produced in our subsequent visions a corresponding tone. The splendors of Arabian fairy-land dyed our dreams. We paced that narrow strip of grass with the tread and port of kings. The song of the *Rana arborea* while he clung to the bark of the ragged plum-tree sounded like the strains of divine orchestras. Houses, walls, and streets melted like rain-clouds, and vistas of unimaginable glory stretched away before us. It was a rapturous companionship. We each of us enjoyed the vast delight more perfectly because, even in our most ecstatic moments, we were ever conscious of each other's presence. Our pleasures, while individual, were still twin, vibrating and moving in musical accord.

On the evening in question, the tenth of July, the Doctor and myself found ourselves in an unusually metaphysical mood. We lit our large meerschaums, filled with fine Turkish tobacco, in the core of which burned a little black nut of opium, that, like the nut in the fairy tale, held within its narrow limits wonders beyond the reach of kings; we paced to and fro, conversing. A strange perversity dominated the currents of our thought. They would *not* flow through the sun-lit channels into which we strove to divert them. For some unaccountable reason they constantly diverged into dark and lonesome beds, where a continual gloom brooded. It was in vain that, after our old fashion, we flung ourselves on the shores of the East, and talked of its gay bazaars, of the splendors of the time of Haroun, of harems and golden palaces. Black afreets continually arose from the depths of our talk, and expanded, like the one the fisherman released from the copper vessel, until they blotted everything bright from our vision. Insensibly we yielded to the occult force that swayed us, and indulged in gloomy speculation. We had talked some time upon the proneness of the human mind to mysticism and the almost universal love of the Terrible, when Hammond suddenly said to me:

"What do you consider to be the greatest element of Terror?"

The question, I own, puzzled me. That many things were terrible, I knew. Stumbling over a corpse in the dark; beholding, as I once did, a woman floating down a deep and rapid river, with wildly-lifted arms and awful, upturned face, uttering, as she sank, shrieks that rent one's heart, while we, the spectators, stood frozen at a window which overhung the river at a height of sixty feet, unable to make the slightest effort to save her, but dumbly watching her last supreme agony and her disappearance. A shattered wreck, with no life visible, encountered floating listlessly on the ocean, is a terrible object, for it suggests a huge terror, the proportions of which are veiled. But it now struck me for the first time that there must be one great and ruling embodiment of fear, a King of Terrors to which all others must succumb. What might it be? To what train of circumstances would it owe its existence?

"I confess, Hammond," I replied to my friend, "I never considered the subject before. That there must be one Something more terrible than any other thing, I feel. I can not attempt, however, even the most vague definition."

"I am somewhat like you, Harry," he answered. "I feel my capacity to experience a terror greater than anything yet conceived by the human mind. Something combining in fearful and unnatural amalgamation hitherto supposed incompatible elements. The calling of the voices in Brockden Brown's novel of 'Wieland' is awful; so is the picture of the Dweller of the Threshold in Bulwer's 'Zanoni;' but," he added, shaking his head gloomily, "there is something more horrible still than these."

"Look here, Hammond," I rejoined; "let us drop this kind of talk for Heaven's sake. We shall suffer for it, depend on it."

"I don't know what's the matter with me tonight," he replied, "but my brain is running upon all sorts of weird and awful thoughts. I feel as if I could write a story like Hoffman tonight, if I were only master of a literary style."

"Well, if we are going to be Hoffmanesque in our talk I'm off to bed. Opium and nightmares should never be brought together. How sultry it is! Good-night, Hammond."

"Good-night, Harry. Pleasant dreams to you."

"To you, gloomy wretch, afreets, ghouls, and enchanters."

We parted, and each sought his respective chamber. I undressed quickly and got into bed, taking with me, according to my usual custom, a book, over which I generally read myself to sleep. I opened the volume as soon as I had laid my head upon the pillow, and instantly flung it to the other side of the room. It was Goudon's "History of Monsters"—a curious French work, which I had lately imported from Paris, but which, in the state of mind I was then in, was anything but an agreeable companion. I resolved to go to sleep at once; so, turning down my gas until nothing but a little blue point of light glimmered on the top of the tube, I composed myself to rest once more.

The room was in total darkness. The atom of gas that still remained lighted did not illuminate a distance of three inches round the burner. I desperately drew my arm across my eyes, as if to shut out even the darkness, and tried to think of nothing. It was in vain. The confounded themes touched on by Hammond in the garden kept obtruding themselves on my brain. I battled against them. I erected ramparts of would-be blankness of intellect to keep them out. They still crowded upon me. While I was lying still as a corpse, hoping that by a perfect physical inaction I would hasten mental repose, an awful incident occurred. A

Something dropped, as it seemed, from the ceiling, plumb upon my chest, and the next instant I felt two bony hands encircling my throat, endeavoring to choke me.

I am no coward, and am possessed of considerable physical strength. The suddenness of the attack instead of stunning me strung every nerve to its highest tension. My body acted from instinct, before my brain had time to realize the terrors of my position. In an instant I wound two muscular arms around the creature, and squeezed it, with all the strength of despair, against my chest. In a few seconds the bony hands that had fastened on my throat loosened their hold, and I was free to breathe once more. Then commenced a struggle of awful intensity. Immersed in the most profound darkness, totally ignorant of the nature of the Thing by which I was so suddenly attacked, finding my grasp slipping every moment by reason, it seemed to me, of the entire nakedness of my assailant, bitten with sharp teeth in the shoulder, neck, and chest, having every moment to protect my throat against a pair of sinewy, agile hands, which my utmost efforts could not confine—these were a combination of circumstances to combat which required all the strength and skill and courage that I possessed.

At last, after a silent, deadly, exhausting struggle, I got my assailant under by a series of incredible efforts of strength. Once pinned, with my knee on what I made out to be its chest, I knew that I was victor. I rested for a moment to breathe. I heard the creature beneath me panting in the darkness, and felt the violent throbbing of a heart. It was apparently as exhausted as I was, that was one comfort. At this moment I remembered that I usually placed under my pillow, before going to bed, a large, yellow silk pocket-handkerchief, for use during the night. I felt for it instantly; it was there. In a few seconds more I had, after a fashion, pinioned the creature's arms.

I now felt tolerably secure. There was nothing more to be done but to turn on the gas, and, having first seen what my midnight assailant was like, arouse the household. I will confess to being actuated by a certain pride in not giving the alarm before; I wished to make the capture alone and unaided.

Never loosing my hold for an instant, I slipped from the bed to the floor, dragging my captive with me. I had but a few steps to make to reach the gas-burner; these I made with the greatest caution, holding the creature in a grip like a vise. At last I got within arm's-length of the tiny speck of blue light, which told me where the gas-burner lay. Quick as lightning I released my grasp with one hand and let on the full flood of light. Then I turned to look at my captive.

I can not even attempt to give any definition of my sensations the instant after I turned on the gas. I suppose I must have shrieked with terror, for in less than a minute afterward my room was crowded with the inmates of the house. I shudder now as I think of that awful moment. *I saw nothing!* Yes; I had one arm firmly clasped round a breathing, panting, corporeal shape, my other hand gripped with all its strength a throat as warm, and apparently fleshly, as my own; and yet, with this living substance in my grasp, with its body pressed against my own, and all in the bright glare of a large jet of gas, I absolutely beheld nothing! Not even an outline—a vapor!

I do not, even at this hour, realize the situation in which I found myself. I can not recall the astounding incident thoroughly. Imagination in vain tries to compass the awful paradox.

It breathed. I felt its warm breath upon my cheek. It struggled fiercely. It had hands. They clutched me. Its skin was smooth, just like my own. There it lay, pressed close up against me, solid as stone—and yet utterly invisible!

I wonder that I did not faint or go mad on the instant. Some wonderful instinct must have sustained me; for, absolutely, in place of loosening my hold on the terrible Enigma, I seemed to gain an additional strength in my moment of horror, and tightened my grasp with such wonderful force that I felt the creature shivering with agony.

Just then Hammond entered my room at the head of the household. As soon as he beheld my face—which, I suppose, must have been an awful sight to look at—he hastened forward, crying,

"Great Heaven, Harry! what has happened?"

"Hammond! Hammond!" I cried, "come here. Oh! this is awful! I have been attacked in bed by something or other, which I have hold of; but I can't see it—I can't see it!"

Hammond, doubtless struck by the unfeigned horror expressed in my countenance, made one or two steps forward with an anxious yet puzzled expression. A very audible titter burst from the remainder of my visitors. This suppressed laughter made me furious. To laugh at a human being in my position! It was the worst species of cruelty. *Now,* I can understand why the appearance of a man struggling violently, as it would seem, with an airy nothing, and calling for assistance against a vision, should have appeared ludicrous. *Then,* so great was my rage against the mocking crowd that had I the power I would have stricken them dead where they stood.

"Hammond! Hammond!" I cried again, despairingly, "for God's sake come to me. I can hold the—the Thing but a short while longer. It is overpowering me. Help me. Help me!"

"Harry," whispered Hammond, approaching me, "you have been smoking too much opium."

"I swear to you, Hammond, that this is no vision," I answered, in the same low tone. "Don't you see how it shakes my whole frame with its struggles? If you don't believe me convince yourself. Feel it—touch it."

Hammond advanced and laid his hand in the spot I indicated. A wild cry of horror burst from him. He had felt it!

In a moment he had discovered somewhere in my room a long piece of cord, and was the next instant winding it, and knotting it about the body of the unseen being that I clasped tightly in my arms.

"Harry," he said, in a hoarse, agitated voice, for, though he preserved his presence of mind, he was deeply moved, "Harry, it's all safe now. You may let go, old fellow, if you're tired. The Thing can't move."

I was utterly exhausted, and I gladly loosed my hold.

Hammond stood holding the ends of the cord that bound the Invisible, twisted round his hand, while before him, self-supporting, as it were, he beheld a rope laced and interlaced, and stretching tightly around a vacant space. I never saw a man look so thoroughly stricken with awe. Nevertheless his face expressed all the courage and determination which I knew him to possess. His lips, although white, were set firmly, and one could perceive at a glance that, although stricken with fear, he was not daunted.

The confusion that ensued among the guests of the house, who were witnesses of this extraordinary scene between Hammond and myself—who beheld the pantomime of binding this struggling Something—who beheld me almost sinking from physical exhaustion when my task of jailer was over—the confusion and terror that took possession of the by-standers, when they saw all this, was beyond description. Many of the weaker ones fled from the apartment. The few who remained behind clustered near the door, and could not be induced to approach Hammond and his Charge. Still incredulity broke out through their terror. They had not the courage to satisfy themselves, and yet they doubted. It was in vain that I begged of some of the men to come near and convince themselves by touch of the existence of a living being in that room which was invisible. They were incredulous, but did not dare to undeceive themselves. How could a solid, living, breathing body be invisible? they asked. My reply was this. I gave a sign to Hammond, and both of us—conquering our fearful repugnance to touching the invisible creature—lifted it from the ground, manacled as it was, and took it to my bed. Its weight was about that of a boy of fourteen.

"Now my friends," I said, as Hammond and myself held the creature suspended over the bed, "I can give you self-evident proof that here is a solid, ponderable body which, nevertheless, you can not see. Be good enough to watch the surface of the bed attentively."

I was astonished at my own courage in treating this strange event so calmly; but I had recovered from my first terror, and felt a sort of scientific pride in the affair which dominated every other feeling.

The eyes of the by-standers were immediately fixed on my bed. At a given signal Hammond and I let the creature fall. There was the dull sound of a heavy body alighting on a soft mass. The timbers of the bed creaked. A deep impression marked itself distinctly on the pillow, and on the bed itself. The crowd who witnessed this gave a sort of low, universal cry, and rushed from the room. Hammond and I were left alone with our Mystery.

We remained silent for some time, listening to the low, irregular breathing of the creature on the bed, and watching the rustle of the bedclothes as it impotently struggled to free itself from confinement. Then Hammond spoke.

"Harry, this is awful."

"Ay, awful."

"But not unaccountable."

"Not unaccountable! What do you mean? Such a thing has never occurred since the birth of the world. I know not what to think, Hammond. God grant that I am not mad, and that this is not an insane fantasy!"

"Let us reason a little, Harry. Here is a body which we touch, but which we cannot see. The fact is so unusual that it strikes us with terror. Is there no parallel, though, for such a phenomenon? Take a piece of pure glass. It is tangible and transparent. A certain chemical coarseness is all that prevents its being so entirely transparent as to be totally invisible. It is not *theoretically impossible,* mind you, to fabricate a glass which shall not reflect a single ray of light—a glass so pure and homogeneous in its atoms that the rays from the sun shall pass through it as they do through the air, refracted but not reflected. We do not see the air, and yet we feel it."

"That's all very well, Hammond, but these are inanimate substances. Glass does not breathe, air does not breathe. *This* thing has a heart that palpitates. A will that moves it. Lungs that play and inspire and respire."

"You forget the strange phenomena of which we have so often heard of late," answered the Doctor, gravely. "At the meetings called 'spirit circles,' invisible hands have been thrust into the hands of those persons round the table—warm, fleshly hands that seemed to pulsate with mortal life."

"What? Do you think, then, that this thing is—"

"I don't know what it is," was the solemn reply; "but please the gods I will, with your assistance, thoroughly investigate it."

We watched together, smoking many pipes, all night long by the bedside of the unearthly being that tossed and panted until it was apparently wearied out. Then we learned by the low, regular breathing that it slept.

The next morning the house was all astir. The boarders congregated on the landing outside my room, and Hammond and myself were lions. We had to answer a thousand questions as to the state of our extraordinary prisoner, for as yet not one person in the house except ourselves could be induced to set foot in the apartment.

The creature was awake. This was evidenced by the convulsive manner in which the bedclothes were moved in its efforts to escape. There was something truly terrible in beholding, as it were, those second-hand indications of the terrible writhings and agonized struggles for liberty, which themselves were invisible.

Hammond and myself had racked our brains during the long night to discover some means by which we might realize the shape and general appearance of the Enigma. As well as we could make out by passing our hands over the creature's form, its outlines and lineaments were human. There was a mouth; a round, smooth head without hair; a nose, which, however, was little elevated above the cheeks; and its hands and feet felt like those of a boy. At first we thought of placing the being on a smooth surface and tracing its outline with chalk, as shoemakers trace the outline of the foot. This plan was given up as being of no value. Such an outline would give not the slightest idea of its conformation.

A happy thought struck me. We would take a cast of it in plaster of Paris. This would give us the solid figure, and satisfy all our wishes. But how to do it? The movements of the creature would disturb the setting of the plastic covering, and distort the mould. Another thought. Why not give it chloroform? It had respiratory organs—that was evident by its breathing. Once reduced to a state of insensibility, we could do with it what we would. Doctor X—was sent for; and after the worthy physician had recovered from the first shock of amazement, he proceeded to administer the chloroform. In three minutes afterward we were enabled to remove the fetters from the creature's body, and a well-known modeler of this city was busily engaged in covering the invisible form with the moist clay. In five minutes more we had a mould, and before evening a rough *facsimile* of the Mystery. It was shaped like a man. Distorted, uncouth, and horrible, but still a man. It was small, not over four feet and some inches in height, and its limbs betrayed a muscular development that was unparalleled. Its face surpassed in hideousness anything I had ever seen. Gustave Doré, or Callot, or Tony Johannot never conceived anything so horrible. There is a face in one of the latter's illustrations to *"Un voyage ou il vous plaira,"* which somewhat approaches the countenance of this creature, but does not equal it. It was the physiognomy of what I should have fancied a ghoul to be. It looked as if it was capable of feeding on human flesh.

Having satisfied our curiosity, and bound every one in the

house over to secrecy, it became a question what was to be done with our Enigma? It was impossible that we should keep such a horror in our house; it was equally impossible that such an awful being should be let loose upon the world. I confess that I would have gladly voted for the creature's destruction. But who would shoulder the responsibility? Who would undertake the execution of this horrible semblance of a human being? Day after day this question was deliberated gravely. The boarders all left the house. Mrs. Moffat was in despair, and threatened Hammond and myself with all sorts of legal penalties if we did not remove the Horror. Our answer was, "We will go if you like, but we decline taking this creature with us. Remove it yourself if you please. It appeared in your house. On you the responsibility rests." To this there was, of course, no answer. Mrs. Moffat could not obtain for love or money a person who would even approach the Mystery.

The most singular part of the transaction was, that we were entirely ignorant of what the creature habitually fed on. Everything in the way of nutriment that we could think of was placed before it, but was never touched. It was awful to stand by, day after day, and see the clothes toss and hear the hard breathing, and know that it was starving.

Ten, twelve days, a fortnight passed, and it still lived. The pulsations of the heart, however, were daily growing fainter, and had now nearly ceased altogether. It was evident that the creature was dying for want of sustenance. While this terrible life-struggle was going on I felt miserable. I could not sleep of nights. Horrible as the creature was, it was pitiful to think of the pangs it was suffering. At last it died. Hammond and I found it cold and stiff one morning in the bed. The heart had ceased to beat, the lungs to inspire. We hastened to bury it in the garden. It was a strange funeral, the dropping of that viewless corpse into the damp hole. The cast of its form I gave to Doctor X——, who keeps it in his museum in Tenth Street.

As I am on the eve of a long journey from which I may not return, I have drawn up this narrative of an event the most singular that has ever come to my knowledge.

THE MIDDLE TOE OF THE RIGHT FOOT
Ambrose Bierce
[1842–c1913]

"Closer to real greatness was the eccentric and saturnine journalist
Ambrose Bierce, born in 1842; who likewise entered the Civil War,
but survived to write some immortal tales and to disappear in 1913
in as great a cloud of mystery as any he ever evoked from his nightmare fancy. . . . Virtually all of Bierce's tales are tales of horror; and
whilst many of them treat only of the physical and psychological
horrors within Nature, a substantial proportion admit the malignly
supernatural and form a leading element in America's fund of weird
literature.

"*The Middle Toe of the Right Foot* is clumsily developed, but has
a powerful climax. A man named Manton has horribly killed his two
children and his wife, the latter of whom lacked the middle toe of
her right foot. Ten years later he returns much altered to the neighbourhood; and, being secretly recognised, is provoked into a bowie-
knife duel in the dark, to be held in the now abandoned house where
his crime was committed. When the moment of the duel arrives a
trick is played upon him; and he is left without an antagonist, shut
in a night-black ground floor room of the reputedly haunted edifice,
with the thick dust of a decade on every hand."

—H.P. Lovecraft

I

T IS WELL-KNOWN that the old Manton house is haunted. In all the rural district near about, and even in the town of Marshall, a mile away, not one person of unbiased mind entertains a doubt of it; incredulity is confined to those opinionated persons who will be called "cranks" as soon as the useful word shall have penetrated the intellectual demesne of the Marshall *Advance*. The evidence that the house is haunted is of two kinds: the testimony of disinterested witnesses who have had ocular proof, and that of the house itself. The former may be disregarded and ruled out on any of the various grounds of objection which may be urged against it by the ingenious; but facts within the observation of all are material and controlling.

In the first place, the Manton house has been unoccupied by mortals for more than ten years, and with its outbuildings is slowly falling into decay—a circumstance which in itself the judicious will hardly venture to ignore. It stands a little way off the loneliest reach of the Marshall and Harriston road, in an opening which was once a farm and is still disfigured with strips of rotting fence and half covered with brambles overrunning a stony and sterile soil long unacquainted with the plow. The house itself is in tolerably good condition, though badly weather-stained and in dire need of attention from the glazier, the smaller male population of the region having attested in the manner of its kind its disapproval of dwelling without dwellers. It is two stories in height, nearly square, its front pierced by a single doorway flanked on each side by a window boarded up to the very top. Corresponding windows above, not protected, serve to admit light and rain to the rooms of the upper floor. Grass and weeds grow pretty rankly all about, and a few shade trees, somewhat the worse for wind, and leaning all in one direction, seem to be making a concerted effort to run away. In short, as the Marshall town humorist explained in the columns of the *Advance,* "the proposition that the Manton house is badly haunted is the only logical conclusion from the premises." The fact that in this dwelling Mr. Manton thought it expedient one night some ten years ago to rise and cut the throats of his wife and two small children, removing at once to another part of the country, has no doubt done its share in directing public attention to the fitness of the place for supernatural phenomena.

To this house, one summer evening, came four men in a wagon. Three of them promptly alighted, and the one who had been driving hitched the team to the only remaining post of what had been a fence. The fourth remained seated in the wagon. "Come," said one of his companions, approaching him, while the others moved away in the direction of the dwelling—"this is the place."

The man addressed did not move. "By God!" he said harshly, "this is a trick, and it looks to me as if you were in it."

"Perhaps I am," the other said, looking him straight in the face and speaking in a tone which had something of contempt in it. "You will remember, however, that the choice of place was with your own assent left to the other side. Of course if you are afraid of spooks—"

"I am afraid of nothing," the man interrupted with another oath, and sprang to the ground. The two then joined the others at the door, which one of them had already opened with some difficulty, caused by rust of lock and hinge. All entered. Inside it was dark, but the man who had unlocked the door produced a candle and matches and made a light. He then unlocked a door on their right as they stood in the passage. This gave them entrance to a large, square room that the candle but dimly lighted. The floor had a thick carpeting of dust, which partly muffled their footfalls. Cobwebs were in the angles of the walls and depended from the ceiling like strips of rotting lace, making undulatory movements in the disturbed air. The room had two windows in adjoining sides, but from neither could anything be seen except the rough inner surfaces of boards a few inches from the glass. There was no fireplace, no furniture; there was nothing: besides the cobwebs and the dust, the four men were the only objects there which were not a part of the structure.

Strange enough they looked in the yellow light of the candle. The one who had so reluctantly alighted was especially spectac-ular—he might have been called sensational. He was of middle age, heavily built, deep chested and broad shouldered. Looking at his figure, one would have said that he had a giant's strength; at his features, that he would use it like a giant. He was clean shaven, his hair rather closely cropped and gray. His low forehead was seamed with wrinkles above the eyes, and over the nose these became vertical. The heavy black brows followed the same law, saved from meeting only by an upward turn at what would oth-erwise have been the point of contact. Deeply sunken beneath these, glowed in the obscure light a pair of eyes of uncertain color, but obviously enough too small. There was something forbidding in their expression, which was not bettered by the cruel mouth and wide jaw. The nose was well enough, as noses go; one does not expect much of noses. All that was sinister in the man's face seemed accentuated by an unnatural pallor—he appeared alto-gether bloodless.

The appearance of the other men was sufficiently common-place: they were such persons as one meets and forgets that he met. All were younger than the man described, between whom and the eldest of the others, who stood apart, there was apparently no kindly feeling. They avoided looking at each other.

"Gentlemen," said the man holding the candle and keys, "I believe everything is right. Are you ready, Mr. Rosser?"

The man standing apart from the group bowed and smiled.

"And you, Mr. Grossmith?"

The heavy man bowed and scowled.

"You will be pleased to remove your outer clothing."

Their hats, coats, waistcoats and neckwear were soon removed and thrown outside the door, in the passage. The man with the candle now nodded, and the fourth man—he who had urged Grossmith to leave the wagon—produced from the pocket of his overcoat two long, murderous-looking bowie-knives, which he drew now from their leather scabbards.

"They are exactly alike," he said, presenting one to each of the two principals—for by this time the dullest observer would have understood the nature of this meeting. It was to be a duel to the death.

Each combatant took a knife, examined it critically near the candle and tested the strength of blade and handle across his lifted knee. Their persons were then searched in turn, each by the second of the other.

"If it is agreeable to you, Mr. Grossmith," said the man holding the light, "you will place yourself in that corner."

He indicated the angle of the room farthest from the door, whither Grossmith retired, his second parting from him with a grasp of the hand which had nothing of cordiality in it. In the angle nearest the door Mr. Rosser stationed himself, and after a whispered consultation his second left him, joining the other near the door. At that moment the candle was suddenly extinguished, leaving all in profound darkness. This may have been done by a draught from the opened door; whatever the cause, the effect was startling.

"Gentlemen," said a voice which sounded strangely unfamiliar in the altered condition affecting the relations of the senses—"gentlemen, you will not move until you hear the closing of the outer door."

A sound of trampling ensued, then the closing of the inner door; and finally the outer one closed with a concussion which shook the entire building.

A few minutes afterward a belated farmer's boy met a light wagon which was being driven furiously toward the town of Marshall. He declared that behind the two figures on the front seat stood a third, with its hands upon the bowed shoulders of the others, who appeared to struggle vainly to free themselves from its grasp. This figure, unlike the others, was clad in white, and had undoubtedly boarded the wagon as it passed the haunted house. As the lad could boast a considerable former experience with the supernatural thereabouts his word had the weight justly due in the testimony of an expert. The story (in connection with the next day's events) eventually appeared in the *Advance,* with some slight literary embellishments and a concluding intimation that the gentlemen referred to would be allowed the use of the paper's columns for their version of the night's adventure. But the privilege remained without a claimant.

II

The events that led up to this "duel in the dark" were simple enough. One evening three young men of the town of Marshall were sitting in a quiet corner of the porch of the village hotel, smoking and discussing such matters as three educated young men of a Southern village would naturally find interesting. Their names were King, Sancher and Rosser. At a little distance, within easy hearing, but taking no part in the conversation, sat a fourth. He was a stranger to the others. They merely knew that on his arrival by the stage-coach that afternoon he had written in the hotel register the name Robert Grossmith. He had not been observed to speak to anyone except the hotel clerk. He seemed, indeed, singularly fond of his own company—or, as the *personnel* of the *Advance* expressed it, "grossly addicted to evil associations." But then it should be said in justice to the stranger that the *personnel* was himself of a too convivial disposition fairly to judge one differently gifted, and had, moreover, experienced a slight rebuff in an effort at an "interview."

"I hate any kind of deformity in a woman," said King, "whether natural or—acquired. I have a theory that any physical defect has its correlative mental and moral defect."

"I infer, then," said Rosser, gravely, "that a lady lacking the moral advantage of a nose would find the struggle to become Mrs. King an arduous enterprise."

"Of course you may put it that way" was the reply; "but, seriously, I once threw over a most charming girl on learning quite accidentally that she had suffered amputation of a toe. My conduct was brutal if you like, but if I had married that girl I should have been miserable for life and should have made her so."

"Whereas," said Sancher, with a light laugh, "by marrying a gentleman of more liberal views she escaped with a parted throat."

"Ah, you know to whom I refer. Yes, she married Manton, but I don't know about his liberality; I'm not sure but he cut her throat because he discovered that she lacked that excellent thing in woman, the middle toe of the right foot."

"Look at that chap!" said Rosser in a low voice, his eyes fixed upon the stranger.

That chap was obviously listening intently to the conversation.

"Damn his impudence!" muttered King—"what ought we to do?"

"That's an easy one," Rosser replied, rising. "Sir," he continued, addressing the stranger, "I think it would be better if you would remove your chair to the other end of the veranda. The presence of gentlemen is evidently an unfamiliar situation to you."

The man sprang to his feet and strode forward with clenched hands, his face white with rage. All were now standing. Sancher stepped between the belligerents.

"You are hasty and unjust," he said to Rosser; "this gentleman has done nothing to deserve such language."

But Rosser would not withdraw a word. By the custom of the country and the time there could be but one outcome to the quarrel.

"I demand the satisfaction due to a gentleman," said the stranger, who had become more calm. "I have not an acquaintance in this region. Perhaps you, sir," bowing to Sancher, "will be kind enough to represent me in this matter."

Sancher accepted the trust—somewhat reluctantly it must be confessed, for the man's appearance and manner were not at all to his liking. King, who during the colloquy had hardly removed his eyes from the stranger's face and had not spoken a word, consented with a nod to act for Rosser, and the upshot of it was that, the principals having retired, a meeting was arranged for the next evening. The nature of the arrangements has been already disclosed. The duel with knives in a dark room was once a commoner feature of Southwestern life than it is likely to be again. How thin a veneering of "chivalry" covered the essential brutality of the code under which such encounters were possible we shall see.

III

In the blaze of a midsummer noonday the old Manton house was hardly true to its traditions. It was of the earth, earthy. The sunshine caressed it warmly and affectionately, with evident disregard of its bad reputation. The grass greening all the expanse in its front seemed to grow, not rankly, but with a natural and joyous exuberance, and the weeds blossomed quite like plants. Full of charming lights and shadows and populous with pleasant-voiced birds, the neglected shade trees no longer struggled to run away, but bent reverently beneath their burdens of sun and song. Even in the glassless upper windows was an expression of peace and contentment, due to the light within. Over the stony fields the visible heat danced with a lively tremor incompatible with the gravity which is an attribute of the supernatural.

Such was the aspect under which the place presented itself to Sheriff Adams and two other men who had come out from Marshall to look at it. One of these men was Mr. King, the sheriff's deputy; the other, whose name was Brewer, was a brother of the late Mrs. Manton. Under a beneficent law of the State relating to property which has been for a certain period abandoned by an owner whose residence cannot be ascertained, the sheriff was legal custodian of the Manton farm and appurtenances thereunto belonging. His present visit was in mere perfunctory compliance with some order of a court in which Mr. Brewer had an action to get possession of the property as heir to his deceased sister. By a mere coincidence, the visit was made on the day after the night that Deputy King had unlocked the house for another and very different purpose. His presence now was not of his own choosing: he had been ordered to accompany his superior and at the moment could think of nothing more prudent than simulated alacrity in obedience to the command.

Carelessly opening the front door, which to his surprise was not locked, the sheriff was amazed to see, lying on the floor of the passage into which it opened, a confused heap of men's apparel. Examination showed it to consist of two hats, and the same number of coats, waistcoats and scarves, all in a remarkably good state of preservation, albeit somewhat defiled by the dust in which they lay. Mr. Brewer was equally astonished, but Mr. King's emotion is not of record. With a new and lively interest in his own actions the sheriff now unlatched and pushed open a door on the right, and the three entered. The room was apparently vacant—no; as their eyes became accustomed to the dimmer light something was visible in the farthest angle of the wall. It was a human figure—that of a man crouching close in the corner. Something in the attitude made the intruders halt when they had barely passed the threshold. The figure more and more clearly defined itself. The man was upon one knee, his back in the angle of the wall, his shoulders elevated to the level of his ears, his hands before his face, palms outward, the fingers spread and crooked like claws; the white face turned upward on the retracted neck had an expression of unutterable fright, the mouth half open, the eyes incredibly expanded. He was stone dead. Yet, with the exception of a bowie-knife, which had evidently fallen from his own hand, not another object was in the room.

In the thick dust that covered the floor were some confused footprints near the door and along the wall through which it opened. Along one of the adjoining walls, too, past the boarded-up windows, was the trail made by the man himself in reaching his corner. Instinctively in approaching the body the three men followed that trail. The sheriff grasped one of the outthrown arms; it was as rigid as iron, and the application of a gentle force rocked the entire body without altering the relation of its parts. Brewer, pale with excitement, gazed intently into the distorted face. "God of mercy!" he suddenly cried, "it is Manton!"

"You are right," said King, with an evident attempt at calmness: "I knew Manton. He then wore a full beard and his hair long, but this is he."

He might have added: "I recognized him when he challenged Rosser. I told Rosser and Sancher who he was before we played him this horrible trick. When Rosser left this dark room at our heels, forgetting his outer clothing in the excitement, and driving away with us in his shirtsleeves—all through the discreditable proceedings we knew whom we were dealing with, murderer and coward that he was!"

But nothing of this did Mr. King say. With his better light he was trying to penetrate the mystery of the man's death. That he had not once moved from the corner where he had been stationed; that his posture was that of neither attack nor defense; that he had dropped his weapon; that he had obviously perished of sheer horror of something that he *saw*—these were circumstances which Mr. King's disturbed intelligence could not rightly comprehend.

Groping in intellectual darkness for a clew to his maze of doubt, his gaze, directed mechanically downward in the way of one who ponders momentous matters, fell upon something which, there, in the light of day and in the presence of living companions, affected him with terror. In the dust of years that lay thick upon the floor—leading from the door by which they had entered, straight across the room to within a yard of Manton's crouching corpse—were three parallel lines of footprints—light but definite impressions of bare feet, the outer ones those of small children, the inner a woman's. From the point at which they ended they did not return; they pointed all one way. Brewer, who had observed them at the same moment, was leaning forward in an attitude of rapt attention, horribly pale.

"Look at that!" he cried, pointing with both hands at the nearest print of the woman's right foot, where she had apparently stopped and stood. "The middle toe is missing—it was Gertrude!"

Gertrude was the late Mrs. Manton, sister to Mr. Brewer.

THE TURN OF THE SCREW
Henry James
[1843–1916]

"Much of the best in American horror-literature has come from pens not mainly devoted to that medium. . . . In *The Turn of the Screw* Henry James triumphs over his inevitable pomposity and prolixity sufficiently well to create a truly potent air of sinister menace; depicting the hideous influence of two dead and evil servants, Peter Quint and the governess, Miss Jessel, over a small boy and girl who had been under their care. James is perhaps too diffuse, too unctuously urbane, and too much addicted to subtleties of speech to realise fully all the wild and devastating horror in his situations; but for all that there is a rare and mounting tide of fright, culminating in the death of the little boy, which gives the novelette a permanent place in its special class."
—H.P. Lovecraft

THE STORY HAD HELD US, round the fire, sufficiently breathless, but except the obvious remark that it was gruesome, as on Christmas Eve in an old house a strange tale should essentially be, I remember no comment uttered till somebody happened to note it as the only case he had met in which such a visitation had fallen on a child. The case, I may mention, was that of an apparition in just such an old house as had gathered us for the occasion—an appearance, of a dreadful kind, to a little boy sleeping in the room with his mother and waking her up in the terror of it; waking her not to dissipate his dread and soothe him to sleep again, but to encounter also herself, before she had succeeded in doing so, the same sight that had shocked him. It was this observation that drew from Douglas—not immediately, but later in the evening—a reply that had the interesting consequence to which I call attention. Some one else told a story not particularly effective, which I saw he was not following. This I took for a sign that he had himself something to produce and that we should only have to wait. We waited in fact till two nights later; but that same evening, before we scattered, he brought out what was in his mind.

"I quite agree—in regard to Griffin's ghost, or whatever it was—that its appearing first to the little boy, at so tender an age, adds a particular touch. But it's not the first occurrence of its charming kind that I know to have been concerned with a child. If the child gives the effect another turn of the screw, what do you say to *two* children—?"

"We say of course," somebody exclaimed, "that two children give two turns! Also that we want to hear about them."

I can see Douglas there before the fire, to which he had got up to present his back, looking down at this converser with his hands in his pockets. "Nobody but me, till now, has ever heard. It's quite too horrible." This was naturally declared by several voices to give the thing the utmost price, and our friend, with quiet art, prepared his triumph by turning his eyes over the rest of us and going on: "It's beyond everything. Nothing at all that I know touches it."

"For sheer terror?" I remember asking.

He seemed to say it wasn't so simple as that; to be really at a loss how to qualify it. He passed his hand over his eyes, made a little wincing grimace. "For dreadful—dreadfulness!"

"Oh how delicious!" cried one of the women.

He took no notice of her; he looked at me, but as if, instead of me, he saw what he spoke of. "For general uncanny ugliness and horror and pain."

"Well then," I said, "just sit right down and begin."

He turned round to the fire, gave a kick to a log, watched it an instant. Then as he faced us again: "I can't begin. I shall have to send to town." There was a unanimous groan at this, and much reproach; after which, in his preoccupied way, he explained. "The story's written. It's in a locked drawer—it has not been out for years. I could write to my man and enclose the key; he could send down the packet as he finds it." It was to me in particular that he appeared to propound this—appeared almost to appeal for aid not to hesitate. He had broken a thickness of ice, the formation of many a winter; had had his reasons for a long silence. The others resented postponement, but it was just his scruples that charmed me. I adjured him to write by the first post and to agree with us for an early hearing; then I asked him if the experience in question had been his own. To this his answer was prompt. "Oh thank God, no!"

"And is the record yours? You took the thing down?"

"Nothing but the impression. I took that *here*"—he tapped his heart. "I've never lost it."

"Then your manuscript—?"

"Is in old faded ink and in the most beautiful hand." He hung fire again. "A woman's. She has been dead these twenty years. She sent me the pages in question before she died." They were all listening now, and of course there was somebody to be arch, or at any rate to draw the inference. But if he put the inference by without a smile it was also without irritation. "She was a most charming person, but she was ten years older than I. She was my sister's governess," he quietly said. "She was the most agreeable woman I've ever known in her position; she'd have been worthy of any whatever. It was long ago, and this episode was long before. I was at Trinity, and I found her at home on my coming down the second summer. I was much there that year—it was a beautiful one; and we had, in her off-hours, some strolls and talks in the garden—talks in which she struck me as awfully clever and nice. Oh yes; don't grin: I liked her extremely and am glad to this day to think she liked me too. If she hadn't she wouldn't have told me. She had never told any one. It wasn't simply that she said so, but that I knew she hadn't. I was sure; I could see. You'll easily judge why when you hear."

"Because the thing had been such a scare?"

He continued to fix me. "You'll easily judge," he repeated: "*you* will."

I fixed him too. "I see. She was in love."

He laughed for the first time. "You *are* acute. Yes, she was in love. That is she *had* been. That came out—she couldn't tell her story without its coming out. I saw it, and she saw I saw it; but neither of us spoke of it. I remember the time and the place—the corner of the lawn, the shade of the great beeches and the long hot summer afternoon. It wasn't a scene for a shudder; but oh—!" He quitted the fire and dropped back into his chair.

"You'll receive the packet Thursday morning?" I said.

"Probably not till the second post."

"Well then; after dinner—"

"You'll all meet me here?" He looked us round again. "Isn't anybody going?" It was almost the tone of hope.

"Everybody will stay!"

"*I* will—and *I* will!" cried the ladies whose departure had been fixed. Mrs. Griffin, however, expressed the need for a little more light. "Who was it she was in love with?"

"The story will tell," I took upon myself to reply.

"Oh I can't wait for the story!"

"The story *won't* tell," said Douglas; "not in any literal vulgar way."

"More's the pity then. That's the only way I ever understand."

"Won't *you* tell, Douglas?" somebody else required.

He sprang to his feet again. "Yes—to-morrow. Now I must go to bed. Good-night." And, quickly catching up a candlestick, he left us slightly bewildered. From our end of the great brown hall we heard his step on the stair; whereupon Mrs. Griffin spoke. "Well, if I don't know who she was in love with I know who *he* was."

"She was ten years older," said her husband.

"*Raison de plus*—at that age! But it's rather nice, his long reticence."

"Forty years!" Griffin put in.

"With this outbreak at last."

"The outbreak," I returned, "will make a tremendous occasion of Thursday night"; and every one so agreed with me that in the light of it we lost all attention for everything else. The last story, however incomplete and like the mere opening of a serial, had been told; we handshook and "candlestuck," as somebody said, and went to bed.

I knew the next day that a letter containing the key had, by the first post, gone off to his London apartments; but in spite of—or perhaps just on account of—the eventual diffusion of this knowledge we quite let him alone till after dinner, till such an hour of the evening in fact as might best accord with the kind of emotion on which our hopes were fixed. Then he became as communicative as we could desire, and indeed gave us his best reason for being so. We had it from him again before the fire in the hall, as we had had our mild wonders of the previous night. It appeared that the narrative he had promised to read us really required for a proper intelligence a few words of prologue. Let me say here distinctly, to have done with it, that this narrative, from an exact transcript of my own made much later, is what I shall presently give. Poor Douglas, before his death—when it was in sight—committed to me the manuscript that reached him on the third of these days and that, on the same spot, with immense effect, he began to read to our hushed little circle on the night of the fourth. The departing ladies who had said they would stay didn't, of course, thank heaven, stay: they departed, in consequence of arrangements made, in a rage of curiosity, as they professed, produced by the touches with which he had already worked us up. But that only made his little final auditory more compact and select, kept it, round the hearth, subject to a common thrill.

The first of these touches conveyed that the written statement took up the tale at a point after it had, in a manner, begun. The fact to be in possession of was therefore that his old friend, the youngest of several daughters of a poor country parson, had at the age of twenty, on taking service for the first time in the schoolroom, come up to London, in trepidation, to answer in person an advertisement that had already placed her in brief correspondence with the advertiser. This person proved, on her presenting herself for judgment at a house in Harley Street that impressed her as vast and imposing—this prospective patron proved a gentleman, a bachelor in the prime of life, such a figure as had never risen, save in a dream or an old novel, before a fluttered anxious girl out of a Hampshire vicarage. One could easily fix his type; it never, happily, dies out. He was handsome and bold and pleasant, off-hand and gay and kind. He struck her, inevitably, as gallant and splendid, but what took her most of all and gave her the courage she afterwards showed was that he put the whole thing to her as a favour, an obligation he should gratefully incur. She figured him as rich, but as fearfully extravagant—saw him all in a glow of high fashion, of good looks, of expensive habits, of charming ways with women. He had for his town residence a big house filled with the spoils of travel and the trophies of the chase; but it was to his country home, an old family place in Essex, that he wished her immediately to proceed.

He had been left, by the death of his parents in India, guardian to a small nephew and a small niece, children of a younger, a military brother whom he had lost two years before. These children were, by the strangest of chances for a man in his position—a lone man without the right sort of experience or a gram of patience—very heavy on his hands. It had all been a great worry and, on his own part doubtless, a series of blunders, but he immensely pitied the poor chicks and had done all he could; had in particular sent them down to his other house, the proper place for them being of course the country, and kept them there from the first with the best people he could find to look after them, parting even with his own servants to wait on them and going down himself, whenever he might, to see how they were doing. The awkward thing was that they had practically no other relations and that his own affairs took up all his time. He had put them in possession of Bly, which was healthy and secure, and had placed at the head of their little establishment—but below-stairs only—an excellent woman, Mrs. Grose, whom he was sure his visitor would like and who had formerly been maid to his mother. She was now housekeeper and was also acting for the time as superintendent to the little girl, of whom, without children of her own, she was by good luck extremely fond. There were plenty of people to help, but of course the young lady who should go down as governess would be in supreme authority. She would also have, in holidays, to look after the small boy, who had been for a term at school—young as he was to be sent, but what else could be done?—and who, as the holidays were about to begin, would be back from one day to the other. There had been for the two children at first a young lady whom they had had the misfortune to lose. She had done for them quite beautifully—she was a most respectable person—till her death, the great awkwardness of which had, precisely, left no alternative but the school for little Miles. Mrs. Grose, since then, in the way of manners and things, had done as she could for Flora; and there were, further, a cook, a housemaid, a dairy-woman, an old pony, an old groom and an old gardener, all likewise thoroughly respectable.

So far had Douglas presented his picture when some one put a question. "And what did the former governess die of? Of so much respectability?"

Our friend's answer was prompt. "That will come out. I don't anticipate."

"Pardon me—I thought that was just what you *are* doing."

"In her successor's place," I suggested, "I should have wished to learn if the office brought with it—"

"Necessary danger to life?" Douglas completed my thought. "She did wish to learn, and she did learn. You shall hear to-morrow what she learnt. Meanwhile of course the prospect struck her as slightly grim. She was young, untried, nervous: it was a vision of serious duties and little company, of really great loneliness. She hesitated—took a couple of days to consult and consider. But the salary offered much exceeded her modest measure, and on a second interview she faced the music, she engaged." And Douglas, with this, made a pause that, for the benefit of the company, moved me to throw in—

"The moral of which was of course the seduction exercised by the splendid young man. She succumbed to it."

He got up and, as he had done the night before, went to the fire, gave a stir to a log with his foot, then stood a moment with his back to us. "She saw him only twice."

"Yes, but that's just the beauty of her passion."

A little to my surprise, on this, Douglas turned round to me. "It *was* the beauty of it. There were others," he went on, "who hadn't succumbed. He told her frankly all his difficulty—that for several applicants the conditions had been prohibitive. They were somehow simply afraid. It sounded dull—it sounded strange; and all the more so because of his main condition."

"Which was—?"

"That she should never trouble him—but never, never: neither appeal nor complain nor write about anything; only meet all questions herself, receive all moneys from his solicitor, take the whole thing over and let him alone. She promised to do this, and she mentioned to me that when, for a moment, disburdened, delighted, he held her hand, thanking her for the sacrifice, she already felt rewarded."

"But was that all her reward?" one of the ladies asked.

"She never saw him again."

"Oh!" said the lady; which, as our friend immediately again left us, was the only other word of importance contributed to the subject till, the next night, by the corner of the hearth, in the best chair, he opened the faded red cover of a thin old-fashioned gilt-edged album. The whole thing took indeed more nights than one, but on the first occasion the same lady put another question. "What's your title?"

"I haven't one."

"Oh *I* have!" I said. But Douglas, without heeding me, had begun to read with a fine clearness that was like a rendering to the ear of the beauty of his author's hand.

I

I remember the whole beginning as a succession of flights and drops, a little see-saw of the right throbs and the wrong. After rising, in town, to met his appeal I had at all events a couple of very bad days—found all my doubts bristle again, felt indeed sure I had made a mistake. In this state of mind I spent the long hours of bumping swinging coach that carried me to the stopping-place at which I was to be met by a vehicle from the house. This convenience, I was told, had been ordered, and I found, toward the close of the June afternoon, a commodious fly in waiting for me. Driving at that hour, on a lovely day, through a country the summer sweetness of which served as a friendly welcome, my fortitude revived and, as we turned into the avenue, took a flight that was probably but a proof of the point to which it had sunk. I suppose I had expected, or had dreaded, something so dreary that what greeted me was a good surprise. I remember as a thoroughly pleasant impression the broad clear front, its open windows and fresh curtains and the pair of maids looking out; I remember the lawn and the bright flowers and the crunch of my wheels on the gravel and the clustered tree-tops over which the rooks circled and cawed in the golden sky. The scene had a greatness that made a different affair from my own scant home, and there immediately appeared at the door, with a little girl in her hand, a civil person who dropped me as decent a curtsey as if I had been the mistress or a distinguished visitor. I had received in Harley Street a narrower notion of the place, and that, as I recalled it, made me think the proprietor still more of a gentleman, suggested that what I was to enjoy might be a matter beyond his promise.

I had no drop again till the next day, for I was carried triumphantly through the following hours by my introduction to the younger of my pupils. The little girl who accompanied Mrs. Grose affected me on the spot as a creature too charming not to make it a great fortune to have to do with her. She was the most beautiful child I had ever seen, and I afterwards wondered why my employer hadn't made more of a point to me of this. I slept little that night— I was too much excited; and this astonished me too, I recollect, remained with me, adding to my sense of the liberality with which I was treated. The large impressive room, one of the best in the house, the great state bed, as I almost felt it, the figured full draperies, the long glasses in which, for the first time, I could see myself from head to foot, all struck me—like the wonderful appeal of my small charge—as so many things thrown in. It was thrown in as well, from the first moment, that I should get on with Mrs. Grose in a relation over which, on my way, in the coach, I fear I had rather brooded. The one appearance indeed that in this early outlook might have made me shrink again was that of her being so inordinately glad to see me. I felt within half an hour that she was so glad—stout simple plain clean wholesome woman—as to be positively on her guard against showing it too much. I wondered even then a little why she should wish *not* to show it, and that, with reflexion, with suspicion, might of course have made me uneasy.

But it was a comfort that there could be no uneasiness in a connexion with anything so beatific as the radiant image of my little girl, the vision of whose angelic beauty had probably more than anything else to do with the restlessness that, before morning, made me several times rise and wander about my room to take in the whole picture and prospect; to watch from my open window the faint summer dawn, to look at such stretches of the rest of the house as I could catch, and to listen, while in the fading dusk the first birds began to twitter, for the possible recurrence of a sound or two, less natural and not without but within, that I had fancied I heard. There had been a moment when I believed I recognised, faint and far, the cry of a child; there had been another when I found myself just consciously starting as at the passage, before my door, of a light footstep. But these fancies were not marked enough not to be thrown off, and it is only in the light, or the gloom, I should rather say, of other and subsequent matters that they now come back to me. To watch, teach, "form" little Flora would too evidently be the making of a happy and useful life. It had been agreed between us downstairs that after this first occasion I should have her as a matter of course at night, her small white bed being already arranged, to that end, in my room. What I had undertaken was the whole care of her, and she had remained just this last time with Mrs. Grose only as an effect of our consideration for my inevitable strangeness and her natural timidity. In spite of this timidity—which the child herself, in the oddest way in the world, had been perfectly frank and brave about, allowing it, without a sign of uncomfortable consciousness, with the deep sweet serenity indeed of one of Raphael's holy infants, to be discussed, to be imputed to her and to determine us—I felt quite sure she would presently like me. It was part of what I already liked Mrs. Grose herself for, the pleasure I could see her feel in my admiration and wonder as I sat at supper with four tall candles and with my pupil, in a high chair and a bib, brightly facing me between them over bread and milk. There were naturally things that in Flora's presence could pass between us only as prodigious and gratified looks, obscure and roundabout allusions.

"And the little boy—does he look like her? Is he too so very remarkable?"

One wouldn't, it was already conveyed between us, too grossly flatter a child. "Oh Miss, *most* remarkable. If you think well of this one!"—and she stood there with a plate in her hand, beaming at our companion, who looked from one of us to the other with placid heavenly eyes that contained nothing to check us.

"Yes; if I do—?"

"You *will* be carried away by the little gentleman!"

"Well, that, I think, is what I came for—to be carried away I'm afraid, however," I remember feeling the impulse to add, "I'm rather easily carried away. I was carried away in London!"

I can still see Mrs. Grose's broad face as she took this in. "In Harley Street?"

"In Harley Street."

"Well, Miss, you're not the first—and you won't be the last."

"Oh I've no pretensions," I could laugh, "to being the only one. My other pupil, at any rate, as I understand, comes back tomorrow?"

"Not to-morrow—Friday, Miss. He arrives, as you did, by the coach, under care of the guard, and is to be met by the same carriage."

I forthwith wanted to know if the proper as well as the pleasant and friendly thing wouldn't therefore be that on the arrival of the public conveyance I should await him with his little sister; a proposition to which Mrs. Grose assented so heartily that I somehow took her manner as a kind of comforting pledge—never falsified, thank heaven!—that we should on every question be quite at one. Oh she was glad I was there!

What I felt the next day was, I suppose, nothing that could be fairly called a reaction from the cheer of my arrival; it was probably at the most only a slight oppression produced by a fuller measure of the scale, as I walked round them, gazed up at them, took them in, of my new circumstances. They had, as it were, an extent and mass for which I had not been prepared and in the presence of which I found myself, freshly, a little scared not less than a little proud. Regular lessons, in this agitation, certainly suffered some wrong; I reflected that my first duty was, by the gentlest arts I could contrive, to win the child into the sense of knowing me. I spent the day with her out of doors; I arranged with her, to her great satisfaction, that it should be she, she only, who might show me the place. She showed it step by step and room by room and secret by secret, with droll delightful childish talk about it and with the result, in half an hour, of our becoming tremendous friends. Young as she was I was struck, throughout our little tour, with her confidence and courage, with the way, in empty chambers and dull corridors, on crooked staircases that made me pause and even on the summit of an old machicolated square tower that made me dizzy, her morning music, her disposition to tell me so many more things than she asked, rang out and led me on. I have not seen Bly since the day I left it, and I dare say that to my present older and more informed eyes it would show a very reduced importance. But as my little conductress, with her hair of gold and her frock of blue, danced before me round corners and pattered down passages, I had the view of a castle of romance inhabited by a rosy sprite, such a place as would somehow, for diversion of the young idea, take all colour out of story-books and fairy-tales. Wasn't it just a story-book over which I had fallen a-doze and a-dream? No; it was a big ugly antique but convenient house, embodying a few features of a building still older, half-displaced and half-utilised, in which I had the fancy of our being almost as lost as a handful of passengers in a great drifting ship. Well, I was strangely at the helm!

II

This came home to me when, two days later, I drove over with Flora to meet, as Mrs. Grose said, the little gentleman; and all the more for an incident that, presenting itself the second evening, had deeply disconcerted me. The first day had been, on the whole, as I have expressed, reassuring; but I was to see it wind up to a change of note. The postbag that evening—it came late—contained a letter for me which, however, in the hand of my employer, I found to be composed but of a few words enclosing another, addressed to himself, with a seal still unbroken. "This, I recognise, is from the head-master, and the head-master's an awful bore. Read him please; deal with him; but mind you don't report. Not a word. I'm off!" I broke the seal with a great effort—so great a one that I was a long time coming to it; took the unopened missive at last up to my room and only attacked it just before going to bed. I had better have let it wait till morning, for it gave me a second sleepless night. With no counsel to take, the next day, I was full of distress; and it finally got so the better of me that I determined to open myself at least to Mrs. Grose.

"What does it mean? The child's dismissed his school."

She gave me a look that I remarked at the moment; then,

visibly, with a quick blankness, seemed to try to take it back. "But aren't they all—?"

"Sent home—yes. But only for the holidays. Miles may never go back at all."

Consciously, under my attention, she reddened. "They won't take him?"

"They absolutely decline."

At this she raised her eyes, which she had turned from me; I saw them fill with good tears. "What has he done?"

I cast about; then I judged best simply to hand her my document—which, however, had the effect of making her, without taking it, simply put her hands behind her. She shook her head sadly. "Such things are not for me, Miss."

My counsellor couldn't read! I winced at my mistake, which I attentuated as I could, and opened the letter again to repeat it to her; then, faltering in the act and folding it up once more, I put it back in my pocket. "Is he really *bad?*"

The tears were still in her eyes. "Do the gentlemen say so?"

"They go into no particulars. They simply express their regret that it should be impossible to keep him. That can have but one meaning." Mrs. Grose listened with dumb emotion; she forbore to ask me what this meaning might be; so that, presently, to put the thing with some coherence and with the mere aid of her presence to my own mind, I went on: "That he's an injury to the others."

At this, with one of the quick turns of simple folk, she suddenly flamed up. "Master Miles!—*him* an injury?"

There was such a flood of good faith in it that, though I had not yet seen the child, my very fears made me jump to the absurdity of the idea. I found myself, to meet my friend the better, offering it, on the spot, sarcastically. "To his poor little innocent mates!"

"It's too dreadful," cried Mrs. Grose, "to say such cruel things! Why he's scarce ten years old."

"Yes, yes; it would be incredible."

She was evidently grateful for such a profession. "See him, Miss, first. *Then* believe it!" I felt forthwith a new impatience to see him; it was the beginning of a curiosity that, all the next hours, was to deepen almost to pain. Mrs. Grose was aware, I could judge, of what she had produced in me, and she followed it up with assurance. "You might as well believe it of the little lady. Bless her," she added the next moment—"*look* at her!"

I turned and saw that Flora, whom, ten minutes before, I had established in the schoolroom with a sheet of white paper, a pencil and a copy of nice "round O's," now presented herself to view at the open door. She expressed in her little way an extraordinary detachment from disagreeable duties, looking at me, however, with a great childish light that seemed to offer it as a mere result of the affection she had conceived for my person, which had rendered necessary that she should follow me. I needed nothing more than this to feel the full force of Mrs. Grose's comparison, and, catching my pupil in my arms, covered her with kisses in which there was a sob of atonement.

None the less, the rest of the day, I watched for further occasion to approach my colleague, especially as, toward evening, I began to fancy she rather sought to avoid me. I overtook her, I remember, on the staircase; we went down together and at the bottom I detained her, holding her there with a hand on her arm. "I take what you said to me at noon as a declaration that *you've* never known him to be bad."

She threw back her head; she had clearly by this time, and very honestly, adopted an attitude. "Oh never known him—I don't pretend *that!*"

I was upset again. "Then you *have* known him—?"

"Yes indeed, Miss, thank God!"

On reflexion I accepted this. "You mean that a boy who never is—?"

"Is no boy for *me!*"

I held her tighter. "You like them with the spirit to be naughty?" Then, keeping pace with her answer, "So do I!" I eagerly brought out. "But not to the degree to contaminate—"

"To contaminate?"—my big word left her at a loss.

I explained it. "To corrupt."

She stared, taking my meaning in; but it produced in her an odd laugh. "Are you afraid he'll corrupt *you?*" She put the question with such a fine bold humour that with a laugh, a little silly doubtless, to match her own, I gave way for the time to the apprehension of ridicule.

But the next day, as the hour for my drive approached, I cropped up in another place. "What was the lady who was here before?"

"The last governess? She was also young and pretty—almost as young and almost as pretty, Miss, even as you."

"Ah then I hope her youth and her beauty helped her!" I recollect throwing off. "He seems to like us young and pretty!"

"Oh he *did,*" Mrs. Grose assented: "it was the way he liked every one!" She had no sooner spoken indeed than she caught herself up. "I mean that's *his* way—the master's."

I was struck. "But of whom did you speak first?"

She looked blank, but she coloured. "Why of *him.*"

"Of the master?"

"Of who else?"

There was so obviously no one else that the next moment I

had lost my impression of her having accidentally said more than she meant; and I merely asked what I wanted to know. "Did *she* see anything in the boy—?"

"That wasn't right? She never told me."

I had a scruple, but I overcame it. "Was she careful—particular?"

Mrs. Grose appeared to try to be conscientious. "About some things—yes."

"But not about all?"

Again she considered. "Well, Miss—she's gone. I won't tell tales."

"I quite understand your feeling," I hastened to reply; but I thought it after an instant not opposed to this concession to pursue: "Did she die here?"

"No—she went off."

I don't know what there was in this brevity of Mrs. Grose's that struck me as ambiguous. "Went off to die?" Mrs. Grose looked straight out of the window, but I felt that, hypothetically, I had a right to know what young persons engaged for Bly were expected to do. "She was taken ill, you mean, and went home?"

"She was not taken ill, so far as appeared, in this house. She left it, at the end of the year, to go home, as she said, for a short holiday, to which the time she had put in had certainly given her a right. We had then a young woman—a nursemaid who had stayed on and who was a good girl and clever; and *she* took the children altogether for the interval. But our young lady never came back, and at the very moment I was expecting her I heard from the master that she was dead."

I turned this over. "But of what?"

"He never told me! But please, Miss," said Mrs. Grose, "I must get to my work."

III

Her thus turning her back on me was fortunately not, for my just preoccupations, a snub that could check the growth of our mutual esteem. We met, after I had brought home little Miles, more intimately than ever on the ground of my stupefaction, my general emotion: so monstrous was I then ready to pronounce it that such a child as had now been revealed to me should be under an interdict. I was a little late on the scene of his arrival, and I felt, as he stood wistfully looking out for me before the door of the inn at which the coach had put him down, that I had seen him on the instant, without and within, in the great glow of freshness, the same positive fragrance of purity, in which I had from the first moment seen his little sister. He was incredibly beautiful, and Mrs. Grose had put her finger on it: everything but a sort of passion of tenderness for him was swept away by his presence. What I then and there took him to my heart for was something divine that I have never found to the same degree in any child—his indescribable little air of knowing nothing in the world but love. It would have been impossible to carry a bad name with a greater sweetness of innocence, and by the time I had got back to Bly with him I remained merely bewildered—so far, that is, as I was not outraged—by the sense of the horrible letter locked up in one of the drawers of my room. As soon as I could compass a private word with Mrs. Grose I declared to her that it was grotesque.

She promptly understood me. "You mean the cruel charge—?"

"It doesn't live an instant. My dear woman, *look* at him!"

She smiled at my pretension to have discovered his charm. "I assure you, Miss, I do nothing else! What will you say then?" she immediately added.

"In answer to the letter?" I had made up my mind. "Nothing at all."

"And to his uncle?"

I was incisive. "Nothing at all."

"And to the boy himself?"

I was wonderful. "Nothing at all."

She gave with her apron a great wipe to her mouth. "Then I'll stand by you. We'll see it out."

"We'll see it out!" I ardently echoed, giving her my hand to make it a vow.

She held me there a moment, then whisked up her apron again with her detached hand. "Would you mind, Miss, if I used the freedom—"

"To kiss me? No!" I took the good creature in my arms and after we had embraced like sisters felt still more fortified and indignant.

This at all events was for the time: a time so full that as I recall the way it went it reminds me of all the art I now need to make it a little distinct. What I look back at with amazement is the situation I accepted. I had undertaken, with my companion, to see it out, and I was under a charm apparently that could smooth away the extent and the far and difficult connexions of such an effort. I was lifted aloft on a great wave of infatuation and pity. I found it simple, in my ignorance, my confusion and perhaps my conceit, to assume that I could deal with a boy whose education for the world was all on the point of beginning. I am unable even to remember at this day what proposal I framed for the end of his holidays and the resumption of his studies. Lessons with me indeed, that charming summer, we all had a theory that he was to have; but I now feel that for weeks the lessons must have been rather my own. I learnt something—at first certainly—that had not been one of the teachings of my small smothered life; learnt to be amused, and even amusing, and not to think for the morrow. It was the first time, in a manner, that I had known space and air and freedom, all the music of summer and all the mystery of nature. And then there was consideration—and consideration was sweet. Oh it was a trap—not designed but deep—to my imagination, to my delicacy, perhaps to my vanity; to whatever in me was most excitable. The best way to picture it all is to say that I was off my guard. They gave me so little trouble—they were of a gentleness so extraordinary. I used to speculate—but even this with a dim disconnectedness—as to how the rough future (for all futures are rough!) would handle them and might bruise them. They had the bloom of health and happiness; and yet, as if I had been in charge of a pair of little grandees, of princes of the blood, for whom everything, to be right, would have to be fenced about and ordered and arranged, the only form that in my fancy the after-years could take for them was that of a romantic, a really royal extension of the garden and the park. It may be of course above all that what suddenly broke into this gives the previous time a charm of stillness—that hush in which something gathers or crouches. The change was actually like the spring of a beast.

In the first weeks the days were long; they often, at their finest, gave me what I used to call my own hour, the hour when, for my pupils, tea-time and bed-time having come and gone, I had before my final retirement a small interval alone. Much as I liked my companions this hour was the thing in the day I liked most; and I liked it best of all when, as the light faded—or rather, I should say, the day lingered and the last calls of the last birds sounded, in a flushed sky, from the old trees—I could take a turn into the grounds and enjoy, almost with a sense of property that amused and flattered me, the beauty and dignity of the place. It

was a pleasure at these moments to feel myself tranquil and justified; doubtless perhaps also to reflect that by my discretion, my
quiet good sense and general high propriety, I was giving
pleasure—if he ever thought of it!—to the person to whose pressure I had yielded. What I was doing was what he had earnestly
hoped and directly asked of me, and that I *could,* after all, do it
proved even a greater joy than I had expected. I dare say I fancied
myself in short a remarkable young woman and took comfort in
the faith that this would more publicly appear. Well, I needed to
be remarkable to offer a front to the remarkable things that
presently gave their first sign.

It was plump, one afternoon, in the middle of my very hour:
the children were tucked away and I had come out for my stroll.
One of the thoughts that, as I don't in the least shrink now from
noting, used to be with me in these wanderings was that it would be
as charming as a charming story suddenly to meet some one. Some
one would appear there at the turn of a path and would stand before
me and smile and approve. I didn't ask more than that—I only
asked that he should *know;* and the only way to be sure he knew
would be to see it, and the kind light of it, in his handsome face.
That was exactly present to me—by which I mean the face was—
when, on the first of these occasions, at the end of a long June day, I
stopped short on emerging from one of the plantations and coming
into view of the house. What arrested me on the spot—and with a
shock much greater than any vision had allowed for—was the sense
that my imagination had, in a flash, turned real. He did stand
there!—but high up, beyond the lawn and at the very top of the
tower to which, on that first morning, little Flora had conducted
me. This tower was one of a pair—square incongruous crenellated
structures—that were distinguished, for some reason, though I

could see little difference, as the new and the old. They flanked opposite ends of the house and were probably architectural absurdities, redeemed in a measure indeed by not being wholly disengaged nor of a height too pretentious, dating, in their gingerbread antiquity, from a romantic revival that was already a respectable past. I admired them, had fancies about them, for we could all profit in a degree, especially when they loomed through the dusk, by the grandeur of their actual battlements; yet it was not at such an elevation that the figure I had so often invoked seemed most in place.

It produced in me, this figure, in the clear twilight, I remember, two distinct gasps of emotion, which were, sharply, the shock of my first and that of my second surprise. My second was a violent perception of the mistake of my first: the man who met my eyes was not the person I had precipitately supposed. There came to me thus a bewilderment of vision of which, after these years, there is no living view that I can hope to give. An unknown man in a lonely place is a permitted object of fear to a young woman privately bred; and the figure that faced me was—a few more seconds assured me—as little any one else I knew as it was the image that had been in my mind. I had not seen it in Harley Street—I had not seen it anywhere. The place moreover, in the strangest way in the world, had on the instant and by the very fact of its appearance become a solitude. To me at least, making my statement here with a deliberation with which I have never made it, the whole feeling of the moment returns. It was as if, while I took in, what I did take in, all the rest of the scene had been stricken with death. I can hear again, as I write, the intense hush in which the sounds of evening dropped. The rooks stopped cawing in the golden sky and the friendly hour lost for the unspeakable minute all its voice. But there was no other change in nature, unless indeed it were a change that I saw with a stranger sharpness. The gold was still in the sky, the clearness in the air, and the man who looked at me over the battlements was as definite as a picture in a frame. That's how I thought, with extraordinary quickness, of each person he might have been and that he wasn't. We were confronted across our distance quite long enough for me to ask myself with intensity who then he was and to feel, as an effect of my inability to say, a wonder that in a few seconds more became intense.

The great question, or one of these, is afterwards, I know, with regard to certain matters, the question of how long they have lasted. Well, this matter of mine, think what you will of it, lasted while I caught at a dozen possibilities, none of which made a difference for the better, that I could see, in there having been in the house—and for how long, above all?—a person of whom I was in ignorance. It lasted while I just bridled a little with the sense of how my office seemed to require that there should be no such ignorance and no such person. It lasted while this visitant, at all events—and there was a touch of the strange freedom, as I remember, in the sign of familiarity of his wearing no hat—seemed to fix me, from his position, with just the question, just the scrutiny through the fading light, that his own presence provoked. We were too far apart to call to each other, but there was a moment at which, at shorter range, some challenge between us, breaking the hush, would have been the right result of our straight mutual stare. He was in one of the angles, the one away from the house, very erect, as it struck me, and with both hands on the ledge. So I saw him as I see the letters I form on this page; then, exactly, after a minute, as if to add to the spectacle, he slowly changed his place—passed, looking at me hard all the while, to the opposite corner of the platform. Yes, it was intense to me that during this transit he never took his eyes from me, and I can see at this moment the way his hand, as he went, moved from one of the crenellations to the next. He stopped at the other corner, but less long, and even as he turned away still markedly fixed me. He turned away; that was all I knew.

IV

It was not that I didn't wait, on this occasion, for more, since I was as deeply rooted as shaken. Was there a "secret" at Bly—a mystery of Udolpho or an insane, an unmentionable relative kept in unsuspected confinement? I can't say how long I turned it over, or how long, in a confusion of curiosity and dread, I remained where I had had my collision; I only recall that when I re-entered the house darkness had quite closed in. Agitation, in the interval, certainly had held me and driven me, for I must, in circling about the place, have walked three miles; but I was to be later on so much more overwhelmed that this mere dawn of alarm was a comparatively human chill. The most singular part of it in fact—singular as the rest had been—was the part I became, in the hall, aware of in meeting Mrs. Grose. This picture comes back to me in the general train—the impression, as I received it on my return, of the wide white panelled space, bright in the lamplight and with its portraits and red carpet, and of the good surprised look of my friend, which immediately told me she had missed me. It came to me straightway, under her contact, that, with plain heartiness, mere relieved anxiety at my appearance, she knew nothing whatever that could bear upon the incident I had there ready for her. I had not suspected in advance that her comfortable face would pull me up, and I somehow measured the importance of what I had seen by my thus finding myself hesitate to mention it. Scarce anything in the whole history seems to me so odd as this fact that my real beginning of fear was one, as I may say, with the instinct of sparing my companion. On the spot, accordingly, in the pleasant hall and with her eyes on me, I, for a reason that I couldn't then have phrased, achieved an inward revolution—offered a vague pretext for my lateness and, with the plea of the beauty of the night and of the heavy dew and wet feet, went as soon as possible to my room.

Here it was another affair; here, for many days after, it was a queer affair enough. There were hours, from day to day—or at least there were moments, snatched even from clear duties—when I had to shut myself up to think. It wasn't so much yet that I was more nervous than I could bear to be as that I was remarkably afraid of becoming so; for the truth I had now to turn over was simply and clearly the truth that I could arrive at no account whatever of the visitor with whom I had been so inexplicably and yet, as it seemed to me, so intimately concerned. It took me little time to see that I might easily sound, without forms of enquiry and without exciting remark, any domestic complication. The shock I had suffered must have sharpened all my senses; I felt sure, at the end of three days and as the result of mere closer attention, that I had not been practised upon by the servants nor made the object of any "game." Of whatever it was that I knew nothing was known around me. There was but one sane inference: some one had taken a liberty rather monstrous. That was what, repeatedly, I dipped into my room and locked the door to say to myself. We had been, collectively, subject to an intrusion; some unscrupulous traveller, curious in old houses, had made his way in unobserved, enjoyed the prospect from the best point of view and then stolen out as he came. If he had given me such a bold hard stare, that was but a part of his indiscretion. The good thing, after all, was that we should surely see no more of him.

This was not so good a thing, I admit, as not to leave me to judge that what, essentially, made nothing else much signify was simply my charming work. My charming work was just my life with Miles and Flora, and through nothing could I so like it as through feeling that to throw myself into it was to throw myself out of my trouble. The attraction of my small charges was a constant joy, leading me to wonder afresh at the vanity of my original fears, the distaste I had begun by entertaining for the probable grey prose of my office. There was to be no grey prose, it appeared, and no long grind; so how could work not be charming that presented itself as daily beauty? It was all the romance of the nursery and the poetry of the schoolroom. I don't mean by this of course that we studied only fiction and verse; I mean that I can express no otherwise the sort of interest my companions inspired. How can I describe that except by saying that instead of growing deadly used to them—and it's a marvel for a governess: I call the sisterhood to witness!—I made constant fresh discoveries. There was one direction, assuredly, in which these discoveries stopped: deep obscurity continued to cover the region of the boy's conduct at school. It had been promptly given me, I have noted, to face that mystery without a pang. Per- haps even it would be nearer the truth to say that—without a word—he himself had cleared it up. He had made the whole charge absurd. My conclusion bloomed there with the real rose-flush of his innocence: he was only too fine and fair for the little horrid unclean school-world, and he had paid a price for it. I reflected acutely that the sense of such individual differences, such superiorities of quality, always, on the part of the majority—which could include even stupid sordid head-masters—turns infallibly to the vindictive.

Both the children had a gentleness—it was their only fault, and it never made Miles a muff—that kept them (how shall I express it?) almost impersonal and certainly quite unpunishable. They were like those cherubs of the anecdote who had—morally at any rate—nothing to whack! I remember feeling with Miles in especial as if he had had, as it were, nothing to call even an infinitesimal history. We expect of a small child scant enough "antecedents," but there was in this beautiful little boy something extraordinarily sensitive, yet extraordinarily happy, that, more than in any creature of his age I have seen, struck me as beginning anew each day. He had never for a second suffered. I took this as a direct disproof of his having really been chastised. If he had been wicked he would have "caught" it, and I should have caught it by the rebound—I should have found the trace, should have felt the wound and the dishonour. I could reconstitute nothing at all, and he was therefore an angel. He never spoke of his school, never mentioned a comrade or a master; and I, for my part, was quite too much disgusted to allude to them. Of course I was under the spell, and the wonderful part is that, even at the time, I perfectly knew I was. But I gave myself up to it; it was an antidote to any pain, and I had more pains than one. I was in receipt in these days of disturbing letters from home, where things were not going well. But with this joy of my children what things in the world mattered? That was the question I used to put to my scrappy retirements. I was dazzled by their loveliness.

There was a Sunday—to get on—when it rained with such force and for so many hours that there could be no procession to church; in consequence of which, as the day declined, I had arranged with Mrs. Grose that, should the evening show improvement, we would attend together the late service. The rain happily stopped, and I prepared for our walk, which, through the park and by the good road to the village, would be a matter of twenty minutes. Coming downstairs to meet my colleague in the hall, I remembered a pair of gloves that had required three stitches and that had received them—with a publicity perhaps not edifying—while I sat with the children at their tea, served on Sundays, by exception, in that cold clean temple of mahogany and brass, the "grown-up" dining-room. The gloves had been dropped there, and I turned in to recover them. The day was grey enough, but the afternoon light still lingered, and it enabled me, on crossing the threshold, not only to recognise, on a chair near the wide window, then closed, the articles I wanted, but to become aware of a person on the other side of the window and looking straight in. One step into the room had sufficed; my vision was instantaneous; it was all there. The person looking straight in was the person who had already appeared to me. He appeared thus again with I won't say greater distinctness, for that was impossible, but with a nearness that represented a forward stride in our intercourse and made me, as I met him, catch my breath and turn cold. He was the same—he was the same, and seen, this time, as he had been seen before, from the waist up, the window, though the dining-room was on the ground floor, not going down to the terrace on which he stood. His face was close to the glass, yet the effect of this better view was, strangely, just to show me how intense the former had been. He remained but a few seconds—long enough to convince me he also saw and recognised; but it was as if I had been looking at him for years and had known him always. Something, however, happened this time that had not happened before; his stare into my face, through the glass and across the room, was as deep and hard as then, but it quitted me for a moment during which I could still watch it, see it fix successively several other things. On the spot there came to me the added shock of a certitude that it was not for me he had come. He had come for some one else.

The flash of this knowledge—for it was knowledge in the midst of dread—produced in me the most extraordinary effect, starting, as I stood there, a sudden vibration of duty and courage. I say courage because I was beyond all doubt already far gone. I bounded straight out of the door again, reached that of the house, got in an instant upon the drive and, passing along the terrace as fast as I could rush, turned a corner and came full in sight. But it was in sight of nothing now—my visitor had vanished. I stopped, almost dropped, with the real relief of this; but I took in the whole scene—I gave him time to reappear. I call it time, but how long was it? I can't speak to the purpose to-day of the duration of these things. That kind of measure must have left me: they couldn't have lasted as they actually appeared to me to last. The terrace and the whole place, the lawn and the garden beyond it, all I could see of the park, were empty with a great emptiness. There were shrubberies and big trees, but I remember the clear assurance I felt that none of them concealed him. He was there or was not there: not there if I didn't see him. I got hold of this; then, instinctively, instead of returning as I had come, went to the window. It was confusedly present to me that I ought to place myself where he had stood. I did so; I applied my face to the pane and looked, as he had looked, into the room. As if, at this moment, to show me exactly what his range had been, Mrs. Grose, as I had done for himself just before, came in from the hall. With this I had the full image of a repetition of what had already occurred. She saw me as I had seen my own visitant; she pulled up short as I had done; I gave her something of the shock that I had received. She turned white, and this made me ask myself if I had blanched as much. She stared, in short, and retreated just on *my* lines, and I knew she had then passed out and come round to me and that I should presently meet her. I remained where I was, and while I waited I thought of more things than one. But there's only one I take space to mention. I wondered why *she* should be scared.

V

Oh she let me know as soon as, round the corner of the house, she loomed again into view. "What in the name of goodness is the matter—?" She was now flushed and out of breath.

I said nothing till she came quite near. "With me?" I must have made a wonderful face. "Do I show it?"

"You're as white as a sheet. You look awful."

I considered; I could meet on this, without scruple, any degree of innocence. My need to respect the bloom of Mrs. Grose's had dropped, without a rustle, from my shoulders, and if I wavered for the instant it was not with what I kept back. I put out my hand to her and she took it; I held her hard a little, liking to feel her close to me. There was a kind of support in the shy heave of her surprise. "You came for me for church, of course, but I can't go."

"Has anything happened?"

"Yes. You must know now. Did I look very queer?"

"Through this window? Dreadful!"

"Well," I said, "I've been frightened." Mrs. Grose's eyes expressed plainly that *she* had no wish to be, yet also that she knew too well her place not to be ready to share with me any marked inconvenience. Oh it was quite settled that she *must* share! "Just what you saw from the dining-room a minute ago was the effect of that. What *I* saw—just before—was much worse."

Her hand tightened. "What was it?"

"An extraordinary man. Looking in."

"What extraordinary man?"

"I haven't the least idea."

Mrs. Grose gazed round us in vain. "Then where is he gone?"

"I know still less."

"Have you seen him before?"

"Yes—once. On the old tower."

She could only look at me harder. "Do you mean he's a stranger?"

"Oh very much!"

"Yet you didn't tell me?"

"No—for reasons. But now that you've guessed—"

Mrs. Grose's round eyes encountered this charge. "Ah I haven't guessed!" she said very simply. "How can I if *you* don't imagine?"

"I don't in the very least."

"You've seen him nowhere but on the tower?"

"And on this spot just now."

Mrs. Grose looked round again. "What was he doing on the tower?"

"Only standing there and looking down at me."

She thought a minute. "Was he a gentleman?"

I found I had no need to think. "No." She gazed in deeper wonder.

"No."

"Then nobody about the place? Nobody from the village?"

"Nobody—nobody. I didn't tell you, but I made sure."

She breathed a vague relief: this was, oddly, so much to the good. It only went indeed a little way. "But if he isn't a gentleman—"

"What *is* he? He's a horror."

"A horror?"

"He's—God help me if I know *what* he is!"

Mrs. Grose looked round once more; she fixed her eyes on the duskier distance and then, pulling herself together, turned to me with full inconsequence. "It's time we should be at church."

"Oh, I'm not fit for church!"

"Won't it do you good?"

"It won't do *them*—!" I nodded at the house.

"The children?"

"I can't leave them now."

"You're afraid—"

I spoke boldly "I'm afraid of *him*."

Mrs. Grose's large face showed me, at this, for the first time, the far-away faint glimmer of a consciousness more acute: I somehow made out in it the delayed dawn of an idea I myself had not given her and that was as yet quite obscure to me. It comes back to me that I thought instantly of this as something I could get from her; and I felt it to be connected with the desire she presently showed to know more. "When was it—on the tower?"

"About the middle of the month. At this same hour."

"Almost at dark," said Mrs. Grose.

"Oh no, not nearly. I saw him as I see you."

"Then how did he get in?"

"And how did he get out?" I laughed. "I had no opportunity to ask him! This evening, you see," I pursued, "he has not been able to get in."

"He only peeps?"

"I hope it will be confined to that!" She had now let go my hand; she turned away a little. I waited an instant; then I brought out: "Go to church. Goodbye. I must watch."

Slowly she faced me again. "Do you fear for them?"

We met in another long look. "Don't *you?*" Instead of answering she came nearer to the window and, for a minute, applied her face to the glass. "You see how he could see," I meanwhile went on.

She didn't move. "How long was he here?"

"Till I came out. I came to meet him."

Mrs. Grose at last turned round, and there was still more in her face. "*I* couldn't have come out."

"Neither could I!" I laughed again. "But I did come. I've my duty."

"So have I mine," she replied; after which she added: "What's he like?"

"I've been dying to tell you. But he's like nobody."

"Nobody?" she echoed.

"He has no hat." Then seeing in her face that she already, in this, with a deeper dismay, found a touch of picture, I quickly added stroke to stroke. "He has red hair, very red, close-curling, and a pale face, long in shape, with straight good features and little rather queer whiskers that are as red as his hair. His eyebrows are somehow darker; they look particularly arched and as if they might move a great deal. His eyes are sharp, strange—awfully; but I only know clearly that they're rather small and very fixed. His mouth's wide, and his lips are thin, except for his little whiskers he's quite cleanshaven. He gives me a sort of sense of looking like an actor."

"An actor!" It was impossible to resemble one less, at least, than Mrs. Grose at that moment.

"I've never seen one, but so I suppose them. He's tall, active, erect," I continued, "but never no, never!—a gentleman."

My companion's face had blanched as I went on; her round eyes started and her mild mouth gaped. "A gentleman?" she gasped, confounded, stupefied: "a gentleman *he?*"

"You know him then?"

She visibly tried to hold herself. "But he *is* handsome?"

I saw the way to help her. "Remarkably!"

"And dressed—?"

"In somebody's clothes. They're smart, but they're not his own."

She broke into a breathless affirmative groan. "They're the master's!"

I caught it up. "You *do* know him?"

She faltered but a second. "Quint!" she cried.

"Quint?"

"Peter Quint—his own man, his valet, when he was here!"

"When the master was?"

Gaping still, but meeting me, she pieced it all together. "He never wore his hat, but he did wear—well, there were waistcoats missed! They were both here—last year. Then the master went, and Quint was alone."

I followed, but halting a little. "Alone?"

"Alone with *us*." Then as from a deeper depth, "In charge," she added.

"And what became of him?"

She hung fire so long that I was still more mystified. "He went too," she brought out at last.

"Went where?"

Her expression, at this, became extraordinary. "God knows where! He died."

"Died?" I almost shrieked.

She seemed fairly to square herself, plant herself more firmly to express the wonder of it. "Yes. Mr. Quint's dead."

VI

It took of course more than that particular passage to place us together in presence of what we had now to live with as we could, my dreadful liability to impressions of the order so vividly exemplified, and my companion's knowledge henceforth—a knowledge half consternation and half compassion—of that liability. There had been this evening, after the revelation that left me for an hour so prostrate—there had been for either of us not attendance on any service but a little service of tears and vows, of prayers and promises, a climax to the series of mutual challenges and pledges that had straightway ensued on our retreating together to the schoolroom and shutting ourselves up there to have everything out. The result of our having everything out was simply to reduce our situation to the last rigour of its elements. She herself had seen nothing, not the shadow of a shadow, and nobody in the house but the governess was in the governess's plight; yet she accepted without directly impugning my sanity the truth as I gave it to her, and ended by showing me on this ground an awestricken tenderness, a deference to my more than questionable privilege, of which the very breath has remained with me as that of the sweetest of human charities.

What was settled between us accordingly that night was that we thought we might bear things together; and I was not even sure that in spite of her exemption it was she who had the best of the burden. I knew at this hour, I think, as well as I knew later, what I was capable of meeting to shelter my pupils; but it took me some time to be wholly sure of what my honest comrade was prepared for to keep terms with so stiff an agreement. I was queer company enough—quite as queer as the company I received; but as I trace over what we went through I see how much common ground we must have found in the one idea that, by good fortune, *could* steady us. It was the idea, the second movement, that led me straight out, as I may say, of the inner chamber of my dread. I could take the air in the court, at least, and there Mrs. Grose could join me. Perfectly can I recall now the particular way strength came to me before we separated for the night. We had gone over and over every feature of what I had seen.

"He was looking for some one else, you say—some one who was not you?"

"He was looking for little Miles." A portentous clearness now possessed me. "*That's* whom he was looking for."

"But how do you know?"

"I know, I know, I know!" My exaltation grew. "And *you* know, my dear!"

She didn't deny this, but I required, I felt, not even so much telling as that. She took it up again in a moment. "What if *he* should see him?"

"Little Miles? That's what he wants!"

She looked immensely scared again. "The child?"

"Heaven forbid! The man. He wants to appear to *them*." That he might was an awful conception, and yet somehow I could keep it at bay; which moreover, as we lingered there, was what I succeeded in practically proving. I had an absolute certainty that I should see again what I had already seen, but something within me said that by offering myself bravely as the sole subject of such experience, by accepting, by inviting, by surmounting it all, I should serve as an expiatory victim and guard the tranquillity of the rest of the household. The children in special I should thus fence about and absolutely save. I recall one of the last things I said that night to Mrs. Grose.

"It does strike me that my pupils have never mentioned—!"

She looked at me hard as I musingly pulled up. "His having been here and the time they were with him?"

"The time they were with him, and his name, his presence, his history, in any way. They've never alluded to it."

"Oh the little lady doesn't remember. She never heard or knew."

"The circumstances of his death?" I thought with some intensity. "Perhaps not. But Miles would remember—Miles would know."

"Ah don't try him!" broke from Mrs. Grose.

I returned her the look she had given me. "Don't be afraid." I continued to think. "It *is* rather odd."

"That he has never spoken of him?"

"Never by the least reference. And you tell me they were 'great friends.' "

"Oh it wasn't *him!*" Mrs. Grose with emphasis declared. "It was Quint's own fancy. To play with him, I mean—to spoil him." She paused a moment; then she added: "Quint was much too free."

This gave me, straight from my vision of his face—*such* a face!—a sudden sickness of disgust. "Too free with *my* boy?"

"Too free with every one!"

I forbore for the moment to analyse this description further than by the reflexion that a part of it applied to several of the members of the household, of the half-dozen maids and men who were still of our small colony. But there was everything, for our apprehension, in the lucky fact that no discomfortable legend, no perturbation of scullions, had ever, within any one's memory, attached to the kind old place. It had neither bad name nor ill fame, and Mrs. Grose, most apparently, only desired to cling to me and to quake in silence. I even put her, the very last thing of all, to the test. It was when, at midnight, she had her hand on the schoolroom door to take leave. "I *have* it from you then—for it's of great importance—that he was definitely and admittedly bad?"

"Oh not admittedly. *I* knew it—but the master didn't."

"And you never told him?"

"Well, he didn't like tale-bearing—he hated complaints. He was terribly short with anything of that kind, and if people were all right to *him*—"

"He wouldn't be bothered with more?" This squared well enough with my impression of him: he was not a trouble-loving gentleman, nor so very particular perhaps about some of the company he himself kept. All the same, I pressed my informant. "I promise you *I* would have told!"

She felt my discrimination. "I dare say I was wrong. But really I was afraid."

"Afraid of what?"

"Of things that man could do. Quint was so clever—he was so deep."

I took this in still more than I probably showed. "You weren't afraid of anything else? Not of his effect—?"

"His effect?" she repeated with a face of anguish and waiting while I faltered.

"On innocent little precious lives. They were in your charge."

"No, they weren't in mine!" she roundly and distressfully returned. "The master believed in him and placed him here because he was supposed not to be quite in health and the country air so good for him. So he had everything to say. Yes"—she let me have it—"even about *them*."

"Them—that creature?" I had to smother a kind of howl. "And you could bear it?"

"No. I couldn't—and I can't now!" And the poor woman burst into tears.

A rigid control, from the next day, was, as I have said, to follow them; yet how often and how passionately, for a week, we came back together to the subject! Much as we had discussed it that Sunday night, I was, in the immediate later hours in especial —for it may be imagined whether I slept—still haunted with the shadow of something she had not told me. I myself had kept back nothing, but there was a word Mrs. Grose had kept back. I was sure moreover by morning that this was not from a failure of frankness, but because on every side there were fears. It seems to me indeed, in raking it all over, that by the time the morrow's sun was high I had restlessly read into the facts before us almost all the meaning they were to receive from subsequent and more cruel occurrences. What they gave me above all was just the sinister figure of the living man—the dead one would keep a while!—and of the months he had continuously passed at Bly, which, added up, made a formidable stretch. The limit of this evil time had arrived only when, on the dawn of a winter's morning, Peter Quint was found, by a labourer going to early work, stone dead on the road from the village: a catastrophe explained—superficially at least—by a visible wound to his head; such a wound as might have been produced (and as, on the final evidence, *had* been) by a fatal slip, in the dark and after leaving the public-house, on the steepish icy slope, a wrong path altogether, at the bottom of which he lay. The icy slope, the turn mistaken at night and in liquor, accounted for much—practically, in the end and after the inquest and boundless chatter, for everything; but there had been matters in his life, strange passages and perils, secret disorders, vices more than suspected, that would have accounted for a good deal more.

I scarce know how to put my story into words that shall be a credible picture of my state of mind; but I was in these days literally able to find a joy in the extraordinary flight of heroism the occasion demanded of me. I now saw that I had been asked for a service admirable and difficult; and there would be a greatness in letting it be seen—oh in the right quarter!—that I could succeed where many another girl might have failed. It was an immense help to me—I confess I rather applaud myself as I look back!—that I saw my response so strongly and so simply. I was there to protect and defend the little creatures in the world the most bereaved and the most loveable, the appeal of whose helplessness had suddenly become only too explicit, a deep constant ache of one's own engaged affection. We were cut off, really, together; we were united in our danger. They had nothing but me, and I— well, I had *them*. It was in short a magnificent chance. This chance presented itself to me in an image richly material. I was a screen—I was to stand before them. The more I saw the less they would. I began to watch them in a stifled suspense, a disguised tension, that might well, had it continued too long, have turned to something like madness. What saved me, as I now see, was that it turned to another matter altogether. It didn't last as suspense— it was superseded by horrible proofs. Proofs, I say, yes—from the moment I really took hold.

This moment dated from an afternoon hour that I happened to spend in the grounds with the younger of my pupils alone. We had left Miles indoors, on the red cushion of a deep window-seat; he had wished to finish a book, and I had been glad to encourage a purpose so laudable in a young man whose only defect was a certain ingenuity of restlessness. His sister, on the contrary, had been alert to come out, and I strolled with her half an hour, seeking the shade, for the sun was still high and the day exceptionally warm. I was aware afresh with her, as we went, of how, like her brother, she contrived—it was the charming thing in both children—to let me alone without appearing to drop me and to accompany me without appearing to oppress. They were never importunate and yet never listless. My attention to them all really went to seeing them amuse themselves immensely without me: this was a spectacle they seemed actively to prepare and that employed me as an active admirer. I walked in a world of their invention—they had no occasion whatever to draw upon mine; so that my time was taken only with being for them some remarkable person or thing that the game of the moment required and that was merely, thanks to my superior, my exalted stamp, a happy and highly distinguished sinecure. I forget what I was on the present occasion; I only remember that I was something very important and very quiet and that Flora was playing very hard. We were on the edge of the lake, and, as we had lately begun geography, the lake was the Sea of Azof.

Suddenly, amid these elements, I became aware that on the other side of the Sea of Azof we had an interested spectator. The way this knowledge gathered in me was the strangest thing in the world—the strangest, that is, except the very much stranger in which it quickly merged itself. I had sat down with a piece of work—for I was something or other that could sit—on the old stone bench which overlooked the pond; and in this position I began to take in with certitude and yet without direct vision the presence, a good way off, of a third person. The old trees, the thick shrubbery, made a great and pleasant shade, but it was all suffused with the brightness of the hot still hour. There was no ambiguity in anything; none whatever at least in the conviction I from one moment to another found myself forming as to what I should see straight before me and across the lake as a consequence of raising my eyes. They were attached at this juncture to the stitching in which I was engaged, and I can feel once more the spasm of my effort not to move them till I should so have steadied myself as to be able to make up my mind what to do. There was an alien object in view—a figure whose right of presence I instantly and passionately questioned. I recollect counting over perfectly the possibilities, reminding myself that nothing was more natural for instance than the appearance of one of the men about the place, or even of a messenger, a postman or a tradesman's boy, from the village. That reminder had as little effect on my practical certitude as I was conscious—still even without looking—of its having upon the character and attitude of our visitor. Nothing was more natural than that these things should be the other things they absolutely were not.

Of the positive identity of the apparition I would assure myself as soon as the small clock of my courage should have ticked out the right second; meanwhile, with an effort that was already sharp enough, I transfered my eyes straight to little Flora, who, at the moment, was about ten yards away. My heart had stood still for an instant with the wonder and terror of the question whether she too would see; and I held my breath while I waited for what a cry from her, what some sudden innocent sign either of interest or of alarm, would tell me. I waited, but nothing came; then in the first place—and there is something more dire in this, I feel, than in anything I have to relate—I was determined by a sense that within a minute all spontaneous sounds from her had dropped; and in the second by the circumstance that also within the minute she had, in her play, turned her back to the water. This was her attitude when I at last looked at her—looked with the confirmed conviction that we were still, together, under direct personal notice. She had picked up a small flat piece of wood which happened to have in it a little hole that had evidently suggested to her the idea of sticking in another fragment that might figure as a mast and make the thing a boat. This second morsel, as I watched her, she was very markedly and intently attempting to tighten in its place. My apprehension of what she was doing sustained me so that after some seconds I felt I was ready for more. Then I again shifted my eyes—I faced what I had to face.

VII

I got hold of Mrs. Grose as soon after this as I could; and I can give no intelligible account of how I fought out the interval. Yet I still hear myself cry as I fairly threw myself into her arms; "They *know*—it's too monstrous: they know, they know!"

"And what on earth—?" I felt her incredulity as she held me.

"Why all that *we* know—and heaven knows what more besides!" Then as she released me I made it out to her, made it out perhaps only now with full coherency even to myself. "Two hours ago, in the garden"—I could scarce articulate—"Flora *saw!*"

Mrs. Grose took it as she might have taken a blow in the stomach. "She has told you?" she panted.

"Not a word—that's the horror. She kept it to herself! The child of eight, *that* child!" Unutterable still for me was the stupefaction of it.

Mrs. Grose of course could only gape the wider. "Then how do you know?"

"I was there—I saw with my eyes: saw she was perfectly aware."

"Do you mean aware of *him?*"

"No—of *her.*" I was conscious as I spoke that I looked prodigious things, for I got the slow reflexion of them in my companion's face. "Another person—this time; but a figure of quite as unmistakeable horror and evil: a woman in black, pale and dreadful—with such an air also, and such a face!—on the other side of the lake. I was there with the child—quiet for the hour; and in the midst of it she came."

"Came how—from where?"

"From where they come from! She just appeared and stood there—but not so near."

"And without coming nearer?"

"Oh for the effect and the feeling she might have been as close as you!"

My friend, with an odd impulse, fell back a step. "Was she some one you've never seen?"

"Never. But some one the child has. Some one *you* have." Then to show how I had thought it all out: "My predecessor—the one who died."

"Miss Jessel?"

"Miss Jessel. You don't believe me?" I pressed.

She turned right and left in her distress. "How can you be sure?"

This drew from me, in the state of my nerves, a flash of impatience. "Then ask Flora—*she's* sure!" But I had no sooner spoken than I caught myself up. "No, for God's sake *don't!* She'll say she isn't—she'll lie!"

Mrs. Grose was not too bewildered instinctively to protest. "Ah how *can* you?"

"Because I'm clear. Flora doesn't want me to know."

"It's only then to spare you."

"No, no—there are depths, depths! The more I go over it the

more I see in it, and the more I see in it the more I fear. I don't
know what I *don't* see, what I *don't* fear!"

Mrs. Grose tried to keep up with me. "You mean you're afraid
of seeing her again?"

"Oh no; that's nothing—now!" Then I explained. "It's of *not*
seeing her."

But my companion only looked wan. "I don't understand."

"Why, it's that the child may keep it up—and that the child
assuredly *will*—without my knowing it."

At the image of this possibility Mrs. Grose for a moment collapsed, yet presently to pull herself together again as from the positive force of the sense of what, should we yield an inch, there
would really be to give way to. "Dear, dear—we must keep our
heads! And after all, if she doesn't mind it—!" She even tried a
grim joke. "Perhaps she likes it!"

"Like *such* things—a scrap of an infant!"

"Isn't it just a proof of her blest innocence?" my friend bravely
enquired.

She brought me, for the instant, almost round. "Oh we must
clutch at *that*—we must cling to it! If it isn't a proof of what you
say, it's a proof of—God knows what! For the woman's a horror of
horrors."

Mrs. Grose, at this, fixed her eyes a minute on the ground,
then at last raising them, "Tell me how you know," she said.

"Then you admit it's what she was?" I cried.

"Tell me how you know," my friend simply repeated.

"Know? By seeing her! By the way she looked."

"At you, do you mean—so wickedly?"

"Dear me, no—I could have borne that. She gave me never a
glance. She only fixed the child."

Mrs. Grose tried to see it. "Fixed her?"

"Ah with such awful eyes!"

She stared at mine as if they might really have resembled them. "Do you mean of dislike?"

"God help us, no. Of something much worse."

"Worse than dislike?"—this left her indeed at a loss.

"With a determination—indescribable. With a kind of fury of intention."

I made her turn pale. "Intention?"

"To get hold of her." Mrs. Grose—her eyes just lingering on mine—gave a shudder and walked to the window; and while she stood there looking out I completed my statement. "*That's* what Flora knows."

After a little she turned round. "The person was in black, you say?"

"In mourning—rather poor, almost shabby. But—yes—with extraordinary beauty." I now recognised to what I had at last, stroke by stroke, brought the victim of my confidence, for she quite visibly weighted this. "Oh handsome—very, very" I insisted; "wonderfully handsome. But infamous."

She slowly came back to me. "Miss Jessel—*was* infamous." She once more took my hand in both her own, holding it as tight as if to fortify me against the increase of alarm I might draw from this disclosure. "They were both infamous," she finally said.

So for a little we faced it once more together; and I found absolutely a degree of help in seeing it now so straight. "I appreciate," I said, "the great decency of your not having hitherto spoken; but the time has certainly come to give me the whole thing." She appeared to assent to this, but still only in silence;

seeing which I went on: "I must have it now. Of what did she die? Come, there was something between them."

"There was everything."

"In spite of the difference—?"

"Oh of their rank, their condition"—she brought it woefully out. "*She* was a lady."

I turned it over; I again saw. "Yes—she was a lady."

"And he so dreadfully below," said Mrs. Grose.

I felt that I doubtless needn't press too hard, in such company, on the place of a servant in the scale; but there was nothing to prevent an acceptance of my companion's own measure of my predecessor's abasement. There was a way to deal with that, and I dealt; the more readily for my full vision—on the evidence—of our employer's late clever good-looking "own" man; impudent, assured, spoiled, depraved. "The fellow was a hound."

Mrs. Grose considered as if it were perhaps a little a case for a sense of shades. "I've never seen one like him. He did what he wished."

"With *her?*"

"With them all."

It was as if now in my friend's own eyes Miss Jessel had again appeared. I seemed at any rate for an instant to trace their evocation of her as distinctly as I had seen her by the pond; and I brought out with decision: "It must have been also what *she* wished!"

Mrs. Grose's face signified that it had been indeed, but she said at the same time: "Poor woman—she paid for it!"

"Then you do know what she died of?" I asked.

"No—I know nothing. I wanted not to know; I was glad enough I didn't; and I thanked heaven she was well out of this!"

"Yet you had then your idea—"

"Of her real reason for leaving? Oh yes—as to that. She couldn't have stayed. Fancy it here—for a governess! And afterwards I imagined—and I still imagine. And what I imagine is dreadful."

"Not so dreadful as what *I* do," I replied; on which I must have shown her—as I was indeed but too conscious—a front of miserable defeat. It brought out again all her compassion for me, and at the renewed touch of her kindness my power to resist broke down. I burst, as I had the other time made her burst, into tears; she took me to her motherly breast, where my lamentation overflowed. "I don't do it!" I sobbed in despair; "I don't save or shield them! It's far worse than I dreamed. They're lost."

VIII

What I had said to Mrs. Grose was true enough: there were in the matter I had put before her depths and possibilities that I lacked resolution to sound; so that when we met once more in the wonder of it we were of a common mind about the duty of resistance to extravagant fancies. We were to keep our heads if we should keep nothing else—difficult indeed as that might be in the face of all that, in our prodigious experience, seemed least to be questioned. Late that night, while the house slept, we had another talk in my room; when she went all the way with me as to its being beyond doubt that I had seen exactly what I had seen. I found that to keep her thoroughly in the grip of this I had only to ask her how, if I had "made it up," I came to be able to give, of each of the persons appearing to me, a picture disclosing, to the last detail, their special marks—a portrait on the exhibition of which she had instantly recognised and named them. She wished, of course—small blame to her!—to sink the whole subject; and I was quick to assure her that my own interest in it had now violently taken the form of a search for the way to escape from it. I closed with her cordially on the article of the likelihood that with recurrence—for recurrence we took for granted—I should get used to my danger; distinctly professing that my personal exposure had suddenly become the least of my discomforts. It was my new suspicion that was intolerable; and yet even to this complication the later hours of the day had brought a little ease.

On leaving her, after my first outbreak, I had of course returned to my pupils, associating the right remedy for my dismay with that sense of their charm which I had already recognised as a resource I could positively cultivate and which had never failed me yet. I had simply, in other words, plunged afresh into Flora's special society and there become aware—it was almost a luxury!—that she could put her little conscious hand straight upon the spot that ached. She had looked at me in sweet speculation and then had accused me to my face of having "cried." I had supposed the ugly signs of it brushed away; but I could literally—for the time at all events—rejoice, under this fathomless charity, that they had not entirely disappeared. To gaze into the depths of blue of the child's eyes and pronounce their loveliness a trick of premature cunning was to be guilty of a cynicism in preference to which I naturally preferred to abjure my judgement and, so far as might be, my agitation. I couldn't abjure for merely wanting to, but I could repeat to Mrs. Grose—as I did there, over and over, in the small hours—that with our small friends' voices in the air, their pressure on one's heart and their fragrant faces against one's cheek, everything fell to the ground but their incapacity and their beauty. It was a pity that, somehow, to settle this once for all, I had equally to re-enumerate the signs of subtlety that, in the afternoon, by the lake, had made a miracle of my show of self-possession. It was a pity to be obliged to re-investigate the certitude of the moment itself and repeat how it had come to me as a revelation that the inconceivable communion I then surprised must have been for both parties a matter of habit. It was a pity I should have had to quaver out again the reasons for my not having, in my delusion, so much as questioned that the little girl saw our visitant even as I actually saw Mrs. Grose herself, and that she wanted, by just so much as she did thus see, to make me suppose she didn't, and at the same time, without showing anything, arrive at a guess as to whether I myself did! It was a pity I needed to recapitulate the portentous little activities by which she sought to divert my attention—the perceptible increase of movement, the greater intensity of play, the singing, the gabbling of nonsense and the invitation to romp.

Yet if I had not indulged, to prove there was nothing in it, in this review, I should have missed the two or three dim elements of comfort that still remained to me. I shouldn't for instance have been able to asseverate to my friend that I was certain—which was so much to the good—that *I* at least had not betrayed myself. I shouldn't have been prompted, by stress of need, by desperation of mind—I scarce know what to call it—to invoke such further aid to intelligence as might spring from pushing my colleague fairly to the wall. She had told me, bit by bit, under pressure, a great deal; but a small shifty spot on the wrong side of it all still sometimes brushed my brow like the wing of a bat; and I remember how on this occasion—for the sleeping house and the concentration alike of our danger and our watch seemed to help—I felt the importance of giving the last jerk to the curtain. "I don't believe anything so horrible," I recollect saying; "no, let us put it definitely, my dear, that I don't. But if I did, you know, there's a thing I should require now, just without sparing you the least bit more—oh not a scrap, come!—to get out of you. What was it you had in mind when, in our distress, before Miles came back, over the letter from his school, you said, under my insistence, that you didn't pretend for him he hadn't literally *ever* been 'bad'? He has *not*, truly, 'ever,' in these weeks that I myself have lived with him and so closely watched him; he has been an imperturbable little prodigy of delightful loveable goodness. Therefore you might perfectly have made the claim for him if you had not, as it happened, seen an exception to take. What was your exception, and to what passage in your personal observation of him did you refer?"

It was a straight question enough, but levity was not our note, and in any case I had before the grey dawn admonished us to separate got my answer. What my friend had had in mind proved immensely to the purpose. It was neither more nor less than the particular fact that for a period of several months Quint and the boy had been perpetually together. It was indeed the very appropriate item of evidence of her having ventured to criticise the propriety, to hint at the incongruity, of so close an alliance, and even to go so far on the subject as a frank overture to Miss Jessel would take her. Miss Jessel had, with a very high manner about it, requested her to mind her business, and the good woman had on this directly approached little Miles. What she had said to him, since I pressed, was that *she* liked to see young gentlemen not forget their station.

I pressed again, of course, the closer for that. "You reminded him that Quint was only a base menial?"

"As you might say! And it was his answer, for one thing, that was bad."

"And for another thing?" I waited. "He repeated your words to Quint?"

"No, not that. It's just what he *wouldn't!*" she could still impress on me.

"I was sure, at any rate," she added, "that he didn't. But he denied certain occasions."

"What occasions?"

"When they had been about together quite as if Quint were his tutor—and a very grand one—and Miss Jessel only for the little lady. When he had gone off with the fellow, I mean, and spent hours with him."

"He then prevaricated about it—he said he hadn't?" Her assent was clear enough to cause me to add in a moment: "I see. He lied."

"Oh!" Mrs. Grose mumbled. This was a suggestion that it didn't matter; which indeed she backed up by a further remark. "You see, after all, Miss Jessel didn't mind. She didn't forbid him."

I considered. "Did he put that to you as a justification?"

At this she dropped again. "No, he never spoke of it."

"Never mentioned her in connexion with Quint?"

She saw, visibly flushing, where I was coming out. "Well, he didn't show anything. He denied," she repeated; "he denied."

Lord, how I pressed her now! "So that you could see he knew what was between the two wretches?"

"I don't know—I don't know!" the poor woman wailed.

"You do know, you dear thing," I replied; "only you haven't my dreadful boldness of mind, and you keep back, out of timidity and modesty and delicacy, even the impression that in the past, when you had, without my aid, to flounder about in silence, most of all made you miserable. But I shall get it out of you yet! There was something in the boy that suggested to you," I continued, "his covering and concealing their relation."

"Oh he couldn't prevent—"

"Your learning the truth? I dare say! But, heavens," I fell, with vehemence, a-thinking, "what it shows that they must, to that extent, have succeeded in making of him!"

"Ah nothing that's not nice *now!*" Mrs. Grose lugubriously pleaded.

"I don't wonder you looked queer," I persisted, "when I mentioned to you the letter from his school!"

"I doubt if I looked as queer as you!" she retorted with homely force. "And if he was so bad then as that comes to, how is he such an angel now?"

"Yes indeed—and if he was a fiend at school! How, how, how? Well," I said in my torment, "you must put it to me again, though I shall not be able to tell you for some days. Only put it to me again!" I cried in a way that made my friend stare. "There are directions in which I mustn't for the present let myself go." Meanwhile I returned to her first example—the one to which she had just previously referred—of the boy's happy capacity for an occasional slip. "If Quint—on your remonstrance at the time you speak of—was a base menial, one of the things Miles said to you, I find myself guessing, was that you were another." Again her admission was so adequate that I continued: "And you forgave him that?"

"Wouldn't *you?*"

"Oh yes!" And we exchanged there, in the stillness, a sound of the oddest amusement. Then I went on: "At all events, while he was with the man—"

"Miss Flora was with the woman. It suited them all!"

It suited me too, I felt, only too well; by which I mean that it suited exactly the particular deadly view I was in the very act of fobidding myself to entertain. But I so far succeeded in checking the expression of this view that I will throw, just here, no further

light on it than may be offered by the mention of my final observation to Mrs. Grose. "His having lied and been impudent are, I
confess, less engaging specimens than I had hoped to have from
you of the outbreak in him of the little natural man. Still," I
mused, "they must do, for they make me feel more than ever that
I must watch." It made me blush, the next minute, to see in my
friend's face how much more unreservedly she had forgiven him
than her anecdote struck me as pointing out to my own tenderness any way to do. This was marked, when, at the schoolroom
door, she quitted me. "Surely you don't accuse *him*—"

"Of carrying on an intercourse that he conceals from me? Ah
remember that, until further evidence, I now accuse nobody."
Then before shutting her out to go by another passage to her own
place, "I must just wait," I wound up.

IX

I waited and waited, and the days took as they elapsed something
from my consternation. A very few of them, in fact, passing, in
constant sight of my pupils, without a fresh incident, sufficed to
give to grievous fancies and even to odious memories a kind of
brush of the sponge. I have spoken of the surrender to their
extraordinary childish grace as a thing I could actively promote in
myself, and it may be imagined if I neglected now to apply at this
source for whatever balm it would yield. Stranger than I can
express certainly, was the effort to struggle against my new lights. It
would doubtless have been a greater tension still, however, had it
not been so frequently successful. I used to wonder how my little
charges could help guessing that I thought strange things about
them; and the circumstance that these things only made them

more interesting was not by itself a direct aid to keeping them in the dark. I trembled lest they should see that they *were* so immensely more interesting. Putting things at the worst, at all events, as in meditation I so often did, any clouding of their innocence could only be—blameless and fore-doomed as they were—a reason the more for taking risks. There were moments when I knew myself to catch them up by an irresistible impulse and press them to my heart. As soon as I had done so I used to wonder— "What will they think of that? Doesn't it betray too much?" It would have been easy to get into a sad wild tangle about how much I might betray; but the real account, I feel, of the hours of peace I could still enjoy was that the immediate charm of my companions was a beguilement still effective even under the shadow of the possibility that it was studied. For if it occurred to me that I might occasionally excite suspicion by the little outbreaks of my sharper passion for them, so too I remember asking if I mightn't see a queerness in the traceable increase of their own demonstrations.

They were at this period extravagantly and preternaturally fond of me; which, after all, I could reflect, was no more than a graceful response in children perpetually bowed down over and hugged. The homage of which they were so lavish succeeded in truth for my nerves quite as well as if I never appeared to myself, as I may say, literally to catch them at a purpose in it. They had never, I think, wanted to do so many things for their poor protectress; I mean—though they got their lessons better and better, which was naturally what would please her most—in the way of diverting, entertaining, surprising her; reading her passages, telling her stories, acting her charades, pouncing out at her, in disguises, as animals and historical characters, and above all astonishing her by the "pieces" they had secretly got by heart and could interminably recite. I should never get to the bottom—were I to let myself go even now—of the prodigious private commentary, all under still more private correction, with which I in these days overscored their full hours. They had shown me from the first a facility for everything, a general faculty which, taking a fresh start, achieved remarkable flights. They got their little tasks as if they loved them; they indulged, from the mere exuberance of the gift, in the most unimposed little miracles of memory. They not only popped out at me as tigers and as Romans, but as Shakespeareans, astronomers and navigators. This was so singularly the case that it had presumably much to do with the fact as to which, at the present day, I am at a loss for a different explanation: I allude to my unnatural composure on the subject of another school for Miles. What I remember is that I was content for the time not to open the question, and that contentment must have sprung from the sense of his perpetually striking show of cleverness. He was too clever for a bad governess, for a parson's daughter, to spoil; and the strangest if not the brightest thread in the pensive embroidery I just spoke of was the impression I might have got, if I had dared to work it out, that he was under some influence operating in his small intellectual life as a tremendous incitement.

If it was easy to reflect, however, that such a boy could postpone school, it was at least as marked that for such a boy to have been "kicked out" by a school-master was a mystification without end. Let me add that in their company now—and I was careful almost never to be out of it—I could follow no scent very far. We lived in a cloud of music and affection and success and private theatricals. The musical sense in each of the children was of the quickest, but the elder in especial had a marvellous knack of catching and repeating. The schoolroom piano broke into all gruesome fancies;

and when that failed there were confabulations in corners, with a sequel of one of them going out in the highest spirits in order to "come in" as something new. I had had brothers myself, and it was no revelation to me that little girls could be slavish idolaters of little boys. What surpassed everything was that there was a little boy in the world who could have for the inferior age, sex and intelligence so fine a consideration. They were extraordinarily at one, and to say that they never either quarrelled or complained is to make the note of praise coarse for their quality of sweetness. Sometimes perhaps indeed (when I dropped into coarseness) I came across traces of little understandings between them by which one of them should keep me occupied while the other slipped away. There is a naïf side, I suppose, in all diplomacy; but if my pupils practised upon me it was surely with the minimum of grossness. It was all in the other quarter that, after a lull, the grossness broke out.

I find that I really hang back; but I must take my horrid plunge. In going on with the record of what was hideous at Bly I not only challenge the most liberal faith—for which I little care; but (and this is another matter) I renew what I myself suffered, I again push my dreadful way through it to the end. There came suddenly an hour after which, as I look back, the business seems to me to have been all pure suffering; but I have at least reached the heart of it, and the straightest road out is doubtless to advance. One evening—with nothing to lead up or prepare it—I felt the cold touch of the impression that had breathed on me the night of my arrival and which, much lighter then as I have mentioned, I should probably have made little of in memory had my subsequent sojourn been less agitated. I had not gone to bed; I sat reading by a couple of candles. There was a roomful of old books at Bly—last-century fiction some of it, which, to the extent of a distinctly deprecated renown, but never to so much as that of a stray specimen, had reached the sequestered home and appealed to the unavowed curiosity of my youth. I remember that the book I had in my hand was Fielding's "Amelia"; also that I was wholly awake. I recall further both a general conviction that it was horribly late and a particular objection to looking at my watch. I figure finally that the white curtain draping, in the fashion of those days, the head of Flora's little bed, shrouded, as I had assured myself long before, the perfection of childish rest. I recollect in short that though I was deeply interested in my author I found myself, at the turn of a page and with his spell all scattered, looking straight up from him and hard at the door of my room. There was a moment during which I listened, reminded of the faint sense I had had, the first night, of there being something undefinably astir in the house, and noted the soft breath of the open casement just move the half-drawn blind. Then, with all the marks of a deliberation that must have seemed magnificent had there been any one to admire it, I laid down my book, rose to my feet and, taking a candle, went straight out of the room and, from the passage, on which my light made little impression, noiselessly closed and locked the door.

I can say now neither what determined nor what guided me, but I went straight along the lobby, holding my candle high, till I came within sight of the tall window that presided over the great turn of the staircase. At this point I precipitately found myself aware of three things. They were practically simultaneous, yet they had flashes of succession. My candle, under a bold flourish, went out, and I perceived by the uncovered window, that the yielding dusk of earliest morning rendered it unnecessary. Without it, the next instant, I knew that there was a figure on the stair. I speak of sequences, but I require no lapse of seconds to stiffen myself for a third encounter with Quint. The apparition had reached the landing halfway up and was therefore on the spot nearest the window, where, at sight of me, it stopped short and fixed me exactly as it had fixed me from the tower and from the garden. He knew me as well as I knew him; and so, in the cold faint twilight, with a glimmer in the high glass and another on the polish of the oak stair below, we faced each other in our common intensity. He was absolutely, on this occasion, a living detestable dangerous presence. But that was not the wonder of wonders; I reserve this distinction for quite another circumstance: the circumstance that dread had unmistakeably quitted me and that there was nothing in me unable to meet and measure him.

I had plenty of anguish after that extraordinary moment, but I had, thank God, no terror. And he knew I hadn't—I found myself at the end of an instant magnificently aware of this. I felt, in a fierce rigour of confidence, that if I stood my ground a minute I should cease—for the time at least—to have him to reckon with; and during the minute, accordingly, the thing was as human and hideous as a real interview: hideous just because it *was* human, as human as to have met alone, in the small hours, in a sleeping house, some enemy, some adventurer, some criminal. It was the dead silence of our long gaze at such close quarters that gave the whole horror, huge as it was, its only note of the unnatural. If I had met a murderer in such a place and at such an hour we still at least would have spoken. Something would have passed, in life, between us; if nothing had passed one of us would have moved. The moment was so prolonged that it would have taken but little more to make me doubt if even *I* were in life. I can't express what followed it save by saying that the silence itself—

which was indeed in a manner an attestation of my strength—
became the element into which I saw the figure disappear; in
which I definitely saw it turn, as I might have seen the low wretch
to which it had once belonged turn on receipt of an order, and
pass, with my eyes on the villainous back that no hunch could
have more disfigured, straight down the staircase and into the
darkness in which the next bend was lost.

X

I remained a while at the top of the stair, but with the effect
presently of understanding that when my visitor had gone, he had
gone; then I returned to my room. The foremost thing I saw there
by the light of the candle I had left burning was that Flora's little
bed was empty; and on this I caught my breath with all the terror
that, five minutes before, I had been able to resist. I dashed at the
place in which I had left her lying and over which—for the small
silk counterpane and the sheets were disarranged—the white curtains had been deceivingly pulled forward; then my step, to my
unutterable relief, produced an answering sound: I noticed an agitation of the window-blind, and the child, ducking down,
emerged rosily from the other side of it. She stood there in so
much of her candour and so little of her night-gown, with her
pink bare feet and the golden glow of her curls. She looked
intensely grave, and I had never had such a sense of losing an
advantage acquired (the thrill of which had just been so prodigious) as on my consciousness that she addressed me with a
reproach—"You naughty: where *have* you been?" Instead of chal-
lenging her own irregularity I found myself arraigned and
explaining. She herself explained, for that matter, with the

loveliest eagerest simplicity. She had known suddenly, as she lay there, that I was out of the room, and had jumped up to see what had become of me. I had dropped, with the joy of her reappearance, back into my chair—feeling then, and then only, a little faint; and she had pattered straight over to me, thrown herself upon my knee, given herself to be held with the flame of the candle full in the wonderful little face that was still flushed with sleep. I remember closing my eyes an instant, yieldingly, consciously, as before the excess of something beautiful that shone out of the blue of her own. "You were looking for me out of the window?" I said. "You thought I might be walking in the grounds?"

"Well, you know, I thought some one was"—she never blanched as she smiled out that at me.

Oh how I looked at her now! "And did you see any one?"

"Ah *no!*" she returned almost (with the full privilege of childish inconsequence) resentfully, though with a long sweetness in her little drawl of the negative.

At that moment, in the state of my nerves, I absolutely believed she lied; and if I once more closed my eyes it was before the dazzle of the three or four possible ways in which I might take this up. One of these for a moment tempted me with such singular force that, to resist it, I must have gripped my little girl with a spasm that, wonderfully, she submitted to without a cry or a sign of fright. Why not break out at her on the spot and have it all over?—give it to her straight in her lovely little lighted face? "You see, you see, you *know* that you do and that you already quite suspect I believe it; therefore why not frankly confess it to me, so that we may at least live with it together and learn perhaps, in the strangeness of our fate, where we are and what it means?" This solicitation dropped, alas, as it came: if I could immediately have succumbed to it I might have spared myself—well, you'll see what. Instead of succumbing I sprang again to my feet, looked at her bed and took a helpless middle way. "Why did you pull the curtain over the place to make me think you were still there?"

Flora luminously considered; after which, with her little divine smile: "Because I don't like to frighten you!"

"But if I had, by your idea, gone out—?"

She absolutely declined to be puzzled; she turned her eyes to the flame of the candle as if the question were as irrelevant, or at any rate as impersonal, as Mrs. Marcet or nine-times-nine. "Oh but you know," she quite adequately answered, "that you might come back, you dear, and that you *have!*" And after a little, when she had got into bed, I had, a long time, by almost sitting on her for the retention of her hand, to show how I recognised the pertinence of my return.

You may imagine the general complexion, from that moment, of my nights. I repeatedly sat up till I didn't know when; I selected moments when my room-mate unmistakeably slept, and, stealing out, took noiseless turns in the passage. I even pushed as far as to where I had last met Quint. But I never met him there again, and I may as well say at once that I on no other occasion saw him in the house. I just missed, on the staircase, nevertheless, a different adventure. Looking down it from the top I once recognised the presence of a woman seated on one of the lower steps with her back presented to me, her body half-bowed and her head, in an attitude of woe, in her hands. I had been there but an instant, however, when she vanished without looking round at me. I knew, for all that, exactly what dreadful face she had to show; and I wondered whether, if instead of being above I had been below, I should have had the same nerve for going up that I had lately shown Quint.

Well, there continued to be plenty of call for nerve. On the eleventh night after my latest encounter with that gentleman— they were all numbered now—I had an alarm that perilously skirted it and that indeed, from the particular quality of its unexpectedness, proved quite my sharpest shock. It was precisely the first night during this series that, weary with vigils, I had conceived I might again without laxity lay myself down at my old hour. I slept immediately and, as I afterwards knew, till about one o'clock; but when I woke it was to sit straight up, as completely roused as if a hand had shaken me. I had left a light burning, but it was now out, and I felt an instant certainly that Flora had extinguished it. This brought me to my feet and straight, in the darkness, to her bed, which I found she had left. A glance at the window enlightened me further, and the striking of a match completed the picture.

The child had again got up—this time blowing out the taper, and had again, for some purpose of observation or response, squeezed in behind the blind and was peering out into the night. That she now saw—as she had not, I had satisfied myself, the previous time—was proved to me by the fact that she was disturbed neither by my re-illumination nor by the haste I made to get into slippers and into a wrap. Hidden, protected, absorbed, she evidently rested on the sill—the casement opened forward—and gave herself up. There was a great still moon to help her, and this fact had counted in my quick decision. She was face to face with the apparition we had met at the lake, and could now communicate with it as she had not then been able to do. What I, on my side, had to care for was, without disturbing her, to reach, from the corridor, some other window turned to the same quarter. I got to the door without her hearing me; I got out of it, closed it and listened, from the other side, for some sound from her. While I stood in the passage I had my eyes on her brother's door, which was but ten steps off and which, indescribably, produced in me a renewal of the strange impulse that I lately spoke of as my temptation. What if I should go straight in and march to *his* window?—what if, by risking to his boyish bewilderment a revelation of my motive, I should throw across the rest of the mystery the long halter of my boldness?

This thought held me sufficiently to make me cross to his threshold and pause again. I preternaturally listened; I figured to myself what might portentously be; I wondered if his bed were also empty and he also secretly at watch. It was a deep soundless minute, at the end of which my impulse failed. He was quiet; he might be innocent; the risk was hideous; I turned away. There was a figure in the grounds—a figure prowling for a sight, the visitor with whom Flora was engaged; but it wasn't the visitor most concerned with my boy. I hesitated afresh, but on other grounds and only a few seconds; then I had made my choice. There were empty rooms enough at Bly, and it was only a question of choosing the right one. The right one suddenly presented itself to me as the lower one—though high above the gardens—in the solid corner of the house that I have spoken of as the old tower. This was a large square chamber, arranged with some state as a bedroom, the extravagant size of which made it so inconvenient that it had not for years, though kept by Mrs. Grose in exemplary order, been occupied. I had often admired it and I knew my way about in it; I had only, after just faltering at the first chill gloom of its disuse, to pass across it and unbolt in all quietness one of the shutters. Achieving this transit I uncovered the glass without a sound and, applying my face to the pane, was able, the darkness without being much less than within, to see that I commanded the right direction. Then I saw something more. The moon made the night extraordinarily penetrable and showed me on the lawn a person, diminished by distance, who stood there motionless as if fascinated, looking up to where I had appeared—looking, that is, not so much straight at me as at something that was apparently above me. There was clearly another person above me—there was a person on the tower; but the presence on the lawn was not in the least what I had conceived and had confidently hurried to meet. The presence on the lawn—I felt sick as I made it out—was poor little Miles himself.

XI

It was not till late next day that I spoke to Mrs. Grose; the rigour with which I kept my pupils in sight making it often difficult to meet her privately: the more as we each felt the importance of not provoking—on the part of the servants quite as much as on that of the children—any suspicion of a secret flurry or of a discussion of mysteries. I drew a great security in this particular from her mere smooth aspect. There was nothing in her fresh face to pass on to others the least of my horrible confidences. She believed me, I was sure, absolutely: if she hadn't I don't know what would have become of me, for I couldn't have borne the strain alone. But she was a magnificent monument to the blessing of a want of imagination, and if she could see in our little charges nothing but their beauty and amiability, their happiness and cleverness, she had no direct communication with the sources of my trouble. If they had been at all visibly blighted or battered she would doubtless have grown, on tracing it back, haggard enough to match them; as matters stood, however, I could feel her, when she surveyed them with her large white arms folded and the habit of serenity in all her look, thank the Lord's mercy that if they were ruined the pieces would still serve. Flights of fancy gave place, in her mind, to a steady fireside glow, and I had already begun to perceive how, with the development of the conviction that—as time went on without a public accident—our young things could, after all, look out for themselves, she addressed her greatest solicitude to the sad case presented by their deputy-guardian. That, for myself, was a sound simplification: I could engage that, to the world, my face should tell no tales, but it would have been, in the conditions, an immense added worry to find myself anxious about hers.

At the hour I now speak of she had joined me, under pressure, on the terrace, where, with the lapse of the season, the afternoon sun was now agreeable; and we sat there together while before us and at a distance, yet within call if we wished, the children strolled to and fro in one of their most manageable moods. They moved slowly, in unison, below us, over the lawn, the boy, as they went, reading aloud from a story-book and passing his arm round his sister to keep her quite in touch. Mrs. Grose watched them with positive placidity; then I caught the suppressed intellectual creak with which she conscientiously turned to take from me a view of the back of the tapestry. I had made her a receptacle of lurid things, but there was an odd recognition of my superiority—my accomplishments and my function—in her patience under my pain. She offered her mind to my disclosures as, had I wished to mix a witch's broth and propose it with assurance, she would have held out a large clean saucepan. This had become thoroughly her attitude by the time that, in my recital of the events of the night, I reached the point of what Miles had said to me when, after seeing him, at such a monstrous hour, almost on the very spot where he happened now to be, I had gone down to bring him in; choosing then, at the window, with a concentrated need of not alarming the house, rather that method than any noisier process. I had left her meanwhile in little doubt of my small hope of representing with success even to her actual sympathy my sense of the real splendour of the little inspiration with which, after I had got him into the house, the boy met my final articulate challenge. As soon as I appeared in the moonlight on the terrace he had come to me as straight as possible; on which I had taken his hand without a word and led him, through the dark spaces, up the staircase where Quint had so hungrily hovered for him, along the lobby where I had listened and trembled, and so to his forsaken room.

Not a sound, on the way, had passed between us, and I had wondered—oh *how* I had wondered!—if he were groping about in his dreadful little mind for something plausible and not too grotesque. It would tax his invention certainly, and I felt, this time, over his real embarrassment, a curious thrill of triumph. It was a sharp trap for any game hitherto successful. He could play no longer at perfect propriety, nor could he pretend to it; so how the deuce would he get out of the scrape? There beat in me indeed, with the passionate throb of this question, an equal dumb appeal as to how the deuce *I* should. I was confronted at last, as never yet, with all the risk attached even now to sounding my own horrid note. I remember in fact that as we pushed into his little chamber, where the bed had not been slept in at all and the window, uncovered to the moonlight, made the place so clear that there was no need of striking a match—I remember how I suddenly dropped, sank upon the edge of the bed from the force of the idea that he must know how he really, as they say, "had" me. He could do what he liked, with all his cleverness to help him, so long as I should continue to defer to the old tradition of the criminality of those caretakers of the young who minister to superstitions and fears.

He "had" me indeed, and in a cleft stick; for who would ever absolve me, who would consent that I should go unhung, if, by the faintest tremor of an overture, I were the first to introduce into our perfect intercourse an element so dire? No, no: it was useless to attempt to convey to Mrs. Grose, just as it is scarcely less so to attempt to suggest here, how, during our short stiff brush there in the dark, he fairly shook me with admiration. I was of course thoroughly kind and merciful; never, never yet had I placed on his small shoulders hands of such tenderness as those with which, while I rested against the bed, I held him there well under fire. I had no alternative but, in form at least, to put it to him.

"You must tell me now—and all the truth. What did you go out for? What were you doing there?"

I can still see his wonderful smile, the whites of his beautiful eyes and the uncovering of his clear teeth, shine to me in the dusk. "If I tell you why, will you understand?" My heart, at this, leaped into my mouth. *Would* he tell me why? I found no sound on my lips to press it, and I was aware of answering only with a vague repeated grimacing nod. He was gentleness itself, and while I wagged my head at him he stood there more than ever a little fairy prince. It was his brightness indeed that gave me a respite. Would it be so great if he were really going to tell me? "Well," he said at last, "just exactly in order that you should do this."

"Do what?"

"Think me—for a change—*bad!*" I shall never forget the sweetness and gaiety with which he brought out the word, nor how, on top of it, he bent forward and kissed me. It was practically the end of everything. I met his kiss and I had to make, while I folded him for a minute in my arms, the most stupendous effort not to cry. He had given exactly the account of himself that permitted least my going behind it, and it was only with the effect of confirming my acceptance of it that, as I presently glanced about the room, I could say—

"Then you didn't undress at all?"

He fairly glittered in the gloom. "Not at all. I sat up and read."

"And when did you go down?"

"At midnight. When I'm bad I *am* bad!"

"I see, I see—it's charming. But how could you be sure I should know it?"

"Oh I arranged that with Flora." His answers rang out with a readiness! "She was to get up and look out."

"Which is what she did do." It was I who fell into the trap!

"So she disturbed you, and, to see what she was looking at, you also looked—you saw."

"While you," I concurred, "caught your death in the night air!"

He literally bloomed so from this exploit that he could afford radiantly to assent. "How otherwise should I have been bad enough?" he asked. Then, after another embrace, the incident and our interview closed on my recognition of all the reserves of goodness that, for his joke, he had been able to draw upon.

XII

The particular impression I had received proved in the morning light, I repeat, not quite successfully presentable to Mrs. Grose, though I re-enforced it with the mention of still another remark that he had made before we separated. "It all lies in half a dozen words," I said to her, "words that really settle the matter. 'Think, you know, what I *might* do!' He threw that off to show me how good he is. He knows down to the ground what he 'might do.' That's what he gave them a taste of at school."

"Lord, you do change!" cried my friend.

"I don't change—I simply make it out. The four, depend upon it, perpetually meet. If on either of these last nights you had been with either child you'd clearly have understood. The more I've watched and waited the more I've felt that if there were nothing else to make it sure it would be made so by the systematic silence of each. *Never,* by a slip of the tongue, have they so much as alluded to either of their old friends, any more than Miles has alluded to his expulsion. Oh yes, we may sit here and look at them, and they may show off to us there to their fill; but even while they pretend to be lost in their fairy-tale they're steeped in their vision of the dead restored to them. He's not reading to her," I declared; "they're talking of *them*—they're talking horrors! I go on, I know, as if I were crazy; and it's a wonder I'm not. What I've seen would have made *you* so; but it has only made me more lucid, made me get hold of still other things."

My lucidity must have seemed awful, but the charming creatures who were victims of it, passing and repassing in their interlocked sweetness, gave my colleague something to hold on by; and I felt how tight she held as, without stirring in the breath of my passion, she covered them still with her eyes. "Of what other things have you got hold?"

"Why of the very things that have delighted, fascinated and yet, at bottom, as I now so strangely see, mystified and troubled me. Their more than earthly beauty, their absolutely unnatural goodness. It's a game," I went on; "It's a policy and a fraud!"

"On the part of little darlings—?"

"As yet mere lovely babies? Yes, mad as that seems!" The very act of bringing it out really helped me to trace it—follow it all up and piece it all together. "They haven't been good—they've only been absent. It has been easy to live with them because they're simply leading a life of their own. They're not mine—they're not ours. They're his and they're hers!"

"Quint's and that woman's?"

"Quint's and that woman's. They want to get to them."

Oh how, at this, poor Mrs. Grose appeared to study them! "But for what?"

"For the love of all the evil that, in those dreadful days, the pair put into them. And to ply them with that evil still, to keep up the work of demons, is what brings the others back."

"Laws!" said my friend under her breath. The exclamation was homely, but it revealed a real acceptance of my further proof of what, in the bad time—for there had been a worse even than this!—must have occurred. There could have been no such justification for me as the plain assent of her experience to whatever depth of depravity I found credible in our brace of scoundrels. It was in obvious submission of memory that she brought out after a moment: "They *were* rascals! But what can they now do?" she pursued.

"Do?" I echoed so loud that Miles and Flora, as they passed at their distance, paused an instant in their walk and looked at us. "Don't they do enough?" I demanded in a lower tone, while the children, having smiled and nodded and kissed hands to us, resumed their exhibition. We were held by it a minute; then I answered: "They can destroy them!" At this my companion did turn, but the appeal she launched was a silent one, the effect of which was to make me more explicit. "They don't know as yet quite how—but they're trying hard. They're seen only across, as it were, and beyond—in strange places and on high places, the top of towers, the roof of houses, the outside of windows, the further edge of pools; but there's a deep design, on either side, to shorten the distance and overcome the obstacle: so the success of the tempters is only a question of time. They've only to keep to their suggestions of danger."

"For the children to come?"

"And perish in the attempt!" Mrs. Grose slowly got up, and I scrupulously added: "Unless, of course, we can prevent!"

Standing there before me while I kept my seat she visibly turned things over. "Their uncle must do the preventing. He must take them away."

"And who's to make him?"

She had been scanning the distance, but she now dropped on me a foolish face. "You, Miss."

"By writing to him that his house is poisoned and his little nephew and niece mad?"

"But if they *are*, Miss?"

"And if I am myself, you mean? That's charming news to be sent him by a person enjoying his confidence and whose prime undertaking was to give him no worry."

Mrs. Grose considered, following the children again. "Yes, he do hate worry. That was the great reason—"

"Why those fiends took him in so long? No doubt, though his indifference must have been awful. As I'm not a fiend, at any rate, I shouldn't take him in."

My companion, after an instant and for all answer, sat down again and grasped my arm. "Make him at any rate come to you."

I stared. "To *me?*" I had a sudden fear of what she might do. " 'Him'?"

"He ought to *be* here—he ought to help."

I quickly rose and I think I must have shown her a queerer face than ever yet. "You see me asking him for a visit?" No, with her eyes on my face she evidently couldn't. Instead of it even—as a woman reads another—she could see what I myself saw: his derision, his amusement, his contempt for the breakdown of my resignation at being left alone and for the fine machinery I had set in motion to attract his attention to my slighted charms. She didn't know—no one knew—how proud I had been to serve him and to stick to our terms; yet she none the less took the measure, I think, of the warning I now gave her. "If you should so lose your head as to appeal to him for me—"

She was really frightened. "Yes, Miss?"

"I would leave, on the spot, both him and you."

XIII

It was all very well to join them, but speaking to them proved quite as much as ever an effort beyond my strength—offered, in close quarters, difficulties as insurmountable as before. This situation continued a month, and with new aggravations and particular notes, the note above all, sharper and sharper, of the small ironic consciousness on the part of my pupils. It was not, I am as sure to-day as I was sure then, my mere infernal imagination: it was absolutely traceable that they were aware of my predicament and that this strange relation made, in a manner, for a long time, the air in which we moved. I don't mean that they had their tongues in their cheeks or did anything vulgar, for that was not one of their dangers: I do mean, on the other hand, that the element of the unnamed and untouched became, between us, greater than any other, and that so much avoidance couldn't have been made successful without a great deal of tacit arrangement. It was as if, at moments, we were perpetually coming into sight of subjects before which we must stop short, turning suddenly out of alleys that we perceived to be blind, closing with a little bang that made us look at each other—for, like all bangs, it was something louder than we had intended—the doors we had indiscreetly opened. All roads lead to Rome, and there were times when it might have struck us that almost every branch of study or subject of conversation skirted forbidden ground. Forbidden ground was the question of the return of the dead in general and of whatever, in especial, might survive, for memory, of the friends little children had lost. There were days when I could have sworn that one of them had, with a small invisible nudge, said to the other: "She thinks she'll do it this time—but she *won't!*" To "do it" would have been to indulge for instance—and for once in a way—in some direct reference to the lady who had prepared them for my discipline. They had a delightful endless appetite for passages in my own history to which I had again and again treated them; they were in possession of everything that had ever happened to me, had had, with every circumstance, the story of my smallest adventures and of those of my brothers and sisters and of the cat and the dog at home, as well as many particulars of the whimsical bent of my father, of the furniture and arrangement of our house and of the conversation of the old women of our village. There were things enough, taking one with another, to chatter about, if one went very fast and knew by instinct when to go round. They pulled with an art of their own the strings of my invention and my memory; and nothing else perhaps, when I thought of such occasions afterwards, gave me so the suspicion of being watched from under cover. It was in any case over *my* life, *my* past and *my* friends alone that we could take anything like our ease; a state of affairs that led them sometimes without the least pertinence to break out into sociable reminders. I was invited—with no visible connexion—to repeat afresh Goody

Gosling's celebrated *mot* or to confirm the details already supplied as to the cleverness of the vicarage pony.

It was partly at such junctures as these and partly at quite different ones that, with the turn my matters had now taken, my predicament, as I have called it, grew most sensible. The fact that the days passed for me without another encounter ought, it would have appeared, to have done something toward soothing my nerves. Since the light brush, that second night on the upper landing, of the presence of a woman at the foot of the stair, I had seen nothing, whether in or out of the house, that one had better not have seen. There was many a corner round which I expected to come upon Quint, and many a situation that, in a merely sinister way, would have favoured the appearance of Miss Jessel. The summer had turned, the summer had gone; the autumn had dropped upon Bly and had blown out half our lights. The place, with its grey sky and withered garlands, its bared spaces and scattered dead leaves, was like a theatre after the performance—all strewn with crumpled playbills. There were exactly states of the air, conditions of sound and of stillness, unspeakable impressions of the *kind* of ministering moment, that brought back to me, long enough to catch it, the feeling of the medium in which, that June evening out of doors, I had had my first sight of Quint, and in which too, at those other instants, I had, after seeing him through the window, looked for him in vain in the circle of shrubbery. I recognised the signs, the portents—I recognised the moment, the spot. But they remained unaccompanied and empty, and I continued unmolested; if unmolested one could call a young woman whose sensibility had, in the most extraordinary fashion, not declined but deepened. I had said in my talk with Mrs. Grose on that horrid scene of Flora's by the lake—and had perplexed her by so saying—that it would from that moment distress me much more to lose my power than to keep it. I had then expressed what was vividly in my mind: the truth that, whether the children really saw or not—since, that is, it was not yet definitely proved—I greatly preferred, as a safeguard, the fulness of my own exposure. I was ready to know the very worst that was to be known. What I had then had an ugly glimpse of was that my eyes might be sealed just while theirs were most opened. Well, my eyes *were* sealed, it appeared, at present—a consummation for which it seemed blasphemous not to thank God. There was, alas, a difficulty about that: I would have thanked him with all my soul had I not had in a proportionate measure this conviction of the secret of my pupils.

How can I retrace to-day the strange steps of my obsession? There were times of our being together when I would have been ready to swear that, literally, in my presence, but with my direct sense of it closed, they had visitors who were known and were welcome. Then it was that, had I not been deterred by the very chance that such an injury might prove greater than the injury to be averted, my exaltation would have broken out. "They're here, they're here, you little wretches," I would have cried, "and you can't deny it now!" The little wretches denied it with all the added volume of their sociability and their tenderness, just in the crystal depths of which—like the flash of a fish in a stream—the mockery of their advantage peeped up. The shock had in truth sunk into me still deeper than I knew on the night when, looking out either for Quint or for Miss Jessel under the stars, I had seen there the boy over whose rest I watched and who had immediately brought in with him—had straightway there turned on me—the lovely upward look with which, from the battlements above us, the hideous apparition of Quint had played. If it was a question of a scare my discovery on this occasion had scared me more than any other, and it was essentially in the scared state that I drew my actual conclusions. They harassed me so that sometimes, at odd moments, I shut myself up audibly to rehearse—it was at once a fantastic relief and a renewed despair—the manner in which I might come to the point. I approached it from one side and the other while, in my room, I flung myself about, but I always broke down in the monstrous utterance of names. As they died away on my lips I said to myself that I should indeed help them to represent something infamous if by pronouncing them I should violate as rare a little case of instinctive delicacy as any schoolroom probably had ever known. When I said to myself: "*They* have the manners to be silent, and you, trusted as you are, the baseness to speak!" I felt myself crimson and covered my face with my hands. After these secret scenes I chattered more than ever, going on volubly enough till one of our prodigious palpable hushes occurred—I can call them nothing else—the strange dizzy lift or swim (I try for terms!) into a stillness, a pause of all life, that had nothing to do with the more or less noise we at the moment might be engaged in making and that I could hear through any intensified mirth or quickened recitation or louder strum of the piano. Then it was that the others, the outsiders, were there. Though they were not angels they "passed," as the French say, causing me, while they stayed, to tremble with the fear of their addressing to their younger victims some yet more infernal message or more vivid image than they had thought good enough for myself.

What it was least possible to get rid of was the cruel idea that, whatever I had seen, Miles and Flora saw *more*—things terrible and unguessable and that sprang from dreadful passages of intercourse in the past. Such things naturally left on the surface, for the time, a chill that we vociferously denied we felt; and we had all three, with repetition, got into such splendid training that we went, each time, to mark the close of the incident, almost automatically through the very same movements. It was striking of the children at all events to kiss me inveterately with a wild irrelevance and never to fail—one or the other—of the precious question that had helped us through many a peril. "When do you think he *will* come? Don't you think we *ought* to write?"—there was nothing like that enquiry, we found by experience, for carrying off an awkwardness. "He" of course was their uncle in Harley Street; and we lived in much profusion of theory that he might at any moment arrive to mingle in our circle. It was impossible to have given less encouragement than he had administered to such a doctrine, but if we had not had the doctrine to fall back upon we should have deprived each other of some of our finest exhibitions. He never wrote to them—that may have been selfish, but it was a part of the flattery of his trust of myself; for the way in which a man pays his highest tribute to a woman is apt to be but by the more festal celebration of one of the sacred laws of his comfort. So I held that I carried out the spirit of the pledge given not to appeal to him when I let our young friends understand that their own letters were but charming literary exercises. They were too beautiful to be posted; I kept them myself; I have them all to this hour. This was a rule indeed which only added to the satiric effect of my being plied with the supposition that he might at any moment be among us. It was exactly as if our young friends knew how almost more awkward than anything else that might be for me. There appears to me moreover as I look back no note in all this more extraordinary than the mere fact that, in spite of my tension and of their triumph, I never lost patience with them. Adorable they must in truth have been, I now feel, since I didn't in these days hate them! Would exasperation, however, if relief had longer been postponed, finally have betrayed me? It little matters, for relief arrived. I call it relief though it was only the relief that a snap brings to a strain or the burst of a thunderstorm to a day of suffocation. It was at least change, and it came with a rush.

XIV

Walking to church a certain Sunday morning, I had little Miles at my side and his sister, in advance of us and at Mrs. Grose's, well in sight. It was a crisp clear day, the first of its order for some time; the night had brought a touch of frost and the autumn air, bright and sharp, made the church-bells almost gay. It was an odd accident of thought that I should have happened at such a moment to be particularly and very gratefully struck with the obedience of my little charges. Why did they never resent my inexorable, my perpetual society? Something or other had brought nearer home to me that I had all but pinned the boy to my shawl, and that in the way our companions were marshalled before me I might have appeared to provide against some danger of rebellion. I was like a gaoler with an eye to possible surprises and escapes. But all this belonged—I mean their magnificent little surrender—just to the special array of the facts that were most abysmal. Turned out for Sunday by his uncle's tailor, who had had a free hand and a notion of pretty waistcoats and of his grand little air, Miles's whole title to independence, the rights of his sex and situation, were so stamped upon him that if he had suddenly struck for freedom I should have had nothing to say. I was by the strangest of chances wondering how I should meet him when the revolution unmistakeably occurred. I call it a revolution because I now see how, with the word he spoke, the curtain rose on the last act of my dreadful drama and the catastrophe was precipitated. "Look here, my dear, you know," he charmingly said, "when in the world, please, am I going back to school?"

Transcribed here the speech sounds harmless enough, particularly as uttered in the sweet, high, casual pipe with which, at all interlocutors, but above all at his eternal governess, he threw off intonations as if he were tossing roses. There was something in them that always made one "catch," and I caught at any rate now so effectually that I stopped as short as if one of the trees of the park had fallen across the road. There was something new, on the spot, between us, and he was perfectly aware I recognised it, though to enable me to do so he had no need to look a whit less candid and charming than usual. I could feel in him how he already, from my at first finding nothing to reply, perceived the advantage he had gained. I was so slow to find anything that he had plenty of time, after a minute, to continue with his suggestive but inconclusive smile: "You know, my dear, that for a fellow to be with a lady *always*—!" His "my dear" was constantly on his lips for me, and nothing could have expressed more the exact shade of the sentiment with which I desired to inspire my pupils than its fond familiarity. It was so respectfully easy.

But oh how I felt that at present I must pick my own phrases! I remember that, to gain time, I tried to laugh, and I seemed to see in the beautiful face with which he watched me how ugly and queer I looked. "And always with the same lady?" I returned.

He neither blenched nor winked. The whole thing was virtually out between us. "Ah of course she's a jolly 'perfect' lady; but after all I'm a fellow, don't you see? who's—well, getting on."

I lingered there with him an instant ever so kindly. "Yes, you're getting on." Oh but I felt helpless!

I have kept to this day the heartbreaking little idea of how he seemed to know that and to play with it. "And you can't say I've not been awfully good, can you?"

I laid my hand on his shoulder, for though I felt how much better it would have been to walk on I was not yet quite able. "No, I can't say that, Miles."

"Except just that one night, you know—!"

"That one night?" I couldn't look as straight as he.

"Why when I went down—went out of the house."

"Oh yes. But I forget what you did it for."

"You forget?"—he spoke with the sweet extravagance of childish reproach. "Why it was just to show you I could!"

"Oh yes—you could."

"And I can again."

I felt I might perhaps after all succeed in keeping my wits about me. "Certainly. But you won't."

"No, not *that* again. It was nothing."

"It was nothing," I said. "But we must go on."

He resumed our walk with me, passing his hand into my arm. "Then when *am* I going back?"

I wore, in turning it over, my most responsible air. "Were you very happy at school?"

He just considered. "Oh I'm happy enough anywhere!"

"Well then," I quavered, "if you're just as happy here—!"

"Ah but that isn't everything! Of course *you* know a lot—"

"But you hint that you know almost as much?" I risked as he paused.

"Not half I want to!" Miles honestly professed. "But it isn't so much that."

"What is it then?"

"Well—I want to see more life."

"I see; I see." We had arrived within sight of the church and of various persons, including several of the household of Bly, on their way to it and clustered about the door to see us go in. I quickened our step; I wanted to get there before the question between us opened up much further; I reflected hungrily that he would have for more than an hour to be silent; and I thought with envy of the comparative dusk of the pew and of the almost spiritual help of the hassock on which I might bend my knees. I seemed literally to be running a race with some confusion to which he was about to reduce me, but I felt he had got in first when, before we had even entered the churchyard, he threw out—

"I want my own sort!"

It literally made me bound forward. "There aren't many of your own sort, Miles!" I laughed. "Unless perhaps dear little Flora!"

"You really compare me to a baby girl?"

This found me singularly weak. "Don't you then *love* our sweet Flora?"

"If I didn't—and you too; if I didn't—!" he repeated as if retreating for a jump, yet leaving his thought so unfinished that, after we had come into the gate, another stop, which he imposed on me by the pressure of his arm, had become inevitable. Mrs. Grose and Flora had passed into the church, the other worshippers had followed and we were, for the minute, alone among the old thick graves. We had paused, on the path from the gate, by a low oblong table-like tomb.

"Yes, if you didn't—?"

He looked, while I waited, about at the graves. "Well, you know what!" But he didn't move, and he presently produced something that made me drop straight down on the stone slab as if suddenly to rest. "Does my uncle think what *you* think?"

I markedly rested. "How do you know what I think?"

"Ah well, of course I don't; for it strikes me you never tell me. But I mean does *he* know?"

"Know what, Miles?"

"Why the way I'm going on."

I recognised quickly enough that I could make, to this enquiry, no answer that wouldn't involve something of a sacrifice of my employer. Yet it struck me that we were all, at Bly, sufficiently sacrificed to make that venial. "I don't think your uncle much cares."

Miles, on this, stood looking at me. "Then don't you think he can be made to?"

"In what way?"

"Why by his coming down."

"But who'll get him to come down?"

"*I* will!" the boy said with extraordinary brightness and emphasis. He gave me another look charged with that expression and then marched off alone into church.

XV

The business was practically settled from the moment I never followed him. It was a pitiful surrender to agitation, but my being aware of this had somehow no power to restore me. I only sat there on my tomb and read into what our young friend had said to me the fulness of its meaning; by the time I had grasped the whole of which, I had also embraced, for absence, the pretext that I was ashamed to offer my pupils and the rest of the congregation such an example of delay. What I said to myself above all was that

Miles had got something out of me and that the gage of it for him would be just this awkward collapse. He had got out of me that there was something I was much afraid of, and that he should probably be able to make use of my fear to gain, for his own purpose, more freedom. My fear was of having to deal with the intolerable question of the grounds of his dismissal from school, since that was really but the question of the horrors gathered behind. That his uncle should arrive to treat with me of these things was a solution that, strictly speaking, I ought now to have desired to bring on; but I could so little face the ugliness and the pain of it that I simply procrastinated and lived from hand to mouth. The boy, to my deep discomposure, was immensely in the right, was in a position to say to me: "Either you clear up with my guardian the mystery of this interruption of my studies, or you cease to expect me to lead with you a life that's so unnatural for a boy." What was so unnatural for the particular boy I was concerned with was this sudden revelation of a consciousness and a plan.

That was what really overcame me, what prevented my going in. I walked round the church, hesitating, hovering; I reflected that I had already, with him, hurt myself beyond repair. Therefore I could patch up nothing and it was too extreme an effort to squeeze beside him into the pew: he would be so much more sure than ever to pass his arm into mine and make me sit there for an hour in close mute contact with his commentary on our talk. For the first minute since his arrival I wanted to get away from him. As I paused beneath the high east window and listened to the sounds of worship I was taken with an impulse that might master me, I felt, and completely, should I give it the least encouragement. I might easily put an end to my ordeal by getting away altogether. Here was my chance; there was no one to stop me; I could give the whole thing up—turn my back and bolt. It was only a question of hurrying again, for a few preparations, to the house which the attendance at church of so many of the servants would practically have left unoccupied. No one, in short, could blame me if I should just drive desperately off. What was it to get away if I should get away only till dinner? That would be in a couple of hours, at the end of which—I had the acute prevision—my little pupils would play at innocent wonder about my non-appearance in their tram.

"What *did* you do, you naughty bad thing? Why in the world, to worry us so—and take our thoughts off too, don't you know?—did you desert us at the very door?" I couldn't meet such questions nor, as they asked them, their false little lovely eyes; yet it was all so exactly what I should have to meet that, as the prospect grew sharp to me, I at last let myself go.

I got, so far as the immediate moment was concerned, away; I came straight out of the churchyard and, thinking hard, retraced my steps through the park. It seemed to me that by the time I reached the house I had made up my mind to cynical flight. The Sunday stillness both of the approaches and of the interior, in which I met no one, fairly stirred me with a sense of opportunity. Were I to get off quickly this way I should get off without a scene, without a word. My quickness would have to be remarkable, however, and the question of a conveyance was the great one to settle. Tormented, in the hall, with difficulties and obstacles, I remember sinking down at the foot of the staircase—suddenly collapsing there on the lowest step and then, with a revulsion, recalling that it was exactly where, more than a month before, in the darkness of night and just so bowed with evil things, I had seen the spectre of the most horrible of women. At this I was able to straighten myself; I went the rest of the way up; I made, in my turmoil, for the schoolroom, where there were objects belonging to me that I should have to take. But I opened the door to find again, in a flash, my eyes unsealed. In the presence of what I saw I reeled straight back upon resistance. Seated at my own table in the clear noonday light I saw a person whom, without my previous experience, I should have taken at the first blush for some housemaid who might have stayed at home to look after the place and who, availing herself of rare relief from observation and of the schoolroom table and my pens, ink and paper, had applied herself to the considerable effort of a letter to her sweetheart. There was an effort in the way that, while her arms rested on the table, her hands, with evident weariness, supported her head; but at the moment I took this in I had already become aware that, in spite of my entrance, her attitude strangely persisted. Then it was—with the very act of its announcing itself— that her identity flared up in a change of posture. She rose, not as if she had heard me, but with an indescribable grand melancholy of indifference and detachment, and, within a dozen feet of me, stood there as my vile predecessor. Dishonoured and tragic, she was all before me; but even as I fixed and, for memory, secured it, the awful image passed away. Dark as midnight in her black dress, her haggard beauty and her unutterable woe, she had looked at me long enough to appear to say that her right to sit at my table was as good as mine to sit at hers. While these instants lasted indeed I had the extraordinary chill of a feeling that it was I who was the intruder. It was as a wild protest against it that, actually addressing her—"You terrible miserable woman!"—I heard myself break into a sound that, by the open door, rang through the long passage and the empty house. She looked at me as if she heard me, but I had recovered myself and cleared the air. There was nothing in the room the next minute but the sunshine and the sense that I must stay.

XVI

I had so perfectly expected the return of the others to be marked by a demonstration that I was freshly upset at having to find them merely dumb and discreet about my desertion. Instead of gaily denouncing and caressing me they made no allusion to my having failed them, and I was left, for the time, on perceiving that she too said nothing, to study Mrs. Grose's odd face. I did this to such purpose that I made sure they had in some way bribed her to silence; a silence that, however, I would engage to break down on the first private opportunity. This opportunity came before tea: I secured five minutes with her in the housekeeper's room, where, in the twilight, amid a smell of lately-baked bread, but with the place all swept and garnished, I found her sitting in pained placidity before the fire. So I see her still, so I see her best: facing the flame from her straight chair in the dusky shining room, a large clean picture of the "put away"— of drawers closed and locked and rest without a remedy.

"Oh yes, they asked me to say nothing; and to please them— so long as they were there—of course I promised. But what had happened to you?"

"I only went with you for the walk," I said. "I had then to come back to meet a friend."

She showed her surprise. "A friend—*you?*"

"Oh yes, I've a couple!" I laughed. "But did the children give you a reason?"

"For not alluding to your leaving us? Yes; they said you'd like it better. Do you like it better?"

My face had made her rueful. "No, I like it worse!" But after an instant I added: "Did they say why I should like it better?"

"No; Master Miles only said 'We must do nothing but what she likes!' "

"I wish indeed he would! And what did Flora say?"

"Miss Flora was too sweet. She said 'Oh of course, of course!'—and I said the same."

I thought a moment. "You were too sweet too—I can hear you all. But none the less, between Miles and me, it's now all out."

"All out?" My companion stared. "But what, Miss?"

"Everything. It doesn't matter. I've made up my mind. I came home, my dear," I went on, "for a talk with Miss Jessel."

I had by this time formed the habit of having Mrs. Grose literally well in hand in advance of my sounding that note; so that even now, as she bravely blinked under the signal of my word, I could keep her comparatively firm. "A talk! Do you mean she spoke?"

"It came to that. I found her, on my return, in the schoolroom."

"And what did she say?" I can hear the good woman still, and the candour of her stupefaction.

"That she suffers the torments—!"

It was this, of a truth, that made her, as she filled out my picture, gape. "Do you mean," she faltered "—of the lost?"

"Of the lost. Of the damned. And that's why, to share them—" I faltered myself with the horror of it.

But my companion, with less imagination, kept me up. "To share them—?"

"She wants Flora." Mrs. Grose might, as I gave it to her, fairly have fallen away from me had I not been prepared. I still held her there, to show I was. "As I've told you, however, it doesn't matter."

"Because you've made up your mind? But to what?"

"To everything."

"And what do you call 'everything'?"

"Why to sending for their uncle."

"Oh Miss, in pity do," my friend broke out.

"Ah but I will, I *will!* I see it's the only way. What's 'out,' as I told you, with Miles is that if he thinks I'm afraid to—and has ideas of what he gains by that—he shall see he's mistaken. Yes, yes; his uncle shall have it here from me on the spot (and before the boy himself if necessary) that if I'm to be reproached with having done nothing again about more school—"

"Yes, Miss—" my companion pressed me.

"Well, there's that awful reason."

There were now clearly so many of these for my poor colleague that she was excusable for being vague. "But—a—which?"

"Why the letter from his old place."

"You'll show it to the master?"

"I ought to have done so on the instant."

"Oh no!" said Mrs. Grose with decision.

"I'll put it before him," I went on inexorably, "that I can't undertake to work the question on behalf of a child who has been expelled—"

"For we've never in the least known what!" Mrs. Grose declared.

"For wickedness. For what else—when he's so clever and beautiful and perfect? Is he stupid? Is he untidy? Is he infirm? Is he illnatured? He's exquisite—so it can be only *that;* and that would open up the whole thing. After all," I said, "it's their uncle's fault. If he left here such people—!"

"He didn't really in the least know them. The fault's mine." She had turned quite pale.

"Well, you shan't suffer," I answered.

"The children shan't!" she emphatically returned.

I was silent a while; we looked at each other. "Then what am I to tell him?"

"You needn't tell him anything. *I'll* tell him."

I measured this. "Do you mean you'll write—?" Remembering she couldn't, I caught myself up. "How do you communicate?"

"I tell the bailiff. *He* writes."

"And should you like him to write our story?"

My question had a sarcastic force that I had not fully intended, and it made her after a moment inconsequently break down. The tears were again in her eyes. "Ah Miss, *you* write!"

"Well—to-night," I at last returned; and on this we separated.

XVII

I went so far, in the evening, as to make a beginning. The weather had changed back, a great wind was abroad, and beneath the lamp, in my room, with Flora at peace beside me, I sat for a long time before a blank sheet of paper and listened to the lash of the rain and the batter of the gusts. Finally I went out, taking a candle; I crossed the passage and listened a minute at Miles's door. What, under my endless obsession, I had been impelled to listen for was some betrayal of his not being at rest, and I presently caught one, but not in the form I had expected. His voice tinkled out. "I say, you there—come in." It was gaiety in the gloom!

I went in with my light and found him in bed, very wide awake but very much at his ease. "Well, what are *you* up to?" he asked with a grace of sociability in which it occurred to me that Mrs. Grose, had she been present, might have looked in vain for proof that anything was "out."

I stood over him with my candle. "How did you know I was there?"

"Why of course I heard you. Did you fancy you made no noise? You're like a troop of cavalry!" he beautifully laughed.

"Then you weren't asleep?"

"Not much! I lie awake and think."

I had put my candle, designedly, a short way off, and then, as he held out his friendly old hand to me, had sat down on the edge of his bed. "What is it," I asked, "that you think of?"

"What in the world, my dear, but *you?*"

"Ah the pride I take in your appreciation doesn't insist on that! I had so far rather you slept."

"Well, I think also, you know, of this queer business of ours."

I marked the coolness of his firm little hand. "Of what queer business, Miles?"

"Why the way you bring me up. And all the rest!"

I fairly held my breath a minute, and even from my glimmering taper there was light enough to show how he smiled up at me from his pillow. "What do you mean by all the rest?"

"Oh you know, you know!"

I could say nothing for a minute, though I felt as I held his hand and our eyes continued to meet that my silence had all the air of admitting his charge and that nothing in the whole world of reality was perhaps at that moment so fabulous as our actual relation. "Certainly you shall go back to school," I said, "if it be that that troubles you. But not to the old place—we must find another, a better. How could I know it did trouble you, this question, when you never told me so, never spoke of it at all?" His clear listening face, framed in its smooth whiteness, made him for the minute as appealing as some wistful patient in a children's hospital; and I would have given, as the resemblance came to me, all I possessed on earth really to be the nurse or the sister of charity who might have helped to cure him. Well, even as it was I perhaps might help! "Do you know you've never said a word to me about your school—I mean the old one; never mentioned it in any way?"

He seemed to wonder; he smiled with the same loveliness. But he clearly gained time; he waited, he called for guidance. "Haven't I?" It wasn't for *me* to help him—it was for the thing I had met!

Something in his tone and the expression of his face, as I got this from him, set my heart aching with such a pang as it had never yet known; so unutterably touching was it to see his little brain puzzled and his little resources taxed to play, under the spell laid on him, a part of innocence and consistency. "No, never—from the hour you came back. You've never mentioned to me one of your masters, one of your comrades, nor the least little thing that ever happened to you at school. Never, little Miles— no never—have you given me an inkling of anything that *may* have happened there. Therefore you can fancy how much I'm in the dark. Until you came out, that way, this morning, you had since the first hour I saw you scarce even made a reference to anything in your previous life. You seemed so perfectly to accept the present." It was extraordinary how my absolute conviction of his secret precocity—or whatever I might call the poison of an influence that I dared but half-phrase—made him, in spite of the faint breath of his inward trouble, appear as accessible as an older person, forced me to treat him as an intelligent equal. "I thought you wanted to go on as you are."

It struck me that at this he just faintly coloured. He gave, at any rate, like a convalescent slightly fatigued, a languid shake of his head. "I don't—I don't. I want to get away."

"You're tired of Bly?"

"Oh no, I like Bly."

"Well then—?"

"Oh *you* know what a boy wants!"

I felt I didn't know so well as Miles, and I took temporary refuge. "You want to go to your uncle?"

Again, at this, with his sweet ironic face, he made a movement on the pillow. "Ah you can't get off with that!"

I was silent a little, and it was I now, I think, who changed colour. "My dear, I don't want to get off!"

"You can't even if you do. You can't, you can't!"—he lay beautifully staring. "My uncle must come down and you must completely settle things."

"If we do," I returned with some spirit, "you may be sure it will be to take you quite away."

"Well, don't you understand that that's exactly what I'm working for? You'll have to *tell* him—about the way you've let it all drop: you'll have to tell him a tremendous lot!"

The exultation with which he uttered this helped me somehow for the instant to meet him rather more. "And how much will *you*, Miles, have to tell him? There are things he'll ask you!"

He turned it over. "Very likely. But what things?"

"The things you've never told me. To make up his mind what to do with you. He can't send you back—"

"I don't want to go back!" he broke in. "I want a new field."

He said it with admirable serenity, with positive unimpeachable gaiety; and doubtless it was that very note that most evoked for me the poignancy, the unnatural childish tragedy, of his probable reappearance at the end of three months with all this bravado and still more dishonour. It overwhelmed me now that I should never be able to bear that, and it made me let myself go. I threw myself upon him and in the tenderness of my pity I embraced him. "Dear little Miles, dear little Miles—!"

My face was close to his, and he let me kiss him, simply taking it with indulgent good humour. "Well, old lady?"

"Is there nothing—nothing at all that you want to tell me?"

He turned off a little, facing round toward the wall and holding up his hand to look at as one had seen sick children look. "I've told you—I told you this morning."

Oh I was sorry for him! "That you just want me not to worry you?"

He looked round at me now as if in recognition of my understanding him; then ever so gently. "To let me alone," he replied.

There was even a strange little dignity in it, something that made me release him, yet when I had slowly risen, linger beside him. God knows *I* never wished to harass him, but I felt that merely, at this, to turn my back on him was to abandon or, to put it more truly, lose him. "I've just begun a letter to your uncle," I said.

"Well then, finish it!"

I waited a minute. "What happened before?"

He gazed up at me again. "Before what?"

"Before you came back. And before you went away."

For some time he was silent, but he continued to meet my eyes. "What happened?"

It made me, the sound of the words, in which it seemed to me I caught for the very first time a small faint quaver of consenting consciousness—it made me drop on my knees beside the bed and seize once more the chance of possessing him. "Dear little Miles, dear little Miles, if you *knew* how I want to help you! It's only that, it's nothing but that, and I'd rather die than give you a pain or do you a wrong—I'd rather die than hurt a hair of you. Dear little Miles"—oh I brought it out now even if I *should* go too far—"I just want you to help me to save you!" But I knew in a moment after this that I had gone too far. The answer to my appeal was instantaneous, but it came in the form of an extraordinary blast and chill, a gust of frozen air and a shake of the room as great as if, in the wild wind, the casement had crashed in. The boy gave a loud high shriek which, lost in the rest of the shock of sound, might have seemed, indistinctly, though I was so close to him, a note either of jubilation or of terror. I jumped to my feet again and was conscious of darkness. So for a moment we remained, while I stared about me and saw the drawn curtains unstirred and the window still tight. "Why the candle's out!" I then cried.

"It was I who blew it, dear!" said Miles.

XVIII

The next day, after lessons, Mrs. Grose found a moment to say to me quietly: "Have you written, Miss?"

"Yes—I've written." But I didn't add—for the hour—that my letter, sealed and directed, was still in my pocket. There would be time enough to send it before the messenger should go to the village. Meanwhile there had been on the part of my pupils no more brilliant, more exemplary morning. It was exactly as if they had both had at heart to gloss over any recent little friction. They performed the dizziest feats of arithmetic, soaring quite out of *my* feeble range, and perpetrated, in higher spirits than ever, geographical and historical jokes. It was conspicuous of course in Miles in particular that he appeared to wish to show how easily he could let me down. This child, to my memory, really lives in a setting of beauty and misery that no words can translate; there was a distinction all his own in every impulse he revealed; never was a small natural creature, to the uninformed eye all frankness and freedom, a more ingenious, a more extraordinary little gentleman. I had perpetually to guard against the wonder of contemplation into which my initiated view betrayed me; to check the irrelevant gaze and discouraged sigh in which I constantly both attacked and renounced the enigma of what such a little gentleman could have done that deserved a penalty. Say that, by the dark prodigy I knew, the imagination of all evil *had* been opened up to him: all the justice within me ached for the proof that it could ever have flowered into an act.

He had never at any rate been such a little gentleman as when, after our early dinner on this dreadful day, he came round to me and asked if I shouldn't like him for half an hour to play to me. David playing to Saul could never have shown a finer sense of the occasion. It was literally a charming exhibition of tact, of magnanimity, and quite tantamount to his saying outright: "The true knights we love to read about never push an advantage too far. I know what you mean now: you mean that—to be let alone yourself and not followed up—you'll cease to worry and spy upon me, won't keep me so close to you, will let me go and come. Well, I 'come,' you see—but I don't go! There'll be plenty of time for that. I do really delight in your society and I only want to show you that I contended for a principle." It may be imagined whether I resisted this appeal or failed to accompany him again, hand in hand, to the schoolroom. He sat down at the old piano and played as he had never played; and if there are those who think he had better have been kicking a football I can only say that I wholly agree with them. For at the end of a time that under his influence I had quite ceased to measure I started up with a strange sense of having literally slept at my post. It was after luncheon, and by the schoolroom fire, and yet I hadn't really in the least slept; I had only done something much worse—I had forgotten. Where all this time was Flora? When I put the question to Miles he played on a minute before answering, and then could only say: "Why, my dear, how do *I* know?"—breaking moreover into a happy laugh which immediately after, as if it were a vocal accompaniment, he prolonged into incoherent extravagant song.

I went straight to my room, but his sister was not there; then, before going downstairs, I looked into several others. As she was nowhere about she would surely be with Mrs. Grose, whom in the comfort of that theory I accordingly proceeded in quest of. I found her where I had found her the evening before, but she met my quick challenge with blank scared ignorance. She had only supposed that, after the repast, I had carried off both the children; as to which she was quite in her right, for it was the very first time I had allowed the little girl out of my sight without some special provision. Of course now indeed she might be with the maids, so that the immediate thing was to look for her without an air of alarm. This we promptly arranged between us; but when, ten minutes later and in pursuance of our arrangement, we met in the hall, it was only to report on either side that after guarded enquiries we had altogether failed to trace her. For a minute there, apart from observation, we exchanged mute alarms, and I could feel with what high interest my friend returned me all those I had from the first given her.

"She'll be above," she presently said—"in one of the rooms you haven't searched."

"No; she's at a distance." I had made up my mind. "She has gone out."

Mrs. Grose stared. "Without a hat?"

I naturally also looked volumes. "Isn't that woman always without one?"

"She's with *her?*"

"She's with *her!*" I declared. "We must find them."

My hand was on my friend's arm, but she failed for the moment, confronted with such an account of the matter, to respond to my pressure. She communed, on the contrary, where she stood, with her uneasiness. "And where's Master Miles?"

"Oh *he's* with Quint. They'll be in the schoolroom."

"Lord, Miss!" My view, I was myself aware—and therefore I suppose my tone—had never yet reached so calm an assurance.

"The trick's played," I went on; "they've successfully worked their plan. He found the most divine little way to keep me quiet while she went off."

" 'Divine'?" Mrs. Grose bewilderedly echoed.

"Infernal then!" I almost cheerfully rejoined. "He has provided for himself as well. But come!"

She had helplessly gloomed at the upper regions. "You leave him—?"

"So long with Quint? Yes—I don't mind that now."

She always ended at these moments by getting possession of my hand, and in this manner she could at present still stay me. But after gasping an instant at my sudden resignation, "Because of your letter?" she eagerly brought out.

I quickly, by way of answer, felt for my letter, drew it forth, held it up, and then, freeing myself, went and laid it on the great hall-table. "Luke will take it," I said as I came back. I reached the house-door and opened it; I was already on the steps.

My companion still demurred: the storm of the night and the early morning had dropped, but the afternoon was damp and grey. I came down to the drive while she stood in the doorway. "You go with nothing on?"

"What do I care when the child has nothing? I can't wait to dress," I cried, "and if you must do so I leave you. Try meanwhile yourself upstairs."

"With *them?*" Oh on this the poor woman promptly joined me!

XIX

We went straight to the lake, as it was called at Bly, and I dare say rightly called, though it may have been a sheet of water less remarkable than my untravelled eyes supposed it. My acquaintance with sheets of water was small, and the pool of Bly, at all events on the few occasions of my consenting, under the protection of my pupils, to affront its surface in the old flat-bottomed boat moored there for our use, had impressed me both with its extent and its agitation. The usual place of embarkation was half a mile from the house, but I had an intimate conviction that, wherever Flora might be, she was not near home. She had not given me the slip for any small adventure, and, since the day of the very great one that I had shared with her by the pond, I had been aware, in our walks, of the quarter to which she most inclined. This was why I had now given to Mrs. Grose's steps so marked a direction—a direction making her, when she perceived it, oppose a resistance that showed me she was freshly mystified. "You're going to the water, Miss?—you think she's *in*—?"

"She may be, though the depth is, I believe, nowhere very great. But what I judge most likely is that she's on the spot from which, the other day, we saw together what I told you."

"When she pretended not to see—?"

"With that astounding self-possession! I've always been sure she wanted to go back alone. And now her brother has managed it for her."

Mrs. Grose still stood where she had stopped. "You suppose they really *talk* of them?"

I could meet this with an assurance! "They say things that, if we heard them, would simply appal us."

"And if she *is* there—?"

"Yes?"

"Then Miss Jessel is?"

"Beyond a doubt. You shall see."

"Oh thank you!" my friend cried, planted so firm that, taking it in, I went straight on without her. By the time I reached the pool, however, she was close behind me, and I knew that, whatever, to her apprehension, might befall me, the exposure of sticking to me struck her as her least danger. She exhaled a moan of relief as we at last came in sight of the greater part of the water without a sight of the child. There was no trace of Flora on that nearer side of the bank where my observation of her had been most startling, and none on the opposite edge, where, save for a margin of some twenty yards, a thick copse came down to the pond. This expanse, oblong in shape, was so narrow compared to its length that, with its ends out of view, it might have been taken for a scant river. We looked at the empty stretch, and then I felt the suggestion in my friend's eyes. I knew what she meant and I replied with a negative headshake.

"No, no; wait! She has taken the boat."

My companion stared at the vacant mooring-place and then again across the lake. "Then where is it?"

"Our not seeing it is the strongest of proofs. She has used it to go over, and then has managed to hide it."

"All alone—that child?"

"She's not alone, and at such times she's not a child: she's an old, old woman." I scanned all the visible shore while Mrs. Grose took again, into the queer element I offered her, one of her plunges of submission; then I pointed out that the boat might perfectly be in a small refuge formed by one of the recesses of the pool, an indentation masked, for the hither side, by a projection of the bank and by a clump of trees growing close to the water.

"But if the boat's there, where on earth's *she?*" my colleague anxiously asked.

"That's exactly what we must learn." And I started to walk further.

"By going all the way round?"

"Certainly, far as it is. It will take us but ten minutes, yet it's far enough to have made the child prefer not to walk. She went straight over."

"Laws!" cried my friend again: the chain of my logic was ever too strong for her. It dragged her at my heels even now, and when we had got halfway round—a devious tiresome process, on ground much broken and by a path choked with overgrowth—I paused to give her breath. I sustained her with a grateful arm, assuring her that she might hugely help me; and this started us afresh, so that in the course of but few minutes more we reached a point from which we found the boat to be where I had supposed it. It had been intentionally left as much as possible out of sight and was tied to one of the stakes of a fence that came, just there, down to the brink and that had been an assistance to disembarking. I recognised, as I looked at the pair of short thick oars, quite safely drawn up, the prodigious character of the feat for a little girl; but I had by this time lived too long among wonders and had panted to too many livelier measures. There was a gate in the fence, through which we passed, and that brought us after a trifling interval more into the open. Then "There she is!" we both exclaimed at once.

Flora, a short way off, stood before us on the grass and smiled as if her performance had now become complete. The next thing she did, however, was to stoop straight down and pluck—quite as if it were all she was there for—a big ugly spray of withered fern. I at once felt sure she had just come out of the copse. She waited for us, not herself taking a step, and I was conscious of the rare solemnity with which we presently approached her. She smiled and smiled, and we met; but it was all done in a silence by this time flagrantly ominous. Mrs. Grose was the first to break the spell: she threw herself on her knees and, drawing the child to her breast, clasped in a long embrace the little tender yielding body. While this dumb convulsion lasted I could only watch it—which I did the more intently when I saw Flora's face peep at me over our companion's shoulder. It was serious now—the flicker had left it; but it strengthened the pang with which I at that moment envied Mrs. Grose the simplicity of *her* relation. Still, all this while, nothing more passed between us save that Flora had let her foolish fern again drop to the ground. What she and I had virtually said to each other was that pretexts were useless now. When Mrs. Grose finally got up she kept the child's hand, so that the two were still before me; and the singular reticence of our communion was even more marked in the frank look she addressed me. "I'll be hanged," it said, "if *I'll* speak!"

It was Flora who, gazing all over me in candid wonder, was the first. She was struck with our bareheaded aspect. "Why where are your things?"

"Where yours are, my dear!" I promptly returned.

She had already got back her gaiety and appeared to take this as an answer quite sufficient. "And where's Miles?" she went on.

There was something in the small valour of it that quite finished me: these three words from her were, in a flash like the glitter of a drawn blade, the jostle of the cup that my hand for weeks and weeks had held high and full to the brim and that now, even before speaking, I felt overflow in a deluge. "I'll tell you if you'll tell *me*—" I heard myself say, then heard the tremor in which it broke.

"Well, what?"

Mrs. Grose's suspense blazed at me, but it was too late now, and I brought the thing out handsomely. "Where, my pet, is Miss Jessel?"

XX

Just as in the churchyard with Miles, the whole thing was upon us. Much as I had made of the fact that this name had never once, between us, been sounded, the quick smitten glare with which the child's face now received it fairly likened my breach of the silence to the smash of a pane of glass. It added to the interposing cry, as if to stay the blow, that Mrs. Grose at the same instant uttered over my violence—the shriek of a creature scared, or rather wounded, which, in turn, within a few seconds, was completed by a gasp of my own. I seized my colleague's arm. "She's there, she's there!"

Miss Jessel stood before us on the opposite bank exactly as she had stood the other time, and I remember, strangely, as the first feeling now produced in me, my thrill of joy at having brought on a proof. She was there, so I was justified; she was there, so I was neither cruel nor mad. She was there for poor scared Mrs. Grose, but she was there most for Flora; and no moment of my monstrous time was perhaps so extraordinary as that in which I consciously threw out to her—with the sense that, pale and ravenous demon as she was, she would catch and understand it—an inarticulate message of gratitude. She rose erect on the spot my friend and I had lately quitted, and there wasn't in all the long reach of her desire an inch of her evil that fell short. This first vividness of vision and emotion were things of a few seconds, during which Mrs. Grose's dazed blink across to where I pointed struck me as showing that she too at last saw, just as it carried my own eyes precipitately to the child. The revelation then of the manner in which Flora was affected startled me in truth far more than it would have done to find her also merely agitated, for direct dismay was of course not what I had expected. Prepared and on her guard as our pursuit had actually made her, she would repress every betrayal; and I was therefore at once shaken by my first glimpse of the particular one for which I had not allowed. To see her, without a convulsion of her small pink face, not even feign to glance in the direction of the prodigy I announced, but only, instead of that, turn at *me* an expression of hard still gravity, an expression absolutely new and unprecedented and that appeared to read and accuse and judge me—this was a stroke that somehow converted the little girl herself into a figure portentous. I gaped at her coolness even though my certitude of her thoroughly seeing was never greater than at that instant, and then, in the immediate need to defend myself, I called her passionately to witness. "She's there, you little unhappy thing—there, there, *there,* and you know it as well as you know me!" I had said shortly before to Mrs. Grose that she was not at these times a child, but an old, old woman, and my description of her couldn't have been more strikingly confirmed than in the way in which, for all notice of this, she simply showed me, without an expressional concession or admission, a countenance of deeper and deeper, of indeed suddenly quite fixed reprobation. I was by this time—if I can put the whole thing at all together—more appalled at what I may properly call her manner than at anything else, though it was quite simultaneously that I became aware of having Mrs. Grose also, and very formidably, to reckon with. My elder companion, the next moment, at any rate, blotted out everything but her own flushed face and her loud shocked protest, a burst of high disapproval. "What a dreadful turn, to be sure, Miss! Where on earth do you see anything?"

I could only grasp her more quickly yet, for even while she spoke the hideous plain presence stood undimmed and undaunted. It had already lasted a minute, and it lasted while I continued, seizing my colleague, quite thrusting her at it and presenting her to it, to insist with my pointing hand. "You don't see her exactly as *we* see?—you mean to say you don't now—*now?* She's as big as a blazing fire! Only look, dearest woman, *look*—!" She looked, just as I did, and gave me, with her deep groan of negation, repulsion, compassion—the mixture with her pity of her relief at her exemption—a sense, touching to me even then, that she would have backed me up if she had been able. I might well have needed that, for with this hard blow of the proof that her eyes were hopelessly sealed I felt my own situation horribly crumble, I felt—I *saw*—my livid predecessor press, from her position, on my defeat, and I took this measure, more than all, of what I should have from this instant to deal with in the astounding little attitude of Flora. Into this attitude Mrs. Grose immediately and violently entered, breaking, even while there pierced through my sense of ruin a prodigious private triumph, into breathless reassurance.

"She isn't there, little lady, and nobody's there—and you never see nothing, my sweet! How can poor Miss Jessel—when poor Miss Jessel's dead and buried? *We* know, don't we love?"—and she appealed, blundering in, to the child. "It's all a mere mistake and a worry and a joke—and we'll go home as fast as we can!"

Our companion, on this, had responded with a strange quick primness of propriety, and they were again, with Mrs. Grose on her feet, united, as it were, in shocked opposition to me. Flora continued to fix me with her small mask or disaffection, and even at that minute I prayed God to forgive me for seeming to see that, as she stood there holding tight to our friend's dress, her incomparable childish beauty had suddenly failed, had quite vanished. I've said it already—she was literally, she was hideously hard; she had turned common and almost ugly. "I don't know what you mean. I see nobody, I see nothing. I never *have*. I think you're cruel. I don't like you!" Then, after this deliverance, which might have been that of a vulgarly pert little girl in the street, she hugged Mrs. Grose more closely and buried in her skirts the dreadful little face. In this position she launched an almost furious wail. "Take me away, take me away—oh take me away from *her!*"

"From *me?*" I panted.

"From you—from you!" she cried.

Even Mrs. Grose looked across at me dismayed; while I had nothing to do but communicate again with the figure that, on the opposite bank, without a movement, as rigidly still as if catching, beyond the interval, our voices, was as vividly there for my disaster as it was not there for my service. The wretched child had spoken exactly as if she had got from some outside source each of her stabbing little words, and I could therefore, in the full despair of all I had to accept, but sadly shake my head at her. "If I had ever doubted all my doubt would at present have gone. I've been living with the miserable truth, and now it has only too much closed round me. Of course I've lost you: I've interfered, and you've seen, under *her* dictation"—with which I faced, over the pool again, our infernal witness—"the easy and perfect way to meet it. I've done my best, but I've lost you. Good-bye." For Mrs. Grose I had an imperative, an almost frantic "Go, go!" before which, in infinite distress, but mutely possessed of the little girl and clearly convinced, in spite of her blindness, that something awful had occurred and some collapse engulfed us, she retreated, by the way we had come, as fast as she could move.

Of what first happened when I was left alone I had no subsequent memory. I only knew that at the end of, I suppose, a quarter of an hour, an odorous dampness and roughness, chilling and piercing my trouble, had made me understand that I must have thrown myself, on my face, to the ground and given way to a wildness of grief. I must have lain there long and cried and wailed, for when I raised my head the day was almost done. I got up and looked a moment, through the twilight, at the grey pool and its blank haunted edge, and then I took, back to the house, my dreary and difficult course. When I reached the gate in the fence the boat, to my surprise, was gone, so that I had a fresh reflexion to make on Flora's extraordinary command of the situation. She passed that night, by the most tacit and, I should add, were not the word so grotesque a false note, the happiest of arrangements, with Mrs. Grose. I saw neither of them on my return, but on the other hand I saw, as by an ambiguous compensation, a great deal of Miles. I saw—I can use no other phrase—so much of him that it fairly-measured more than it had ever measured. No evening I had passed at Bly was to have had the portentous quality of this one; in spite of which—and in spite also of the deeper depths of consternation that had opened beneath my feet—there was literally, in the ebbing actual, an extraordinarily sweet sadness. On reaching the house I had never so much as looked for the boy; I had simply gone straight to my room to change what I was wearing and to take in, at a glance, much material testimony to Flora's rupture. Her little belongings had all been removed. When later, by the schoolroom fire, I was served with tea by the usual maid, I indulged, on the article of my other pupil, in no enquiry whatever. He had his freedom now—he might have it to the end! Well, he did have it; and it consisted—in part at least—of his coming in at about eight o'clock and sitting down with me in silence. On the removal of the tea-things I had blown out the candles and drawn my chair closer: I was conscious of a mortal coldness and felt as if I should never again be warm. So when he appeared I was sitting in the glow with my thoughts. He paused a moment by the door as if to look at me; then—as if to share them—came to the other side of the hearth and sank into a chair. We sat there in absolute stillness; yet he wanted, I felt, to be with me.

XXI

Before a new day, in my room, had fully broken, my eyes opened to Mrs. Grose, who had come to my bedside with worse news. Flora was so markedly feverish that an illness was perhaps at hand; she had passed a night of extreme unrest, a night agitated above all by fears that had for their subject not in the least her former but wholly her present governess. It was not against the possible re-entrance of Miss Jessel on the scene that she protested—it was conspicuously and passionately against mine. I was at once on my feet, and with an immense deal to ask; the more that my friend had discernibly now girded her loins to meet me afresh. This I felt as soon as I had put to her the question of her sense of the child's sincerity as against my own. "She persists in denying to you that she saw, or has ever seen, anything?"

My visitor's trouble truly was great. "Ah Miss, it isn't a matter on which I can push her! Yet it isn't either, I must say, as if I much needed to. It has made her, every inch of her, quite old."

"Oh I see her perfectly from here. She resents, for all the world like some high little personage, the imputation on her truthfulness and, as it were, her respectability. 'Miss Jessel indeed—*she!*' Ah she's 'respectable,' the chit! The impression she gave me there yesterday was, I assure you, the very strangest of all: it was quite beyond any of the others. I *did* put my foot in it! She'll never speak to me again."

Hideous and obscure as it all was, it held Mrs. Grose briefly silent; then she granted my point with a frankness which, I made sure, had more behind it. "I think indeed, Miss, she never will. She do have a grand manner about it!"

"And that manner"—I summed it up—"is practically what's the matter with her now."

Oh that manner, I could see in my visitor's face, and not a little else besides! "She asks me every three minutes if I think you're coming in."

"I see—I see." I too, on my side, had so much more than worked it out. "Has she said to you since yesterday—except to repudiate her familiarity with anything so dreadful—a single other word about Miss Jessel?"

"Not one, Miss. And of course, you know," my friend added, "I took it from her by the lake that just then and there at least there *was* nobody."

"Rather! And naturally you take it from her still."

"I don't contradict her. What else can I *do?*"

"Nothing in the world! You've the cleverest little person to deal with. They've made them—their two friends, I mean—still cleverer even than nature did; for it was wondrous material to play on! Flora has now her grievance, and she'll work it to the end."

"Yes, Miss; but to *what* end?"

"Why that of dealing with me to her uncle. She'll make me out to him the lowest creature—!"

I winced at the fair show of the scene in Mrs. Grose's face; she looked for a minute as if she sharply saw them together. "And him who thinks so well of you!"

"He has an odd way—it comes over me now," I laughed, "—of proving it! But that doesn't matter. What Flora wants of course is to get rid of me."

My companion bravely concurred. "Never again to so much as look at you."

"So that what you've come to me now for," I asked, "is to speed me on my way?" Before she had time to reply, however, I had her in check. "I've a better idea—the result of my reflexions. My going *would* seem the right thing, and on Sunday I was terribly near it. Yet that won't do. It's *you* who must go. You must take Flora."

My visitor, at this, did speculate. "But where in the world—?"

"Away from here. Away from *them.* Away, even most of all, now, from me. Straight to her uncle."

"Only to tell on you—?"

"No, not 'only'! To leave me, in addition, with my remedy."

She was still vague. "And what *is* your remedy?"

"Your loyalty, to begin with. And then Miles's."

She looked at me hard. "Do you think he—?"

"Won't, if he has the chance, turn on me? Yes, I venture still to think it. At all events I want to try. Get off with his sister as soon as possible and leave me with him alone." I was amazed, myself, at the spirit I had still in reserve, and therefore perhaps a trifle the more disconcerted at the way in which, in spite of this fine example of it, she hesitated. "There's one thing, of course," I went on: "they mustn't, before she goes, see each other for three seconds." Then it came over me that, in spite of Flora's presumable sequestration from the instant of her return from the pool, it might already be too late. "Do you mean," I anxiously asked, "that they *have* met?"

At this she quite flushed. "Ah, Miss, I'm not such a fool as that! If I've been obliged to leave her three or four times, it has been each time with one of the maids, and at present, though she's alone, she's locked in safe. And yet—and yet!" There were too many things.

"And yet what?"

"Well, are you so sure of the little gentleman?"

"I'm not sure of anything but *you*. But I have, since last evening, a new hope. I think he wants to give me an opening. I do believe that—poor little exquisite wretch!—he wants to speak. Last evening, in the firelight and the silence, he sat with me for two hours as if it were just coming."

Mrs. Grose looked hard through the window at the grey gathering day. "And did it come?"

"No, though I waited and waited I confess it didn't, and it was without a breach of the silence, or so much as a faint allusion to his sister's condition and absence, that we at last kissed for goodnight. All the same," I continued, "I can't, if her uncle sees her, consent to his seeing her brother without my having given the boy—and most of all because things have got so bad—a little more time."

My friend appeared on this ground more reluctant than I could quite understand. "What do you mean by more time?"

"Well, a day or two—really to bring it out. He'll then be on *my* side—of which you see the importance. If nothing comes I shall only fail, and you at the worst have helped me by doing on your arrival in town whatever you may have found possible." So I put it before her, but she continued for a little so lost in other reasons that I came again to her aid. "Unless indeed," I wound up, "you really want *not* to go."

I could see it, in her face, at last clear itself: she put out her hand to me as a pledge. "I'll go—I'll go. I'll go this morning."

I wanted to be very just. "If you *should* wish still to wait I'd engage she shouldn't see me."

"No, no: it's the place itself. She must leave it." She held me a moment with heavy eyes, then brought out the rest. "Your idea's the right one. I myself, Miss—"

"Well?"

"I can't stay."

The look she gave me with it made me jump at possibilities. "You mean that, since yesterday, you *have* seen—?"

She shook her head with dignity. "I've *heard*—!"

"Heard?"

"From that child—horrors! There!" she sighed with tragic relief. "On my honour, Miss, she says things—!" But at this evocation she broke down; she dropped with a sudden cry upon my sofa and, as I had seen her do before, gave way to all the anguish of it.

It was quite in another manner that I for my part let myself go. "Oh thank God!"

She sprang up again at this, drying her eyes with a groan. "'Thank God'?"

"It so justifies me!"

"It does that, Miss!"

I couldn't have desired more emphasis, but I just waited. "She's so horrible?"

I saw my colleague scarce knew how to put it. "Really shocking."

"And about me?"

"About you, Miss—since you must have it. It's beyond everything, for a young lady; and I can't think wherever she must have picked up—"

"The appalling language she applies to me? I can then!" I broke in with a laugh that was doubtless significant enough.

It only in truth left my friend still more grave. "Well, perhaps I ought to also—since I've heard some of it before! Yet I can't bear it," the poor woman went on while with the same movement she glanced, on my dressing-table, at the face of my watch. "But I must go back."

I kept her, however. "Ah if you can't bear it—!"

"How can I stop with her, you mean? Why just *for* that: to get her away. Far from this," she pursued, "far from *them*—"

"She may be different? she may be free?" I seized her almost with joy. "Then in spite of yesterday you *believe*—"

"In such doings?" Her simple description of them required, in the light of her expression, to be carried no further, and she gave me the whole thing as she had never done. "I believe."

Yes, it was a joy, and we were still shoulder to shoulder: if I might continue sure of that I should care but little what else happened. My support in the presence of disaster would be the same as it had been in my early need of confidence, and if my friend would answer for my honesty I would answer for all the rest. On the point of taking leave of her, none the less, I was to some extent embarrassed. "There's one thing of course—it occurs to me—to remember. My letter giving the alarm will have reached town before you."

I now felt still more how she had been beating about the bush and how weary at last it had made her. "Your letter won't have got there. Your letter never went."

"What then became of it?"

"Goodness knows! Master Miles—"

"Do you mean *he* took it?" I gasped.

She hung fire, but she overcame her reluctance. "I mean that I saw yesterday, when I came back with Miss Flora, that it wasn't where you had put it. Later in the evening I had the chance to question Luke, and he declared that he had neither noticed nor touched it." We could only exchange, on this, one of our deeper mutual soundings, and it was Mrs. Grose who first brought up the plumb with an almost elate "You see!"

"Yes, I see that if Miles took it instead he probably will have read it and destroyed it."

"And don't you see anything else?"

I faced her a moment with a sad smile. "It strikes me that by this time your eyes are open even wider than mine."

They proved to be so indeed, but she could still almost blush to show it. "I make out now what he must have done at school." And she gave, in her simple sharpness, an almost droll disillu-sioned nod. "He stole!"

I turned it over—I tried to be more judicial. "Well—perhaps."

She looked as if she found me unexpectedly calm. "He stole *letters!*"

She couldn't know my reasons for a calmness after all pretty shallow; so I showed them off as I might. "I hope then it was to more purpose than in this case! The note, at all events, that I put on the table yesterday," I pursued, "will have given him so scant an advantage—for it contained only the bare demand for an interview—that he's already much ashamed of having gone so far for so little, and that what he had on his mind last evening was precisely the need of confession." I seemed to myself for the instant to have mastered it, to see it all. "Leave us, leave us"—I was already, at the door, hurrying her off. "I'll get it out of him. He'll meet me. He'll confess. If he confesses he's saved. And if he's saved—"

"Then *you* are?" The dear woman kissed me on this, and I took her farewell. "I'll save you without him!" she cried as she went.

XXII

Yet it was when she had got off—and I missed her on the spot—that the great pinch really came. If I had counted on what it would give me to find myself alone with Miles I quickly recognised that it would give me at least a measure. No hour of my stay in fact was so assailed with apprehensions as that of my coming down to learn that the carriage containing Mrs. Grose and my younger pupil had already rolled out of the gates. Now I *was,* I said to myself, face to face with the elements, and for much of the rest of the day, while I fought my weakness, I could consider that I had been supremely rash. It was a tighter place still than I had yet turned round in; all the more that, for the first time, I could see in the aspect of others a confused reflexion of the crisis. What had happened naturally caused them all to stare; there was too little of the explained, throw out whatever we might, in the suddenness of my colleague's act. The maids and the men looked blank; the effect of which on my nerves was an aggravation until I saw the necessity of making it a positive aid. It was in short by just clutching the helm that I avoided total wreck; and I dare say that, to bear up at all, I became that morning very grand and very dry. I welcomed the consciousness that I was charged with much to do, and I caused it to be known as well that, left thus to myself, I was quite remarkably firm. I wandered with that manner, for the next hour or two, all over the place and looked, I have no doubt, as if I were ready for any onset. So, for the benefit of whom it might concern, I paraded with a sick heart.

The person it appeared least to concern proved to be, till dinner, little Miles himself. My perambulations had given me meanwhile no glimpse of him, but they had tended to make more public the change taking place in our relation as a consequence of his having at the piano, the day before, kept me, in Flora's interest, so beguiled and befooled. The stamp of publicity had of course been fully given by her confinement and departure, and the change itself was now ushered in by our non-observance of the regular custom of the schoolroom. He had already disappeared when, on my way down, I pushed open his door, and I learned below that he had breakfasted—in the presence of a couple of the maids—with Mrs. Grose and his sister. He had then gone out, as he said, for a stroll; than which nothing, I reflected, could better have expressed his frank view of the abrupt transformation of my office. What he would now permit this office to consist of was yet to be settled: there was at the least a queer relief—I mean for myself in especial—in the renouncement of one pretension. If so much had sprung to the surface I scarce put it too strongly in saying that

what had perhaps sprung highest was the absurdity of our pro-
longing the fiction that I had anything more to teach him. It sufficiently stuck out that, by tacit little tricks in which even more
than myself he carried out the care for my dignity, I had had to
appeal to him to let me off straining to meet him on the ground of
his true capacity. He had at any rate his freedom now; I was never
to touch it again: as I had amply shown, moreover, when, on his
joining me in the schoolroom the previous night, I uttered, in reference to the interval just concluded, neither challenge nor hint. I
had too much, from this moment, my other ideas. Yet when he at
last arrived the difficulty of applying them, the accumulations of
my problem, were brought straight home to me by the beautiful
little presence on which what had occurred had as yet, for the eye,
dropped neither stain nor shadow.

To mark, for the house, the high state I cultivated I decreed
that my meals with the boy should be served, as we called it, downstairs; so that I had been awaiting him in the ponderous pomp of
the room outside the window of which I had had from Mrs. Grose,
that first scared Sunday, my flash of something it would scarce have
done to call light. Here at present I felt afresh—for I had felt it
again and again—how my equilibrium depended on the success of
my rigid will, the will to shut my eyes as tight as possible to the
truth that what I had to deal with was, revoltingly, against nature.
I could only get on at all by taking "nature" into my confidence
and my account, by treating my monstrous ordeal as a push in a
direction unusual, of course, and unpleasant, but demanding after
all, for a fair front, only another turn of the screw of ordinary
human virtue. No attempt, none the less, could well require more
tact than just this attempt to supply, one's self, *all* the nature. How
could I put even a little of that article into a suppression of reference

to what had occurred? How on the other hand could I make a reference without a new plunge into the hideous obscure? Well, a sort of answer, after a time, had come to me, and it was so far confirmed as that I was met, incontestably, by the quickened vision of what was rare in my little companion. It was indeed as if he had found even now—as he had so often found at lessons—still some other delicate way to ease me off. Wasn't there light in the fact which, as we shared our solitude, broke out with a specious glitter it had never yet quite worn?—the fact that (opportunity aiding, precious opportunity which had now come) it would be preposterous, with a child so endowed, to forego the help one might wrest from absolute intelligence? What had his intelligence been given him for but to save him? Mightn't one, to reach his mind, risk the stretch of a stiff arm across his character? It was as if, when we were face to face in the dining-room, he had literally shown me the way. The roast mutton was on the table and I had dispensed with attendance. Miles, before he sat down, stood a moment with his hands in his pockets and looked at the joint, on which he seemed on the point of passing some humorous judgement. But what he presently produced was: "I say, my dear, is she really very awfully ill?"

"Little Flora? Not so bad but that she'll presently be better. London will set her up. Bly had ceased to agree with her. Come here and take your mutton."

He alertly obeyed me, carried the plate carefully to his seat and, when he was established, went on. "Did Bly disagree with her so terribly all at once?"

"Not so suddenly as you might think. One had seen it coming on."

"Then why didn't you get her off before?"

"Before what?"

"Before she became too ill to travel."

I found myself prompt. "She's *not* too ill to travel; she only might have become so if she had stayed. This was just the moment to seize. The journey will dissipate the influence"—oh I was grand!—"and carry it off."

"I see, I see"—Miles, for that matter, was grand too. He settled to his repast with the charming little "table manner" that, from the day of his arrival, had relieved me of all grossness of admonition. Whatever he had been expelled from school for, it wasn't for ugly feeding. He was irreproachable, as always, today; but was unmistakably more conscious. He was discernibly trying to take for granted more things than he found, without assistance, quite easy; and he dropped into peaceful silence while he felt his situation. Our meal was of the briefest—mine a vain pretence, and I had the things immediately removed. While this was done Miles stood again with his hands in his little pockets and his back to me—stood and looked out of the wide window through which, that other day, I had seen what pulled me up. We continued silent while the maid was with us—as silent, it whimsically occurred to me, as some young couple who, on their wedding-journey, at the inn, feel shy in the presence of the waiter. He turned round only when the waiter had left us. "Well—so we're alone!"

XXIII

"Oh more or less." I imagine my smile was pale. "Not absolutely. We shouldn't like that!" I went on.

"No—I suppose we shouldn't. Of course we've the others."

"We've the others—we've indeed the others," I concurred.

"Yet even though we have them," he returned, still with his hands in his pockets and planted there in front of me, "they don't much count, do they?"

I made the best of it, but I felt wan. "It depends on what you call 'much'!"

"Yes"—with all accommodation—"everything depends!" On this, however, he faced to the window again and presently reached it with his vague restless cogitating step. He remained there a while with his forehead against the glass, in contemplation of the stupid shrubs I knew and the dull things of November. I had always my hypocrisy of "work," behind which I now gained the sofa. Steadying myself with it there as I had repeatedly done at those moments of torment that I have described as the moments of my knowing the children to be given to something from which I was barred, I sufficiently obeyed my habit of being prepared for the worst. But an extraordinary impression dropped on me as I extracted a meaning from the boy's embarrassed back—none other than the impression that I was not barred now. This inference grew in a few minutes to sharp intensity and seemed bound up with the direct perception that it was positively *he* who was. The frames and squares of the great window were a kind of image, for him, of a kind of failure. I felt that I saw him, in my case, shut in or shut out. He was admirable but not comfortable: I took it in with a throb of hope. Wasn't he looking through the haunted pane for something he couldn't see?—and wasn't it the first time in the whole business that he had known such a lapse? The first, the very first: I found it a splendid portent. It made him anxious, though he watched himself; he had been anxious all day and, even while in his usual sweet little manner he sat at table, had needed all his small strange genius to give it a gloss. When he at last turned round to meet me it was almost as if this genius had succumbed. "Well, I think I'm glad Bly agrees with *me!*"

"You'd certainly seem to have seen, these twenty-four hours, a good deal more of it than some time before. I hope," I went on bravely, "that you've been enjoying yourself."

"Oh yes, I've been ever so far; all round about—miles and miles away. I've never been so free."

He had really a manner of his own, and I could only try to keep up with him. "Well, do you like it?"

He stood there smiling; then at last he put into two words— "Do *you?*"— more discrimination than I had ever heard two words contain. Before I had time to deal with that, however, he continued as if with the sense that this was an impertinence to be softened. "Nothing could be more charming than the way you take it, for of course, if we're alone together now it's you that are alone most. But I hope," he threw in, "you don't particularly mind!"

"Having to do with you?" I asked. "My dear child, how can I help minding? Though I've renounced all claim to your company —you're so beyond me—I at least greatly enjoy it. What else should I stay on for?"

He looked at me more directly, and the expression of his face, graver now, struck me as the most beautiful I had ever found in it. "You stay on just for *that?*"

"Certainly. I stay on as your friend and from the tremendous interest I take in you till something can be done for you that may be more worth your while. That needn't surprise you." My voice trembled so that I felt it impossible to suppress the shake. "Don't you remember how I told you, when I came and sat on your bed the night of the storm, that there was nothing in the world I wouldn't do for you?"

"Yes, yes!" He, on his side, more and more visibly nervous, had a tone to master; but he was so much more successful than I that, laughing out through his gravity, he could pretend we were pleasantly jesting. "Only that, I think, was to get me to do something for *you!*"

"It was partly to get you to do something," I conceded. "But, you know, you didn't do it."

"Oh yes," he said with the brightest superficial eagerness, "you wanted me to tell you something."

"That's it. Out, straight out. What you have on your mind, you know."

"Ah then is *that* what you've stayed over for?"

He spoke with a gaiety through which I could still catch the finest little quiver of resentful passion; but I can't begin to express the effect upon me of an implication of surrender even so faint. It was as if what I had yearned for had come at last only to astonish me. "Well, yes—I may as well make a clean breast of it. It was precisely for that."

He waited so long that I supposed it for the purpose of repudiating the assumption on which my action had been founded; but what he finally said was: "Do you mean now—here?"

"There couldn't be a better place or time." He looked round him uneasily, and I had the rare—oh the queer!—impression of the very first symptom I had seen in him of the approach of immediate fear. It was as if he were suddenly afraid of me—which struck me indeed as perhaps the best thing to make him. Yet in the very pang of the effort I felt it vain to try sternness, and I heard myself the next instant so gentle as to be almost grotesque. "You want so to go out again?"

"Awfully!" He smiled at me heroically, and the touching little bravery of it was enhanced by his actually flushing with pain. He had picked up his hat, which he had brought in, and stood twirling it in a way that gave me, even as I was just nearly reaching port, a perverse horror of what I was doing. To do it in *any* way was an act of violence, for what did it consist of but the obtrusion of the idea of grossness and guilt on a small helpless creature who had been for me a revelation of the possibilities of beautiful intercourse? Wasn't it base to create for a being so exquisite a mere alien awkwardness? I suppose I now read into our situation a clearness it couldn't have had at the time, for I seem to see our poor eyes already lighted with some spark of a prevision of the anguish that was to come. So we circled about with terrors and scruples, fighters not daring to close. But it was for each other we feared! That kept us a little longer suspended and unbruised. "I'll tell you everything," Miles said—"I mean I'll tell you anything you like. You'll stay on with me, and we shall both be all right, and I *will* tell you—I *will*. But not now."

"Why not now?"

My insistence turned him from me and kept him once more at his window in a silence during which, between us, you might have heard a pin drop. Then he was before me again with the air of a person for whom, outside, some one who had frankly to be reckoned with was waiting. "I have to see Luke."

I had not yet reduced him to quite so vulgar a lie, and I felt proportionately ashamed. But, horrible as it was, his lies made up my truth. I achieved thoughtfully a few loops of my knitting. "Well then go to Luke, and I'll wait for what you promise. Only in return for that satisfy, before you leave me, one very much smaller request."

He looked as if he felt he had succeeded enough to be able still a little to bargain. "Very much smaller—?"

"Yes, a mere fraction of the whole. Tell me"—oh my work preoccupied me, and I was off-hand!—"if, yesterday afternoon, from the table in the hall, you took, you know, my letter."

XXIV

My grasp of how he received this suffered for a minute from something that I can describe only as a fierce split of my attention—a stroke that at first, as I sprang straight up, reduced me to the mere blind movement of getting hold of him, drawing him close and, while I just fell for support against the nearest piece of furniture, instinctively keeping him with his back to the window. The appearance was full upon us that I had already had to deal with here: Peter Quint had come into view like a sentinel before a prison. The next thing I saw was that, from outside, he had reached the window, and then I knew that, close to the glass and glaring in through it, he offered once more to the room his white face of damnation. It represents but grossly what took place within me at the sight to say that on the second my decision was made; yet I believe that no woman so overwhelmed ever in so short a time recovered her command of the *act*. It came to me in the very horror of the immediate presence that the act would be, seeing and facing what I saw and faced, to keep the boy himself unaware. The inspiration—I can call it by no other name—was that I felt how voluntarily, how transcendently, I *might*. It was like fighting with a demon for a human soul, and when I had fairly so appraised it I saw how the human soul—held out, in the tremor of my hands, at arms' length—had a perfect dew of sweat on a lovely childish forehead. The face that was close to mine was as white as the face against the glass, and out of it presently came a sound, not low nor weak, but as if from much further away, that I drank like a waft of fragrance.

"Yes—I took it."

At this, with a moan of joy, I enfolded, I drew him close; and while I held him to my breast, where I could feel in the sudden fever of his little body the tremendous pulse of his little heart, I kept my eyes on the thing at the window and saw it move and shift its posture. I have likened it to a sentinel, but its slow wheel, for a moment, was rather the prowl of a baffled beast. My present quickened courage, however, was such that, not too much to let it through, I had to shade, as it were, my flame. Meanwhile the glare of the face was again at the window, the scoundrel fixed as if to watch and wait. It was the very confidence that I might now defy him, as well as the positive certitude, by this time, of the child's unconsciousness, that made me go on. "What did you take it for?"

"To see what you said about me."

"You opened the letter?"

"I opened it."

My eyes were now, as I held him off a little again, on Miles's own face, in which the collapse of mockery showed me how complete was the ravage of uneasiness. What was prodigious was that at last, by my success, his sense was sealed and his communication stopped: he knew that he was in presence, but knew not of what, and knew still less that I also was and that I did know. And what did this strain of trouble matter when my eyes went back to the window only to see that the air was clear again and—by my personal triumph—the influence quenched? There was nothing there. I felt that the cause was mine and that I should surely get *all*. "And you found nothing!"—I let my elation out.

He gave the most mournful, thoughtful little headshake. "Nothing."

"Nothing, nothing!" I almost shouted in my joy.

"Nothing, nothing," he sadly repeated.

I kissed his forehead; it was drenched. "So what have you done with it?"

"I've burnt it."

"Burnt it?" It was now or never. "Is that what you did at school?"

Oh what this brought up! "At school?"

"Did you take letters?—or other things?"

"Other things?" He appeared now to be thinking of something far off and that reached him only through the pressure of his anxiety. Yet it did reach him. "Did I *steal?*"

I felt myself redden to the roots of my hair as well as wonder if it were more strange to put to a gentleman such a question or to see him take it with allowances that gave the very distance of his fall in the world. "Was it for that you mightn't go back?"

The only thing he felt was rather a dreary little surprise. "Did you know I mightn't go back?"

"I know everything."

He gave me at this the longest and strangest look. "Everything?"

"Everything. Therefore *did* you—?" But I couldn't say it again. Miles could, very simply. "No. I didn't steal."

My face must have shown him I believed him utterly; yet my hands—but it was for pure tenderness—shook him as if to ask him why, if it was all for nothing, he had condemned me to months of torment. "What then did you do?"

He looked in vague pain all round the top of the room and drew his breath, two or three times over, as if with difficulty. He might have been standing at the bottom of the sea and raising his eyes to some faint green twilight. "Well—I said things."

"Only that?"

"They thought it was enough!"

"To turn you out for?"

Never, truly, had a person "turned out" shown so little to explain it as this little person! He appeared to weigh my question, but in a manner quite detached and almost helpless. "Well, I suppose I oughtn't."

"But to whom did you say them?"

He evidently tried to remember, but it dropped—he had lost it. "I don't know!"

He almost smiled at me in the desolation of his surrender, which was indeed practically, by this time, so complete that I ought to have left it there. But I was infatuated—I was blind with victory, though even then the very effect that was to have brought him so much nearer was already that of added separation. "Was it to every one?" I asked.

"No; it was only to—" But he gave a sick little headshake. "I don't remember their names."

"Were they then so many?"

"No—only a few. Those I liked."

Those he liked? I seemed to float not into clearness, but into a darker obscure, and within a minute there had come to me out of my very pity the appalling alarm of his being perhaps innocent. It was for the instant confounding and bottomless, for if he *were* innocent what then on earth was I? Paralysed, while it lasted, by the mere brush of the question, I let him go a little, so that, with a deep-drawn sigh, he turned away from me again; which, as he faced toward the clear window, I suffered, feeling that I had nothing now there to keep him from. "And did they repeat what you said?" I went on after a moment.

He was soon at some distance from me, still breathing hard and again with the air, though now without anger for it, of being confined against his will. Once more, as he had done before, he looked up at the dim day as if, of what had hitherto sustained him, nothing was left but an unspeakable anxiety. "Oh yes," he nevertheless replied—"they must have repeated them. To those *they* liked," he added.

There was somehow less of it than I had expected; but I turned it over. "And these things came round—?"

"To the masters? Oh yes!" he answered very simply. "But I didn't know they'd tell."

"The masters? They didn't—they've never told. That's why I ask you."

He turned to me again his little beautiful fevered face. "Yes, it was too bad."

"Too bad?"

"What I suppose I sometimes said. To write home."

I can't name the exquisite pathos of the contradiction given to such a speech by such a speaker; I only know that the next instant I heard myself throw off with homely force: "Stuff and nonsense!" But the next after that I must have sounded stern enough. "What *were* these things?"

My sternness was all for his judge, his executioner; yet it made him avert himself again, and that movement made *me*, with a single bound and an irrepressible cry, spring straight upon him. For there again, against the glass, as if to blight his confession and stay his answer, was the hideous author of our woe—the white face of damnation. I felt a sick swim at the drop of my victory and all the return of my battle, so that the wildness of my veritable leap only served as a great betrayal. I saw him, from the midst of my act, meet it with a divination, and on the perception that even now he only guessed, and that the window was still to his own eyes free, I let the impulse flame up to convert the climax of his dismay into the very proof of his liberation. "No more, no more, no more!" I shrieked to my visitant as I tried to press him against me.

"Is she *here?*" Miles panted as he caught with his sealed eyes the direction of my words. Then as his strange "she" staggered me and, with a gasp, I echoed it, "Miss Jessel, Miss Jessel!" he with sudden fury gave me back.

I seized, stupefied, his supposition—some sequel to what we had done to Flora, but this made me only want to show him that it was better still than that. "It's not Miss Jessel! But it's at the window—straight before us. It's *there*—the coward horror, there for the last time!"

At this, after a second, in which his head made the movement of a baffled dog's on a scent and then gave a frantic little shake for air and light, he was at me in a white rage, bewildered, glaring vainly over the place and missing wholly, though it now, to my sense, filled the room like the taste of poison, the wide over-whelming presence. "It's *he?*"

I was so determined to have all my proof that I flashed into ice to challenge him. "Whom do you mean by 'he'?"

"Peter Quint—you devil!" His face gave again, round the room, its convulsed supplication. *"Where?"*

They are in my ears still, his supreme surrender of the name and his tribute to my devotion. "What does he matter now, my own?—what will he *ever* matter? *I* have you," I launched at the beast, "but he has lost you for ever!" Then for the demonstration of my work, "There, *there!*" I said to Miles.

But he had already jerked straight round, stared, glared again, and seen but the quiet day. With the stroke of the loss I was so proud of he uttered the cry of a creature hurled over an abyss, and the grasp with which I recovered him might have been that of catching him in his fall. I caught him, yes, I held him—it may be imagined with what a passion; but at the end of a minute I began to feel what it truly was that I held. We were alone with the quiet day, and his little heart, dispossessed, had stopped.

THE DEAD SMILE

F. Marion Crawford

[1854–1909]

"F. Marion Crawford produced several weird tales of varying quality, now collected in a volume entitled *Wandering Ghosts*. *For the Blood is the Life* touches powerfully on a case of moon-cursed vampirism near an ancient tower on the rocks of the lonely South Italian seacoast. *The Dead Smile* treats of family horrors in an old house and an ancestral vault in Ireland, and introduces the banshee with considerable force."

—*H.P. Lovecraft*

I

SIR HUGH OCKRAM SMILED as he sat by the open window of his study, in the late August afternoon, and just then a curiously yellow cloud obscured the low sun, and the clear summer light turned lurid, as if it had been suddenly poisoned and polluted by the foul vapours of a plague. Sir Hugh's face seemed, at best, to be made of fine parchment drawn skintight over a wooden mask, in which two eyes were sunk out of sight, and peered from far within through crevices under the slanting, wrinkled lids, alive and watchful like two toads in their holes, side by side and exactly alike. But as the light changed, then a little yellow glare flashed in each. Nurse Macdonald said once that

when Sir Hugh smiled he saw the faces of two women in hell—
two dead women he had betrayed. (Nurse Macdonald was a hundred years old.) And the smile widened, stretching the pale lips across the discoloured teeth in an expression of profound self-satisfaction, blended with the most unforgiving hatred and contempt for the human doll. The hideous disease of which he was dying had touched his brain. His son stood beside him, tall, white, and delicate as an angel in a primitive picture, and though there was deep distress in his violet eyes as he looked at his father's face, he felt the shadow of that sickening smile stealing across his own lips and parting them and drawing them against his will. And it was like a bad dream, for he tried not to smile and smiled the more. Beside him, strangely like him in her wan, angelic beauty, with the same shadowy golden hair, the same sad violet eyes, the same luminously pale face, Evelyn Warburton rested one hand upon his arm. And as she looked into her uncle's eyes, and could not turn her own away, she knew that the deathly smile was hovering on her own red lips, drawing them tightly across her little teeth, while two bright tears ran down her cheeks to her mouth, and dropped from the upper to the lower lip while she smiled—and the smile was like the shadow of death and the seal of damnation upon her pure, young face.

"Of course," said Sir Hugh very slowly, and still looking out at the trees, "if you have made up your mind to be married, I cannot hinder you, and I don't suppose you attach the smallest importance to my consent——"

"Father!" exclaimed Gabriel reproachfully.

"No, I do not deceive myself," continued the old man, smiling terribly. "You will marry when I am dead, though there is a very good reason why you had better not—why you had better not," he repeated very emphatically, and he slowly turned his toad eyes upon the lovers.

"What reason?" asked Evelyn in a frightened voice.

"Never mind the reason, my dear. You will marry just as if it did not exist." There was a long pause. "Two gone," he said, his voice lowering strangely, "and two more will be four—all together—for ever and ever, burning, burning, burning bright."

At the last words his head sank slowly back, and the little glare of the toad eyes disappeared under the swollen lids, and the lurid cloud passed from the westering sun, so that the earth was green again and the light pure. Sir Hugh had fallen asleep, as he often did in his last illness, even while speaking.

Gabriel Ockram drew Evelyn away, and from the study they went out into the dim hall, softly closing the door behind them, and each audibly drew breath, as though some sudden danger had been passed. They laid their hands each in the other's, and their strangely-like eyes met in a long look, in which love and perfect understanding were darkened by the secret terror of an unknown thing. Their pale faces reflected each other's fear.

"It is his secret," said Evelyn at last. "He will never tell us what it is."

"If he dies with it," answered Gabriel, "let it be on his own head!"

"On his head!" echoed the dim hall. It was a strange echo, and some were frightened by it, for they said that if it were a real echo it should repeat everything and not give back a phrase here and there, now speaking, now silent. But Nurse Macdonald said that the great hall would never echo a prayer when an Ockram was to die, though it would give back curses ten for one.

"On his head!" it repeated quite softly, and Evelyn started and looked round.

"It is only the echo," said Gabriel, leading her away.

They went out into the late afternoon light, and sat upon a stone seat behind the chapel, which was built across the end of the east wing. It was very still, not a breath stirred, and there was no sound near them. Only far off in the park a song-bird was whistling the high prelude to the evening chorus.

"It is very lonely here," said Evelyn, taking Gabriel's hand nervously, and speaking as if she dreaded to disturb the silence. "If it were dark, I should be afraid."

"Of what? Of me?" Gabriel's sad eyes turned to her.

"Oh no! How could I be afraid of you? But of the old Ockrams —they say they are just under our feet here in the north vault outside the chapel, all in their shrouds, with no coffins, as they used to bury them."

"As they always will—as they will bury my father, and me. They say an Ockram will not lie in a coffin."

"But it cannot be true—these are fairy tales—ghost stories!" Evelyn nestled nearer to her companion, grasping his hand more tightly, and the sun began to go down.

"Of course. But there is a story of old Sir Vernon, who was beheaded for treason under James II. The family brought his body back from the scaffold in an iron coffin with heavy locks, and they put it in the north vault. But ever afterwards, whenever the vault was opened to bury another of the family, they found the coffin wide open, and the body standing upright against the wall, and the head rolled away in a corner, smiling at it."

"As Uncle Hugh smiles?" Evelyn shivered.

"Yes, I suppose so," answered Gabriel, thoughtfully. "Of course I never saw it, and the vault has not been opened for thirty years—none of us have died since then."

"And if—if Uncle Hugh dies—shall you—" Evelyn stopped, and her beautiful thin face was quite white.

"Yes. I shall see him laid there too—with his secret, whatever it is." Gabriel sighed and pressed the girl's little hand.

"I do not like to think of it," she said unsteadily. "O Gabriel, what can the secret be? He said we had better not marry—not that he forbade it—but he said it so strangely, and he smiled—ugh!" Her small white teeth chattered with fear, and she looked over her shoulder while drawing still closer to Gabriel. "And, somehow, I felt it in my own face——"

"So did I," answered Gabriel in a low, nervous voice. "Nurse Macdonald—" He stopped abruptly.

"What? What did she say?"

"Oh—nothing. She has told me things—they would frighten you, dear. Come, it is growing chilly." He rose, but Evelyn held his hand in both of hers, still sitting and looking up into his face.

"But we shall be married, just the same—Gabriel! Say that we shall!"

"Of course, darling—of course. But while my father is so very ill, it is impossible——"

"O Gabriel, Gabriel dear! I wish we were married now!" cried Evelyn in sudden distress. "I know that something will prevent it and keep us apart."

"Nothing shall!"

"Nothing?"

"Nothing human," said Gabriel Ockram, as she drew him down to her.

And their faces, that were so strangely alike, met and touched—and Gabriel knew that the kiss had a marvellous savour of evil, but on Evelyn's lips it was like the cool breath of a sweet and mortal fear. And neither of them understood, for they were innocent and young. Yet she drew him to her by her lightest touch, as a sensitive plant shivers and waves its thin leaves, and bends and closes softly upon what it wants, and he let himself be drawn to her willingly, as he would if her touch had been deadly and poisonous; for she strangely loved that half voluptuous breath of fear, and he passionately desired the nameless evil something that lurked in her maiden lips.

"It is as if we loved in a strange dream," she said.

"I fear the waking," he murmured.

"We shall not wake, dear—when the dream is over it will have already turned into death, so softly that we shall not know it. But until then——"

She paused, and her eyes sought his, and their faces slowly came nearer. It was as if they had thoughts in their red lips that foresaw and foreknew the deep kiss of each other.

"Until then—" she said again, very low, and her mouth was nearer to his.

"Dream—till then," murmured his breath.

II

Nurse Macdonald was a hundred years old. She used to sleep sitting all bent together in a great old leathern arm-chair with wings, her feet in a bag footstool lined with sheepskin, and many warm blankets wrapped about her, even in summer. Beside her a little lamp always burned at night by an old silver cup, in which there was something to drink.

Her face was very wrinkled, but the wrinkles were so small and fine and near together that they made shadows instead of lines. Two thin locks of hair, that was turning from white to a smoky yellow again, were drawn over her temples from under her starched white cap. Every now and then she woke, and her eyelids were drawn up in tiny folds like little pink silk curtains, and her queer blue eyes looked straight before her through doors and walls and worlds to a far place beyond. Then she slept again, and her hands lay one upon the other on the edge of the blanket, the thumbs had grown longer than the fingers with age, and the joints shone in the low lamplight like polished crab-apples.

It was nearly one o'clock in the night, and the summer breeze was blowing the ivy branch against the panes of the window with a hushing caress. In the small room beyond, with the door ajar, the girl-maid who took care of Nurse Macdonald was fast asleep. All was very quiet. The old woman breathed regularly, and her indrawn lips trembled each time as the breath went out, and her eyes were shut.

But outside the closed window there was a face, and violet eyes were looking steadily at the ancient sleeper, for it was like the face of Evelyn Warburton, though there were eighty feet from the sill of the window to the foot of the tower. Yet the cheeks were thinner than Evelyn's, and as white as a gleam, and her eyes stared, and the lips were not red with life, they were dead and painted with new blood.

Slowly Nurse Macdonald's wrinkled eyelids folded themselves back, and she looked straight at the face at the window while one might count ten.

"Is it time?" she asked in her little old, far-away voice.

While she looked the face at the window changed, for the eyes opened wider and wider till the white glared all round the bright violet, and the bloody lips opened over gleaming teeth, and stretched and widened and stretched again, and the shadow golden hair rose and streamed against the window in the night breeze. And in answer to Nurse Macdonald's question came the sound that freezes the living flesh.

That low moaning voice that rises suddenly, like the scream of storm, from a moan to a wail, from a wail to a howl, from a howl to the fear-shriek of the tortured dead—he who had heard knows, and he can bear witness that the cry of the banshee is an evil cry to hear alone in the deep night. When it was over and the face was gone, Nurse Macdonald shook a little in her great chair, and still she looked at the black square of the window, but there was nothing more there, nothing but the night, and the whispering ivy branch. She turned her head to the door that was ajar, and there stood the girl in her white gown, her teeth chattering with fright.

"It is time, child," said Nurse Macdonald. "I must go to him, for it is the end."

She rose slowly, leaning her withered hands upon the arms of the chair, and the girl brought her a woollen gown and a great mantle, and her crutch-stick, and made her ready. But very often the girl looked at the window and was unjointed with fear, and often Nurse Macdonald shook her head and said words which the maid could not understand.

"It was like the face of Miss Evelyn," said the girl at last trembling.

But the ancient woman looked up sharply and angrily, and her queer blue eyes glared. She held herself by the arm of the great chair with her left hand, and lifted up her crutch-stick to strike the maid with all her might. But she did not.

"You are a good girl," she said, "but you are a fool. Pray for wit, child, pray for wit—or else find service in another house than Ockram Hall. Bring the lamp and help me under my left arm."

The crutch-stick clacked on the wooden floor, and the low heels of the woman's slippers clappered after her in slow triplets, as Nurse Macdonald got towards the door. And down the stairs each step she took was a labour in itself, and by the clacking noise the waking servants knew that she was coming, very long before they saw her.

No one was sleeping now, and there were lights and whisperings and pale faces in the corridors near Sir Hugh's bedroom, and now someone went in, and now someone came out, but every one made way for Nurse Macdonald, who had nursed Sir Hugh's father more than eighty years ago.

The light was soft and clear in the room. There stood Gabriel Ockram by his father's bedside, and there knelt Evelyn Warburton, her hair lying like a golden shadow down her shoulders, and her hands clasped nervously together. And opposite Gabriel, a nurse was trying to make Sir Hugh drink. But he would not, and though his lips were parted, his teeth were set. He was very, very thin and yellow now, and his eyes caught the light sideways and were as yellow coals.

"Do not torment him," said Nurse Macdonald to the woman who held the cup. "Let me speak to him, for his hour is come."

"Let her speak to him," said Gabriel in a dull voice.

So the ancient woman leaned to the pillow and laid the featherweight of her withered hand, that was like a brown moth, upon Sir Hugh's yellow fingers, and she spoke to him earnestly, while only Gabriel and Evelyn were left in the room to hear.

"Hugh Ockram," she said, "this is the end of your life; and as I saw you born, and saw your father born before you, I am come to see you die. Hugh Ockram, will you tell me the truth?"

The dying man recognised the little far-away voice he had

known all his life, and he very slowly turned his yellow face to Nurse Macdonald; but he said nothing. Then she spoke again.

"Hugh Ockram, you will never see the daylight again. Will you tell the truth?"

His toad-like eyes were not dull yet. They fastened themselves on her face.

"What do you want of me?" he asked, and each word struck hollow on the last. "I have no secrets. I have lived a good life."

Nurse Macdonald laughed—a tiny, cracked laugh, that made her old head bob and tremble a little, as if her neck were on a steel spring. But Sir Hugh's eyes grew red, and his pale lips began to twist.

"Let me die in peace," he said slowly.

But Nurse Macdonald shook her head, and her brown, moth-like hand left his and fluttered to his forehead.

"By the mother that bore you and died of grief for the sins you did, tell me the truth!"

Sir Hugh's lips tightened on his discoloured teeth.

"Not on earth," he answered slowly.

"By the wife who bore your son and died heart-broken, tell me the truth!"

"Neither to you in life, nor to her in eternal death."

His lips writhed, as if the words were coals between them, and a great drop of sweat rolled across the parchment of his forehead. Gabriel Ockram bit his hand as he watched his father die. But Nurse Macdonald spoke a third time.

"By the woman whom you betrayed, and who waits for you this night, Hugh Ockram, tell me the truth!"

"It is too late. Let me die in peace."

The writhing lips began to smile across the set yellow teeth, and the toad eyes glowed like evil jewels in his head.

"There is time," said the ancient woman. "Tell me the name of Evelyn Warburton's father. Then I will let you die in peace."

Evelyn started back, kneeling as she was, and stared at Nurse Macdonald, and then at her uncle.

"The name of Evelyn's father?" he repeated slowly, while the awful smile spread upon his dying face.

The light was growing strangely dim in the great room. As Evelyn looked, Nurse Macdonald's crooked shadow on the wall grew gigantic. Sir Hugh's breath came thick, rattling in his throat, as death crept in like a snake and choked it back. Evelyn prayed aloud, high and clear.

Then something rapped at the window, and she felt her hair rise upon her head in a cool breeze, as she looked around in spite of herself. And when she saw her own white face looking in at the window, and her own eyes staring at her through the glass, wide and fearful, and her own hair streaming against the pane, and her own lips dashed with blood, she rose slowly from the floor and stood rigid for one moment, till she screamed once and fell straight back into Gabriel's arms. But the shriek that answered hers was the fear-shriek of the tormented corpse, out of which the soul cannot pass for shame of deadly sins, though the devils fight in it with corruption, each for their due share.

Sir Hugh Ockram sat upright in his death-bed, and saw and cried aloud:

"Evelyn!" His harsh voice broke and rattled in his chest as he sank down. But still Nurse Macdonald tortured him, for there was a little life left in him still.

"You have seen the mother as she waits for you, Hugh Ockram. Who was this girl Evelyn's father? What was his name?"

For the last time the dreadful smile came upon the twisted

lips, very slowly, very surely now, and the toad eyes glared red, and the parchment face glowed a little in the flickering light. For the last time words came.

"They know it in hell."

Then the glowing eyes went out quickly, the yellow face turned waxen pale, and a great shiver ran through the thin body as Hugh Ockram died.

But in death he still smiled, for he knew his secret and kept it still, on the other side, and he would take it with him, to lie with him for ever in the north vault of the chapel where the Ockrams lie uncoffined in their shrouds—all but one. Though he was dead, he smiled, for he had kept his treasure of evil truth to the end, and there was none left to tell the name he had spoken, but there was all the evil he had not undone left to bear fruit.

As they watched—Nurse Macdonald and Gabriel, who held Evelyn still unconscious in his arms while he looked at the father—they felt the dead smile crawling along their own lips— the ancient crone, and the youth with the angel's face. Then they shivered a little, and both looked at Evelyn as she lay with her head on his shoulder, and, though she was very beautiful, the same sickening smile was twisting her young mouth too, and it was like the foreshadowing of a great evil which they could not understand.

But by and by they carried Evelyn out, and she opened her eyes and the smile was gone. From far away in the great house the sound of weeping and crooning came up the stairs and echoed along the dismal corridors, for the women had begun to mourn the dead master, after the Irish fashion, and the hall had echoes of its own all that night, like the far-off wail of the banshee among forest trees.

When the time was come they took Sir Hugh in his winding-sheet on a trestle bier, and bore him to the chapel and through the iron door and down the long descent to the north vault, with tapers, to lay him by his father. And two men went in first to prepare the place, and came back staggering like drunken men, and white, leaving behind their lights behind them.

But Gabriel Ockram was not afraid, for he knew. And he went in alone and saw that the body of Sir Vernon Ockram was leaning upright against the stone wall, and that his head lay on the ground near by with the face turned up, and the dried leathern lips smiled horribly at the dried-up corpse, while the iron coffin, lined with black velvet, stood open on the floor.

Then Gabriel took the thing in his hands, for it was very light, being quite dried by the air of the vault, and those who peeped in from the door saw him lay it in the coffin again, and it rustled a little, like a bundle of reeds, and sounded hollow as it touched the sides and the bottom. He also placed the head upon the shoulders and shut down the lid, which fell to with a rusty spring that snapped.

After that they laid Sir Hugh beside his father, with the trestle bier on which they had brought him, and they went back to the chapel.

But when they saw one another's faces, master and men, they were all smiling with the dead smile of the corpse they had left in the vault, so that they could not bear to look at one another until it had faded away.

III

Gabriel Ockram became Sir Gabriel, inheriting the baronetcy

with the half-ruined fortune left by his father, and still Evelyn
Warburton lived at Ockram Hall, in the south room that had
been hers ever since she could remember anything. She could not
go away, for there were no relatives to whom she could have gone,
and, besides there seemed to be no reason why she should not
stay. The world would never trouble itself to care what the Ockrams did on their Irish estates, and it was long since the Ockrams
had asked anything of the world.

So Sir Gabriel took his father's place at the dark old table
in the dining-room, and Evelyn sat opposite to him, until such
time as their mourning should be over, and they might be married at last. And meanwhile their lives went on as before, since
Sir Hugh had been a hopeless invalid during the last year of his
life, and they had seen him but once a day for the little while,
spending most of their time together in a strangely perfect
companionship.

But though the late summer saddened into autumn, and
autumn darkened into winter, and storm followed storm, and rain
poured on rain through the short days and the long nights, yet
Ockram Hall seemed less gloomy since Sir Hugh had been laid in
the north vault beside his father. And at Christmastide Evelyn
decked the great hall with holly and green boughs, and huge fires
blazed on every hearth. Then the tenants were all bidden to a New
Year's dinner, and they ate and drank well, while Sir Gabriel sat at
the head of the table. Evelyn came in when the port wine was
brought, and the most respected of the tenants made a speech to
propose her health.

It was long, he said, since there had been a Lady Ockram. Sir
Gabriel shaded his eyes with his hand and looked down at the
table, but a faint colour came into Evelyn's transparent cheeks.

But, said the grey-haired farmer, it was longer still since there had been a Lady Ockram so fair as the next was to be, and he gave the health of Evelyn Warburton.

Then the tenants all stood up and shouted for her, and Sir Gabriel stood up likewise, beside Evelyn. And when the men gave the last and loudest cheer of all there was a voice not theirs, above them all, higher, fiercer, louder—a scream not earthly, shrieking for the bride of Ockram Hall. And the holly and the green boughs over the great chimney-piece shook and slowly waved as if a cool breeze were blowing over them. But the men turned very pale, and many of them set down their glasses, but others let them fall upon the floor for fear. And looking into one another's faces, they were all smiling strangely, a dead smile, like dead Sir Hugh's. One cried out words in Irish, and the fear of death was suddenly upon them all so that they fled in panic, falling over one another like wild beasts in the burning forest, when the thick smoke runs along before the flame, and the tables were overset, and drinking glasses and bottles were broken in heaps, and the dark red wine crawled like blood upon the polished floor.

Sir Gabriel and Evelyn stood alone at the head of the table before the wreck of the feast, not daring to turn to see each other, for each knew that the other smiled. But his right arm held her and his left hand clasped her right as they stared before them, and but for the shadows of her hair one might not have told their two faces apart. They listened long, but the cry came not again, and the dead smile faded from their lips, while each remembered that Sir Hugh Ockram lay in the north vault, smiling in his winding-sheet, in the dark, because he had died with his secret.

So ended the tenants' New Year's dinner. But from that time on Sir Gabriel grew more and more silent, and his face grew even paler and thinner than before. Often without warning and without words, he would rise from his seat, as if something moved him against his will, and he would go out into the rain or the sunshine to the north side of the chapel, and sit on the stone bench, staring at the ground as if he could see through it, and through the vault below, and through the white winding-sheet in the dark, to the dead smile that would not die.

Always when he went out in that way Evelyn came out presently and sat beside him. Once, too, as in summer, their beautiful faces came suddenly near, and their lids drooped, and their red lips were almost joined together. But as their eyes met, they grew wide and wild, so that the white showed in a ring all round the deep violet, and their teeth chattered, and their hands were like hands of corpses, each in the other's for the terror of what was under their feet, and of what they knew but could not see.

Once, also, Evelyn found Sir Gabriel in the chapel alone, standing before the iron door that led down to the place of death, and in his hand there was the key to the door, but he had not put it in the lock. Evelyn drew him away, shivering, for she had also been driven in waking dreams to see that terrible thing again, and to find out whether it had changed since it had lain there.

"I'm going mad," said Sir Gabriel, covering his eyes with his hand as he went with her. "I see it in my sleep, I see it when I am awake—it draws me to it, day and night—and unless I see it I shall die!"

"I know," answered Evelyn, "I know. It is as if threads were spun from it, like a spider's, drawing us down to it." She was silent for a moment, and then she started violently and grasped his arm with a man's strength, and almost screamed the words she spoke. "But we must not go there!" she cried. "We must not go!"

Sir Gabriel's eyes were half shut, and he was not moved by the agony of her face.

"I shall die, unless I see it again," he said, in a quiet voice not like his own. And all that day and that evening he scarcely spoke, thinking of it, always thinking, while Evelyn Warburton quivered from head to foot with a terror she had never known.

She went alone, on a grey winter's morning, to Nurse Macdonald's room in the tower, and sat down beside the great leathern easy-chair, laying her thin white hand upon the withered fingers.

"Nurse," she said, "what was it that Uncle Hugh should have told you, that night before he died? It must have been an awful secret—and yet, though you asked him, I feel somehow that you know it, and that you know why he used to smile so dreadfully."

The old woman's head moved slowly from side to side.

"I only guess—I shall never know," she answered slowly in her cracked little voice.

"But what do you guess? Who am I? Why did you ask who my father was? You know I am Colonel Warburton's daughter, and my mother was Lady Ockram's sister, so that Gabriel and I are cousins. My father was killed in Afghanistan. What secret can there be?"

"I do not know. I can only guess."

"Guess what?" asked Evelyn imploringly, and pressing the soft withered hands, as she leaned forward. But Nurse Macdonald's wrinkled lids dropped suddenly over her queer blue eyes, and her lips shook a little with her breath, as if she were asleep.

Evelyn waited. By the fire the Irish maid was knitting fast, and the needles clicked like three or four clocks ticking against each other. And the real clock on the wall solemnly ticked alone, checking off the seconds of the woman who was a hundred years old, and had not many days left. Outside the ivy branch beat the window in the wintry blast, as it had beaten against the glass a hundred years ago.

Then as Evelyn sat there she felt again the waking of a horrible desire—the sickening wish to go down, down to the thing in the north vault, and to open the winding-sheet, and see whether it had changed, and she held Nurse Macdonald's hands as if to keep herself in her place and fight against the appalling attraction of the evil dead.

But the old cat that kept Nurse Macdonald's feet warm, lying always on the bag footstool, got up and stretched itself, and looked up into Evelyn's eyes, while its back arched, and its tail thickened and bristled, and its ugly pink lips drew back in a devilish grin, showing its sharp teeth. Evelyn stared at it, half fascinated by its ugliness. Then the creature suddenly put out one paw with all its claws spread, and spat at the girl, and all at once the grinning cat was like the smiling corpse far down below, so that Evelyn shivered down to her small feet, and covered her face with her free hand lest Nurse Macdonald should wake and see the dead smile there, for she could feel it.

The old woman had already opened her eyes again, and she touched her cat with the end of her crutch-stick, whereupon its back went down and its tail shrunk, and it sidled back to its place on the bag footstool. But its yellow eyes looked up sideways at Evelyn, between the slits of its lids.

"What is it that you guess, nurse?" asked the young girl again.

"A bad thing—a wicked thing. But I dare not tell you, lest it might not be true, and the very thought should blast your life. For if I guess right, he meant that you should not know, and that you two should marry, and pay for his old sin with your souls."

"He used to tell us that we ought not to marry——"

"Yes—he told you that, perhaps—but it was as if a man put poisoned meat before a starving beast, and said 'do not eat' but never raised his hand to take the meat away. And if he told you that you should not marry, it was because he hoped you would, for of all men living or dead, Hugh Ockram was the falsest man that ever told a cowardly lie, and the crudest that ever hurt a weak woman, and the worst that ever loved a sin."

"But Gabriel and I love each other," said Evelyn very sadly.

Nurse Macdonald's old eyes looked far away, at sights seen long ago, and that rose in the grey winter air amid the mists of an ancient youth.

"If you love, you can die together," she said, very slowly. "Why should you live, if it is true? I am a hundred years old. What has life given me? The beginning is fire, the end is a heap of ashes, and between the end and the beginning lies all the pain in the world. Let me sleep, since I cannot die."

Then the old woman's eyes closed again, and her head sank a little lower upon her breast.

So Evelyn went away and left her asleep, with the cat asleep on the bag footstool; and the young girl tried to forget Nurse Macdonald's words, but she could not, for she heard them over and over again in the wind, and behind her on the stairs. And as she grew sick with fear of the frightful unknown evil to which her soul was bound, she felt a bodily something pressing her, and pushing her, and forcing her on, and from the other side she felt the threads that drew her mysteriously, and when she shut her eyes, she saw in the chapel behind the altar, the low iron door through which she must pass to go to the thing.

And as she lay awake at night, she drew the sheet over her

face, lest she should see shadows on the wall beckoning her and the sound of her own warm breath made whisperings in her ears, while she held the mattress with her hands, to keep from getting up and going to the chapel. It would have been easier if there had not been a way thither through the library, by a door which was never locked. It would be fearfully easy to take her candle and go softly through the sleeping house. And the key of the vault lay under the altar behind a stone that turned. She knew the little secret. She could go alone and see.

But when she thought of it, she felt her hair rise on her head, and first she shivered so that the bed shook, and then the horror went through her in a cold thrill that was agony again, like myriads of icy needles, boring into her nerves.

IV

The old clock in Nurse Macdonald's tower struck midnight. From her room she could hear the creaking chains and weights in their box in the corner of the staircase, and overhead the jarring of the rusty lever that lifted the hammer. She had heard it all her life. It struck eleven strokes clearly and then came the twelfth, with a dull half stroke, as though the hammer were too weary to go on, and had fallen asleep against the bell.

The old cat got up from the bag footstool and stretched itself, and Nurse Macdonald opened her ancient eyes and looked slowly round the room by the dim light of the night lamp. She touched the cat with her crutch-stick, and it lay down upon her feet. She drank a few drops from her cup and went to sleep again.

But downstairs Sir Gabriel sat straight up as the clock struck, for he had dreamed a fearful dream of horror, and his heart stood still, till he awoke at its stopping, and it beat again furiously with his breath, like a wild thing set free. No Ockram had ever known fear waking, but sometimes it came to Sir Gabriel in his sleep.

He pressed his hands to his temples as he sat up in bed, and his hands were icy cold, but his head was hot. The dream faded far, and in its place there came the master thought that racked his life; with the thought also came the sick twisting of his lips in the dark that would have been a smile. Far off, Evelyn Warburton dreamed that the dead smile was on her mouth, and awoke, starting with a little moan, her face in her hands shivering.

But Sir Gabriel struck a light and got up and began to walk up and down his great room. It was midnight, and he had barely slept an hour, and in the north of Ireland the winter nights are long.

"I shall go mad," he said to himself, holding his forehead. He knew that it was true. For weeks and months the possession of the thing had grown upon him like a disease, till he could think of nothing without thinking first of that. And now all at once it outgrew his strength, and he knew that he must be its instrument or lose his mind—that he must do the deed he hated and feared, if he could fear anything, or that something would snap in his brain and divide him from life while he was yet alive. He took the candlestick in his hand, the old-fashioned heavy candlestick that had always been used by the head of the house. He did not think of dressing, but went as he was, in his silk night-clothes and his slippers, and he opened the door. Everything was very still in the great old house. He shut the door behind him and walked noiselessly on the carpet through the long corridor. A cool breeze blew over his shoulder and blew the flame of his candle straight out from him. Instinctively he stopped and looked round, but all was still, and the upright flame burned steadily. He walked on, and instantly a strong draught was behind him, almost extinguishing the light. It seemed to blow him on his way, ceasing whenever he turned, coming again when he went on—invisible, icy.

Down the great staircase to the echoing hall he went, seeing nothing but the flaring flame of the candle standing away from him over the guttering wax, while the cold wind blew over his shoulder and through his hair. On he passed through the open door into the library, dark with old books and carved bookcases, on through the door in the shelves, with painted shelves on it, and the imitated backs of books, so that one needed to know where to find it—and it shut itself after him with a soft click. He entered the low-arched passage, and though the door was shut behind him and fitted tightly in its frame, still the cold breeze blew the flame forward as he walked. And he was not afraid, but his face was very pale, and his eyes were wide and bright, looking before him, seeing already in the dark air the picture of the thing beyond. But in the chapel he stood still, his hand on the little turning stone tablet in the back of the stone altar. On the tablet were engraved words, *"Clavis sepulchri Clarissimorum Dominorum De Ockram"*—("the key to the vault of the most illustrious lords of Ockram.") Sir Gabriel paused and listened. He fancied that he heard a sound far off in the great house where all had been so still, but it did not come again. Yet he waited at the last, and looked at the low iron door. Beyond it, down the long descent, lay his father uncoffined, six months dead, corrupt, terrible in his clinging shroud. The strangely preserving air of the vault could not yet have done its work completely. But on the thing's ghastly features, with their half-dried, open eyes, there would still be the frightful smile with which the man had died—the smile that haunted——

As the thought crossed Sir Gabriel's mind, he felt his lips

writhing, and he struck his own mouth in wrath with the back of his hand so fiercely that a drop of blood ran down his chin and another, and more, falling back in the gloom upon the chapel pavement. But still his bruised lips twisted themselves. He turned the tablet by the simple secret. It needed no safer fastening, for had each Ockram been confined in pure gold, and had the door been wide, there was not a man in Tyrone brave enough to go down to that place, saving Gabriel Ockram himself, with his angel's face and his thin, white hands, and his sad unflinching eyes. He took the great gold key and set it into the lock of the iron door, and the heavy, rattling noise echoed down the descent beyond like footsteps, as if a watcher had stood behind the iron and were running away within, with heavy dead feet. And though he was standing still, the cool wind was from behind him, and blew the flame of the candle against the iron panel. He turned the key.

Sir Gabriel saw that his candle was short. There were new ones on the altar, with long candlesticks and he lit one, and left his own burning on the floor. As he set it down on the pavement his lip began to bleed again, and another drop fell upon the stones.

He drew the iron door open and pushed it back against the chapel wall, so that it should not shut of itself, while he was within, and the horrible draught of the sepulchre came up out of the depths in his face, foul and dark. He went in, but though the fetid air met him, yet the flame of the tall candle was blown straight from him against the wind while he walked down the easy incline with steady steps, his loose slippers slapping the pavement as he trod.

He shaded the candle with his hand, and his fingers seemed to be made of wax and blood as the light shone through them. And in spite of him the unearthly draught forced the flame forward, till it was blue over the black wick, and it seemed as if it must go out. But he went straight on, with shining eyes.

The downward passage was wide, and he could not always see the walls by the struggling light, but he knew when he was in the place of death by the larger, drearier echo of his steps in the greater space and by the sensation of a distant blank wall. He stood still, almost enclosing the flame of the candle in the hollow of his hand. He could see a little, for his eyes were growing used to the gloom. Shadowy forms were outlined in the dimness, where the biers of the Ockrams stood crowded together, side by side, each with its straight, shrouded corpse, strangely preserved by the dry air, like the empty shell that the locust sheds in summer. And a few steps before him he saw clearly the dark shape of headless Sir Vernon's iron coffin, and he knew that nearest to it lay the thing he sought.

He was as brave as any of those dead men had been, and they were his fathers, and he knew that sooner or later he should lie there himself, beside Sir Hugh, slowly drying to a parchment shell. But he was still alive, and he closed his eyes a moment, and three great drops stood on his forehead.

Then he looked again, and by the whiteness of the winding-sheet he knew his father's corpse, for all the others were brown with age; and, moreover, the flame of the candle was blown toward it. He made four steps till he reached it, and suddenly the light burned straight and high, shedding a dazzling yellow glare upon the fine linen that was all white, save over the face, and where the joined hands were laid on the breast. And at those places ugly stains had spread, darkened with outlines of the features and of the tight-clasped fingers. There was a frightful stench of drying death.

As Sir Gabriel looked down, something stirred behind him, softly at first, then more noisily, and something fell to the stone floor with a dull thud and rolled up to his feet; he started back, and saw a withered head lying almost face upward on the pavement, grinning at him. He felt the cold sweat standing on his face, and his heart beat painfully.

For the first time in all his life that evil thing which men call fear was getting hold of him, checking his heart-strings as a cruel driver checks a quivering horse, clawing at his backbone with icy hands, lifting his hair with freezing breath climbing up and gathering in his midriff with leaden weight.

Yet presently he bit his lip and bent down, holding the candle in one hand, to lift the shroud back from the head of the corpse with the other. Slowly he lifted it. Then it clove to the half-dried skin of the face, and his hand shook as if some one had struck him on the elbow, but half in fear and half in anger at himself, he pulled it, so that it came away with a little ripping sound. He caught his breath as he held it, not yet throwing it back, and not yet looking. The horror was working in him, and he felt that old Vernon Ockram was standing up in his iron coffin, headless, yet watching him with the stump of his severed neck.

While he held his breath he felt the dead smile twisting his lips. In sudden wrath at his own misery, he tossed the death-stained linen backward, and looked at last. He ground his teeth lest he should shriek aloud.

There it was, the thing that haunted him, that haunted Evelyn Warburton, that was like a blight on all that came near him.

The dead face was blotched with dark stains, and the thin, grey hair was matted about the discoloured forehead. The sunken lids were half open, and the candle light gleamed on something foul where the toad eyes had lived.

But yet the dead thing smiled, as it had smiled in life; the ghastly lips were parted and drawn wide and tight upon the wolfish teeth, cursing still, and still defying hell to do its worst—defying, cursing, and always and for ever smiling alone in the dark.

Sir Gabriel opened the winding-sheet where the hands were, and the blackened, withered fingers were closed upon something stained and mottled. Shivering from head to foot, but fighting like a man in agony for his life, he tried to take the package from the dead man's hold. But as he pulled at it the claw-like fingers seemed to close more tightly, and when he pulled harder the shrunken hands and arms rose from the corpse with a horrible look of life following his motion—then as he wrenched the sealed packet loose at last, the hands fell back into their place still folded.

He set down the candle on the edge of the bier to break the seals from the stout paper. And, kneeling on one knee, to get a better light, he read what was within, written long ago in Sir Hugh's queer hand.

He was no longer afraid.

He read how Sir Hugh had written it all down that it might perchance be a witness of evil and of his hatred; how he had loved Evelyn Warburton, his wife's sister; and how his wife had died of a broken heart with his curse upon her, and how Warburton and he had fought side by side in Afghanistan, and Warburton had fallen; but Ockram had brought his comrade's wife back a full year later, and little Evelyn, her child, had been born in Ockram Hall. And next, how he had wearied of the mother, and she had died like her sister with his curse on her. And then, how Evelyn had been brought up as his niece, and how he had trusted that his son Gabriel and his daughter, innocent and unknowing, might love and marry, and the souls of the women he had betrayed might suffer another anguish before eternity was out. And, last of all, he hoped that some day, when nothing could be undone, the two might find his writing and live on, not daring to tell the truth for their children's sake and the world's word, man and wife.

This he read, kneeling beside the corpse in the north vault, by the light of the altar candle; and when he had read it all, he thanked God aloud that he had found the secret in time. But when he rose to his feet and looked down at the dead face it was changed, and the smile was gone from it for ever, and the jaw had fallen a little, and the tired, dead lips were relaxed. And then there was a breath behind him and close to him, not cold like that which had blown the flame of the candle as he came, but warm and human. He turned suddenly.

There she stood, all in white, with her shadowy golden hair—for she had risen from her bed and had followed him noiselessly, and had found him reading, and had herself read over his shoulder. He started violently when he saw her, for his nerves were unstrung—and then he cried out her name in the still place of death:

"Evelyn!"

"My brother!" she answered, softly and tenderly, putting out both hands to meet his.

THE WIND IN THE ROSE-BUSH
Mary E. Wilkins-Freeman
[1852–1930]

"Horror material of authentic force may be found in the work of the New England realist Mary E. Wilkins, whose volume of short tales, *The Wind in the Rose-Bush*, contains a number of noteworthy achievements."

—*H.P. Lovecraft*

FORD VILLAGE HAS NO RAILROAD STATION, being on the other side of the river from Porter's Falls, and accessible only by the ford which gives it its name, and a ferry line. The ferry-boat was waiting when Rebecca Flint got off the train with her bag and lunch basket. When she and her small trunk were safely embarked she sat stiff and straight and calm in the ferry-boat as it shot swiftly and smoothly across stream. There was a horse attached to a light country wagon on board, and he pawed the deck uneasily. His owner stood near, with a wary eye upon him, although he was chewing, with as dully reflective an expression as a cow. Beside Rebecca sat a woman of about her own age, who kept looking at her with furtive curiosity; her husband, short and stout and saturnine, stood near her. Rebecca paid no attention to either of them. She was tall and spare and pale, the type of a spinster, yet with rudimentary lines and expressions of matronhood. She all unconsciously held her shawl, rolled up in a canvas bag, on her left hip, as if it had been a child. She wore a settled frown of dissent at life, but it was the frown of a mother who regarded life as a froward child, rather than as an overwhelming fate.

The other woman continued staring at her; she was mildly stupid, except for an overdeveloped curiosity which made her at times sharp beyond belief. Her eyes glittered, red spots came on her flaccid cheeks; she kept opening her mouth to speak, making little abortive motions. Finally she could endure it no longer; she nudged Rebecca boldly.

"A pleasant day," said she.

Rebecca looked at her and nodded coldly.

"Yes, very," she assented.

"Have you come far?"

"I have come from Michigan."

"Oh!" said the woman, with awe. "It's a long way," she remarked presently.

"Yes, it is," replied Rebecca, conclusively.

Still the other woman was not daunted; there was something which she determined to know, possibly roused thereto by a vague sense of incongruity in the other's appearance. "It's a long ways to come and leave a family," she remarked with painful slyness.

"I ain't got any family to leave," returned Rebecca shortly.

"Then you ain't . . ."

"No, I ain't."

"Oh!" said the woman.

Rebecca looked straight ahead at the race of the river.

It was a long ferry. Finally Rebecca herself waxed unexpectedly loquacious. She turned to the other woman and inquired if she knew John Dent's widow who lived in Ford Village. "Her husband died about three years ago," said she, by way of detail.

The woman started violently. She turned pale, then she flushed; she cast a strange glance at her husband, who was regarding both women with a sort of stolid keenness.

"Yes, I guess I do," faltered the woman finally.

"Well, his first wife was my sister," said Rebecca with the air of one imparting important intelligence.

"Was she?" responded the other woman feebly. She glanced at her husband with an expression of doubt and terror, and he shook his head forbiddingly.

"I'm going to see her, and take my niece Agnes home with me," said Rebecca.

Then the woman gave such a violent start that she noticed it.

"What is the matter?" she asked.

"Nothin', I guess," replied the woman with eyes on her husband, who was slowly shaking his head like a Chinese toy.

"Is my niece sick?" asked Rebecca with quick suspicion.

"No, she ain't sick," replied the woman with alacrity, then she caught her breath again.

"She ought to have grown up real pretty, if she takes after my sister. She was a real pretty woman," Rebecca said wistfully.

"Yes, I guess she did grow up pretty," replied the woman in a trembling voice.

"What kind of a woman is the second wife?"

The woman glanced at her husband's warning face. She continued to gaze at him while she replied in a choking voice to Rebecca:

"I—guess she's a nice woman," she replied. "I—don't know, I—guess so. I—don't see much of her."

"I felt kind of hurt that John married again so quick," said Rebecca; "but I suppose he wanted his house kept, and Agnes wanted care. I wasn't so situated that I could take her when her mother died. I had my own mother to care for, and I was school-teaching. Now mother has gone, and my uncle died six months ago and left me quite a little property, and I've come for Agnes. I guess she'll be glad to go with me, though I suppose her stepmother is a good woman, and has always done for her."

The man's warning shake at his wife was fairly portentous.

"I guess so," said she.

"John always wrote that she was a beautiful woman," said Rebecca.

Then the ferry-boat grated on the shore.

John Dent's widow had sent a horse and wagon to meet her sister-in-law. When the woman and her husband went down the road, on which Rebecca in the wagon with her trunk soon passed them, she said reproachfully:

"Seems as if I'd ought to have told her, Thomas."

"Let her find it out herself," replied the man. "Don't you go to burnin' your fingers in other folks' puddin', Maria."

"Do you s'pose she'll see anything?" asked the woman with a spasmodic shudder and a terrified roll of her eyes.

"See!" returned her husband with stolid scorn. "Better be sure there's anything to see."

"Oh, Thomas, they say . . ."

"Lord, ain't you found out that what they say is mostly lies?"

"But if it should be true, and she's a nervous woman, she might be scared enough to lose her wits," said his wife, staring uneasily after Rebecca's erect figure in the wagon disappearing over the crest of the hilly road.

"Wits that so easy upset ain't worth much," declared the man. "You keep out of it, Maria."

Rebecca in the meantime rode on in the wagon, beside a flaxen-headed boy, who looked, to her understanding, not very bright. She asked him a question, and he paid no attention. She repeated it, and he responded with a bewildered and incoherent grunt. Then she let him alone, after making sure that he knew how to drive straight.

They had traveled about half a mile, passed the village square, and gone a short distance beyond, when the boy drew up with a sudden *Whoa!* before a very prosperous-looking house. It had been one of the aboriginal cottages of the vicinity, small and white, with a roof extending on one side over a piazza, and a tiny "L" jutting out in the rear, on the right hand. Now the cottage was transformed by dormer windows, a bay window on the piazzaless side, a carved railing down the front steps, and a modern hard-wood door.

"Is this John Dent's house?" asked Rebecca.

The boy was as sparing of speech as a philosopher. His only response was in flinging the reins over the horse's back, stretching out one foot to the shaft, and leaping out of the wagon, then going around to the rear for the trunk. Rebecca got out and went toward the house. Its white paint had a new gloss; its blinds were an immaculate apple green; the lawn was trimmed as smooth as velvet, and it was dotted with scrupulous groups of hydrangeas and cannas.

"I always understood that John Dent was well-to-do," Rebecca reflected comfortably. "I guess Agnes will have considerable. I've got enough, but it will come in handy for her schooling. She can have advantages."

The boy dragged the trunk up the fine gravel-walk, but before he reached the steps leading up to the piazza, for the house stood on a terrace, the front door opened and a fair, frizzled head of a very large and handsome woman appeared. She held up her black silk skirt, disclosing voluminous ruffles of starched embroidery, and waited for Rebecca. She smiled placidly, her pink, double-chinned face widened and dimpled, but her blue eyes were wary and calculating. She extended her hand as Rebecca climbed the steps.

"This is Miss Flint, I suppose," said she.

"Yes, ma'am," replied Rebecca, noticing with bewilderment a curious expression compounded of fear and defiance on the other's face.

"Your letter only arrived this morning," said Mrs. Dent, in a steady voice. Her great face was a uniform pink, and her china-blue eyes were at once aggressive and veiled with secrecy.

"Yes, I hardly thought you'd get my letter," replied Rebecca. "I felt as if I could not wait to hear from you before I came. I supposed you would be so situated that you could have me a little while without putting you out too much, from what John used to write me about his circumstances, and when I had that money so unexpected I felt as if I must come for Agnes. I suppose you will be willing to give her up. You know she's my own blood, and of course she's no relation to you, though you must have got attached to her. I know from her picture what a sweet girl she must be, and John always said she looked like her own mother, and Grace was a beautiful woman, if she was my sister."

Rebecca stopped and stared at the other woman in amazement and alarm. The great handsome blonde creature stood speechless, livid, gasping, with her hand to her heart, her lips parted in a horrible caricature of a smile.

"Are you sick!" cried Rebecca, drawing near. "Don't you want me to get you some water!"

Then Mrs. Dent recovered herself with a great effort. "It is nothing," she said. "I am subject to—spells. I am over it now. Won't you come in, Miss Flint?"

As she spoke, the beautiful deep-rose color suffused her face, her blue eyes met her visitor's with the opaqueness of turquoise— with a revelation of blue, but a concealment of all behind.

Rebecca followed her hostess in, and the boy, who had waited quiescently, climbed the steps with the trunk. But before they entered the door a strange thing happened. On the upper terrace, close to the piazza-post, grew a great rose-bush, and on it, late in the season though it was, one small red, perfect rose.

Rebecca looked at it, and the other woman extended her hand with a quick gesture. "Don't you pick that rose!" she brusquely cried.

Rebecca drew herself up with stiff dignity.

"I ain't in the habit of picking other folks' roses without leave," said she.

As Rebecca spoke she started violently, and lost sight of her resentment, for something singular happened. Suddenly the rose-bush was agitated violently as if by a gust of wind, yet it was a remarkably still day. Not a leaf of the hydrangea standing on the terrace close to the rose trembled.

"What on earth . . ." began Rebecca, then she stopped with a gasp at the sight of the other woman's face. Although a face, it gave somehow the impression of a desperately clutched hand of secrecy.

"Come in!" said she in a harsh voice, which seemed to come

forth from her chest with no intervention of the organs of speech. "Come into the house. I'm getting cold out here."

"What makes that rose-bush blow so when there isn't any wind?" asked Rebecca, trembling with vague horror, yet resolute.

"I don't see as it is blowing," returned the woman calmly. And as she spoke, indeed, the bush was quiet.

"It was blowing," declared Rebecca.

"It isn't now," said Mrs. Dent. "I can't try to account for everything that blows out-of-doors. I have too much to do."

She spoke scornfully and confidently, with defiant, unflinching eyes, first on the bush, then on Rebecca, and led the way into the house.

"It looked queer," persisted Rebecca, but she followed, and also the boy with the trunk.

Rebecca entered an interior, prosperous, even elegant, according to her simple ideas. There were Brussels carpets, lace curtains, and plenty of brilliant upholstery and polished wood.

"You're real nicely situated," remarked Rebecca, after she had become a little accustomed to her new surroundings and the two women were seated at the tea-table.

Mrs. Dent stared with a hard complacency from behind her silver-plated service. "Yes, I be," said she.

"You got all the things new?" said Rebecca hesitatingly, with a jealous memory of her dead sister's bridal furnishings.

"Yes," said Mrs. Dent; "I was never one to want dead folks' things, and I had money enough of my own, so I wasn't beholden to John. I had the old duds put up at auction. They didn't bring much."

"I suppose you saved some for Agnes. She'll want some of her poor mother's things when she is grown up," said Rebecca with some indignation.

The defiant stare of Mrs. Dent's blue eyes waxed more intense. "There's a few things up garret," said she.

"She'll be likely to value them," remarked Rebecca. As she spoke she glanced at the window. "Isn't it most time for her to be coming home?" she asked.

"Most time," answered Mrs. Dent carelessly; "but when she gets over to Addie Slocum's she never knows when to come home."

"Is Addie Slocum her intimate friend?"

"Intimate as any."

"Maybe we can have her come out to see Agnes when she's living with me," said Rebecca wistfully. "I suppose she'll be likely to be homesick at first."

"Most likely," answered Mrs. Dent.

"Does she call you mother?" Rebecca asked.

"No, she calls me Aunt Emeline," replied the other woman shortly. "When did you say you were going home?"

"In about a week, I thought, if she can be ready to go so soon," answered Rebecca with a surprised look.

She reflected that she would not remain a day longer than she could help after such an inhospitable look and question.

"Oh, as far as that goes," said Mrs. Dent, "it wouldn't make any difference about her being ready. You could go home whenever you felt that you must, and she could come afterward."

"Alone?"

"Why not? She's a big girl now, and you don't have to change cars."

"My niece will go home when I do, and not travel alone; and

if I can't wait here for her, in the house that used to be her mother's and my sister's home, I'll go and board somewhere," returned Rebecca with warmth.

"Oh, you can stay here as long as you want to. You're welcome," said Mrs. Dent.

Then Rebecca started. "There she is!" she declared in a trembling, exultant voice. Nobody knew how she longed to see the girl.

"She isn't as late as I thought she'd be," said Mrs. Dent, and again that curious, subtle change passed over her face, and again it settled into that stony impassiveness.

Rebecca stared at the door, waiting for it to open. "Where is she?" she asked presently.

"I guess she's stopped to take off her hat in the entry," suggested Mrs. Dent.

Rebecca waited. "Why don't she come? It can't take her all this time to take off her hat."

For answer Mrs. Dent rose with a stiff jerk and threw open the door.

"Agnes!" she called. "Agnes!" Then she turned and eyed Rebecca. "She ain't there."

"I saw her pass the window," said Rebecca in bewilderment.

"You must have been mistaken."

"I know I did," persisted Rebecca.

"You couldn't have."

"I did. I saw first a shadow go over the ceiling, then I saw her in the glass there"—she pointed to a mirror over the sideboard opposite—"and then the shadow passed the window."

"How did she look in the glass?"

"Little and light-haired, with the light hair kind of tossing over her forehead."

"You couldn't have seen her."

"Was that like Agnes?"

"Like enough; but of course you didn't see her. You've been thinking so much about her that you thought you did."

"You thought *you* did."

"I thought I saw a shadow pass the window, but I must have been mistaken. She didn't come in, or we would have seen her before now. I knew it was too early for her to get home from Addie Slocum's, anyhow."

When Rebecca went to bed Agnes had not returned. Rebecca had resolved that she would not retire until the girl came, but she was very tired, and she reasoned with herself that she was foolish. Besides, Mrs. Dent suggested that Agnes might go to the church social with Addie Slocum. When Rebecca suggested that she be sent for and told that her aunt had come, Mrs. Dent laughed meaningly.

"I guess you'll find out that a young girl ain't so ready to leave a sociable, where there's boys, to see her aunt," said she.

"She's too young," said Rebecca incredulously and indignantly.

"She's sixteen," replied Mrs. Dent; "and she's always been great for the boys."

"She's going to school four years after I get her before she thinks of boys," declared Rebecca.

"We'll see," laughed the other woman.

After Rebecca went to bed, she lay awake a long time listening for the sound of girlish laughter and a boy's voice under her window; then she fell asleep.

The next morning she was down early. Mrs. Dent, who kept no servants, was busily preparing breakfast.

"Don't Agnes help you about breakfast?" asked Rebecca.

"No, I let her lay," replied Mrs. Dent shortly.

"What time did she get home last night?"

"She didn't get home. She stayed with Addie. She often does."

"Without sending you word?"

"Oh, she knew I wouldn't worry."

"When will she be home?"

"Oh, I guess she'll be along pretty soon."

Rebecca was uneasy, but she tried to conceal it, for she knew of no good reason for uneasiness. What was there to occasion alarm in the fact of one young girl staying overnight with another? She could not eat much breakfast. Afterward she went out on the little piazza, although her hostess strove furtively to stop her.

"Why don't you go out back of the house? It's real pretty—a view over the river," she said.

"I guess I'll go out here," replied Rebecca. She had a purpose: to watch for the absent girl.

Presently Rebecca came hustling into the house through the sitting-room, into the kitchen where Mrs. Dent was cooking.

"That rose-bush!" she gasped.

Mrs. Dent turned and faced her.

"What of it?"

"It's a-blowing."

"What of it?"

"There isn't a mite of wind this morning."

Mrs. Dent turned with an inimitable toss of her fair head. "If you think I can spend my time puzzling over such nonsense as . . ." she began, but Rebecca interrupted her with a cry and a rush to the door.

"There she is now!" she cried.

She flung the door wide open, and curiously enough a breeze came in and her own gray hair tossed, and a paper blew off the table to the floor with a loud rustle, but there was nobody in sight.

"There's nobody here," Rebecca said.

She looked blankly at the other woman, who brought her rolling-pin down on a slab of pie-crust with a thud.

"I didn't hear anybody," she said calmly.

"I saw somebody pass that window!"

"You were mistaken again."

"I *know* I saw somebody."

"You couldn't have. Please shut that door."

Rebecca shut the door. She sat down beside the window and looked out on the autumnal yard, with its little curve of footpath to the kitchen door.

"What smells so strong of roses in this room?" she said presently. She sniffed hard.

"I don't smell anything but these nutmegs."

"It is not nutmeg."

"I don't smell anything else."

"Where do you suppose Agnes is?"

"Oh, perhaps she has gone over the ferry to Porter's Falls with Addie. She often does. Addie's got an aunt over there, and Addie's got a cousin, a real pretty boy."

"You suppose she's gone over there?"

"Mebbe. I shouldn't wonder."

"When should she be home?"

"Oh, not before afternoon."

Rebecca waited with all the patience she could muster. She kept reassuring herself, telling herself that it was all natural, that the other woman could not help it, but she made up her mind that if Agnes did not return that afternoon she should be sent for.

When it was four o'clock she started up with resolution. She had been furtively watching the onyx clock on the sitting-room mantel; she had timed herself. She had said that if Agnes was not home by that time she should demand that she be sent for. She rose and stood before Mrs. Dent, who looked up coolly from her embroidery.

"I've waited just as long as I'm going to," she said. "I've come 'way from Michigan to see my own sister's daughter and take her home with me. I've been here ever since yesterday—twenty-four hours— and I haven't seen her. Now I'm going to. I want her sent for."

Mrs. Dent folded her embroidery and rose.

"Well, I don't blame you," she said. "It is high time she came home. I'll go right over and get her myself."

Rebecca heaved a sigh of relief. She hardly knew what she had suspected or feared, but she knew that her position had been one of antagonism if not accusation, and she was sensible of relief.

"I wish you would," she said gratefully, and went back to her chair, while Mrs. Dent got her shawl and her little white head-tie. "I wouldn't trouble you, but I do feel as if I couldn't wait any longer to see her," she remarked apologetically.

"Oh, it ain't any trouble at all," said Mrs. Dent as she went out. "I don't blame you; you have waited long enough."

Rebecca sat at the window watching breathlessly until Mrs. Dent came stepping through the yard alone. She ran to the door and saw, hardly noticing it this time, that the rose-bush was again violently agitated, yet with no wind evident elsewhere.

"Where is she?" she cried.

Mrs. Dent laughed with stiff lips as she came up the steps over the terrace. "Girls will be girls," said she. "She's gone with Addie to

Lincoln. Addie's got an uncle who's conductor on the train, and lives there, and he got 'em passes, and they're goin' to stay to Addie's Aunt Margaret's a few days. Mrs. Slocum said Agnes didn't have time to come over and ask me before the train went, but she took it on herself to say it would be all right, and . . ."

"Why hadn't she been over to tell you?" Rebecca was angry, though not suspicious. She even saw no reason for her anger.

"Oh, she was putting up grapes. She was coming over just as soon as she got the black off her hands. She heard I had company, and her hands were a sight. She was holding them over sulphur matches."

"You say she's going to stay a few days?" repeated Rebecca dazedly.

"Yes; till Thursday, Mrs. Slocum said."

"How far is Lincoln from here?"

"About fifty miles. It'll be a real treat to her. Mrs. Slocum's sister is a real nice woman."

"It is goin' to make it pretty late about my goin' home."

"If you don't feel as if you could wait, I'll get her ready and send her on just as soon as I can," Mrs. Dent said sweetly.

"I'm going to wait," said Rebecca grimly.

The two women sat down again, and Mrs. Dent took up her embroidery.

"Is there any sewing I can do for her?" Rebecca asked finally in a desperate way. "If I can get her sewing along some . . ."

Mrs. Dent arose with alacrity and fetched a mass of white from the closet. "Here," she said, "if you want to sew the lace on this nightgown. I was going to put her to it, but she'll be glad enough to get rid of it. She ought to have this and one more before she goes. I don't like to send her away without some good underclothing."

Rebecca snatched at the little white garment and sewed feverishly.

That night she wakened from a deep sleep a little after midnight and lay a minute trying to collect her faculties and explain to herself what she was listening to. At last she discovered that it was the then popular strains of "The Maiden's Prayer" floating up through the floor from the piano in the sitting-room below. She jumped up, threw a shawl over her nightgown, and hurried downstairs trembling. There was nobody in the sitting-room; the piano was silent. She ran to Mrs. Dent's bedroom and called hysterically:

"Emeline! Emeline!"

"What is it?" asked Mrs. Dent's voice from the bed. The voice was stern, but had a note of consciousness in it.

"Who—who was that playing 'The Maiden's Prayer' in the sitting-room, on the piano?"

"I didn't hear anybody."

"There was some one."

"I didn't hear anything."

"I tell you there was some one. But—*there ain't anybody there.*"

"I didn't hear anything."

"I did—somebody playing 'The Maiden's Prayer' on the piano. Has Agnes got home? I *want to know.*"

"Of course Agnes hasn't got home," answered Mrs. Dent with rising inflection. "Be you gone crazy over that girl? The last boat from Porter's Falls was in before we went to bed. Of course she ain't come."

"I heard . . ."

"You were dreaming."

"I wasn't; I was broad awake."

Rebecca went back to her chamber and kept her lamp burning all night.

The next morning her eyes upon Mrs. Dent were wary and blazing with suppressed excitement. She kept opening her mouth as if to speak, then frowning, and setting her lips hard. After breakfast she went upstairs, and came down presently with her coat and bonnet.

"Now, Emeline," she said, "I want to know where the Slocums live."

Mrs. Dent gave a strange, long, half-lidded glance at her. She was finishing her coffee.

"Why?" she asked.

"I'm going over there and find out if they have heard anything from her daughter and Agnes since they went away. I don't like what I heard last night."

"You must have been dreaming."

"It don't make any odds whether I was or not. Does she play 'The Maiden's Prayer' on the piano? I want to know."

"What if she does? She plays it a little, I believe. I don't know. She don't half play it, anyhow; she ain't got an ear."

"That wasn't half played last night. I don't like such things happening. I ain't superstitious, but I don't like it. I'm going. Where do the Slocums live?"

"You go down the road over the bridge past the old grist mill, then you turn to the left; it's the only house for half a mile. You can't miss it. It has a barn with a ship in full sail on the cupola."

"Well, I'm going. I don't feel easy."

About two hours later Rebecca returned. There were red spots on her cheeks. She looked wild. "I've been there," she said, "and there isn't a soul at home. Something *has* happened."

"What has happened?"

"I don't know. Something. I had a warning last night. There wasn't a soul there. They've been sent for to Lincoln."

"Did you see anybody to ask?" asked Mrs. Dent with thinly concealed anxiety.

"I asked the woman that lives on the turn of the road. She's stone deaf. I suppose you know. She listened while I screamed at her to know where the Slocums were, and then she said, 'Mrs. Smith don't live here.' I didn't see anybody on the road, and that's the only house. What do you suppose it means?"

"I don't suppose it means much of anything," replied Mrs. Dent coolly. "Mr. Slocum is conductor on the railroad, and he'd be away anyway, and Mrs. Slocum often goes early when he does, to spend the day with her sister in Porter's Falls. She'd be more likely to go away than Addie."

"And you don't think anything has happened?" Rebecca asked with diminishing distrust before the reasonableness of it.

"Land, no!"

Rebecca went upstairs to lay aside her coat and bonnet. But she came hurrying back with them still on.

"Who's been in my room?" she gasped. Her face was pale as ashes.

Mrs. Dent also paled as she regarded her.

"What do you mean?" she asked slowly.

"I found when I went upstairs that—little nightgown of— Agnes's on—the bed, laid out. It was—*laid out*. The sleeves were folded across the bosom, and there was that little rose between them. Emeline, what is it? Emeline, what's the matter? Oh!"

Mrs. Dent was struggling for breath in great, choking gasps. She clung to the back of a chair. Rebecca, trembling herself so she could scarcely keep on her feet, got her some water.

As soon as she recovered herself Mrs. Dent regarded her with eyes full of the strangest mixture of fear and horror and hostility.

"What do you mean talking so?" she said in a hard voice.

"It *is there.*"

"Nonsense. You threw it down and it fell that way."

"It was folded in my bureau drawer."

"It couldn't have been."

"Who picked that red rose?"

"Look at the bush," Mrs. Dent replied shortly.

Rebecca looked at her; her mouth gaped. She hurried out of the room. When she came back her eyes seemed to protrude. (She had in the meantime hastened upstairs, and come down with tottering steps, clinging to the banisters.)

"Now I want to know what all this means?" she demanded.

"What what means?"

"The rose is on the bush, and it's gone from the bed in my room! Is this house haunted, or what?"

"I don't know anything about a house being haunted. I don't believe in such things. Be you crazy?" Mrs. Dent spoke with gathering force. The color flashed back to her cheeks.

"No," said Rebecca shortly. "I ain't crazy yet, but I shall be if this keeps on much longer. I'm going to find out where that girl is before night."

Mrs. Dent eyed her.

"What be you going to do?"

"I'm going to Lincoln."

A faint triumphant smile overspread Mrs. Dent's large face.

"You can't," said she; "there ain't any train."

"No train?"

"No; there ain't any afternoon train from the Falls to Lincoln."

"Then I'm going over to the Slocums' again tonight."

However, Rebecca did not go; such a rain came up as deterred even her resolution, and she had only her best dresses with her. Then in the evening came the letter from the Michigan village which she had left nearly a week ago. It was from her cousin, a single woman, who had come to keep her house while she was away. It was a pleasant unexciting letter enough, all the first of it, and related mostly how she missed Rebecca; how she hoped she was having pleasant weather and kept her health; and how her friend, Mrs. Greenaway, had come to stay with her since she had felt lonesome the first night in the house; how she hoped Rebecca would have no objections to this, although nothing had been said about it, since she had not realized that she might be nervous alone. The cousin was painfully conscientious, hence the letter. Rebecca smiled in spite of her disturbed mind as she read it, then her eye caught the postscript. That was in a different hand, purporting to be written by the friend, Mrs. Hannah Greenaway, informing her that the cousin had fallen down the cellar stairs and broken her hip, and was in a dangerous condition, and begging Rebecca to return at once, as she herself was rheumatic and unable to nurse her properly, and no one else could be obtained.

Rebecca looked at Mrs. Dent, who had come to her room with the letter quite late; it was half-past nine, and she had gone upstairs for the night.

"Where did this come from?" she asked.

"Mr. Amblecrom brought it," she replied.

"Who's he?"

"The postmaster. He often brings the letters that come on the late mail. He knows I ain't anybody to send. He brought yours about your coming. He said he and his wife came over on the ferry-boat with you."

"I remember him," Rebecca replied shortly. "There's bad news in this letter."

Mrs. Dent's face took on an expression of serious inquiry.

"Yes, my Cousin Harriet has fallen down the cellar stairs— they were always dangerous—and she's broken her hip, and I've got to take the first train home tomorrow."

"You don't say so. I'm dreadfully sorry."

"No, you ain't sorry!" said Rebecca, with a look as if she leaped. "You're glad. I don't know why, but you're glad. You're glad. You've wanted to get rid of me for some reason ever since I came. I don't know why. You're a strange woman. Now you've got your way, and I hope you're satisfied."

"How you talk."

Mrs. Dent spoke in a faintly injured voice, but there was a light in her eyes.

"I talk the way it is. Well, I'm going tomorrow morning, and I want you, just as soon as Agnes Dent comes home, to send her out to me. Don't you wait for anything. You pack what clothes she's got, and don't wait even to mend them, and you buy her ticket. I'll leave money, and you send her along. She don't have to change cars. You start her off, when she gets home, on the next train!"

"Very well," replied the other woman. She had an expression of covert amusement.

"Mind you do it."

"Very well, Rebecca."

Rebecca started on her journey the next morning. When she

arrived, two days later, she found her cousin in perfect health. She found, moreover, that the friend had not written the postscript in the cousin's letter. Rebecca would have returned to Ford Village the next morning, but the fatigue and nervous strain had been too much for her. She was not able to move from her bed. She had a species of low fever induced by anxiety and fatigue. But she could write, and she did, to the Slocums, and she received no answer. She also wrote to Mrs. Dent; she even sent numerous telegrams, with no response. Finally she wrote to the postmaster, and an answer arrived by the first possible mail. The letter was short, curt, and to the purpose. Mr. Amblecrom, the postmaster, was a man of few words, and especially wary as to his expressions in a letter.

"Dear madam," he wrote, "Your favour rec'ed. No Slocums in Ford's Village. All dead. Addie ten years ago, her mother two years later, her father five. House vacant. Mrs. John Dent said to have neglected stepdaughter. Girl was sick. Medicine not given. Talk of taking action. Not enough evidence. House said to be haunted. Strange sights and sounds. Your niece, Agnes Dent, died a year ago, about this time.

"Yours truly,

"Thomas Amblecrom."

THE YELLOW WALLPAPER
Charlotte Perkins Gilman
[1850–1904]

"Charlotte Perkins Gilman, in *The Yellow Wall Paper*, rises to a classic level in subtly delineating the madness which crawls over a woman dwelling in the hideously papered room where a madwoman was once confined."

—H.P. Lovecraft

T IS VERY SELDOM that mere ordinary people like John and myself secure ancestral halls for the summer.

A colonial mansion, a hereditary estate, I would say a haunted house and reach the height of romantic felicity—but that would be asking too much of fate!

Still I will proudly declare that there is something queer about it.

Else, why should it be let so cheaply? And why have stood so long untenanted?

John laughs at me, of course, but one expects that.

John is practical in the extreme. He has no patience with faith, an intense horror of superstition, and he scoffs openly at any talk of things not to be felt and seen and put down in figures.

John is a physician, and *perhaps*—(I would not say it to a

living soul, of course, but this is dead paper and a great relief to my mind)—*perhaps* that is one reason I do not get well faster.

You see, he does not believe I am sick! And what can one do?

If a physician of high standing, and one's own husband assures friends and relatives that there is really nothing the matter with one but temporary nervous depression—a slight hysterical tendency—what is one to do?

My brother is also a physician, and also of high standing, and he says the same thing.

So I take phosphates or phosphites—whichever it is—and tonics, and air and exercise, and journeys, and am absolutely forbidden to "work" until I am well again.

Personally, I disagree with their ideas.

Personally, I believe that congenial work, with excitement and change, would do me good.

But what is one to do?

I did write for a while in spite of them; but it *does* exhaust me a good deal—having to be so sly about it, or else meet with heavy opposition.

I sometimes fancy that in my condition, if I had less opposition and more society and stimulus—but John says the very worst thing I can do is to think about my condition, and I confess it always makes me feel bad.

So I will let it alone and talk about the house.

The most beautiful place! It is quite alone, standing well back from the road, quite three miles from the village. It makes me think of English places that you read about, for there are hedges and walls and gates that lock, and lots of separate little houses for the gardeners and people.

There is a *delicious* garden! I never saw such a garden—large and shady, full of box-bordered paths, and lined with long grape-covered arbors with seats under them.

There were greenhouses, but they are all broken now.

There was some legal trouble, I believe, something about the heirs and co-heirs; anyhow, the place has been empty for years.

That spoils my ghostliness, I am afraid, but I don't care— there is something strange about the house—I can feel it.

I even said so to John one moonlight evening, but he said what I felt was a draught, and shut the window.

I get unreasonably angry with John sometimes. I'm sure I never used to be so sensitive. I think it is due to this nervous condition.

But John says if I feel so I shall neglect proper self-control; so I take pains to control myself—before him, at least, and that makes me very tired.

I don't like our room a bit. I wanted one downstairs that opened onto the piazza and had roses all over the window, and such pretty old-fashioned chintz hangings! But John would not hear of it.

He said there was only one window and not room for two beds, and no near room for him if he took another.

He is very careful and loving, and hardly lets me stir without special direction.

I have a schedule prescription for each hour in the day; he takes all care from me, and so I feel basely ungrateful not to value it more.

He said he came here solely on my account, that I was to have perfect rest and all the air I could get. "Your exercise depends on your strength, my dear," said he, "and your food somewhat on your appetite; but air you can absorb all the time." So we took the nursery at the top of the house.

It is a big, airy room, the whole floor nearly, with windows that look all ways, and air and sunshine galore. It was nursery first, and then playroom and gymnasium, I should judge, for the windows are barred for little children, and there are rings and things in the walls.

The paint and paper look as if a boys' school had used it. It is stripped off—the paper—in great patches all around the head of my bed, about as far as I can reach, and in great places on the other side of the room low down. I never saw a worse paper in my life. One of those sprawling, flamboyant patterns commiting every artistic sin.

It is dull enough to confuse the eye in following, pronounced enough constantly to irritate and provoke study, and when you follow the lame uncertain curves for a little distance they suddenly commit suicide—plunge off at outrageous angles, destroy themselves in unheard-of contradictions.

The color is repellent, almost revolting: a smouldering unclean yellow, strangely faded by the slow-turning sunlight. It is a dull yet lurid orange in some places, a sickly sulphur tint in others.

No wonder the children hated it! I should hate it myself if I had to live in this room long.

There comes John, and I must put this away—he hates to have me write a word.

We have been here two weeks, and I haven't felt like writing before, since that first day.

I am sitting by the window now, up in this atrocious nursery, and there is nothing to hinder my writing as much as I please, save lack of strength.

John is away all day, and even some nights when his cases are serious.

I am glad my case is not serious!

But these nervous troubles are dreadfully depressing.

John does not know how much I really suffer. He knows there is no *reason* to suffer, and that satisfies him.

Of course it is only nervousness. It does weigh on me so not to do my duty in any way!

I meant to be such a help to John, such a real rest and comfort, and here I am a comparative burden already!

Nobody would believe what an effort it is to do what little I am able—to dress and entertain, and order things.

It is fortunate Mary is so good with the baby. Such a dear baby!

And yet I *cannot* be with him, it makes me so nervous.

I suppose John never was nervous in his life. He laughs at me so about this wallpaper!

At first he meant to repaper the room, but afterward he said that I was letting it get the better of me, and that nothing was worse for a nervous patient than to give way to such fancies.

He said that after the wallpaper was changed it would be the heavy bedstead, and then the barred windows, and then that gate at the head of the stairs, and so on.

"You know the place is doing you good," he said, "and really, dear, I don't care to renovate the house just for a three months' rental."

"Then do let us go downstairs," I said. "There are such pretty rooms there."

Then he took me in his arms and called me a blessed little goose, and said he would go down cellar, if I wished, and have it whitewashed into the bargain.

But he is right enough about the beds and windows and things.

It is as airy and comfortable a room as anyone need wish, and, of course, I would not be so silly as to make him uncomfortable just for a whim.

I'm really getting quite fond of the big room, all but that horrid paper.

Out of one window I can see the garden—those mysterious deep-shaded arbors, the riotous old-fashioned flowers, and bushes and gnarly trees.

Out of another I get a lovely view of the bay and a little private wharf belonging to the estate. There is a beautiful shaded lane that runs down there from the house. I always fancy I see people walking in these numerous paths and arbors, but John has cautioned me not to give way to fancy in the least. He says that with my imaginative power and habit of story-making, a nervous weakness like mine is sure to lead to all manner of excited fancies, and that I ought to use my will and good sense to check the tendency. So I try.

I think sometimes that if I were only well enough to write a little it would relieve the press of ideas and rest me.

But I find I get pretty tired when I try.

It is so discouraging not to have any advice and companionship about my work. When I get really well, John says we will ask Cousin Henry and Julia down for a long visit; but he says he would as soon put fireworks in my pillow-case as to let me have those stimulating people about now.

I wish I could get well faster.

But I must not think about that. This paper looks to me as if it *knew* what a vicious influence it had!

There is a recurrent spot where the pattern lolls like a broken neck and two bulbous eyes stare at you upside down.

I get positively angry with the impertinence of it and the everlastingness. Up and down and sideways they crawl, and those absurd unblinking eyes are everywhere. There is one place where two breadths didn't match, and the eyes go all up and down the line, one a little higher than the other.

I never saw so much expression in an inanimate thing before, and we all know how much expression they have! I used to lie awake as a child and get more entertainment and terror out of blank walls and plain furniture than most children could find in a toy-store.

I remember what a kindly wink the knobs of our big old bureau used to have, and there was one chair that always seemed like a strong friend.

I used to feel that if any of the other things looked too fierce I could always hop into that chair and be safe.

The furniture in this room is no worse than inharmonious, however, for we had to bring it all from downstairs. I suppose when this was used as a playroom they had to take the nursery things out, and no wonder! I never saw such ravages as the children have made here.

The wallpaper, as I said before, is torn off in spots, and it sticketh closer than a brother—they must have had perseverance as well as hatred.

Then the floor is scratched and gouged and splintered, the plaster itself is dug out here and there, and this great heavy bed, which is all we found in the room, looks as if it had been through the wars.

But I don't mind it a bit—only the paper.

There comes John's sister. Such a dear girl as she is, and so careful of me! I must not let her find me writing.

She is a perfect and enthusiastic housekeeper, and hopes for no better profession. I verily believe she thinks it is the writing which made me sick!

But I can write when she is out, and see her a long way off from these windows.

There is one that commands the road, a lovely shaded winding road, and one that just looks off over the country. A lovely country, too, full of great elms and velvet meadows.

This wallpaper has a kind of sub-pattern in a different shade, a particularly irritating one, for you can only see it in certain lights, and not clearly then.

But in the places where it isn't faded and where the sun is just so—I can see a strange, provoking, formless sort of figure that seems to skulk about behind that silly and conspicuous front design.

There's sister on the stairs!

Well, the Fourth of July is over! The people are all gone, and I am tired out. John thought it might do me good to see a little company, so we just had Mother and Nellie and the children down for a week.

Of course I didn't do a thing. Jennie sees to everything now.

But it tired me all the same.

John says if I don't pick up faster he shall send me to Weir Mitchell in the fall.

But I don't want to go there at all. I had a friend who was in his hands once, and she says he is just like John and my brother, only more so!

Besides, it is such an undertaking to go so far.

I don't feel as if it was worthwhile to turn my hand over for anything, and I'm getting dreadfully fretful and querulous.

I cry at nothing, and cry most of the time.

Of course, I don't when John is here, or anybody else, but when I am alone.

And I am alone a good deal just now. John is kept in town very often by serious cases, and Jennie is good and lets me alone when I want her to.

So I walk a little in the garden or down that lovely lane, sit on the porch under the roses, and lie down up here a good deal.

I'm getting really fond of the room in spite of the wallpaper. Perhaps *because* of the wallpaper.

It dwells in my mind so!

I lie on this great immovable bed—it is nailed down, I believe—and follow that pattern about by the hour. It is as good as gymnastics, I assure you. I start, we'll say, at the bottom, down in the corner over there where it has not been touched, and I determine for the thousandth time that I *will* follow that pointless pattern to some sort of a conclusion.

I know a little of the principle of design, and I know this thing was not arranged on any laws of radiation, or alternation, or repetition, or symmetry, or anything else that I ever heard of.

It is repeated, of course, by the breadths, but not otherwise.

Looked at in one way, each breadth stands alone; the bloated curves and flourishes—a kind of "debased Romanesque" with *delirium tremens*—go waddling up and down in isolated columns of fatuity.

But, on the other hand, they connect diagonally, and the sprawling outlines run off in great slanting waves of optic horror, like a lot of wallowing sea-weeds in full chase.

The whole thing goes horizontally, too, at least it seems so, and I exhaust myself trying to distinguish the order of its going in that direction.

They have used a horizontal breadth for a frieze, and that adds wonderfully to the confusion.

There is one end of the room where it is almost intact, and there, when the crosslights fade and the low sun shines directly upon it, I can almost fancy radiation after all—the interminable grotesque seems to form around a common center and rush off in headlong plunges of equal distraction.

It makes me tired to follow it. I will take a nap, I guess.

I don't know why I should write this.

I don't want to.

I don't feel able.

And I think John would think it absurd. But I *must* say what I feel and think in some way—it is such a relief!

But the effort is getting to be greater than the relief.

Half the time now I am awfully lazy, and lie down ever so much.

John says I mustn't lose my strength, and has me take cod liver oil and lots of tonics and things, to say nothing of ale and wine and rare meat.

Dear John! He loves me very dearly, and hates to have me sick. I tried to have a real earnest reasonable talk with him the other day, and tell him how I wish he would let me go and make a visit to Cousin Henry and Julia.

But he said I wasn't able to go, nor able to stand it after I got there, and I did not make out a very good case for myself, for I was crying before I had finished.

It is getting to be a great effort for me to think straight. Just this nervous weakness, I suppose.

And dear John gathered me up in his arms, and just carried me upstairs and laid me on the bed, and sat by me and read to me till it tired my head.

He said I was his darling and his comfort and all he had, and that I must take care of myself for his sake, and keep well.

He says no one but myself can help me out of it, that I must use my will and self-control and not let any silly fancies run away with me.

There's one comfort—the baby is well and happy, and does not have to occupy this nursery with the horrid wallpaper.

If we had not used it, that blessed child would have! What a fortunate escape! Why, I wouldn't have a child of mine, an impressionable little thing, live in such a room for worlds.

I never thought of it before, but it is lucky that John kept me here after all; I can stand it so much easier than a baby, you see.

Of course I never mention it to them any more—I am too wise—but I keep watch of it all the same.

There are things in that paper that nobody knows about but me, or ever will.

Behind that outside pattern the dim shapes get clearer every day.

It is always the same shape, only very numerous.

And it is like a woman stooping down and creeping about behind that pattern. I don't like it a bit. I wonder—I begin to think—I wish John would take me away from here!

It is so hard to talk with John about my case, because he is so wise, and because he loves me so.

But I tried it last night.

It was moonlight. The moon shines in all around just as the sun does.

I hate to see it sometimes, it creeps so slowly, and always comes in by one window or another.

John was asleep and I hated to waken him, so I kept still and watched the moonlight on that undulating wallpaper till I felt creepy.

The faint figure behind seemed to shake the pattern, just as if she wanted to get out.

I got up softly and went to feel and see if the paper *did* move, and when I came back John was awake.

"What is it, little girl?" he said. "Don't go walking about like that—you'll get cold."

I thought it was a good time to talk, so I told him that I really was not gaining here, and that I wished he would take me away.

"Why, darling!" said he. "Our lease will be up in three weeks, and I can't see how to leave before.

"The repairs are not done at home, and I cannot possibly leave town just now. Of course, if you were in any danger, I could and would, but you really are better, dear, whether you can see it or not. I am a doctor, dear, and I know. You are gaining flesh and color, your appetite is better, I feel really much easier about you."

"I don't weigh a bit more," said I, "nor as much; and my appetite may be better in the evening when you are here but it is worse in the morning when you are away!"

"Bless her little heart!" said he with a big hug. "She shall be as sick as she pleases! But now let's improve the shining hours by going to sleep, and talk about it in the morning!"

"And you won't go away?" I asked gloomily.

"Why, how can I, dear? It is only three weeks more and then we will take a nice little trip of a few days while Jennie is getting the house ready. Really, dear, you are better!"

"Better in body perhaps—" I began, and stopped short, for he sat up straight and looked at me with such a stern, reproachful look that I could not say another word.

"My darling," said he, "I beg of you, for my sake and for our child's sake, as well as for your own, that you will never for one instant let that idea enter your mind! There is nothing so dangerous, so fascinating, to a temperament like yours. It is a false and foolish fancy. Can you not trust me as a physician when I tell you so?"

So of course I said no more on that score, and we went to sleep before long. He thought I was asleep first, but I wasn't and lay there for hours trying to decide whether that front pattern and the back pattern really did move together or separately.

On a pattern like this, by daylight, there is a lack of sequence, a defiance of law, that is a constant irritant to a normal mind.

The color is hideous enough, and unreliable enough, and infuriating enough, but the pattern is torturing.

You think you have mastered it, but just as you get well under way in following, it turns a back-somersault and there you are. It slaps you in the face, knocks you down, and tramples upon you. It is like a bad dream.

The outside pattern is a florid arabesque, reminding one of a fungus. If you can imagine a toadstool in joints, an interminable string of toadstools, budding and sprouting in endless convolutions—why, that is something like it.

That is sometimes!

There is one marked peculiarity about this paper, a thing

nobody seems to notice but myself, and that is that it changes as the light changes.

When the sun shoots in through the east window—I always watch for that first long, straight ray—it changes so quickly that I never can quite believe it.

That is why I watch it always.

By moonlight—the moon shines in all night when there is a moon—I wouldn't know it was the same paper.

At night in any kind of light, in twilight, candlelight, camplight, and worst of all by moonlight, it becomes bars! The outside pattern, I mean, and the woman behind it is as plain as can be.

I didn't realize for a long time what the thing was that showed behind, that dim sub-pattern, but now I am quite sure it is a woman.

By daylight she is subdued, quiet. I fancy it is the pattern that keeps her so still. It is so puzzling. It keeps me quiet by the hour.

I lie down ever so much now. John says it is good for me, and to sleep all I can.

Indeed he started the habit by making me lie down for an hour after each meal.

It is a very bad habit, I am convinced, for you see, I don't sleep.

And that cultivates deceit, for I don't tell them I'm awake—oh, no!

The fact is I am getting a little afraid of John.

He seems very queer sometimes, and even Jennie has an inexplicable look.

It strikes me occasionally, just as a scientific hypothesis, that perhaps it is the paper!

I have watched John when he did not know I was looking, and come into the room suddenly on the most innocent excuses, and I've caught him several times *looking at the paper!* And Jennie too. I caught Jennie with her hand on it once.

She didn't know I was in the room, and when I asked her in a quiet, a very quiet voice, with the most restrained manner possible, what she was doing with the paper, she turned around as if she had been caught stealing, and looked quite angry—asked me why I should frighten her so!

Then she said that the paper stained everything it touched, that she had found yellow smooches on all my clothes and John's and she wished we would be more careful!

Did not that sound innocent? But I know she was studying that pattern, and I am determined that nobody shall find it out but myself.

Life is very much more exciting now than it used to be. You see, I have something more to expect, to look forward to, to watch, I really do eat better, and am more quiet than I was.

John is so pleased to see me improve! He laughed a little the other day, and said I seemed to be flourishing in spite of my wallpaper.

I turned it off with a laugh. I had no intention of telling him it was *because* of the wallpaper—he would make fun of me. He might even want to take me away.

I don't want to leave now until I have found it out. There is a week more, and I think that will be enough.

I'm feeling ever so much better! I don't sleep much at night, for it is so interesting to watch developments; but I sleep a good deal during the daytime.

In the daytime it is tiresome and perplexing.

There are always new shoots on the fungus, and new shades of yellow all over it. I cannot keep count of them, though I have tried conscientiously.

It is the strangest yellow, that wallpaper! It makes me think of all the yellow things I ever saw—not beautiful ones like buttercups, but old, foul, bad yellow things.

But there is something else about that paper—the smell! I noticed it the moment we came into the room, but with so much air and sun it was not bad. Now we have had a week of fog and rain, and whether the windows are open or not, the smell is here.

It creeps all over the house.

I find it hovering in the dining-room, skulking in the parlor, hiding in the hall, lying in wait for me on the stairs.

It gets into my hair.

Even when I go to ride, if I turn my head suddenly and surprise it—there is that smell!

Such a peculiar odor, too! I have spent hours in trying to analyze it, to find what it smelled like.

It is not bad—at first—and very gentle, but quite the subtlest, most enduring odor I ever met.

In this damp weather it is awful. I wake up in the night and find it hanging over me.

It used to disturb me at first. I thought seriously of burning the house—to reach the smell.

But now I am used to it. The only thing I can think of that it is like is the *color* of the paper! A yellow smell!

There is a very funny mark on this wall, low down, near the mopboard. A streak that runs round the room. It goes behind every piece of furniture, except the bed, a long, straight, even *smooch,* as if it had been rubbed over and over.

I wonder how it was done and who did it, and what they did it for. Round and round and round—round and round and round—it makes me dizzy!

I really have discovered something at last.

Through watching so much at night, when it changes so, I have finally found out.

The front pattern *does* move—and no wonder! The woman behind shakes it!

Sometimes I think there are a great many women behind, and sometimes only one, and she crawls around fast, and her crawling shakes it all over.

Then in the very bright spots she keeps still, and in the very shady spots she just takes hold of the bars and shakes them hard.

And she is all the time trying to climb through. But nobody could climb through that pattern—it strangles so; I think that is why it has so many heads.

They get through, and then the pattern strangles them off and turns them upside down, and makes their eyes white!

If those heads were covered or taken off it would not be half so bad.

I think that woman gets out in the daytime!

And I'll tell you why—privately—I've seen her!

I can see her out of every one of my windows!

It is the same woman, I know, for she is always creeping, and most women do not creep by daylight.

I see her in that long shaded lane, creeping up and down. I see her in those dark grape arbors, creeping all around the garden.

I see her on that long road under the trees, creeping along, and when a carriage comes she hides under the blackberry vines.

I don't blame her a bit. It must be very humiliating to be caught creeping by daylight!

I always lock the door when I creep by daylight. I can't do it at night, for I know John would suspect something at once.

And John is so queer now that I don't want to irritate him. I wish he would take another room! Besides, I don't want anybody to get that woman out at night but myself.

I often wonder if I could see her out of all the windows at once.

But, turn as fast as I can, I can only see out of one at one time.

And though I always see her, she may be able to creep faster than I can turn! I have watched her sometimes away off in the open country, creeping as fast as a cloud shadow in a high wind.

If only that top pattern could be gotten off from the under one! I mean to try it, little by little.

I have found out another funny thing, but I shan't tell it this time! It does not do to trust people too much.

There are only two more days to get this paper off, and I believe John is beginning to notice. I don't like the look in his eyes.

And I heard him ask Jennie a lot of professional questions about me. She had a very good report to give. She said I slept a good deal in the daytime. John knows I don't sleep very well at night, for all I'm so quiet!

He asked me all sorts of questions, too, and pretended to be very loving and kind.

As if I couldn't see through him!

Still, I don't wonder he acts so, sleeping under this paper for three months.

It only interests me, but I feel sure John and Jennie are affected by it.

Hurrah! This is the last day, but it is enough. John is to stay in town over night, and won't be out until this evening.

Jennie wanted to sleep with me—the sly thing; but I told her I should undoubtedly rest better for a night all alone.

That was clever, for really I wasn't alone a bit. As soon as it was moonlight and that poor thing began to crawl and shake the pattern, I got up and ran to help her.

I pulled and she shook. I shook and she pulled, and before morning we had peeled off yards of that paper.

A strip about as high as my head and half around the room.

And then when the sun came and that awful pattern began to laugh at me, I declared I would finish it today!

We go away tomorrow, and they are moving all my furniture down again to leave things as they were before.

Jennie looked at the wall in amazement, but I told her merrily that I did it out of pure spite at the vicious thing.

She laughed and said she wouldn't mind doing it herself, but I must not get tired.

How she betrayed herself that time!

But I am here, and no person touches this paper but Me— not *alive!*

She tried to get me out of the room—it was too patent! But I said it was so quiet and empty and clean now that I believed I would lie down again and sleep all I could, and not to wake me even for dinner—I would call when I woke.

So now she is gone, and the servants are gone, and the things are gone, and there is nothing left but that great bedstead nailed down, with the canvas mattress we found on it.

We shall sleep downstairs tonight, and take the boat home tomorrow.

I quite enjoy the room, now it is bare again.

How those children did tear about here!

This bedstead is fairly gnawed!

But I must get to work.

I have locked the door and thrown the key down into the front path.

I don't want to go out, and I don't want to have anybody come in, till John comes.

I want to astonish him.

I've got a rope up here that even Jennie did not find. If that woman does get out, and tries to get away, I can tie her!

But I forgot I could not reach far without anything to stand on! This bed will *not* move!

I tried to lift and push it until I was lame, and then I got so angry I bit off a little piece at one corner—but it hurt my teeth.

Then I peeled off all the paper I could reach standing on the floor. It sticks horribly and the pattern just enjoys it. All those strangled heads and bulbous eyes and waddling fungus growths just shriek with derision!

I was getting angry enough to do something desperate. To jump out of the window would be admirable exercise, but the bars are too strong even to try.

Besides I wouldn't do it. Of course not. I know well enough that a step like that is improper and might be misconstrued.

I don't like to *look* out of the windows even—there are so many of those creeping women, and they creep so fast.

I wonder if they all come out of that wallpaper as I did!

But I am securely fastened now by my well-hidden rope—you don't get *me* out in the road there!

I suppose I shall have to get back behind the pattern when it comes night, and that is hard!

It is so pleasant to be out in this great room and creep around as I please!

I don't want to go outside. I won't even if Jennie asks me to.

For outside you have to creep on the ground, and everything is green instead of yellow.

But here I can creep smoothly on the floor, and my shoulder just fits in that long smooch around the wall, so I cannot lose my way.

Why, there's John at the door!

It is no use, young man, you can't open it!

How he does call and pound!

Now he's crying to Jennie for an axe.

It would be a shame to break down that beautiful door!

"John, dear!" said I in the gentlest voice. "The key is down by the front steps, under a plantain leaf!"

That silenced him for a few moments.

Then he said, very quietly indeed, "Open the door, my darling!"

"I can't," said I. "The key is down by the front door under a plantain leaf!" And then I said it again, several times, very gently and slowly, and said it so often that he had to go and see, and he got it of course, and came in. He stopped short by the door.

"What is the matter?" he cried. "For God's sake, what are you doing!"

I kept on creeping just the same, but I looked at him over my shoulder.

"I've got out at last," said I, "in spite of you and Jane. And I've pulled off most of the paper, so you can't put me back!"

Now why should that man have fainted? But he did, and right across my path by the wall, so that I had to creep over him every time!

THE RECRUDESCENCE OF IMRAY
Rudyard Kipling
[1865–1936]

"Recent British literature, besides including the three or four greatest fantasists of the present age, has been gratifyingly fertile in the element of the weird. Rudyard Kipling has often approached it, and has, despite the omnipresent mannerisms, handled it with indubitable mastery in such tales as *The Phantom Rickshaw*, *The Finest Story in the World*, *The Recrudescence of Imray*, and *The Mark of the Beast*."
—*H.P. Lovecraft*

The doors were wide, the story saith,
Out of the night came the patient wraith,
He might not speak, and he could not stir
A hair of the Baron's minniver—
Speechless and strengthless, a shadow thin,
He roved the castle to seek his kin.
And oh, 'twas a piteous thing to see
The dumb ghost follow his enemy!

—The Baron.

Imray achieved the impossible. Without warning, for no conceivable motive, in his youth, at the threshold of his career he chose to disappear from the world—which is to say, the little Indian station where he lived.

Upon a day he was alive, well, happy, and in great evidence among the billiard-tables at his Club. Upon a morning he was not, and no manner of search could make sure where he might be. He had stepped out of his place; he had not appeared at his office at the proper time, and his dogcart was not upon the public roads. For these reasons, and because he was hampering, in a microscopical degree, the administration of the Indian Empire, that Empire paused for one microscopical moment to make inquiry into the fate of Imray. Ponds were dragged, wells were plumbed, telegrams were despatched down the lines of railways and to the nearest seaport town—twelve hundred miles away; but Imray was not at the end of the drag-ropes nor the telegraph wires. He was gone, and his place knew him no more. Then the work of the great Indian Empire swept forward, because it could not be delayed, and Imray from being a man became a mystery—such a thing as men talk over at their tables in the Club for a month, and then forget utterly. His guns, horses, and carts were sold to the highest bidder. His superior officer wrote an altogether absurd letter to his mother, saying that Imray had unaccountably disappeared, and his bungalow stood empty.

After three or four months of the scorching hot weather had gone by, my friend Strickland, of the Police, saw fit to rent the bungalow from the native landlord. This was before he was engaged to Miss Youghal—an affair which has been described in another place—and while he was pursuing his investigations into native life. His own life was sufficiently peculiar, and men complained of his manners and customs. There was always food in his house, but there were no regular times for meals. He ate, standing up and walking about, whatever he might find at the sideboard, and this is not good for human beings. His domestic equipment was limited to six rifles, three shot-guns, five saddles, and a collection of stiff-jointed mahseer-rods, bigger and stronger than the largest salmon-rods. These occupied one-half of his bungalow, and the other half was given up to Strickland and his dog Tietjens —an enormous Rampur slut who devoured daily the rations of two men. She spoke to Strickland in a language of her own; and whenever, walking abroad, she saw things calculated to destroy the peace of Her Majesty the Queen-Empress, she returned to her master and laid information. Strickland would take steps at once, and at the end of his labours was trouble and fine and imprisonment for other people. The natives believed that Tietjens was a familiar spirit, and treated her with the great reverence that is born of hate and fear. One room in the bungalow was set apart for her special use. She owned a bedstead, a blanket, and a drinking-trough, and if anyone came into Strickland's room at night her custom was to knock down the invader and give tongue till someone came with a light. Strickland owed his life to her when he was on the Frontier, in search of a local murderer, who came in the grey dawn to send Strickland much farther than the Andaman Islands. Tietjens caught the man as he was crawling into Strickland's tent with a dagger between his teeth; and after his record of iniquity was established in the eyes of the law he was hanged. From that date Tietjens wore a collar of rough silver, and employed a monogram on her night-blanket; and the blanket was of double woven Kashmir cloth, for she was a delicate dog.

Under no circumstances would she be separated from Strickland; and once, when he was ill with fever, made great trouble for the doctors, because she did not know how to help her master and would not allow another creature to attempt aid. Macarnaght, of the Indian Medical Service, beat her over her head with a gun-butt before she could understand that she must give room for those who could give quinine.

A short time after Strickland had taken Imray's bungalow, my business took me through that Station, and naturally, the Club quarters being full, I quartered myself upon Strickland. It was a desirable bungalow, eight-roomed and heavily thatched against any chance of leakage from rain. Under the pitch of the roof ran a ceiling-cloth which looked just as neat as a white-washed ceiling. The landlord had repainted it when Strickland took the bungalow. Unless you knew how Indian bungalows were built you would never have suspected that above the cloth lay the dark three-cornered cavern of the roof, where the beams and the underside of the thatch harboured all manner of rats, bats, ants and foul things.

Tietjens met me in the verandah with a bay like the boom of the bell of St Paul's, putting her paws on my shoulder to show she was glad to see me. Strickland had contrived to claw together a sort of meal which he called lunch, and immediately after it was finished went out about his business. I was left alone with Tietjens and my own affairs. The heat of the summer had broken up and turned to the warm damp of the rains. There was no motion in the heated air, but the rain fell like ramrods on the earth, and flung up a blue mist when it splashed back. The bamboos, and the custard-apples, the poinsettias, and the mango-trees in the garden stood still while the warm water lashed through them, and the frogs began to sing among the aloe hedges. A little before the light failed, and when the rain was at its worst, I sat in the back verandah and heard the water roar from the eaves, and scratched myself because I was covered with the thing called prickly-heat. Tietjens came out with me and put her head in my lap and was very sorrowful; so I gave her biscuits when tea was ready, and I took tea in the back verandah on account of the little coolness found there. The rooms of the house were dark behind me. I could smell Strickland's saddlery and the oil on his guns, and I had no desire to sit among these things. My own servant came to me in the twilight, the muslin of his clothes clinging tightly to his drenched body, and told me that a gentleman had called and wished to see someone. Very much against my will, but only because of the darkness of the rooms, I went into the naked drawing-room, telling my man to bring the lights. There might or might not have been a caller waiting—it seemed to me that I saw a figure by one of the windows—but when the lights came there was nothing save the spikes of the rain without, and the smell of the drinking earth in my nostrils. I explained to my servant that he was no wiser than he ought to be, and went back to the verandah to talk to Tietjens. She had gone out into the wet, and I could hardly coax her back to me, even with biscuits with sugar tops. Strickland came home, dripping wet, just before dinner, and the first thing he said was:

"Has anyone called?"

I explained, with apologies, that my servant had summoned me into the drawing-room on a false alarm; or that some loafer had tried to call on Strickland, and thinking better of it had fled after giving his name. Strickland ordered dinner, without comment, and since it was a real dinner with a white tablecloth attached, we sat down.

At nine o'clock Strickland wanted to go to bed, and I was tired too. Tietjens, who had been lying underneath the table, rose up, and swung into the least exposed verandah as soon as her master moved to his own room, which was next to the stately chamber set apart for Tietjens. If a mere wife had wished to sleep out of doors in that pelting rain it would not have mattered; but Tietjens was a dog, and therefore the better animal. I looked at Strickland, expecting to see him flay her with a whip. He smiled queerly, as a man would smile after telling some unpleasant domestic tragedy. "She has done this ever since I moved in here," said he. "Let her go."

The dog was Strickland's dog, so I said nothing, but I felt all that Strickland felt in being thus made light of. Tietjens encamped outside my bedroom window, and storm after storm came up, thundered on the thatch, and died away. The lightning spattered the sky as a thrown egg spatters a barn-door, but the light was pale blue, not yellow; and, looking through my split bamboo blinds, I could see the great dog standing, not sleeping, in the verandah, the hackles alift on her back, and her feet anchored as tensely as the drawn wire-rope of a suspension bridge. In the very short pauses of the thunder I tried to sleep, but it seemed that someone wanted me very urgently. He, whoever he was, was trying to call me by name, but his voice was no more than a husky whisper. The thunder ceased, and Tietjens went into the garden and howled at the low moon. Somebody tried to open my door, walked about and about through the house, and stood breathing heavily in the verandahs, and just when I was falling asleep I fancied that I heard a wild hammering and clamouring above my head or on the door.

I ran into Strickland's room and asked him whether he was ill, and had been calling for me. He was lying on his bed half dressed, a pipe in his mouth. "I thought you'd come," he said. "Have I been walking round the house recently?"

I explained that he had been tramping in the dining-room

and the smoking-room and two or three other places; and he laughed and told me to go back to bed. I went back to bed and slept till the morning, but through all my mixed dreams I was sure I was doing someone an injustice in not attending to his wants. What those wants were I could not tell; but a fluttering, whispering, bolt-tumbling, lurking, loitering Someone was reproaching me for my slackness, and, half awake, I heard the howling of Tietjens in the garden and the threshing of the rain.

I lived in that house for two days. Strickland went to his office daily, leaving me alone for eight or ten hours with Tietjens for my only companion. As long as the full light lasted I was comfortable, and so was Tietjens; but in the twilight she and I moved into the back verandah and cuddled each other for company. We were alone in the house, but none the less it was much too fully occupied by a tenant with whom I did not wish to interfere. I never saw him, but I could see the curtains between the rooms quivering where he had just passed through; I could hear the chairs creaking as the bamboos sprung under a weight that had just quitted them; and I could feel when I went to get a book from the dining-room that somebody was waiting in the shadows of the front verandah till I should have gone away. Tietjens made the twilight more interesting by glaring into the darkened rooms with every hair erect, and following the motions of something that I could not see. She never entered the rooms, but her eyes moved interestedly: that was quite sufficient. Only when my servant came to trim the lamps and make all light and habitable she would come in with me and spend her time sitting on her haunches, watching an invisible extra man as he moved about behind my shoulder. Dogs are cheerful companions.

I explained to Strickland, gently as might be, that I would go over to the Club and find for myself quarters there. I admired his hospitality, was pleased with his guns and rods, but I did not much care for his house and its atmosphere. He heard me out to the end, and then smiled very wearily, but without contempt, for he is a man who understands things. "Stay on," he said, "and see what this thing means. All you have talked about I have known since I took the bungalow. Stay on and wait. Tietjens has left me. Are you going too?"

I had seen him through one little affair, connected with a heathen idol, that had brought me to the doors of a lunatic asylum, and I had no desire to help him through further experiences. He was a man to whom unpleasantnesses arrived as do dinners to ordinary people.

Therefore I explained more clearly than ever that I liked him immensely, and would be happy to see him in the daytime; but that I did not care to sleep under his roof. This was after dinner, when Tietjens had gone out to lie in the verandah.

"'Pon my soul, I don't wonder," said Strickland, with his eyes on the ceiling-cloth. "Look at that!"

The tails of two brown snakes were hanging between the cloth and the cornice of the wall. They threw long shadows in the lamplight.

"If you are afraid of snakes of course—" said Strickland.

I hate and fear snakes, because if you look into the eyes of any snake you will see that it knows all and more of the mystery of man's fall, and that it feels all the contempt that the Devil felt when Adam was evicted from Eden. Besides which its bite is generally fatal, and it twists up trouser legs.

"You ought to get your thatch overhauled," I said. "Give me a mahseer-rod, and we'll poke 'em down."

"They'll hide among the roof-beams," said Strickland. "I can't stand snakes overhead. I'm going up into the roof. If I shake 'em down, stand by with a cleaning-rod and break their backs."

I was not anxious to assist Strickland in his work, but I took the cleaning-rod and waited in the dining-room, while Strickland brought a gardener's ladder from the verandah, and set it against the side of the room. The snake-tails drew themselves up and disappeared. We could hear the dry rushing scuttle of long bodies running over the baggy ceiling cloth. Strickland took a lamp with him, while I tried to make clear to him the danger of hunting roof-snakes between a ceiling-cloth and a thatch, apart from the deterioration of property caused by ripping out ceiling-cloths.

"Nonsense!" said Strickland. "They're sure to hide near the walls by the cloth. The bricks are too cold for 'em, and the heat of the room is just what they like." He put his hand to the corner of the stuff and ripped it from the cornice. It gave with a great sound of tearing, and Strickland put his head through the opening into the dark of the angle of the roof-beams. I set my teeth and lifted the rod, for I had not the least knowledge of what might descend.

"H'm!" said Strickland, and his voice rolled and rumbled in the roof. "There's room for another set of rooms up here, and, by Jove, someone is occupying 'em!"

"Snakes?" I said from below.

"No. It's a buffalo. Hand me up the two last joints of a mahseer-rod, and I'll prod it. It's lying on the main roof-beam."

I handed up the rod.

"What a nest for owls and serpents! No wonder the snakes live here," said Strickland, climbing farther into the roof. I could see his elbow thrusting with the rod. "Come out of that, whoever you are! Heads below there! It's falling."

I saw the ceiling cloth nearly in the centre of the room bag with a shape that was pressing it downwards and downwards towards the lighted lamp on the table. I snatched the lamp out of danger and stood back. Then the cloth ripped out from the walls, tore, split, swayed, and shot down upon the table something that I dared not look at, till Strickland had slid down the ladder and was standing by my side.

He did not say much, being a man of few words; but he picked up the loose end of the tablecloth and threw it over the remnants on the table.

"It strikes me," said he, putting down the lamp, "our friend Imray has come back. Oh! you would, would you?"

There was a movement under the cloth, and a little snake wriggled out, to be back-broken by the butt of the mahseer-rod. I was sufficiently sick to make no remarks worth recording.

Strickland meditated, and helped himself to drinks. The arrangements under the cloth made no more signs of life.

"Is it Imray?" I said.

Strickland turned back the cloth for a moment, and looked.

"It is Imray," he said; "and his throat is cut from ear to ear."

Then we spoke, both together and to ourselves: "That's why he whispered about the house."

Tietjens, in the garden, began to bay furiously. A little later her great nose heaved open the dining-room door.

She snuffed and was still. The tattered ceiling-cloth hung down almost to the level of the table, and there was hardly room to move away from the discovery.

Tietjens came in and sat down; her teeth bared under her lip and her forepaws planted. She looked at Strickland.

"It's a bad business, old lady," said he. "Men don't climb up into the roofs of their bungalows to die, and they don't fasten up the ceiling cloth behind 'em. Let's think it out."

"Let's think it out somewhere else," I said.

"Excellent idea! Turn the lamps out. We'll get into my room."

I did not turn the lamps out. I went into Strickland's room first, and allowed him to make the darkness. Then he followed me, and we lit tobacco and thought. Strickland thought. I smoked furiously, because I was afraid.

"Imray is back," said Strickland. "The question is—who killed Imray? Don't talk, I've a notion of my own. When I took this bungalow I took over most of Imray's servants. Imray was guileless and inoffensive, wasn't he?"

I agreed; though the heap under the cloth had looked neither one thing nor the other.

"If I call in all the servants they will stand fast in a crowd and lie like Aryans. What do you suggest?"

"Call 'em in one by one," I said.

"They'll run away and give the news to all their fellows," said Strickland. "We must segregate 'em. Do you suppose your servant knows anything about it?"

"He may, for aught I know; but I don't think it's likely. He has only been here for two or three days," I answered. "What's your notion?"

"I can't quite tell. How the dickens did the man get the wrong side of the ceiling-cloth?"

There was a heavy coughing outside Strickland's bedroom door. This showed that Bahadur Khan, his body-servant, had waked from sleep and wished to put Strickland to bed.

"Come in," said Strickland. "It's a very warm night, isn't it?"

Bahadur Khan, a great, green-turbaned, six-foot Mahomedan, said that it was a very warm night; but that there was more rain pending, which, by his Honour's favour, would bring relief to the country.

"It will be so, if God pleases," said Strickland, tugging off his boots. "It is in my mind, Bahadur Khan, that I have worked thee remorselessly for many days—ever since that time when thou first camest into my service. What time was that?"

"Has the Heaven-born forgotten? It was when Imray Sahib went secretly to Europe without warning given; and I—even I— came into the honoured service of the protector of the poor."

"And Imray Sahib went to Europe?"

"It is so said among those who were his servants."

"And thou wilt take service with him when he returns?"

"Assuredly, Sahib. He was a good master, and cherished his dependants."

"That is true. I am very tired, but I go buck-shooting tomorrow. Give me the little sharp rifle that I use for black-buck; it is in the case yonder."

The man stooped over the case; handed barrels, stock, and fore-end to Strickland, who fitted all together, yawning dolefully. Then he reached down to the gun-case, took a solid-drawn cartridge, and slipped it into the breech of the .360 Express.

"And Imray Sahib has gone to Europe secretly! That is very strange, Bahadur Khan, is it not?"

"What do I know of the ways of the white man, Heaven-born?"

"Very little, truly. But thou shall know more anon. It has reached me that Imray Sahib has returned from his so long journeyings, and that even now he lies in the next room, waiting his servant."

"Sahib!"

The lamplight slid along the barrels of the rifle as they levelled themselves at Bahadur Khan's broad breast.

"Go and look!" said Strickland. "Take a lamp. Thy master is tired, and he waits thee. Go!"

The man picked up a lamp, and went into the dining-room, Strickland following, and almost pushing him with the muzzle of the rifle. He looked for a moment at the black depths behind the ceiling-cloth; at the writhing snake under foot; and last, a grey glaze settling on his face, at the thing under the tablecloth.

"Hast thou seen?" said Strickland after a pause.

"I have seen. I am clay in the white man's hands. What does the Presence do?"

"Hang thee within the month. What else?"

"For killing him? Nay, Sahib, consider. Walking among us, his servants, he cast his eyes upon my child, who was four years old. Him he bewitched, and in ten days he died of the fever—my child!"

"What said Imray Sahib?"

"He said he was a handsome child, and patted him on the head; wherefore my child died. Wherefore I killed Imray Sahib in the twilight, when he had come back from office, and was sleeping. Wherefore I dragged him up into the roof-beams and made all fast behind him. The Heaven-born knows all things. I am the servant of the Heaven-born."

Strickland looked at me above the rifle, and said, in the vernacular, "Thou art witness to this saying? He has killed."

Bahadur Khan stood ashen grey in the light of the one lamp. The need for justification came upon him very swiftly. "I am trapped," he said, "but the offence was that man's. He cast an evil eye upon my child, and I killed and hid him. Only such as are served by devils," he glared at Tietjens, couched stolidly before him, "only such could know what I did."

"It was clever. But thou shouldst have lashed him to the beam with a rope. Now, thou thyself will hang by a rope. Orderly!"

A drowsy policeman answered Strickland's call. He was followed by another, and Tietjens sat wondrous still.

"Take him to the police station," said Strickland. "There is a case toward."

"Do I hang, then?" said Bahadur Khan, making no attempt to escape, and keeping his eyes on the ground.

"If the sun shines or the water runs—yes!" said Strickland.

Bahadur Khan stepped back one long pace, quivered, and stood still. The two policemen waited further orders.

"Go!" said Strickland.

"Nay; but I go very swiftly," said Bahadur Khan. "Look! I am even now a dead man."

He lifted his foot, and to the little toe there clung the head of the half-killed snake, firm fixed in the agony of death.

"I come of land-holding stock," said Bahadur Khan, rocking where he stood. "It were a disgrace to me to go to the public scaffold: therefore I take this way. Be it remembered that the Sahib's shirts are correctly enumerated, and that there is an extra piece of soap in his wash-basin. My child was bewitched and I slew the wizard. Why should you seek to slay me with the rope? My honour is saved, and—and—I die."

At the end of an hour he died, as they die who are bitten by the little brown *karait,* and the policemen bore him and the thing under the tablecloth to their appointed places. All were needed to make clear the disappearance of Imray.

"This," said Strickland, very calmly, as he climbed into

bed, "is called the nineteenth century. Did you hear what that man said?"

"I heard," I answered. "Imray made a mistake."

"Simply and solely through not knowing the nature of the Oriental, and the coincidence of a little seasonal fever. Bahadur Khan had been with him for four years."

I shuddered. My own servant had been with me for exactly that length of time. When I went over to my own room I found my man waiting, impassive as the copper head on a penny, to pull off my boots.

"What has befallen Bahadur Khan?" said I.

"He was bitten by a snake and died. The rest the Sahib knows," was the answer.

"And how much of this matter has thou known?"

"As much as might be gathered from One coming in in the twilight to seek satisfaction. Gently, Sahib. Let me pull off those boots."

I had just settled to the sleep of exhaustion when I heard Strickland shouting from his side of the house—

"Tietjens has come back to her place!"

And so she had. The great deerhound was couched statelily on her own bedstead on her own blanket, while, in the next room, the idle, empty, ceiling-cloth waggled as it trailed on the table.

THE HANDS OF KARMA
(INGWA-BANASHI)
Lafcadio Hearn
[1850–1904]

"Lafcadio Hearn, strange, wandering, and exotic, departs still farther from the realm of the real; and with the supreme artistry of a sensitive poet weaves phantasies impossible to an author of the solid roast-beef type. His *Fantastics*, written in America, contains some of the most impressive ghoulishness in all literature; whilst his *Kwaidan*, written in Japan, crystallises with matchless skill and delicacy the eerie lore and whispered legends of that richly colourful nation. Still more of Hearn's wizardry of language is shown in some of his translations from the French, especially from Gautier and Flaubert. His version of the latter's *Temptation of St. Anthony* is a classic of fevered and riotous imagery clad in the magic of singing words."

—*H.P. Lovecraft*

THE DAIMYO'S WIFE was dying, and knew that she was dying. She had not been able to leave her bed since the early autumn of the tenth Bunsei. It was now the fourth month of the twelfth Bunsei—the year 1829 by Western counting; and the cherry-trees were blossoming. She thought of the cherry-trees in her garden, and of the gladness of spring. She thought of her children. She thought of her husband's various concubines—especially the Lady Yukiko, nineteen years old.

"My dear wife," said the daimyo, "you have suffered very

much for three long years. We have done all that we could to get
you well—watching beside you night and day, praying for you,
and often fasting for your sake. But in spite of our loving care, and
in spite of the skill of our best physicians, it would now seem that
the end of your life is not far off. Probably we shall sorrow more
than you will sorrow because of your having to leave what the
Buddha so truly termed 'this burning-house of the world.' I shall
order to be performed—no matter what the cost—every religious
rite that can serve you in regard to your next rebirth; and all of us
will pray without ceasing for you, that you may not have to
wander in the Black Space, but may quickly enter Paradise, and
attain to Buddhahood."

He spoke with the utmost tenderness, caressing her the while.
Then, with eyelids closed, she answered him in a voice thin as the
voice of an insect:

"I am grateful—most grateful—for your kind words. . . . Yes,
it is true, as you say, that I have been sick for three long years, and
that I have been treated with all possible care and affection. . . .
Why, indeed, should I turn away from the one true Path at the
very moment of my death? . . . Perhaps to think of worldly matters at such a time is not right—but I have one last request to
make—only one. . . . Call here to me the Lady Yukiko—you
know that I love her like a sister. I want to speak to her about the
affairs of this household."

Yukiko came at the summons of the lord, and, in obedience to a
sign from him, knelt down beside the couch. The daimyo's wife
opened her eyes, and looked at Yukiko, and spoke:

"Ah, here is Yukiko! . . . I am so pleased to see you, Yukiko!
. . . Come a little closer—so that you can hear me well: I am not

able to speak loud. . . . Yukiko, I am going to die. I hope that you will be faithful in all things to our dear lord—for I want you to take my place when I am gone. . . . I hope that you will always be loved by him—yes, even a hundred times more than I have been—and that you will very soon be promoted to a higher rank, and become his honoured wife. . . . And I beg of you always to cherish our dear lord: never allow another woman to rob you of his affection. . . . This is what I wanted to say to you, dear Yukiko. . . . Have you been able to understand?"

"Oh, my dear Lady," protested Yukiko, "do not, I entreat you, say such strange things to me! You well know that I am of poor and mean condition—how could I ever dare to aspire to become the wife of our lord!"

"Nay, nay!" returned the wife, huskily—"this is not a time for words of ceremony: let us speak only the truth to each other. After my death, you will certainly be promoted to a higher place; and I now assure you again that I wish you to become the wife of our lord—yes, I wish this, Yukiko, even more than I wish to become a Buddha! . . . Ah, I had almost forgotten!—I want you to do something for me, Yukiko. You know that in the garden there is a *yaë-zakura*,* which was brought here, the year before last, from Mount Yoshino in Yamato. I have been told that it is now in full bloom— and I wanted so much to see it in flower! In a little while I shall be dead—I must see that tree before I die. Now I wish you to carry me into the garden—at once, Yukiko—so that I can see it. . . . Yes, upon your back, Yukiko—take me upon your back. . . ."

---

* *Yaë-zakura, yaë-no-sakura,* a variety of Japanese cherry-tree that bears double-blossoms.

While thus asking, her voice had gradually become clear and strong—as if the intensity of the wish had given her new force: then she suddenly burst into tears. Yukiko knelt motionless, not knowing what to do; but the lord nodded assent.

"It is her last wish in this world," he said. "She always loved cherry-flowers; and I know that she wanted very much to see that Yamato-tree in blossom. Come, my dear Yukiko, let her have her will."

As a nurse turns her back to a child, that the child may cling to it, Yukiko offered her shoulders to the wife, and said:

"Lady, I am ready: please tell me how I best can help you."

"Why, this way!"—responded the dying woman, lifting herself with an almost super-human effort by clinging to Yukiko's shoulders. But as she stood erect, she quickly slipped her thin hands down over the shoulders, under the robe, and clutched the breasts of the girl, and burst into a wicked laugh.

"I have my wish!" she cried—"I have my wish for the cherry-bloom,* but not the cherry-bloom of the garden! . . . I could not die before I got my wish. Now I have it!—oh, what a delight!"

And with these words she fell forward upon the crouching girl, and died.

The attendants at once attempted to lift the body from Yukiko's shoulders, and to lay it upon the bed. But—strange to say!—this seemingly easy thing could not be done. The cold hands had attached themselves in some unaccountable way to the breasts of

---

* In Japanese poetry and proverbial phraseology, the physical beauty of a woman is compared to the cherry-flower; while feminine moral beauty is compared to the plum-flower.

the girl—appeared to have grown into the quick flesh. Yukiko became senseless with fear and pain.

Physicians were called. They could not understand what had taken place. By no ordinary methods could the hands of the dead woman be unfastened from the body of her victim—they so clung that any effort to remove them brought blood. This was not because the fingers held: it was because the flesh of the palms had united itself in some inexplicable manner to the flesh of the breasts!

At that time the most skilful physician in Yedo was a foreigner —a Dutch surgeon. It was decided to summon him. After a careful examination he said that he could not understand the case, and that for the immediate relief of Yukiko there was nothing to be done except to cut the hands from the corpse. He declared that it would be dangerous to attempt to detach them from the breasts. His advice was accepted; and the hands were amputated at the wrists. But they remained clinging to the breasts; and there they soon darkened and dried up—like the hands of a person long dead.

Yet this was only the beginning of the horror.

Withered and bloodless though they seemed, those hands were not dead. At intervals they would stir—stealthily, like great grey spiders. And nightly thereafter—beginning always at the Hour of the Ox,[*] they would clutch and compress and torture. Only at the Hour of the Tiger the pain would cease.

---

[*] In ancient Japanese time, the Hour of the Ox was the special hour of ghosts. It began at 2 A.M., and lasted until 4 A.M.—for the old Japanese hour was double the length of the modern hour. The Hour of the Tiger began at 4 A.M.

Yukiko cut off her hair, and became a mendicant-nun—taking the religious name of Dassetsu. She had an *ihai* (mortuary tablet) made, bearing the *kaimyo* of her dead mistress—*Myo-Ko-In-Den Chizan-Ryo-Fu Daishi*—and this she carried about with her in all her wanderings; and every day before it she humbly besought the dead for pardon, and performed a Buddhist service in order that the jealous spirit might find rest. But the evil karma that had rendered such an affliction possible could not soon be exhausted. Every night at the Hour of the Ox, the hands never failed to torture her, during more than seventeen years—according to the testimony of those persons to whom she last told her story, when she stopped for one evening at the house of Noguchi Dengozayémon, in the village of Tanaka in the district of Kawachi in the province of Shimotsuké. This was in the third year of Kokwa (1846). Thereafter nothing more was ever heard of her.

THE BURIAL OF THE RATS

Bram Stoker

[1847–1912]

"Better known than [Matthew Phipps] Shiel is the ingenious Bram Stoker, who created many starkly horrific conceptions in a series of novels whose poor technique sadly impairs their net effect. *The Lair of the White Worm*, dealing with a gigantic primitive entity that lurks in a vault beneath an ancient castle, utterly ruins a magnificent idea by a development almost infantile. *The Jewel of Seven Stars*, touching on a strange Egyptian resurrection, is less crudely written. But best of all is the famous *Dracula*, which has become almost the standard modern exploitation of the frightful vampire myth."

—*H.P. Lovecraft*

LEAVING PARIS BY THE ORLEANS ROAD, cross the Enceinte, and, turning to the right, you find yourself in a somewhat wild and not at all savoury district. Right and left, before and behind, on every side rise great heaps of dust and waste accumulated by the process of time.

Paris has its night as well as its day life, and the sojourner who enters his hotel in the Rue de Rivoli or the Rue St. Honore late at night or leaves it early in the morning, can guess, in coming near Montrouge—if he has not done so already—the purpose of those great waggons that look like boilers on wheels which he finds halting everywhere as he passes.

Every city has its peculiar institutions created out of its own needs; and one of the most notable institutions of Paris is its rag-picking population. In the early morning—and Parisian life commences at an early hour—may be seen in most streets standing on the pathway opposite every court and alley and between every few houses, as still in some American cities, even in parts of New York, large wooden boxes into which the domestics or tenement-holders empty the accumulated dust of the past day. Round these boxes gather and pass on, when the work is done, to fresh fields of labour and pastures new, squalid, hungry-looking men and women, the implements of whose craft consist of a coarse bag or basket slung over the shoulder and a little rake with which they turn over and probe and examine in the minutest manner the dustbins. They pick up and deposit in their baskets, by aid of their rakes, whatever they may find, with the same facility as a Chinaman uses his chopsticks.

Paris is a city of centralisation—and centralisation and classification are closely allied. In the early times, when centralisation is becoming a fact, its forerunner is classification. All things which are similar or analogous become grouped together, and from the grouping of groups rises one whole or central point. We see radiating many long arms with innumerable tentaculae, and in the centre rises a gigantic head with a comprehensive brain and keen eyes to look on every side and ears sensitive to hear—and a voracious mouth to swallow.

Other cities resemble all the birds and beasts and fishes whose appetites and digestions are normal. Paris alone is the analogical apotheosis of the octopus. Product of centralisation carried to an *ad absurdum,* it fairly represents the devil fish; and in no respects is the resemblance more curious than in the similarity of the digestive apparatus.

Those intelligent tourists who, having surrendered their individuality into the hands of Messrs. Cook or Gaze, "do" Paris in three days, are often puzzled to know how it is that the dinner which in London would cost about six shillings, can be had for three francs in a café in the Palais Royal. They need have no more wonder if they will but consider the classification which is a theoretic speciality of Parisian life, and adopt all round the fact from which the chiffonier has his genesis.

The Paris of 1850 was not like the Paris of to-day, and those who see the Paris of Napoleon and Baron Hausseman can hardly realise the existence of the state of things forty-five years ago.

Amongst other things, however, which have not changed are those districts where the waste is gathered. Dust is dust all the world over, in every age, and the family likeness of dust-heaps is perfect. The traveller, therefore, who visits the environs of Montrouge can go back in fancy without difficulty to the year 1850.

In this year I was making a prolonged stay in Paris. I was very much in love with a young lady who, though she returned my passion, so far yielded to the wishes of her parents that she had promised not to see me or to correspond with me for a year. I, too, had been compelled to accede to these conditions under a vague hope of parental approval. During the term of probation I had promised to remain out of the country and not to write to my dear one until the expiration of the year.

Naturally the time went heavily with me. There was no one of my own family or circle who could tell me of Alice, and none of her own folk had, I am sorry to say, sufficient generosity to send me even an occasional word of comfort regarding her health and well-being. I spent six months wandering about Europe, but as I could find no satisfactory distraction in travel, I determined to come to

Paris, where, at least, I would be within easy hail of London in case any good fortune should call me thither before the appointed time. That "hope deferred maketh the heart sick" was never better exemplified than in my case, for in addition to the perpetual longing to see the face I loved there was always with me a harrowing anxiety lest some accident should prevent me showing Alice in due time that I had, throughout the long period of probation, been faithful to her trust and my own love. Thus, every adventure which I undertook had a fierce pleasure of its own, for it was fraught with possible consequences greater than it would have ordinarily borne.

Like all travellers I exhausted the places of most interest in the first month of my stay, and was driven in the second month to look for amusement whithersoever I might. Having made sundry journeys to the better-known suburbs, I began to see that there was a *terra incognita,* in so far as the guide book was concerned, in the social wilderness lying between these attractive points. Accordingly I began to systematise my researches, and each day took up the thread of my exploration at the place where I had on the previous day dropped it.

In process of time my wanderings led me near Montrouge, and I saw that hereabouts lay the Ultima Thule of social exploration—a country as little known as that round the source of the White Nile. And so I determined to investigate philosophically the chiffonier—his habitat, his life, and his means of life.

The job was an unsavoury one, difficult of accomplishment, and with little hope of adequate reward. However, despite reason, obstinacy prevailed, and I entered into my new investigation with a keener energy than I could have summoned to aid me in any investigation leading to any end, valuable or worthy.

One day, late in a fine afternoon, toward the end of September,

I entered the holy of holies of the city of dust. The place was evidently the recognised abode of a number of chiffoniers, for some sort of arrangement was manifested in the formation of the dust heaps near the road. I passed amongst these heaps, which stood like orderly sentries, determined to penetrate further and trace dust to its ultimate location.

As I passed along I saw behind the dust heaps a few forms that flitted to and fro, evidently watching with interest the advent of any stranger to such a place. The district was like a small Switzerland, and as I went forward my tortuous course shut out the path behind me.

Presently I got into what seemed a small city or community of chiffoniers. There were a number of shanties or huts, such as may be met with in the remote parts of the Bog of Allan—rude places with wattled walls, plastered with mud and roofs of rude thatch made from stable refuse—such places as one would not like to enter for any consideration, and which even in water-colour could only look picturesque if judiciously treated. In the midst of these huts was one of the strangest adaptations—I cannot say habitations—I had ever seen. An immense old wardrobe, the colossal remnant of some boudoir of Charles VII, or Henry II, had been converted into a dwelling-house. The double doors lay open, so that the entire menage was open to public view. In the open half of the wardrobe was a common sitting-room of some four feet by six, in which sat, smoking their pipes round a charcoal brazier, no fewer than six old soldiers of the First Republic, with their uniforms torn and worn threadbare. Evidently they were of the *mauvais sujet* class; their blear eyes and limp jaws told plainly of a common love of absinthe; and their eyes had that haggard, worn look which stamps the drunkard at his worst, and that look of slumbering ferocity which follows hard in the wake of drink. The other side stood as of old, with its shelves intact, save that they were cut to half their depth, and in each shelf of which there were six, was a bed made with rags and straw. The half-dozen of worthies who inhabited this structure looked at me curiously as I passed; and when I looked back after going a little way I saw their heads together in a whispered conference. I did not like the look of this at all, for the place was very lonely, and the men looked very, very villainous. However, I did not see any cause for fear, and went on my way, penetrating further and further into the Sahara. The way was tortuous to a degree, and from going round in a series of semi-circles, as one goes in skating with the Dutch roll, I got rather confused with regard to the points of the compass.

When I had penetrated a little way I saw, as I turned the corner of a half-made heap, sitting on a heap of straw an old soldier with threadbare coat.

"Hallo!" said I to myself; "the First Republic is well represented here in its soldiery."

As I passed him the old man never even looked up at me, but gazed on the ground with stolid persistency. Again I remarked to myself: "See what a life of rude warfare can do! This old man's curiosity is a thing of the past."

When I had gone a few steps, however, I looked back suddenly, and saw that curiosity was not dead, for the veteran had raised his head and was regarding me with a very queer expression. He seemed to me to look very like one of the six worthies in the press. When he saw me looking he dropped his head; and without thinking further of him I went on my way, satisfied that there was a strange likeness between these old warriors.

Presently I met another old soldier in a similar manner. He, too, did not notice me whilst I was passing.

By this time it was getting late in the afternoon, and I began to think of retracing my steps. Accordingly I turned to go back, but could see a number of tracks leading between different mounds and could not ascertain which of them I should take. In my perplexity I wanted to see someone of whom to ask the way, but could see no one. I determined to go on a few mounds further and so try to see someone—not a veteran.

I gained my object, for after going a couple of hundred yards I saw before me a single shanty such as I had seen before—with, however, the difference that this was not one for living in, but merely a roof with three walls open in front. From the evidences which the neighbourhood exhibited I took it to be a place for sorting. Within it was an old woman wrinkled and bent with age; I approached her to ask the way.

She rose as I came close and I asked her my way. She immediately commenced a conversation; and it occurred to me that here in the very centre of the Kingdom of Dust was the place to gather details of the history of Parisian rag-picking—particularly as I could do so from the lips of one who looked like the oldest inhabitant.

I began my inquiries, and the old woman gave me most interesting answers—she had been one of the ceteuces who sat daily before the guillotine and had taken an active part among the women who signalised themselves by their violence in the revolution. While we were talking she said suddenly: "But m'sieur must be tired standing," and dusted a rickety old stool for me to sit down. I hardly liked to do so for many reasons; but the poor old woman was so civil that I did not like to run the risk of hurting her by refusing, and moreover the conversation of one who had been at the taking of the Bastille was so interesting that I sat down and so our conversation went on.

While we were talking an old man—older and more bent and

wrinkled even than the woman—appeared from behind the shanty. "Here is Pierre," said she. "M'sieur can hear stories now if he wishes, for Pierre was in everything, from the Bastille to Waterloo." The old man took another stool at my request and we plunged into a sea of revolutionary reminiscences. This old man, albeit clothed like a scarecrow, was like any one of the six veterans.

I was now sitting in the centre of the low hut with the woman on my left hand and the man on my right, each of them being somewhat in front of me. The place was full of all sorts of curious objects of lumber, and of many things that I wished far away. In one corner was a heap of rags which seemed to move from the number of vermin it contained, and in the other a heap of bones whose odour was something shocking. Every now and then, glancing at the heaps, I could see the gleaming eyes of some of the rats which infested the place. These loathsome objects were bad enough, but what looked even more dreadful was an old butcher's axe with an iron handle stained with clots of blood leaning up against the wall on the right hand side. Still these things did not give me much concern. The talk of the two old people was so fascinating that I stayed on and on, till the evening came and the dust heaps threw dark shadows over the vales between them.

After a time I began to grow uneasy, I could not tell how or why, but somehow I did not feel satisfied. Uneasiness is an instinct and means warning. The psychic faculties are often the sentries of the intellect; and when they sound alarm the reason begins to act, although perhaps not consciously.

This was so with me. I began to bethink me where I was and by what surrounded, and to wonder how I should fare in case I should be attacked; and then the thought suddenly burst upon me, although without any overt cause, that I was in danger. Prudence whispered: "Be still and make no sign," and so I was still and made no sign, for I knew that four cunning eyes were on me. "Four eyes—if not more." My God, what a horrible thought! The whole shanty might be surrounded on three sides with villains! I might be in the midst of a band of such desperadoes as only half a century of periodic revolution can produce.

With a sense of danger my intellect and observation quickened, and I grew more watchful than was my wont. I noticed that the old woman's eyes were constantly wandering toward my hands. I looked at them too, and saw the cause—my rings. On my left little finger I had a large signet and on the right a good diamond.

I thought that if there was any danger my first care was to avert suspicion. Accordingly I began to work the conversation round to rag-picking—to the drains—of the things found there; and so by easy stages to jewels. Then, seizing a favourable opportunity, I asked the old woman if she knew anything of such things. She answered that she did, a little. I held out my right hand, and, showing her the diamond, asked her what she thought of that. She answered that her eyes were bad, and stooped over my hand. I said as nonchalantly as I could: "Pardon me! You will see better thus!" and taking it off handed it to her. An unholy light came into her withered old face, as she touched it. She stole one glance at me swift and keen as a flash of lightning.

She bent over the ring for a moment, her face quite concealed as though examining it. The old man looked straight out of the front of the shanty before him, at the same time fumbling in his pockets and producing a screw of tobacco in a paper and a pipe, which he proceeded to fill. I took advantage of the pause and the momentary rest from the searching eyes on my face to look carefully round the place, now dim and shadowy in the gloaming. There still lay all the heaps of varied reeking foulness; there the terrible blood-stained axe leaning against the wall in the right hand corner, and everywhere, despite the gloom, the baleful glitter of the eyes of the rats. I could see them even through some of the chinks of the boards at the back low down close to the ground. But stay! these latter eyes seemed more than usually large and bright and baleful!

For an instant my heart stood still, and I felt in that whirling condition of mind in which one feels a sort of spiritual drunkenness, and as though the body is only maintained erect in that there is no time for it to fall before recovery. Then, in another second, I was calm—coldly calm, with all my energies in full vigour, with a self-control which I felt to be perfect and with all my feeling and instincts alert.

Now I knew the full extent of my danger: I was watched and surrounded by desperate people! I could not even guess at how many of them were lying there on the ground behind the shanty, waiting for the moment to strike. I knew that I was big and strong, and they knew it, too. They knew also, as I did, that I was an Englishman and would make a fight for it; and so we waited. I had, I felt, gained an advantage in the last few seconds, for I knew my danger and understood the situation. Now, I thought, is the test of my courage—the enduring test: the fighting test may come later!

The old woman raised her head and said to me in a satisfied kind of way:

"A very fine ring, indeed—a beautiful ring! Oh, me! I once had such rings, plenty of them, and bracelets and earrings! Oh! for in those fine days I led the town a dance! But they've forgotten me now! They've forgotten me! They? Why, they never heard of me! Perhaps their grandfathers remember me, some of them!" and she laughed a harsh, croaking laugh. And then I am bound to say that she

astonished me! for she handed me back the ring with a certain suggestion of old-fashioned grace which was not without its pathos.

The old man eyed her with a sort of sudden ferocity, half
rising from his stool, and said to me suddenly and hoarsely:

"Let me see!"

I was about to hand the ring when the old woman said:

"No! no, do not give it to Pierre! Pierre is eccentric. He loses
things; and such a pretty ring!"

"Cat!" said the old man, savagely. Suddenly the old woman
said, rather more loudly than was necessary:

"Wait! I shall tell you something about a ring." There was
something in the sound of her voice that jarred upon me. Perhaps
it was my hyper-sensitiveness, wrought up as I was to such a pitch
of nervous excitement, but I seemed to think that she was not
addressing me. As I stole a glance round the place I saw the eyes
of the rats in the bone heaps, but missed the eyes along the back.
But even as I looked I saw them again appear. The old woman's
"Wait!" had given me a respite from attack, and the men had sunk
back to their reclining posture.

"I once lost a ring—a beautiful diamond hoop that had
belonged to a queen, and which was given to me by a farmer of the
taxes, who afterwards cut his throat because I sent him away. I
thought it must have been stolen, and taxed my people; but I could
get no trace. The police came and suggested that it had found its
way to the drain. We descended—I in my fine clothes, for I would
not trust them with my beautiful ring! I know more of the drains
since then, and of rats, too! but I shall never forget the horror of that
place—alive with blazing eyes, a wall of them just outside the light of
our torches. Well, we got beneath my house. We searched the outlet
of the drain, and there in the filth found my ring, and we came out.

"But we found something else also before we came! As we were coming toward the opening a lot of sewer rats—human ones this time—came toward us. They told the police that one of their number had gone into the drain, but had not returned. He had gone in only shortly before we had, and, if lost, could hardly be far off. They asked help to seek him, so we turned back. They tried to prevent me going, but I insisted. It was a new excitement, and had I not recovered my ring? Not far did we go till we came on something. There was but little water, and the bottom of the drain was raised with brick, rubbish, and much matter of the kind. He had made a fight for it, even when his torch had gone out. But they were too many for him! They had not been long about it! The bones were still warm; but they were picked clean. They had even eaten their own dead ones and there were bones of rats as well as of the man. They took it cool enough those other—the human ones—and joked of their comrade when they found him dead, though they would have helped him living. Bah! what matters it—life or death?"

"And had you no fear?" I asked her.

"Fear!" she said with a laugh. "Me have fear? Ask Pierre! But I was younger then, and, as I came through that horrible drain with its wall of greedy eyes, always moving with the circle of the light from the torches, I did not feel easy. I kept on before the men, though! It is a way I have! I never let the men get it before me. All I want is a chance and a means! And they ate him up—took every trace away except the bones; and no one knew it, nor no sound of him was ever heard!" Here she broke into a chuckling fit of the ghastliest merriment which it was ever my lot to hear and see. A great poetess describes her heroine singing: "Oh! to see or hear her singing! Scarce I know which is the divinest."

And I can apply the same idea to the old crone—in all save the

divinity, for I scarce could tell which was the most hellish—
the harsh, malicious, satisfied, cruel laugh, or the leering grin, and
the horrible square opening of the mouth like a tragic mask, and the
yellow gleam of the few discoloured teeth in the shapeless gums. In
that laugh and with that grin and the chuckling satisfaction I knew
as well as if it had been spoken to me in words of thunder that my
murder was settled, and the murderers only bided the proper time
for its accomplishment. I could read between the lines of her gruesome story the commands to her accomplices. "Wait," she seemed
to say, "bide your time. I shall strike the first blow. Find the weapon
for me, and I shall make the opportunity! He shall not escape! Keep
him quiet, and then no one will be wiser. There will be no outcry,
and the rats will do their work!"

It was growing darker and darker; the night was coming. I
stole a glance round the shanty, still all the same! The bloody axe
in the corner, the heaps of filth, and the eyes on the bone heaps
and in the crannies of the floor.

Pierre had been still ostensibly filling his pipe; he now struck
a light and began to puff away at it. The old woman said:

"Dear heart, how dark it is! Pierre, like a good lad, light
the lamp!"

Pierre got up and with the lighted match in his hand touched
the wick of a lamp which hung at one side of the entrance to the
shanty, and which had a reflector that threw the light all over the
place. It was evidently that which was used for their sorting at night.

"Not that, stupid! Not that! The lantern!" she called out to him.

He immediately blew it out, saying: "All right, mother, I'll
find it," and he hustled about the left corner of the room—the old
woman saying through the darkness:

"The lantern! the lantern! Oh! That is the light that is most

useful to us poor folks. The lantern was the friend of the revolution! It is the friend of the chiffonier! It helps us when all else fails."

Hardly had she said the word when there was a kind of creaking
of the whole place, and something was steadily dragged over the roof.

Again I seemed to read between the lines of her words. I knew
the lesson of the lantern.

"One of you get on the roof with a noose and strangle him as
he passes out if we fail within."

As I looked out of the opening I saw the loop of a rope outlined black against the lurid sky. I was now, indeed, beset!

Pierre was not long in finding the lantern. I kept my eyes
fixed through the darkness on the old woman. Pierre struck his
light, and by its flash I saw the old woman raise from the ground
beside her where it had mysteriously appeared, and then hide in
the folds of her gown, a long sharp knife or dagger. It seemed to
be like a butcher's sharpening iron fined to a keen point.

The lantern was lit.

"Bring it here, Pierre," she said. "Place it in the doorway
where we can see it. See how nice it is! It shuts out the darkness
from us; it is just right!"

Just right for her and her purposes! It threw all its light on my
face, leaving in gloom the faces of both Pierre and the woman,
who sat outside of me on each side.

I felt that the time of action was approaching; but I knew
now that the first signal and movement would come from the
woman, and so watched her.

I was all unarmed, but I had made up my mind what to do.
At the first movement I would seize the butcher's axe in the right-
hand corner and fight my way out. At least, I would die hard. I
stole a glance round to fix its exact locality so that I could not fail

to seize it at the first effort, for then, if ever, time and accuracy would be precious.

Good God! It was gone! All the horror of the situation burst upon me; but the bitterest thought of all was that if the issue of the terrible position should be against me Alice would infallibly suffer. Either she would believe me false—and any lover, or any one who has ever been one, can imagine the bitterness of the thought—or else she would go on loving long after I had been lost to her and to the world, so that her life would be broken and embittered, shattered with disappointment and despair. The very magnitude of the pain braced me up and nerved me to bear the dread scrutiny of the plotters.

I think I did not betray myself. The old woman was watching me as a cat does a mouse; she had her right hand hidden in the folds of her gown, clutching, I knew, that long, cruel-looking dagger. Had she seen any disappointment in my face she would, I felt, have known that the moment had come, and would have sprung on me like a tigress, certain of taking me unprepared.

I looked out into the night, and there I saw new cause for danger. Before and around the hut were at a little distance some shadowy forms; they were quite still, but I knew that they were all alert and on guard. Small chance for me now in that direction.

Again I stole a glance round the place. In moments of great excitement and of great danger, which is excitement, the mind works very quickly, and the keenness of the faculties which depend on the mind grows in proportion. I now felt this. In an instant I took in the whole situation. I saw that the axe had been taken through a small hole made in one of the rotten boards. How rotten they must be to allow of such a thing being done without a particle of noise.

The hut was a regular murder-trap, and was guarded all around. A garroter lay on the roof ready to entangle me with his noose if I should escape the dagger of the old hag. In front the way was guarded by I know not how many watchers. And at the back was a row of desperate men—I had seen their eyes still through the crack in the boards of the floor, when last I looked—as they lay prone waiting for the signal to start erect. If it was to be ever, now for it!

As nonchalantly as I could I turned slightly on my stool so as to get my right leg well under me. Then with a sudden jump, turning my head, and guarding it with my hands, and with the fighting instinct of the knights of old, I breathed my lady's name, and hurled myself against the back wall of the hut.

Watchful as they were, the suddenness of my movement surprised both Pierre and the old woman. As I crashed through the rotten timbers I saw the old woman rise with a leap like a tiger and heard her low gasp of baffled rage. My feet lit on something that moved, and as I jumped away I knew that I had stepped on the back of one of the row of men lying on their faces outside the hut. I was torn with nails and splinters, but otherwise unhurt. Breathless I rushed up the mound in front of me, hearing as I went the dull crash of the shanty as it collapsed into a mass.

It was a nightmare climb. The mound, though but low, was awfully steep, and with each step I took the mass of dust and cinders tore down with me and gave way under my feet. The dust rose and choked me; it was sickening, foetid, awful; but my climb was, I felt, for life or death, and I struggled on. The seconds seemed hours; but the few moments I had in starting, combined with my youth and strength, gave me a great advantage, and, though several forms struggled after me in deadly silence which was more dreadful than any sound, I easily reached the top. Since then I have climbed the cone of Vesuvius, and as I struggled up that dreary steep amid the sulphurous fumes the memory of that awful night at Montrouge came back to me so vividly that I almost grew faint.

The mound was one of the tallest in the region of dust, and as I struggled to the top, panting for breath and with my heart beating like a sledge-hammer, I saw away to my left the dull red gleam of the sky, and nearer still the flashing of lights. Thank God! I knew where I was now and where lay the road to Paris!

For two or three seconds I paused and looked back. My pursuers were still well behind me, but struggling up resolutely, and in deadly silence. Beyond, the shanty was a wreck—a mass of timber and moving forms. I could see it well, for flames were already bursting out; the rags and straw had evidently caught fire from the lantern. Still silence there! Not a sound! These old wretches could die game, anyhow.

I had no time for more than a passing glance, for as I cast an eye round the mound preparatory to making my descent I saw several dark forms rushing round on either side to cut me off on my way. It was now a race for life. They were trying to head me on my way to Paris, and with the instinct of the moment I dashed down to the right-hand side. I was just in time, for, though I came as it seemed to me down the steep in a few steps, the wary old men who were watching me turned back, and one, as I rushed by into the opening between the two mounds in front, almost struck me a blow with that terrible butcher's axe. There could surely not be two such weapons about!

Then began a really horrible chase. I easily ran ahead of the old men, and even when some younger ones and a few women joined in the hunt I easily distanced them. But I did not know the way, and I could not even guide myself by the light in the sky, for I was running away from it. I had heard that, unless of conscious purpose, hunted men turn always to the left, and so I found it now; and so, I suppose, knew also my pursuers, who were more animals than men, and with cunning or instinct had found out such secrets for themselves: for on finishing a quick spurt, after which I intended to take a moment's breathing space, I suddenly saw ahead of me two or three forms swiftly passing behind a mound to the right.

I was in the spider's web now indeed! But with the thought of this new danger came the resource of the hunted, and so I darted down the next turning to the right. I continued in this direction for some hundred yards, and then, making a turn to the left again, felt certain that I had, at any rate, avoided the danger of being surrounded.

But not of pursuit, for on came the rabble after me, steady, dogged, relentless, and still in grim silence.

In the greater darkness the mounds seemed now to be some-what smaller than before, although—for the night was closing—they looked bigger in proportion. I was now well ahead of my pursuers, so I made a dart up the mound in front.

Oh joy of joys! I was close to the edge of this inferno of dustheaps. Away behind me the red light of Paris in the sky, and towering up behind rose the heights of Montmartre—a dim light, with here and there brilliant points like stars.

Restored to vigour in a moment, I ran over the few remaining mounds of decreasing size, and found myself on the level land beyond. Even then, however, the prospect was not inviting. All before me was dark and dismal, and I had evidently come on one of those dank, low-lying waste places which are found here and there in the neighbourhood of great cities. Places of waste and des-olation, where the space is required for the ultimate agglomeration of all that is noxious, and the ground is so poor as to create no desire of occupancy even in the lowest squatter. With eyes accustomed to the gloom of the evening, and away now from the shadows of those dreadful dustheaps, I could see much more easily than I could a little while ago. It might have been, of course, that the glare in the sky of the lights of Paris, though the city was some miles away, was reflected here. Howsoever it was, I saw well enough to take bearings for certainly some little distance around me.

In front was a bleak, flat waste that seemed almost dead level, with here and there the dark shimmering of stagnant pools. Seemingly far off on the right, amid a small cluster of scattered lights, rose a dark mass of Fort Montrouge, and away to the left in the dim distance, pointed with stray gleams from cottage windows, the lights in the sky showed the locality of Bicêtre. A moment's thought decided me to take to the right and try to reach Montrouge. There at least would be some sort of safety, and I might possibly long before come on some of the cross roads which I knew. Somewhere, not far off, must lie the strategic road made to connect the outlying chain of forts circling the city.

Then I looked back. Coming over the mounds, and outlined black against the glare of the Parisian horizon, I saw several moving figures, and still a way to the right several more deploying out between me and my destination. They evidently meant to cut me off in this direction, and so my choice became constricted; it lay now between going straight ahead or turning to the left. Stooping to the ground, so as to get the advantage of the horizon as a line of sight, I looked carefully in this direction, but could detect no sign of my enemies. I argued that as they had not guarded or were not trying to guard that point, there was evidently danger to me there already. So I made up my mind to go straight on before me.

It was not an inviting prospect, and as I went on the reality grew worse. The ground became soft and oozy, and now and again gave way beneath me in a sickening kind of way. I seemed somehow to be going down, for I saw round me places seemingly more elevated than where I was, and this in a place which from a little way back seemed dead level. I looked around, but could see none of my pursuers. This was strange, for all along these birds of the night had followed me through the darkness as well as though it was broad daylight. How I blamed myself for coming out in my light-coloured tourist suit of tweed. The silence, and my not being able to see my enemies, whilst I felt that they were watching me, grew appalling, and in the hope of some one not of this ghastly crew hearing me I raised my voice and shouted several times. There was not the slightest response; not even an echo rewarded my efforts. For a while I stood stock still and kept my eyes in one direction. On one of the rising places around me I saw something dark move along, then another, and another. This was to my left, and seemingly moving to head me off.

I thought that again I might with my skill as a runner elude my enemies at this game, and so with all my speed darted forward.

Splash!

My feet had given way in a mass of slimy rubbish, and I had fallen headlong into a reeking, stagnant pool. The water and the mud in which my arms sank up to the elbows was filthy and nauseous beyond description, and in the suddenness of my fall I had actually swallowed some of the filthy stuff, which nearly choked me, and made me gasp for breath. Never shall I forget the moments during which I stood trying to recover myself almost fainting from the foetid odour of the filthy pool, whose white mist rose ghostlike around. Worst of all, with the acute despair of the hunted animal when he sees the pursuing pack closing on him, I saw before my eyes whilst I stood helpless the dark forms of my pursuers moving swiftly to surround me.

It is curious how our minds work on odd matters even when the energies of thought are seemingly concentrated on some terrible and pressing need. I was in momentary peril of my life: my safety depended on my action, and my choice of alternatives coming now with almost every step I took, and yet I could not but think of the strange dogged persistency of these old men. Their silent resolution, their steadfast, grim persistency even in such a cause commanded, as well as fear, even a measure of respect. What must they have been in the vigour of their youth. I could understand now that whirlwind rush on the bridge of Arcola, that scornful exclamation of the Old Guard at Waterloo! Unconscious cerebration has its own pleasures, even at such moments; but fortunately it does not in any way clash with the thought from which action springs.

I realised at a glance that so far I was defeated in my object, my enemies as yet had won. They had succeeded in surrounding me on three sides, and were bent on driving me off to the left-hand, where there was already some danger for me, for they had left no guard. I accepted the alternative—it was a case of Hobson's choice and run. I had to keep the lower ground, for my pursuers were on the higher places. However, though the ooze and broken ground impeded me my youth and training made me able to hold my ground, and by keeping a diagonal line I not only kept them from gaining on me but even began to distance them. This gave me new heart and strength, and by this time habitual training was beginning to tell and my second wind had come. Before me the ground rose slightly. I rushed up the slope and found before me a waste of watery slime, with a low dyke or bank looking black and grim beyond. I felt that if I could but reach that dyke in safety I could there, with solid ground under my feet and some kind of path to guide me, find with comparative ease a way out of my troubles. After a glance right and left and seeing no one near, I kept my eyes for a few minutes to their rightful work of aiding my feet whilst I crossed the swamp. It was rough, hard work, but there was little danger, merely toil; and a short time took me to the dyke. I rushed up the slope exciting; but here again I met a new shock. On either side of me rose a number of crouching figures. From right and left they rushed at me. Each body held a rope.

The cordon was nearly complete. I could pass on neither side, and the end was near.

There was only one chance, and I took it. I hurled myself across the dyke, and escaping out of the very clutches of my foes threw myself into the stream.

At any other time I should have thought that water foul and filthy, but now it was as welcome as the most crystal stream to the parched traveller. It was a highway of safety!

My pursuers rushed after me. Had only one of them held the rope it would have been all up with me, for he could have entangled me before I had time to swim a stroke; but the many hands holding it embarrassed and delayed them, and when the rope struck the water I heard the splash well behind me. A few minutes' hard swimming took me across the stream. Refreshed with the immersion and encouraged by the escape, I climbed the dyke in comparative gaiety of spirits.

From the top I looked back. Through the darkness I saw my assailants scattering up and down along the dyke. The pursuit was evidently not ended, and again I had to choose my course. Beyond the dyke where I stood was a wild, swampy space very similar to that which I had crossed. I determined to shun such a place, and thought for a moment whether I would take up or down the dyke. I thought I heard a sound—the muffled sound of oars, so I listened, and then shouted.

No response; but the sound ceased. My enemies had evidently got a boat of some kind. As they were on the up side of me I took the down path and began to run. As I passed to the left of where I had entered the water I heard several splashes, soft and stealthy, like the sound a rat makes as he plunges into the stream, but vastly greater; and as I looked I saw the dark sheen of the water broken by the ripples of several advancing heads. Some of my enemies were swimming the stream also.

And now behind me, up the stream, the silence was broken by the quick rattle and creak of oars; my enemies were in hot pursuit. I put my best leg foremost and ran on. After a break of a couple of minutes I looked back, and by a gleam of light through the ragged clouds I saw several dark forms climbing the bank behind me. The wind had now begun to rise, and the water beside me was ruffled and beginning to break in tiny waves on the bank. I had to keep my eyes pretty well on the ground before me, lest I should stumble, for I knew that to stumble was death. After a few minutes I looked back behind me. On the dyke were only a few dark figures, but crossing the waste, swampy ground were many more. What new danger this portended I did not know—could only guess. Then as I ran it seemed to me that my track kept ever sloping away to the right. I looked up ahead and saw that the river was much wider than before, and that the dyke on which I stood fell quite away, and beyond it was another stream on whose near bank I saw some of the dark forms now across the marsh. I was on an island of some kind.

My situation was now indeed terrible, for my enemies had hemmed me in on every side. Behind came the quickening roll of the oars, as though my pursuers knew that the end was close.

Around me on every side was desolation; there was not a roof or light, as far as I could see. Far off to the right rose some dark mass, but what it was I knew not. For a moment I paused to think what I should do, not for more, for my pursuers were drawing closer. Then my mind was made up. I slipped down the bank and took to the water. I struck out straight ahead, so as to gain the current by clearing the backwater of the island for such I presume it was, when I had passed into the stream. I waited till a cloud came driving across the moon and leaving all in darkness. Then I took off my hat and laid it softly on the water floating with the stream, and a second after dived to the right and struck out under water with all my might. I was, I suppose half a minute under water, and when I rose came up as softly as I could, and turning, looked back. There went my light brown hat floating merrily away. Close behind it came a rickety old boat, driven furiously by a pair of oars. The moon was still partly obscured by the drifting clouds, but in the partial light I could see a man in the bows holding aloft ready to strike what appeared to me to be that same dreadful pole-axe which I had before escaped. As I looked the boat drew closer, closer, and the man struck savagely. The hat disappeared. The man fell forward, almost out of the boat. His comrades dragged him in but without the axe, and then as I turned with all my energies bent on reaching the further bank, I heard the fierce whirr of the muttered "Sacre!" which marked the anger of my baffled pursuers.

That was the first sound I had heard from human lips during all this dreadful chase, and full as it was of menace and danger to me it was a welcome sound for it broke that awful silence which shrouded and appalled me. It was as though an overt sign that my opponents were men and not ghosts, and that with them I had, at least, the chance of a man, though but one against many.

But now that the spell of silence was broken the sounds came thick and fast. From boat to shore and back from shore to boat came quick question and answer, all in the fiercest whispers. I looked back—a fatal thing to do—for in the instant someone caught sight of my face, which showed white on the dark water, and shouted. Hands pointed to me, and in a moment or two the boat was under weigh, and following hard after me. I had but a little way to go, but quicker and quicker came the boat after me. A few more strokes and I would be on the shore, but I felt the oncoming of the boat, and expected each second to feel the crash of an oar or other weapon on my head. Had I not seen that dreadful axe disappear in the water I do not think that I could have won the shore. I heard the muttered curses of those not rowing and the laboured breath of the rowers. With one supreme effort for life or liberty I touched the bank and sprang up it. There was not a single second to spare, for hard behind me the boat grounded and several dark forms sprang after me. I gained the top of the dyke, and keeping to the left ran on again. The boat put off and followed down the stream. Seeing this I feared danger in this direction, and quickly turning, ran down the dyke on the other side, and after passing a short stretch of marshy ground gained a wild, open flat country and sped on.

Still behind me came on my relentless pursuers. Far away, below me, I saw the same dark mass as before, but now grown closer and greater. My heart gave a great thrill of delight, for I knew that it must be the fortress of Bicêtre, and with new courage I ran on. I had heard that between each and all of the protecting forts of Paris there are strategic ways, deep sunk roads, where soldiers marching should be sheltered from an enemy. I knew that if I could gain this road I would be safe, but in the darkness I could not see any sign of it, so, in blind hope of striking it, I ran on.

Presently I came to the edge of a deep cut, and found that down below me ran a road guarded on each side by a ditch of water fenced on either side by a straight, high wall.

Getting fainter and dizzier, I ran on; the ground got more broken—more and more still, till I staggered and fell, and rose again, and ran on in the blind anguish of the hunted. Again the thought of Alice nerved me. I would not be lost and wreck her life: I would fight and struggle for life to the bitter end. With a great effort I caught the top of the wall. As, scrambling like a catamount, I drew myself up, I actually felt a hand touch the sole of my foot. I was now on a sort of causeway, and before me I saw a dim light. Blind and dizzy, I ran on, staggered, and fell, rising, covered with dust and blood.

"Halt la!"

The words sounded like a voice from heaven. A blaze of light seemed to enwrap me, and I shouted with joy.

"Qui va la?" The rattle of musketry, the flash of steel before my eyes. Instinctively I stopped, though close behind me came a rush of my pursuers.

Another word or two, and out from a gateway poured, as it seemed to me, a tide of red and blue, as the guard turned out. All around seemed blazing with light, and the flash of steel, the clink and rattle of arms, and the loud, harsh voices of command. As I fell forward, utterly exhausted, a soldier caught me. I looked back in dreadful expectation, and saw the mass of dark forms disappearing into the night. Then I must have fainted. When I recovered my senses I was in the guard room. They gave me brandy, and after a while I was able to tell them something of what had passed. Then a commissary of police appeared, apparently out of the empty air, as is the way of the Parisian police officer. He listened attentively, and then had a moment's consultation with the officer in command.

Apparently they were agreed, for they asked me if I were ready now to come with them.

"Where to?" I asked, rising to go.

"Back to the dust heaps. We shall, perhaps, catch them yet!"

"I shall try!" said I.

He eyed me for a moment keenly, and said suddenly:

"Would you like to wait a while or till tomorrow, young Englishman?" This touched me to the quick, as, perhaps, he intended, and I jumped to my feet.

"Come now!" I said; "now! now! An Englishman is always ready for his duty!"

The commissary was a good fellow, as well as a shrewd one; he slapped my shoulder kindly. "Brave garçon!" he said. "Forgive me, but I knew what would do you most good. The guard is ready. Come!"

And so, passing right through the guard room, and through a long vaulted passage, we were out into the night. A few of the men in front had powerful lanterns. Through courtyards and down a sloping way we passed out through a low archway to a sunken road, the same that I had seen in my flight. The order was given to get at the double, and with a quick, springing stride, half run, half walk, the soldiers went swiftly along. I felt my strength renewed again—such is the difference between hunter and hunted. A very short distance took us to a low-lying pontoon bridge across the stream, and evidently very little higher up than I had struck it. Some effort had evidently been made to damage it, for the ropes had all been cut, and one of the chains had been broken. I heard the officer say to the commissary:

"We are just in time! A few more minutes, and they would have destroyed the bridge. Forward, quicker still!" and on we went. Again we reached a pontoon on the winding stream; as we came up we heard the hollow boom of the metal drums as the efforts to destroy the bridge were again renewed. A word of command was given, and several men raised their rifles.

"Fire!" A volley rang out. There was a muffled cry, and the dark forms dispersed. But the evil was done, and we saw the far end of the pontoon swing into the stream. This was a serious delay, and it was nearly an hour before we had renewed ropes and restored the bridge sufficiently to allow us to cross.

We renewed the chase. Quicker, quicker we went towards the dust heaps.

After a time we came to a place that I knew. There were the remains of a fire—a few smouldering wood ashes still cast a red glow, but the bulk of the ashes were cold. I knew the site of the hut and the hill behind it up which I had rushed, and in the flickering glow the eyes of the rats still shone with a sort of phosphorescence. The commissary spoke a word to the officer, and he cried:

"Halt!"

The soldiers were ordered to spread around and watch, and then we commenced to examine the ruins. The commissary himself began to lift away the charred boards and rubbish. These the soldiers took and piled together. Presently he started back, then bent down and rising beckoned me.

"See!" he said.

It was a gruesome sight. There lay a skeleton face downwards, a woman by the lines—an old woman by the coarse fibre of the bone. Between the ribs rose a long spike-like dagger made from a butcher's sharpening knife, its keen point buried in the spine.

"You will observe," said the commissary to the officer and to me as he took out his note book, "that the woman must have fallen on her dagger. The rats are many here—see their eyes

glistening among that heap of bones—and you will also notice"—
I shuddered as he placed his hand on the skeleton—"that but little
time was lost by them, for the bones are scarcely cold!"

There was no other sign of any one near, living or dead; and
so deploying again into line the soldiers passed on. Presently we
came to the hut made of the old wardrobe. We approached. In
five of the six compartments was an old man sleeping—sleeping
so soundly that even the glare of the lanterns did not wake them.
Old and grim and grizzled they looked, with their gaunt, wrinkled, bronzed faces and their white moustaches.

The officer called out harshly and loudly a word of command, and in an instant each one of them was on his feet before
us and standing at "attention!"

"What do you here?"

"We sleep," was the answer.

"Where are the other chiffoniers?" asked the commissary.

"Gone to work."

"And you?"

"We are on guard!"

"Peste!" laughed the officer grimly, as he looked at the old
men one after the other in the face and added with cool deliberate
cruelty, "Asleep on duty! Is this the manner of the Old Guard? No
wonder, then, a Waterloo!"

By the gleam of the lantern I saw the grim old faces grow
deadly pale, and almost shuddered at the look in the eyes of the
old men as the laugh of the soldiers echoed the grim pleasantry of
the officer.

I felt in that moment that I was in some measure avenged.

For a moment they looked as if they would throw themselves
on the taunter, but years of their life had schooled them and they
remained still.

"You are but five," said the commissary; "where is the sixth?" The answer came with a grim chuckle.

"He is there!" and the speaker pointed to the bottom of the wardrobe. "He died last night. You won't find much of him. The burial of the rats is quick!"

The commissary stooped and looked in. Then he turned to the officer and said calmly:

"We may as well go back. No trace here now; nothing to prove that man was the one wounded by your soldiers' bullets! Probably they murdered him to cover up the trace. See!" again he stooped and placed his hands on the skeleton. "The rats work quickly and they are many. These bones are warm!"

I shuddered, and so did many more of those around me.

"Form!" said the officer, and so in marching order, with the lanterns swinging in front and the manacled veterans in the midst, with steady tramp we took ourselves out of the dust-heaps and turned backward to the fortress of Bicêtre.

My year of probation has long since ended, and Alice is my wife. But when I look back upon that trying twelvemonth one of the most vivid incidents that memory recalls is that associated with my visit to the City of Dust.

THE RED LODGE

H.R. Wakefield

[1888–1964]

"H.R. Wakefield, in his collections, *They Return at Evening* and *Others Who Return*, manages now and then to achieve heights of horror despite a vitiating air of sophistication. The most notable stories are *The Red Lodge* with its slimy acqueous evil, *He Cometh and He Passeth By, And He Shall Sing, The Cairn, Look Up There, Blind Man's Buff,* and that bit of lurking millennial horror, *The Seventeenth Hole at Doncaster.*"

—*H.P. Lovecraft*

I AM WRITING THIS FROM an imperative sense of duty, for I consider The Red Lodge is a foul death-trap and utterly unfit to be a human habitation—it has its own proper denizens—and because I know its owner to be an unspeakable blackguard to allow it so to be used for his financial advantage. He knows the perils of the place perfectly well; I wrote him of our experiences, and he didn't even acknowledge the letter, and two days ago I saw the ghastly pest-house advertised in *Country Life*. So anyone who rents The Red Lodge in future will receive a copy of this document as well as some uncomfortable words from Sir William, and that scoundrel Wilkes can take what action he pleases.

I certainly didn't carry any prejudice against the place down to it with me: I had been too busy to look over it myself, but my wife reported extremely favourably—I take her word for most things—and I could tell by the photographs that it was a magnificent specimen of the medium-sized Queen Anne house, just the ideal thing for me. Mary said the garden was perfect, and there was the river for Tim at the bottom of it. I had been longing for a holiday, and was in the highest spirits as I travelled down. I was not in the highest spirits for long.

My first vague, faint uncertainty came to me so soon as I had crossed the threshold. I am a painter by profession, and therefore sharply responsive to colour tone. Well, it was a brilliantly fine day, the hall of the Red Lodge was fully lighted, yet it seemed a shade off the key, as it were, as though I were regarding it through a pair of slightly darkened glasses. Only a painter would have noticed it, I fancy.

When Mary came out to greet me, she was not looking as well as I had hoped, or as well as a week in the country should have made her look.

"Everything all right?" I asked.

"Oh, yes," she replied, but I thought she found it difficult to say so, and then my eye detected a curious little spot of green on the maroon rug in front of the fireplace. I picked it up—it seemed like a patch of river slime.

"I suppose Tim brings those in," said Mary. "I've found several; of course, he promises he doesn't." And then for a moment we were silent, and a very unusual sense of constraint seemed to set a barrier between us. I went out into the garden to smoke a cigarette before lunch, and sat myself down under a very fine mulberry tree.

I wondered if, after all, I had been wise to have left it all to

Mary. There was nothing wrong with the house, of course, but I am a bit psychic, and I always know the mood or character of a house. One welcomes you with the tail-writhing enthusiasm of a really nice dog, makes you at home, and at your ease at once. Others are sullen, watchful, hostile, with things to hide. They make you feel that you have obtruded yourself into some curious affairs which are none of your business. I had never encountered so hostile, aloof, and secretive a living place as The Red Lodge seemed when I first entered it. Well, it couldn't be helped, though it was disappointing; and there was Tim coming back from his walk, and the luncheon gong. My son seemed a little subdued and thoughtful, though he looked pretty well, and soon we were all chattering away with those quick changes of key which occur when the respective ages of the conversationalists are forty, thirty-three and six and one-half, and after half a bottle of Meursault and a glass of port I began to think I had been a morbid ass. I was still so thinking when I began my holiday in the best possible way by going to sleep in an exquisitely comfortable chair under the mulberry tree. But I have slept better. I dozed off, but I had a silly impression of being watched, so that I kept waking up in case there might be someone with his eye on me. I was lying back, and could just see a window on the second floor framed by a gap in the leaves, and on one occasion, when I woke rather sharply from one of these dozes, I thought I saw for a moment a face peering down at me, and this face seemed curiously flattened against the pane—just a "carry over" from a dream, I concluded. However, I didn't feel like sleeping any more, and began to explore the garden. It was completely walled in, I found, except at the far end, where there was a door leading through to a path which, running parallel to the right-hand wall, led to the river a few yards away. I noticed on this door several of those patches of green slime for which Tim was supposedly responsible. It was a dark little corner cut off from the rest of the garden by two rowan trees, a cool, silent little place I thought it. And then it was time for Tim's cricket lesson, which was interrupted by the arrival of some infernal callers. But they were pleasant people, as a matter of fact, the Local Knuts, I gathered, who owned the Manor House; Sir William Prowse and his lady and his daughter. I went for a walk with him after tea.

"Who had this house before us?" I asked.

"People called Hawker," he replied. "That was two years ago."

"I wonder the owner doesn't live in it," I said. "It isn't an expensive place to keep up."

Sir William paused as if considering his reply.

"I think he dislikes being so near the river. I'm not sorry, for I detest the fellow. By the way, how long have you taken it for?"

"Three months," I replied, "till the end of October."

"Weill, if I can do anything for you I shall be delighted. If you are in any trouble, come straight to me." He slightly emphasised the last sentence.

I rather wondered what sort of trouble Sir William envisaged for me. Probably he shared the general opinion that artists were quite mad at times, and that when I had one of my lapses I should destroy the peace in some manner. However, I was duly grateful.

I was sorry to find Tim didn't seem to like the river; he appeared nervous of it, and I determined to help him to overcome this, for the fewer terrors one carries through life with one the better, and they can often be laid by delicate treatment in child-hood. Curiously enough the year before at Frinton he seemed to have no fear of the sea.

The rest of the day passed uneventfully—at least I think I can say so. After dinner I strolled down to the end of the garden, meaning to go through the door and have a look at the river. Just as I got my hand on the latch there came a very sharp, furtive whistle. I turned round quickly, but seeing no one, concluded it had come from someone in the lane outside. However, I didn't investigate further, but went back to the house.

I woke up the next morning feeling a shade depressed. My dressing-room smelled stale and bitter, and I flung its windows open. As I did so I felt my right foot slip on something. It was one of those small, slimy, green patches. Now Tim would never come into my dressing-room. An annoying little puzzle. How on earth had that patch—? Which question kept forcing its way into my mind as I dressed. How could a patch of green slime . . . ? How could a patch of green slime . . . ? Dropped from something? From what? I am very fond of my wife—she slaved for me when I was poor, and always has kept me happy, comfortable and faithful, and she gave me my small son Timothy. I must stand between her and patches of green slime! What in hell's name was I talking about? And it was a flamingly fine day. Yet all during breakfast my mind was trying to find some sufficient reason for these funny little patches of green slime, and not finding it.

After breakfast I told Tim I would take him out in a boat on the river.

"Must I, Daddy?" he asked, looking anxiously at me.

"No, of course not," I replied, a trifle irritably, "but I believe you'll enjoy it."

"Should I be a funk if I didn't come?"

"No, Tim, but I think you should try it once, anyway."

"All right," he said.

He's a plucky little chap, and did his very best to pretend to be enjoying himself, but I saw it was a failure from the start.

Perplexed and upset, I asked his nurse if she knew of any reason for this sudden fear of water.

"No, sir," she said. "The first day he ran down to the river just as he used to run down to the sea, but all of a sudden he started crying and ran back to the house. It seemed to me he'd seen something in the water which frightened him."

We spent the afternoon motoring round the neighborhood, and already I found a faint distaste at the idea of returning to the house, and again I had the impression that we were intruding, and that something had been going on during our absence which our return had interrupted.

Mary, pleading a headache, went to bed soon after dinner, and I went to the study to read.

Directly I had shut the door I had again that very unpleasant sensation of being watched. It made the reading of Sidgwick's *The Use of Words in Reasoning*—an old favourite of mine, which requires concentration—a difficult business. Time after time I found myself peeping into dark corners and shifting my position. And there were little sharp sounds; just the oak-panelling cracking, I supposed. After a time I became more absorbed in the book, and less fidgety, and then I heard a very soft cough just behind me. I felt little icy rays pour down and through me, but I would *not* look round, and I *would* go on reading. I had just reached the following passage: "However many things may be said about Socrates, or about any fact observed, there remains still more that might be said if the need arose; the need is the determining factor. Hence the distinction between complete and incomplete description, though perfectly sharp and clear in the abstract, can only have a meaning—can only be applied to actual cases—if it be taken as equivalent to *sufficient* description, the sufficiency being relative to some purpose. Evidently the description of Socrates as a man, scanty though it is, may be fully sufficient for the purpose of the modest enquiry whether he is *mortal* or not"—when my eye was caught by a green patch which suddenly appeared on the floor beside me, and then another and another, following a straight line towards the door. I picked up the nearest one, and it was a bit of soaking slime. I called on all my will power, for I feared something worse to come, and it should *not* materialise—and then no more patches appeared. I got up and walked deliberately, slowly, to the door, turned on the light in the middle of the room, and then came back and turned out the reading lamp and went to my dressing-room. I sat down and thought things over. There was something very wrong with this house. I had passed the stage of pretending otherwise, and my inclination was to take my family away from it the next day. But that meant sacrificing one hundred and sixty-eight pounds, and we had nowhere else to go. It was conceivable that these phenomena were perceptible only to me, being half a Highlander. I might be able to stick it out if I were careful and kept my tail up, for apparitions of this sort are partially subjective—one brings something of oneself to their materialisation. That is a hard saying, but I believe it to be true. If Mary and Tim and the servants were immune it was up to me to face and fight this nastiness. As I undressed, I came to the decision that I would decide nothing then and there, and that I would see what happened. I made this decision against my better judgment, I think.

In bed I tried to thrust all this away from me by a conscious effort to "change the subject," as it were. The easiest subject for me to switch over to is the myriad-sided, useless, consistently abused business of creating things, stories out of pens and ink and paper, representations of things and moods out of paint, brushes and canvas, and our own miseries, perhaps, out of wine, women and song. With a considerable effort, therefore, and with the edges of my brain anxious to be busy with bits of green slime, I recalled an article I had read that day on a glorious word "Jugend-bewegung," the "Youth Movement," that pregnant or merely wind-swollen Teutonism! How ponderously it attempted to canonise with its polysyllabic sonority that inverted Boy-Scoutishness of the said youths and maidens. "One bad, mad deed—sonnet—scribble of some kind—lousy daub—a day." Bunk without spunk, sauce without force, Futurism without a past, merely a *Transition* from one yelping pose to another. And then I suddenly found myself at the end of the garden, attempting desperately to hide myself behind a rowan tree, while my eyes were held relentlessly to face the door. And then it began slowly to open, and something which was horridly unlike anything I had seen before began passing through it, and *I* knew It knew I was there, and then my head seemed to burst and flamed asunder, splintered and destroyed, and I awoke trembling to reel that something in the darkness was poised an inch or two above me, and then drip, drip, drip, something began falling on my face. Mary was in the bed next to mine, and I *would not* scream, but flung the clothes over my head, my eyes streaming with the tears of terror. And so I remained cowering till I heard the clock strike five, and dawn, the ally I longed for, came, and the birds began to sing, and then I slept.

I awoke a wreck, and after breakfast, feeling the need to be alone, I pretended I wanted to sketch, and went out into the

garden. Suddenly I recalled Sir William's remark about coming to see him if there was any trouble. Not much difficulty in guessing what he had meant. I'd go and see him about it at once. I wished I knew whether Mary was troubled too. I hesitated to ask her, for, if she were not, she was certain to become suspicious and uneasy if I questioned her. And then I discovered that, while my brain had been busy with its thoughts my hand had also not been idle, but had been occupied in drawing a very singular design on the sketching block. I watched it as it went automatically on. Was it a design or a figure of some sort? When had I seen something like it before? My God, in my dream last night! I tore it to pieces, and got up in agitation and made my way to the Manor House along a path through tall, bowing, stippled grasses hissing lightly in the breeze. My inclination was to run to the station and take the next train to anywhere; pure undiluted panic—an insufficiently analysed word—that which causes men to trample on women and children when Death is making his choice. Of course, I had Mary and Tim and the servants to keep me from it, but supposing they had no claim on me, should I desert them? No, I should not. Why? Such things aren't done by respectable inhabitants of Great Britain—a people despised and respected by all other tribes. Despised as Philistines, but it took the jaw-bone of an ass to subdue that hardy race! Respected for what? Birkenhead stuff. No, not the noble Lord, for there were no glittering prizes for those who went down to the bottom of the sea in ships. My mind delib- erately restricting itself to such highly debatable jingoism, I reached the Manor House, to be told that Sir William was up in London for the day, but would return that evening. Would he ring me up on his return? "Yes, sir." And then, with lagging steps, back to The Red Lodge.

I took Mary for a drive in the car after lunch. Anything to get out of the beastly place. Tim didn't come, as he preferred to play in the garden. In the light of what happened I suppose I shall be criticised for leaving Tim alone with a nurse, but at that time I held the theory that these appearances were in no way malignant, and that it was more than possible that even if Tim did see anything he wouldn't be frightened, not realising it was out of the ordinary in any way. After all, nothing that I had seen or heard, at any rate during the daytime, would strike him as unusual.

Mary was very silent, and I was beginning to feel sure, from a certain depression and oppression in her manner and appearance, that my trouble was hers. It was on the tip of my tongue to say something, but I resolved to wait until I had heard what Sir William had to say. It was a dark, sombre, and brooding afternoon, and my spirits fell as we turned for home. What a home!

We got back at six, and I had just stopped the engine and helped Mary out when I heard a scream from the garden. I rushed round, to see Tim, his hands to his eyes, staggering across the lawn, the nurse running behind him. And then he screamed again and fell. I carried him into the house and laid him down on a sofa in the drawing-room, and Mary went to him. I took the nurse by the arm and out of the room; she was panting and crying down a face of chalk.

"What happened? What happened?" I asked.

"I don't know what it was, sir, but we had been walking in the lane, and had left the door open. Master Tim was a bit ahead of me, and went through the door first, and then he screamed like that."

"Did you see anything that could have frightened him?"

"No, sir, nothing."

I went back to them. It was no good questioning Tim, and there was nothing coherent to be learnt from his hysterical sobbing. He grew calmer presently, and was taken up to bed. Suddenly he turned to Mary, and looked at her with eyes of terror.

"The green monkey won't get me, will it, Mummy?"

"No, no, it's all right now," said Mary, and soon after he went to sleep, and then she and I went down to the drawing-room. She was on the border of hysteria herself.

"Oh, Tom, what is the matter with this awful house? I'm *terrified*. Ever since I've been here I've been terrified. Do you see things?"

"Yes," I replied.

"Oh, I wish I'd known. I didn't want to worry you if you hadn't. Let me tell you what it's been like. On the day we arrived I saw a man pass ahead of me into my bedroom. Of course, I only *thought* I had. And then I've heard beastly whisperings, and every time I pass that turn in the corridor I *know* there's someone just round the corner. And then the day before you arrived I woke suddenly, and something seemed to force me to go to the window, and I crawled there on hands and knees and peeped through the blind. It was just light enough to see. And suddenly I saw someone running down the lawn, his or her hands outstretched, and there was something ghastly just beside him, and they disappeared behind the trees at the end. I'm terrified every minute."

"What about the servants?"

"Nurse hasn't seen anything, but the others have, I'm certain. And then there are those slimy patches, I think they're the vilest of all. I don't think Tim has been troubled till now, but I'm sure he's been puzzled and uncertain several times."

"Well," I said, "it's pretty obvious we must clear out. I'm seeing Sir William about it to-morrow, I hope, and I'm certain enough of what he'll advise. Meanwhile we must think over where to go. It is a nasty jar, though; I don't mean merely the money, though that's bad enough, but the fuss—just when I hoped we were going to be so happy and settled. However, it's got to be done. We should be mad after a week of this filth-drenched hole."

Just then the telephone bell rang. It was a message to say Sir William would be pleased to see me at half past ten to-morrow.

With the dusk came that sense of being watched, waited for, followed about, plotted against, an atmosphere of quiet, hunting malignancy. A thick mist came up from the river, and as I was changing for dinner I noticed the lights from the windows seemed to project a series of swiftly changing pictures on its grey, crawling screen. The one opposite my window, for example, was unpleasantly suggestive of three figures staring in and seeming to grow nearer and larger. The effect must have been slightly hypnotic, for suddenly I started back, for it was as if they were about to close on me. I pulled down the blind and hurried downstairs. During dinner we decided that unless Sir William had something very reassuring to say we would go back to London two days later and stay at a hotel till we could find somewhere to spend the next six weeks. Just before going to bed we went up to the night nursery to see if Tim was all right. This room was at the top of a short flight of stairs. As these stairs were covered with green slime, and there was a pool of the muck just outside the door, we took him down to sleep with us.

The Permanent Occupants of The Red Lodge waited till the light was out, but then I felt them come thronging, slipping in one by one, their weapon, fear. It seemed to me they were massed for the attack. A yard away my wife was lying with my son in her arms, so I must fight. I lay back, gripped the sides of the bed and strove with all my might to hold my assailants back. As the hours went by I felt myself beginning to get the upper hand, and a sense of exaltation came to me. But an hour before dawn they made their greatest effort. I knew that they were willing me to creep on my hands and knees to the window and peep through the blind, and that if I did so we were doomed. As I set my teeth and tightened my grip till I felt racked with agony, the sweat poured from me. I felt them come crowding round the bed and thrusting their faces into mine; and a voice in my head kept saying insistently, "You must crawl to the window and look through the blind." In my mind's eye I could see myself crawling stealthily across the floor and pulling the blind aside, but who would be staring back at me? Just when I felt my resistance breaking I heard a sweet, sleepy twitter from a tree outside, and saw the blind touched by a faint suggestion of light, and at once those with whom I had been struggling left me and went their way, and, utterly exhausted, I slept.

In the morning I found, somewhat ironically, that Mary had slept better than on any night since she came down.

Half past ten found me entering the Manor House, a delightful nondescript old place, which started wagging its tail as soon as I entered it. Sir William was awaiting me in the library. "I expected this would happen," he said gravely, "and now tell me."

I gave him a short outline of our experiences.

"Yes," he said, "it's always much the same story. Every time that horrible place has been let I have felt a sense of personal responsibility, and yet I cannot give a proper warning, for the letting of haunted houses is not yet a criminal offense—though it ought to be—and I couldn't afford a libel action, and, as a matter of fact, one old couple had the house for fifteen years and were perfectly delighted with it, being troubled in no way. But now let me tell you what I know of The Red Lodge. I have studied it for forty years, and I regard it as my personal enemy.

"The local tradition is that the second owner, early in the eighteenth century, wished to get rid of his wife, and bribed his servants to frighten her to death—just the sort of ancestor I can imagine that blackguard Wilkes being descended from.

"What devilries they perpetrated I don't know, but she is supposed to have rushed from the house just before dawn one day and drowned herself. Whereupon her husband installed a small harem in the house; but it was a failure, for each of these charmers one by one rushed down to the river just before dawn, and finally the husband himself did the same. Of the period between then and forty years ago I have no record, but the local tradition has it that it was the scene of tragedy after tragedy, and then was shut up for a long time. When I first began to study it, it was occupied by two bachelor brothers. One shot himself in the room which I imagine you use as your bedroom, and the other drowned himself in the usual way. I may tell you that the worst room in the house, the one the unfortunate lady is supposed to have occupied, is locked up, you know, the one on the second floor. I imagine Wilkes mentioned it to you."

"Yes, he did," I replied. "Said he kept important papers there."

"Yes; well, he was forced in self-defence to do so ten years ago, and since then the death rate has been lower, but in those forty years twenty people have taken their lives in the house or in the river, and six children have been drowned accidentally. The last case was Lord Passover's butler in 1924. He was seen to run down to the river and leap in. He was pulled out, but had died of shock.

"The people who took the house two years ago left in a week, and threatened to bring an action against Wilkes, but they were warned they had no legal case. And I strongly advise you, more than that, *implore* you, to follow their example, though I can imagine the financial loss and great inconvenience, for that house is a death-trap."

"I will," I replied. "I forgot to mention one thing; when my little boy was so badly frightened he said something about 'a green monkey.' "

"He did!" said Sir William sharply. "Well then, it is absolutely imperative that you should leave at once. You remember I mentioned the death of certain children. Well, in each case they have been found drowned in the reeds just at the end of that lane, and the people about here have a firm belief that 'The Green Thing,' or 'The Green Death'—it is sometimes referred to as the first and sometimes as the other—is connected with danger to children."

"Have you ever seen anything yourself?" I asked.

"I go to the infernal place as little as possible," replied Sir William, "but when I called on your predecessors I most distinctly saw someone leave the drawing-room as we entered it, otherwise all I have noted is a certain dream which recurs with curious regularity. I find myself standing at the end of the lane and watching the river—always in a sort of brassy half-light. And presently something comes floating down the stream. I can see it jerking up and down, and I always feel passionately anxious to see what it may be. At first I think that it is a log, but when it gets exactly opposite me it changes its course and comes towards me, and then I see that it is a dead body, very decomposed. And when it reaches the bank it begins to climb up towards me, and then I am thankful to say I always awake. Sometimes I have thought that one day I shall not wake just then, and that on this occasion something will happen to me, but that is probably merely the silly fancy of an old gentleman who has concerned himself with these singular events rather more than is good for his nerves."

"That is obviously the explanation," I said, "and I am extremely grateful to you. We will leave to-morrow. But don't you think we should attempt to devise some means by which other people may be spared this sort of thing, and this brute Wilkes be prevented from letting the house again?"

"I certainly do so, and we will discuss it further on some other occasion. And now go and pack!"

A very great and charming gentleman, Sir William, I reflected, as I walked back to The Red Lodge.

Tim seemed to have recovered excellently well, but I thought it wise to keep him out of the house as much as possible, so while Mary and the maids packed after lunch I went with him for a walk through the fields. We took our time, and it was only when the sky grew black and there was a distant rumble of thunder and a menacing little breeze came from the west that we turned to come back. We had to hurry, and as we reached the meadow next to the house there came a ripping flash and the storm broke. We started to run for the door into the garden when I tripped over my bootlace, which had come undone, and fell. Tim ran on. I had just tied the lace and was on my feet again when I saw something slip through the door. It was green, thin, tall. It seemed to glance back at me, and what should have been its face was a patch of soused slime. At that moment Tim saw it, screamed, and ran for the river. The figure turned and followed him, and before I could reach him hovered over him. Tim screamed again and flung himself in. A moment later I passed through a green and stenching film and dived after him. I found him writhing in the reeds and brought him to the bank. I ran with him in my arms to the house, and I shall not forget Mary's face as she saw us from the bedroom window.

By nine o'clock we were all in a hotel in London, and The Red Lodge was an evil, fading memory. I shut the front door when I had packed them all into the car. As I took hold of the knob I felt a quick and powerful pressure from the other side, and it shut with a crash. The Permanent Occupants of The Red Lodge were in sole possession once more.

THE CAPTAIN OF THE POLE-STAR
Sir Arthur Conan Doyle
[1859–1930]

"Mention has been made of the weird work of H.G. Wells and
A. Conan Doyle. . . . Doyle now and then struck a powerfully spectral
note, as in *The Captain of the Pole-Star*, a tale of arctic ghostliness, and
Lot No. 249, wherein the reanimated mummy theme is used with
more than ordinary skill."

—*H.P. Lovecraft*

*[Being an extract from the singular journal of JOHN
M'ALISTER RAY, student of medicine.]*

SEPTEMBER 11TH.—LAT. 81° 40' N.; long. 2° E. Still lying-
to amid enormous ice fields. The one which stretches away
to the north of us, and to which our ice-anchor is attached,
can not be smaller than an English county. To the right and left
unbroken sheets extend to the horizon. This morning the mate
reported that there were signs of pack ice to the southward.
Should this form of sufficient thickness to bar our return, we shall
be in a position of danger, as the food, I hear, is already running
somewhat short. It is late in the season, and the nights are beginning to reappear. This morning I saw a star twinkling just over the
foreyard, the first since the beginning of May. There is considerable

discontent among the crew, many of whom are anxious to get back home to be in time for the herring season, when labor always commands a high price upon the Scotch coast. As yet their displeasure is only signified by sullen countenances and black looks, but I heard from the second mate this afternoon that they contemplated sending a deputation to the captain to explain their grievance. I much doubt how he will receive it, as he is a man of fierce temper, and very sensitive about anything approaching to an infringement of his rights. I shall venture after dinner to say a few words to him upon the subject. I have always found that he will tolerate from me what he would resent from any other member of the crew. Amsterdam Island, at the northwest corner of Spitzbergen, is visible upon our starboard quarter—a rugged line of volcanic rocks, intersected by white seams, which represent glaciers. It is curious to think that at the present moment there is probably no human being nearer to us than the Danish settlements in the south of Greenland—a good nine hundred miles as the crow flies. A captain takes a great responsibility upon himself when he risks his vessel under such circumstances. No whaler has ever remained in these latitudes till so advanced a period of the year.

9 P.M.—I have spoken to Captain Craigie, and though the result has been hardly satisfactory, I am bound to say that he listened to what I had to say very quietly and even deferentially. When I had finished he put on that air of iron determination which I have frequently observed upon his face, and paced rapidly backward and forward across the narrow cabin for some minutes. At first I feared that I had seriously offended him, but he dispelled the idea by sitting down again and putting his hand upon my arm with a gesture which almost amounted to a caress. There was a depth of tenderness too in his wild dark eyes which surprised me considerably.

"Look here, doctor," he said, "I'm sorry I ever took you—I am indeed—and I would give fifty pounds this minute to see you standing safe upon the Dundee quay. It's hit or miss with me this time. There are fish to the north of us. How dare you shake your head, sir, when I tell you I saw them blowing from the mast-head?"—this in a sudden burst of fury, though I was not conscious of having shown any signs of doubt. "Two-and-twenty fish in as many minutes, as I am a living man, and not one under ten feet. Now, doctor, do you think I can leave the country when there is only one infernal strip of ice between me and my fortune? If it came on to blow from the north tomorrow we could fill the ship and be away before the frost could catch us. If it came on to blow from the south—well, I suppose the men are paid for risking their lives, and as for myself it matters but little to me, for I have more to bind me to the other world than to this one. I confess that I am sorry for *you*, though. I wish I had old Angus Tait who was with me last voyage, for he was a man that would never be missed, and you—you said once that you were engaged, did you not?"

"Yes," I answered, snapping the spring of the locket which hung from my watch-chain, and holding up the little vignette of Flora.

"Curse you!" he yelled, springing out of his seat, with his very beard bristling with passion. "What is your happiness to me? What have I to do with her that you must dangle her photograph before my eyes?"

I almost thought that he was about to strike me in the frenzy of his rage, but with another imprecation he dashed open the door of the cabin and rushed out upon deck, leaving me considerably astonished at his extraordinary violence. It is the first time that he has ever shown me anything but courtesy and kindness. I can hear him pacing excitedly up and down overhead as I write these lines.

I should like to give a sketch of the character of this man, but it seems presumptuous to attempt such a thing upon paper, when the idea in my own mind is at best a vague and uncertain one. Several times I have thought that I grasped the clue which might explain it, but only to be disappointed by his presenting himself in some new light which would upset all my conclusions. It may be that no human eye but my own shall ever rest upon these lines, yet as a psychological study I shall attempt to leave some record of Captain Nicholas Craigie.

A man's outer case generally gives some indication of the soul within. The captain is tall and well formed, with dark, handsome face, and a curious way of twitching his limbs, which may arise from nervousness, or be simply an outcome of his excessive energy. His jaw and whole cast of countenance are manly and resolute, but the eyes are the distinctive feature of his face. They are of the very darkest hazel, bright and eager, with a singular mixture of recklessness in their expression, and of something else which I have sometimes thought was more allied with horror than any other emotion. Generally the former predominated, but on occasions, and more particularly when he was thoughtfully inclined, the look of fear would spread and deepen until it imparted a new character to his whole countenance. It is at these times that he is most subject to tempestuous fits of anger, and he seems to be aware of it, for I have known him to lock himself up so that no one might approach him until his dark hour was passed. He sleeps badly, and I have heard him shouting during the night, but his cabin is some little distance from mine, and I could never distinguish the words which he said.

This is one phase of his character, and the most disagreeable one. It is only through my close association with him, thrown together as we are day after day, that I have observed it. Otherwise he is an agreeable companion, well-read and entertaining, and as gallant a seaman as ever trod a deck. I shall not easily forget the way in which he handled the ship when we were caught by a gale among the loose ice at the beginning of April. I have never seen him so cheerful, and even hilarious, as he was that night, as he paced backward and forward upon the bridge amid the flashing of the lightning and the howling of the wind. He has told me several times that the thought of death is a pleasant one to him, which is a sad thing for a young man to say; he cannot be much more than thirty, though his hair and mustache are already slightly grizzled. Some great sorrow must have overtaken him and blighted his whole life. Perhaps I should be the same if I lost my Flora—God knows! I think if it were not for her that I should care very little whether the wind blew from the north or the south tomorrow. There, I hear him come down the companion, and he has locked himself up in his room, which shows that he is still in an unamiable mood. And so to bed, as old Pepys would say, for the candle is burning down (we have to use them now since the nights are closing in), and the steward has turned in, so there are no hopes of another one.

September 12th,—Calm, clear day, and still lying in the same position. What wind there is comes from the southeast, but it is very slight. Captain is in a better humor, and apologized to me at breakfast for his rudeness. He still looks somewhat distrait, however, and retains that wild look in his eyes which in a Highlander would mean that he was "fey"—at least so our chief engineer remarked to me, and he has some reputation among the Celtic portion of our crew as a seer and expounder of omens.

It is strange that superstition should have obtained such

mastery over this hard-headed and practical race. I could not have believed to what an extent it is carried had I not observed it for myself. We have had a perfect epidemic of it this voyage, until I have felt inclined to serve out rations of sedatives and nerve tonics with the Saturday allowance of grog. The first symptom of it was that shortly after leaving Shetland the men at the wheel used to complain that they heard plaintive cries and screams in the wake of the ship, as if something were following it and were unable to overtake it. This fiction has been kept up during the whole voyage, and on dark nights at the beginning of the seal-fishing it was only with great difficulty that men could be induced to do their spell. No doubt what they heard was either the creaking of the rudder-chains, or the cry of some passing sea-bird. I have been fetched out of bed several times to listen to it, but I need hardly say that I was never able to distinguish anything unnatural. The men, however, are so absurdly positive upon the subject that it is hopeless to argue with them. I mentioned the matter to the captain once, but to my surprise he took it very gravely, and indeed seemed to be considerably disturbed by what I told him. I should have thought that he at least would have been above such vulgar delusions.

All this disquisition upon superstition leads me up to the fact that Mr. Manson, our second mate, saw a ghost last night—or, at least says that he did, which of course is the same thing. It is quite refreshing to have some new topic of conversation after the eternal routine of bears and whales which has served us for so many months. Manson swears the ship is haunted, and that he would not stay in her a day if he had any other place to go to. Indeed, the fellow is honestly frightened, and I had to give him some chloral and bromide of potassium this morning to steady him down. He seemed quite indignant when I suggested that he had been having an extra glass the night before, and I was obliged to pacify him by keeping as grave a countenance as possible during his story, which he certainly narrated in a very straightforward and matter-of-fact way.

"I was on the bridge," he said, "about four bells in the middle watch, just when the night was at its darkest. There was a bit of a moon, but the clouds were blowing across it so that you couldn't see far from the ship. John M'Leod, the harpooner, came aft from the foc'sle-head and reported a strange noise on the starboard bow. I went forrad and we both heard it, sometimes like a bairn crying and sometimes like a wench in pain. I've been seventeen years to the country and I never heard seal, old or young, make a sound like that. As we were standing there on the foc'sle head the moon came out from behind a cloud, and we both saw a sort of white figure moving across the ice field in the same direction that we had heard the cries. We lost sight of it for a while, but it came back on the port bow, and we could just make it out like a shadow on the ice. I sent a hand aft for the rifles, and M'Leod and I went down on to the pack, thinking that maybe it might be a bear. When we got on the ice I lost sight of M'Leod, but I pushed on in the direction where I could still hear the cries. I followed them for a mile or maybe more, and then running round a hummock I came right on to the top of it standing and waiting for me seemingly. I don't know what it was. It wasn't a bear anyway. It was tall and white and straight, and if it wasn't a man nor a woman, I'll stake my davy it was something worse. I made for the ship as hard as I could run, and precious glad I was to find myself aboard. I signed articles to do my duty by the ship, and on the ship I'll stay, but you don't catch me on the ice again after sundown."

That is his story, given as far as I can in his own words. I fancy what he saw must, in spite of his denial, have been a young bear erect upon its hind legs, an attitude which they often assume when alarmed. In the uncertain light this would bear a resemblance to a human figure, especially to a man whose nerves were already somewhat shaken. Whatever it may have been, the occurrence is unfortunate, for it has produced a most unpleasant effect upon the crew. Their looks are more sullen than before, and their discontent more open. The double grievance of being debarred from the herring fishing and of being detained in what they choose to call a haunted vessel, may lead them to do something rash. Even the harpooners, who are the oldest and steadiest among them, are joining in the general agitation.

Apart from this absurd outbreak of superstition, things are looking rather more cheerful. The pack which was forming to the south of us has partly cleared away, and the water is so warm as to lead me to believe that we are lying in one of those branches of the Gulf Stream which run up between Greenland and Spitzbergen. There are numerous small Medusæ and sea-lemons about the ship, with abundance of shrimps, so that there is every possibility of "fish" being sighted. Indeed, one was seen blowing about dinnertime but in such a position that it was impossible for the boats to follow it.

September 13th.—Had an interesting conversation with the chief mate, Mr. Milne, upon the bridge. It seems that our captain is as great an enigma to the seamen, and even to the owners of the vessel, as he has been to me. Mr. Milne tells me that when the ship is paid off, upon returning from a voyage, Captain Craigie disappears, and is not seen again until the approach of another season, when he walks quietly into the office of the company, and asks whether his services will be required. He has no friend in Dundee, nor does any one pretend to be acquainted with his early history. His position depends entirely upon his skill as a seaman and the name for courage and coolness which he had earned in the capacity of mate, before being trusted with a separate command. The unanimous opinion seems to be that he is not a Scotchman, and that his name is an assumed one. Mr. Milne thinks that he has devoted himself to whaling simply for the reason that it is the most dangerous occupation which he could select, and that he courts death in every possible manner. He mentioned several instances of this, one of which is rather curious, if true. It seems that on one occasion he did not put in an appearance at the office, and a substitute had to be selected in his place. That was at the time of the last Russian and Turkish war. When he turned up again next spring he had a puckered wound in the side of his neck which he used to endeavor to conceal with his cravat. Whether the mate's inference that he had been engaged in the war is true or not I can not say. It was certainly a strange coincidence.

The wind is veering round in an easterly direction, but is still very slight. I think the ice is lying closer than it did yesterday. As far as the eye can reach on every side there is one wide expanse of spotless white, only broken by an occasional rift or the dark shadow of a hummock. To the south there is the narrow lane of blue water which is our sole means of escape, and which is closing up every day. The captain is taking a heavy responsibility upon himself. I hear that the tank of potatoes has been finished, and even the biscuits are running short, but he preserves the same impassable countenance, and spends the greater part of the day at the crow's nest, sweeping the horizon with his glass. His manner is very variable, and he seems to avoid my society, but there has been no repetition of the violence which he showed the other night.

7:30 P.M.—My deliberate opinion is that we are commanded by a madman. Nothing else can account for the extraordinary vagaries of Captain Craigie. It is fortunate that I have kept this journal of our voyage, as it will serve to justify us in case we have to put him under any sort of restraint, a step which I should only consent to as a last resource. Curiously enough it was he himself who suggested lunacy and not mere eccentricity as the secret of his strange conduct. He was standing upon the bridge about an hour ago, peering as usual through his glass, while I was walking up and down the quarterdeck. The majority of the men were below at their tea, for the watches have not been regularly kept of late. Tired of walking, I leaned against the bulwarks, and admired the mellow glow cast by the sinking sun upon the great ice fields which surround us. I was suddenly aroused from the reverie into which I had fallen by a hoarse voice at my elbow, and starting round I found that the captain had descended and was standing by my side. He was staring out over the ice with an expression in which horror, surprise, and something approaching to joy were contending for the mastery. In spite of the cold, great drops of perspiration were coursing down his forehead, and he was evidently fearfully excited. His limbs twitched like those of a man upon the verge of an epileptic fit, and the lines about his mouth were drawn and hard.

"Look!" he gasped, seizing me by the wrist, but still keeping his eyes upon the distant ice, and moving his head slowly in a horizontal direction, as if following some object which was moving across the field of vision. "Look! There, man, there! Between the hummocks! Now coming out from behind the far one! You see her—you *must* see her! There still! Flying from me, by God, flying from me—and gone!"

He uttered the last two words in a whisper of concentrated agony which shall never fade from my remembrance. Clinging to the ratlines, he endeavored to climb upon the top of the bulwarks as if in the hope of obtaining a last glance at the departing object. His strength was not equal to the attempt, however, and he staggered back against the saloon skylights, where he leaned panting and exhausted. His face was so livid that I expected him to become unconscious, so lost no time in leading him down the companion, and stretching him upon one of the sofas in the cabin. I then poured him out some brandy, which I held to his lips, and which had a wonderful effect upon him, bringing the blood back into his white face and steadying his poor shaking limbs. He raised himself up upon his elbow, and looking round to see that we were alone, he beckoned to me to come and sit beside him.

"You saw it, didn't you?" he asked, still in the same subdued awesome tone so foreign to the nature of the man.

"No, I saw nothing."

His head sunk back again upon the cushions. "No, he wouldn't without the glass," he murmured. "He couldn't. It was the glass that showed her to me, and then the eyes of love—the eyes of love. I say, Doc, don't let the steward in! He'll think I'm mad. Just bolt the door, will you?"

I rose and did what he had commanded.

He lay quiet for a while, lost in thought apparently, and then raised himself up upon his elbow again, and asked for some more brandy.

"You don't think I am, do you, Doc?" he asked, as I was putting the bottle back into the after-locker. "Tell me now, as man to man, do you think that I am mad?"

"I think you have something on your mind," I answered, "which is exciting you and doing you a good deal of harm."

"Right there, lad!" he cried, his eyes sparkling from the effects of the brandy. "Plenty on my mind—plenty! But I can work out the latitude and the longitude, and I can handle my sextant and manage my logarithms. You couldn't prove me mad in a court of law, could you, now?" It was curious to hear the man lying back and coolly arguing out the question of his own sanity.

"Perhaps not," I said; "but still I think you would be wise to get home as soon as you can, and settle down to a quiet life for a while."

"Get home, eh?" he muttered, with a sneer upon his face. "One word for me and two for yourself, lad. Settle down with Flora—pretty little Flora. Are bad dreams signs of madness?"

"Sometimes," I answered.

"What else? What would be the first symptoms?"

"Pains in the head, noises in the ears, flashes before the eyes, delusions—"

"Ah! what about them?" he interrupted. "What would you call a delusion?"

"Seeing a thing which is not there is a delusion."

"But she *was* there!" he groaned to himself. "She *was* there!" and rising, he unbolted the door and walked with slow and uncertain steps to his own cabin, where I have no doubt that he will remain until tomorrow morning. His system seems to have received a terrible shock, whatever it may have been that he imagined himself to have seen. The man becomes a greater mystery every day, though I fear that the solution which he has himself suggested is the correct one, and that his reason is affected. I do

THE CAPTAIN OF THE POLE-STAR

not think that a guilty conscience has anything to do with his behavior. The idea is a popular one among the officers, and, I believe, the crew; but I have seen nothing to support it. He has not the air of a guilty man, but of one who has had terrible usage at the hands of fortune, and who should be regarded as a martyr rather than a criminal.

The wind is veering round to the south tonight. God help us if it blocks that narrow pass which is our only road to safety! Situated as we are on the edge of the main Arctic pack, or the "barrier" as it is called by the whalers, any wind from the north has the effect of shredding out the ice around us and allowing our escape, while a wind from the south blows up all the loose ice behind us and hems us in between two packs. God help us, I say again!

September 14th.—Sunday, and a day of rest. My fears have been confirmed, and the thin strip of blue water has disappeared from the southward. Nothing but the great motionless ice fields around us, with their weird hummocks and fantastic pinnacles. There is a deathly silence over their wide expanse which is horrible. No lapping of the waves now, no cries of seagulls or straining of sails, but one deep universal silence in which the murmurs of the seamen, and the creak of their boots upon the white shining deck, seem discordant and out of place. Our only visitor was an Arctic fox, a rare animal upon the pack, though common enough upon the land. He did not come near the ship, however, but after surveying us from a distance fled rapidly across the ice. This was curious conduct, as they generally know nothing of man, and being of an inquisitive nature, become so familiar that they are easily captured. Incredible as it may seem, even this little incident produced a bad effect upon the crew. "Yon puir beastie kens mair, ay, an sees mair nor you nor me!" was the comment of one of the leading harpooners, and the others nodded their acquiescence. It is vain to attempt to argue against such puerile superstition. They have made up their minds that there is a curse upon the ship, and nothing will ever persuade them to the contrary.

The captain remained in seclusion all day except for about half an hour in the afternoon, when he came out upon the quarterdeck. I observe that he kept his eye fixed upon the spot where the vision of yesterday had appeared, and was quite prepared for another outburst, but none such came. He did not seem to see me although I was standing close beside him. Divine service was read as usual by the chief engineer. It is a curious thing that in whaling vessels the Church of England Prayer book is always employed, although there is never a member of that Church among either officers or crew. Our men are all Roman Catholics or Presbyterians, the former predominating. Since a ritual is used which is foreign to both, neither can complain that the other is preferred to them, and they listen with all attention and devotion, so that the system has something to recommend it.

A glorious sunset which made the great fields of ice look like a lake of blood. I have never seen a finer and at the same time more weird effect. Wind is veering round. If it will blow twenty-four hours from the north all will yet be well.

September 15th.—Today is Flora's birthday. Dear lass! It is well that she can not see her boy, as she used to call me, shut up among the ice fields with a crazy captain and a few weeks' provisions. No doubt she scans the shipping list in the *Scotsman* every morning to see if we are reported from Shetland. I have set an example to the men and look cheery and unconcerned; but God knows, my heart is very heavy at times.

The thermometer is at nineteen Fahrenheit today. There is but little wind, and what there is comes from an unfavorable quarter. Captain is in an excellent humor; I think he imagines he has seen some other omen or vision, poor fellow, during the night, for he came into my room early in the morning, and stooping down over my bunk, whispered, "It wasn't a delusion, Doc; it's all right!" After breakfast he asked me to find out how much food was left, which the second mate and I proceeded to do. It is even less than we had expected. Forward they have half a tank full of biscuits, three barrels of salt meat, and a very limited supply of coffee beans and sugar. In the afterhold and lockers there are a good many luxuries, such as tinned salmon, soups, harricot mutton, etc., but they will go a very short way among a crew of fifty men. There are two barrels of flour in the storeroom, and an unlimited supply of tobacco. Altogether there is about enough to keep the men on half rations for eighteen or twenty days—certainly not more. When we reported the state of things to the captain, he ordered all hands to be piped, and addressed them from the quarterdeck. I never saw him to better advantage. With his tall, well-knit figure, and dark animated face, he seemed a man born to command, and he discussed the situation in a cool, sailor-like way which showed that while appreciating the danger he had an eye for every loophole of escape.

"My lads," he said, "no doubt you think I brought you into this fix, if it is a fix, and maybe some of you feel bitter against me on account of it. But you must remember that for many a season no ship that comes to the country has brought in as much oil-money as the old *Pole-Star*, and every one of you has had his share of it. You can leave your wives behind you in comfort while other poor fellows come back to find their lasses on the parish. If you have to thank me for the one you have to thank me for the other, and we may call it quits. We've tried a bold venture before this and succeeded, so now that we've tried one and failed we've no cause to cry out about it. If the worst comes to the worst, we can make the land across the ice, and lay in a stock of seals which will keep us alive until the spring. It won't come to that, though, for you'll see the Scotch coast again before three weeks are out. At present every man must go on half rations, share and share alike, and no favor to any. Keep up your hearts and you'll pull through this as you've pulled through many a danger before." These few simple words of his had a wonderful effect upon the crew. His former unpopularity was forgotten, and the old harpooner whom I have already mentioned for his superstition, led off three cheers, which were heartily joined in by all hands.

September 16th.—The wind has veered round to the north during the night, and the ice shows some symptoms of opening out. The men are in good humor in spite of the short allowance upon which they have been placed. Steam is kept up in the engine room, that there may be no delay should an opportunity for escape present itself. The captain is in exuberant spirits, though he still retains that wild "fey" expression which I have already remarked upon. This burst of cheerfulness puzzles me more than his former gloom. I can not understand it. I think I mentioned in an early part of this journal that one of his oddities is that he never permits any person to enter his cabin, but insists upon making his own bed, such as it is, and performing every other office for himself.

To my surprise he handed me the key today and requested me to go down there and take the time by his chronometer while he measured the altitude of the sun at noon. It was a bare little room, containing a washing-stand and a few books, but little else in the way of luxury, except some pictures upon the walls. The majority of these are small cheap oleographs, but there was one watercolor sketch of the head of a young lady which arrested my attention. It was evidently a portrait, and not one of those fancy types of female beauty which sailors particularly effect. No artist could have evolved from his own mind such a mixture of character and weakness. The languid, dreamy eyes, with their drooping lashes, and the broad, low brow, unruffled by thought or care, were in strong contrast with the clean-cut, prominent jaw, and the resolute set of the lower lip. Underneath it in one of the corners was written, "M. B., æt. 19." That any one in the short space of nineteen years of existence could develop such strength of will as was stamped upon her face seemed to me at the time to be well-nigh incredible. She must have been an extraordinary woman. Her features have thrown such a glamour over me that, though I had but a fleeting glance at them, I could, were I a draughtsman, reproduce them line for line upon this page of the journal. I wonder what part she has played in our captain's life. He has hung her picture at the end of his berth, so that his eyes continually rest upon it. Were he a less reserved man I should make some remark upon the subject. Of the other things in his cabin there was nothing worthy of mention—uniform coats, a camp-stool, small looking glass, tobacco box, and numerous pipes, including an Oriental hookah—which, by-the-by, gives some color to Mr. Milne's story about his participation in the war, though the connection may seem rather a distant one.

11:20 P.M.—Captain has just gone to bed after a long and interesting conversation on general topics. When he chooses he can be a most fascinating companion, being remarkably well read, and having the power of expressing his opinion forcibly without appearing to be dogmatic. I hate to have my intellectual toes trod upon. He spoke about the nature of the soul, and sketched out the views of Aristotle and Plato upon the subject in a masterly manner. He seems to have a leaning for metempsychosis and the doctrines of Pythagoras. In discussing them we touched upon modern spiritualism, and I made some joking allusion to the impostures of Slade, upon which, to my surprise, he warned me most impressively against confusing the innocent with the guilty, and argued that it would be as logical to brand Christianity as an error because Judas, who professed that religion, was a villain. He shortly afterward bid me goodnight and retired to his room.

The wind is freshening up, and blows steadily from the north. The nights are as dark now as they are in England. I hope tomorrow may set us free from our frozen fetters.

September 17th.—The bogie again. Thank Heaven that I have strong nerves! The superstition of these poor fellows, and the circumstantial accounts which they give, with the utmost earnestness and self-conviction, would horrify any man not accustomed to their ways. There are many versions of the matter, but the sum total of them all is that something uncanny has been flitting round the ship all night, and that Sandie McDonald of Peterhead and "lang" Peter Williamson of Shetland saw it, as also did Mr. Milne on the bridge—so, having three witnesses, they can make a better case of it than the second mate did. I spoke to Milne after breakfast, and told him that he should be above such nonsense, and that as an officer he ought to set the men a better example. He shook his weatherbeaten head ominously, but answered with characteristic caution, "Mebbe aye, mebbe na, doctor," he said; "I didna ca' it a ghaist. I canna' say I preen my faith in sea-bogles an' the like, though there's a mony as claims to ha' seen a' that and waur. I'm no easy feared, but maybe your ain bluid would run a bit cauld, mun, if instead o' speerin' aboot it in daylicht ye were wi' me last night, an' seed an awfu' like shape, white an' grew-some, whiles here, whiles there, an' it greetin' and ca'ing in the darkness like a bit lambie that hae lost its mither. Ye would na' be sae ready to put it a' doon to auld wives' clavers then, I'm thinkin'." I saw it was hopeless to reason with him, so contented myself with begging him as a personal favor to call me up the next time the spectre appeared—a request to which he acceded with many ejaculations expressive of his hopes that such an opportunity might never arise.

As I had hoped, the white desert behind us has become broken by many thin streaks of water which intersect it in all directions. Our latitude today was 80° 52' N., which shows that there is a strong southerly drift upon the pack. Should the wind continue favorable it will break up as rapidly as it formed. At present we can do nothing but smoke and wait and hope for the best. I am rapidly becoming a fatalist. When dealing with such uncertain factors as wind and ice a man can be nothing else. Perhaps it was the wind and sand of the Arabian deserts which gave the minds of the original followers of Mohammed their tendency to bow to kismet.

These spectral alarms have a very bad effect upon the captain. I feared that it might excite his sensitive mind, and endeavored to conceal the absurd story from him, but unfortunately he over-heard one of the men making an allusion to it, and insisted upon being informed about it. As I had expected, it brought out all his latent lunacy in an exaggerated form. I can hardly believe that this is the same man who discoursed philosophy last night with the most critical acumen and coolest judgment. He is pacing back-ward and forward upon the quarterdeck like a caged tiger, stop-ping now and again to throw out his hands with a yearning gesture, and stare impatiently out over the ice. He keeps up a continual mutter to himself, and once he called out, "But a little time, love—but a little time!" Poor fellow, it is sad to see a gallant seaman and accomplished gentleman reduced to such a pass, and to think that imagination and delusion can cow a mind to which real danger was but the salt of life. Was ever a man in such a position as I, between a demented captain and a ghost-seeing mate? I sometimes think I am the only real sane man aboard the vessel—except, perhaps, the second engineer, who is a kind of ruminant, and would care nothing for all the fiends in the Red Sea so long as they would leave him alone and not disarrange his tools.

The ice is still opening rapidly, and there is every probability of our being able to make a start tomorrow morning. They will think I am inventing when I tell them at home all the strange things that have befallen me.

12 P.M.—I have been a good deal startled, though I feel steadier now, thanks to a stiff glass of brandy. I am hardly myself yet, however, as this handwriting will testify. The fact is that I have gone through a very strange experience, and am beginning to doubt whether I was justified in branding every one on board as madmen because they professed to have seen things which did not seem reasonable to my understanding. Pshaw! I am a fool to let such a trifle unnerve me; and yet, coming as it does, after all these alarms, it has an additional significance, for I can not doubt either Mr. Manson's story or that of the mate, now that I have experienced that which I used formerly to scoff at.

After all it was nothing very alarming—a mere sound, and that was all. I can not expect that any one reading this, if any one ever should read it, will sympathize with my feelings, or realize the effect which it produced upon me at the time. Supper was over, and I had gone on deck to have a quiet pipe before turning in. The night was very dark—so dark that, standing under the quarter-boat, I was unable to see the officer upon the bridge. I think I have already mentioned the extraordinary silence which prevails in these frozen seas. In other parts of the world, be they ever so barren, there is some slight vibration of the air—some faint hum, be it from the distant haunts of men, or from the leaves of the trees, or the wings of the birds, or even the faint rustle of the grass that covers the ground. One may not actively perceive the sound, and yet if it were withdrawn it would be missed. It is only here in these Arctic seas that stark, unfathomable stillness obtrudes itself upon you in all its gruesome reality. You find your tympanum straining to catch some little murmur, and dwelling eagerly upon every acci-dental sound within the vessel. In this state I was leaning against the bulwarks when there arose from the ice almost directly under-neath me a cry, sharp and shrill, upon the silent air of the night, beginning, as it seemed to me, at a note such as prima donna never reached, and mounting from that ever higher and higher until it culminated in a long wail of agony, which might have been the last cry of a lost soul. The ghastly scream is still ringing in my ears. Grief, unutterable grief, seemed to be expressed in it, and a great longing, and yet through it all there was an occasional wild note of exultation. It shrilled out from close beside me, and yet as I glared into the darkness I could discern nothing. I waited some little time, but without hearing any repetition of the sound, so I came below, more shaken than I have ever been in my life before. As I came down the companion I met Mr. Milne coming up to relieve the watch. "Weel, doctor," he said, "maybe that's auld wives' clavers tae? Did ye no hear it skirling? Maybe that's a supersteetion? What d'ye think o't noo?" I was obliged to apologize to the honest fellow, and acknowledge that I was as puzzled by it as he was. Perhaps tomorrow things may look different. At present I dare hardly write all that I think. Reading it again in days to come, when I have shaken off all these associations, I should despise myself for having been so weak.

September 18th.—Passed a restless and uneasy night still haunted by that strange sound. The captain does not look as if he had had much repose either, for his face is haggard and his eyes bloodshot. I have not told him of my adventure of last night, nor shall I. He is already restless and excited, standing up, sitting down, and apparently utterly unable to keep still.

A fine lead appeared in the pack this morning, as I had expected, and we were able to cast off our ice-anchor, and steam about twelve miles in a west-sou'-westerly direction. We were then brought to a halt by a great floe as massive as any which we have left behind us. It bars our progress completely, so we can do nothing but anchor again and wait until it breaks up, which it will probably do within twenty-four hours, if the wind holds. Several bladder-nosed seals were seen swimming in the water, and one was shot, an immense creature more than eleven feet long. They are fierce, pugnacious animals, and are said to be more than a match for a bear. Fortunately they are slow and clumsy in their movements, so there is little danger in attacking them upon the ice.

The captain evidently does not think we have seen the last of our troubles, though why he should take a gloomy view of the situation is more than I can fathom since every one else on board considers that we have had a miraculous escape, and are sure now to reach the open sea.

"I suppose you think it's all right now, doctor?" he said, as we sat together after dinner.

"I hope so," I answered.

"We mustn't be too sure—and yet no doubt you are right. We'll all be in the arms of our own true loves before long, lad, won't we? But we mustn't be too sure—we mustn't be too sure."

He sat silent a little, swinging his leg thoughtfully backward and forward.

"Look here," he continued; "it's a dangerous place this, even at its best—a treacherous, dangerous place. I have known men cut off very suddenly in a land like this. A slip would do it sometimes—a single slip, and down you go through a crack, and only a bubble on the green water to show where it was that you sank. It's a queer thing," he continued with a nervous laugh, "but all the years I've been in this country I never once thought of making a will—not that I have anything to leave in particular, but still when a man is exposed to danger he should have everything arranged and ready—don't you think so?"

"Certainly," I answered, wondering what on earth he was driving at.

"He feels better for knowing it's all settled," he went on. "Now if anything should ever befall me I hope that you will look after things for me. There is very little in the cabin, but such as it is I should like it to be sold, and the money divided in the same proportion as the oil-money among the crew. The chronometer I wish you to keep yourself as some slight remembrance of our voyage. Of course all this is a mere precaution, but I thought I would take the opportunity of speaking to you about it. I suppose I might rely upon you if there were any necessity?"

"Most assuredly," I answered; "and since you are taking this step, I may as well. . . ."

"You! you!" he interrupted. "*You're* all right. What the devil is the matter with *you?* There, I didn't mean to be peppery, but I don't like to hear a young fellow, that has hardly begun life, speculating about death. Go up on deck and get some fresh air into your lungs instead of talking nonsense in the cabin, and encouraging me to do the same."

The more I think of this conversation of ours the less do I like it. Why should the man be settling his affairs at the very time when we seem to be emerging from all danger? There must be some method in his madness. Can it be that he contemplates suicide? I remember that upon one occasion he spoke in a deeply reverent manner of the heinousness of the crime of self-destruction. I shall keep my eye upon him, however, and though I can not intrude upon the privacy of his cabin, I shall at least make a point of remaining on deck as long as he stays up.

Mr. Milne pooh-poohs my fears, and says it is only the "skipper's little way." He himself takes a very rosy view of the situation. According to him we shall be out of the ice by the day after tomorrow, pass Jan Meyen two days after that, and sight Shetland in little more than a week. I hope he may not be too sanguine. His opinion may be fairly balanced against the gloomy precautions of the captain, for he is an old and experienced seaman and weighs his words well before uttering them.

The long-impending catastrophe has come at last. I hardly know what to write about it. The captain is gone. He may come back to us again alive, but I fear me—I fear me. It is now seven o'clock in the morning of the 19th of September. I have spent the whole night traversing the great ice-floe in front of us with a party of seamen in the hope of coming upon some trace of him, but in vain. I shall try to give some account of the circumstances which attended upon his disappearance. Should any one ever chance to read the words which I put down, I trust they will remember that I do not write from conjecture or from hearsay, but that I, a sane and educated man, am describing accurately what actually occurred before my very eyes. My inferences are my own, but I shall be answerable for the facts.

The captain remained in excellent spirits after the conversation which I have recorded. He appeared to be nervous and impatient, however, frequently changing his position, and moving his limbs in an aimless way which is characteristic of him at times. In a quarter of an hour he went upon deck seven times, only to descend after a few hurried paces. I followed him each time, for there was something about his face which confirmed my resolution of not letting him out of my sight. He seemed to observe the effect which his movements had produced, for he endeavored by an over-done hilarity, laughing boisterously at the very smallest of jokes, to quiet my apprehensions.

After supper he went on to the poop once more, and I with him. The night was dark and very still, save for the melancholy soughing of the wind among the spars. A thick cloud was coming up from the northwest, and the ragged tentacles which it threw out in front of it were drifting across the face of the moon, which only shone now and again through a rift in the wrack. The captain paced rapidly backward and forward, and then seeing me still dogging him he came across and hinted that he thought I should be better below—which I need hardly say, had the effect of strengthening my resolution to remain on deck.

I think he forgot about my presence after this, for he stood silently leaning over the taffrail, and peering out across the great desert of snow, part of which lay in shadow, while part glittered mistily in the moonlight. Several times I could see by his movements that he was referring to his watch, and once he muttered a short sentence, of which I could only catch the one word, "ready." I confess to having felt an eerie feeling creeping over me as I watched the loom of his tall figure through the darkness, and noted how completely he fulfilled the idea of a man who is keeping a tryst. A tryst with whom? Some vague perception began to dawn upon me as I pieced one fact with another, but I was utterly unprepared for the sequel.

By the sudden intensity of his attitude I felt that he saw something. I crept up behind him. He was staring with an eager, questioning gaze at what seemed to be a wreath of mist, blown swiftly in a line with the ship. It was a dim, nebulous body, devoid of shape, sometimes more, sometimes less apparent, as the light fell on it. The moon was dimmed in its brilliancy at the moment by a canopy of thinnest cloud, like the coating of an anemone.

"Coming, lass, coming," cried the skipper, in a voice of unfathomable tenderness and compassion, like one who soothes a beloved one by some favor long looked for and as pleasant to bestow as to receive.

What followed happened in an instant. I had no power to interfere. He gave one spring to the top of the bulwarks, and another which took him on to the ice, almost to the feet of the pale misty figure. He held out his hands as if to clasp it, and so ran into the darkness with outstretched arms and loving words. I still stood rigid and motionless, straining my eyes after his retreating form, until his voice died away in the distance. I never thought to see him again, but at that moment the moon shone out brilliantly through a chink in the cloudy heaven, and illuminated the great field of ice. Then I saw his dark figure, already a very long way off, running with prodigious speed across the frozen plain. That was the last glimpse which we caught of him—perhaps the last we ever shall. A party was organized to follow him, and I accompanied it, but the men's hearts were not in the work, and nothing was found. Another will be formed within a few hours. I can hardly believe I have not been dreaming, or suffering from some hideous nightmare, as I write these things down.

7:30 P.M.—Just returned dead beat and utterly tired out from a second unsuccessful search for the captain. The floe is of enormous extent, for though we have traversed at least twenty miles of its surface, there has been no sign of its coming to an end. The frost has been so severe of late that the overlying snow is frozen as hard as granite, otherwise we might have had the footsteps to guide us. The crew are anxious that we should cast off and steam round the floe and so to the southward, for the ice has opened up during the night, and the sea is visible upon the horizon. They argue that Captain Craigie is certainly dead, and that we are all risking our lives to no purpose by remaining when we have an opportunity of escape. Mr. Milne and I have had the greatest difficulty in persuading them to wait until tomorrow night, and have been compelled to promise that we will not under any circumstances delay our departure longer than that. We propose therefore to take a few hours' sleep, and then to start upon a final search.

September 20th, evening.—I crossed the ice this morning with a party of men exploring the southern part of the floe, while Mr. Milne went off in a northerly direction. We pushed on for ten or twelve miles without seeing a trace of any living thing except a single bird, which fluttered a great way over our heads, and which by its flight I should judge to have been a falcon. The southern extremity of the ice field tapered away into a long narrow spit which projected out into the sea. When we came to the base of this promontory the men halted, but I begged them to continue to the extreme end of it, that we might have the satisfaction of knowing that no possible chance had been neglected.

We had hardly gone a hundred yards before McDonald of Peterhead cried out that he saw something in front of us, and began to run. We all got a glimpse of it and ran too. At first it was only a vague darkness against the white ice, but as we raced along together it took the shape of a man, and eventually of the man of whom we were in search. He was lying face downward upon a frozen bank. Many little crystals of ice and feathers of snow had drifted on to him as he lay, and sparkled upon his dark seaman's jacket. As we came up some wandering puff of wind caught these tiny flakes in its vortex and they whirled up into the air, partially descended again, and then, caught once more in the current, sped rapidly away in the direction of the sea. To my eyes it seemed but a snowdrift, but many of my companions averred that it started up in the shape of a woman, stooped over the corpse and kissed it, and then hurried away across the floe. I have learned never to ridicule any man's opinion, however strange it may seem. Sure it is that Captain Nicholas Craigie had met with no painful end, for there was a bright smile upon his blue, pinched features, and his hands were still outstretched as though grasping at the strange visitor which had summoned him away into the dim world that lies beyond the grave.

We buried him the same afternoon with the ship's ensign around him, and a thirty-two-pound shot at his feet. I read the burial service, while the rough sailors wept like children, for there were many who owed much to his kind heart, and who showed now the affection which his strange ways had repelled during his lifetime. He went off the grating with a dull, sullen splash, and as

I looked into the green water I saw him go down, down, down until he was but a little flickering patch of white hanging upon the outskirts of eternal darkness. Then even that faded away, and he was gone. There he shall lie, with his secret and his sorrows and his mystery all still buried in his breast, until that great day when the sea shall give up its dead, and Nicholas Craigie come out from among the ice with the smile upon his face, and his stiffened arms outstretched in greeting. I pray that his lot may be a happier one in that life than it has been in this.

I shall not continue my journal. Our road to home lies plain and clear before us, and the great ice field will soon be but a remembrance of the past. It will be some time before I get over the shock produced by recent events. When I began this record of our voyage I little thought of how I should be compelled to finish it. I am writing these final words in the lonely cabin, still starting at times and fancying I hear the quick nervous step of the dead man upon the deck above me. I entered his cabin tonight, as was my duty, to make a list of his effects in order that they might be entered in the official log. All was as it had been upon my previous visit, save that the picture which I have described as having hung at the end of his bed had been cut out of its frame, as with a knife, and was gone. With this last link in a strange chain of evidence I close my diary of the voyage of the *Pole-Star.*

[NOTE by Dr. John M'Alister Ray, senior.—I have read over the strange events connected with the death of the captain of the *Pole-Star,* as narrated in the journal of my son. That everything occurred exactly as he describes it I have the fullest confidence, and, indeed, the most positive certainty, for I know him to be a strong-nerved and unimaginative man, with the strictest regard for veracity. Still, the story is, on the face of it, so vague and so improbable, that I was long opposed to its publication. Within the last few days, however, I have had independent testimony upon the subject which throws a new light upon it. I had run down to Edinburgh to attend a meeting of the British Medical Association, when I chanced to come across Dr. P—, an old college chum of mine, now practicing at Saltash, in Devonshire. Upon my telling him of this experience of my son's, he declared to me that he was familiar with the man, and proceeded, to my no small surprise, to give me a description of him, which tallied remarkably well with that given in the journal, except that he depicted him as a younger man. According to his account, he had been engaged to a young lady of singular beauty residing upon the Cornish coast. During his absence at sea his betrothed had died under circumstances of peculiar horror.]

THE VILLA DÉSIRÉE
May Sinclair
[1865–1946]

"May Sinclair's *Uncanny Stories* contain more of traditional 'occultism' than of that creative treatment of fear which marks mastery in this field, and are inclined to lay more stress on human emotions and psychological delving than upon the stark phenomena of a cosmos utterly unreal. It may be well to remark here that occult believers are probably less effective than materialists in delineating the spectral and the fantastic, since to them the phantom world is so commonplace a reality that they tend to refer to it with less awe, remoteness, and impressiveness than do those who see in it an absolute and stupendous violation of the natural order."

—*H.P. Lovecraft*

I

HE HAD ARRANGED IT ALL FOR HER. She was to stay a week in Cannes with her aunt and then to go on to Roquebrune by herself, and he was to follow her there. She, Mildred Eve, supposed he could follow her anywhere, since they were engaged now.

There had been difficulties, but Louis Carson had got over all of them by lending her the Villa Désirée. She would be all right there, he said. The caretakers, Narcisse and Armandine, would look after her; Armandine was an excellent cook; and she wouldn't be five hundred yards from her friends, the Derings. It was so like him to think of it, to plan it all out for her. And when he came down? Oh, when he came down he would go to the Cap Martin Hotel, of course.

He understood everything without any tiresome explaining. She couldn't afford the hotels at Cap Martin and Monte Carlo; and though the Derings had asked her to stay with them, she really couldn't dump herself down on them like that, almost in the middle of their honeymoon.

Their honeymoon—she could have bitten her tongue out for saying it, for not remembering. It was awful of her to go talking to Louis Carson about honeymoons, after the appalling tragedy of *his*.

There were things she hadn't been told, that she hadn't liked to ask: Where it had happened? And how? And how long ago? She only knew it was on his wedding-night, that he had gone in to the poor little girl of a bride and found her dead there, in the bed.

They said she had died in a sort of fit.

You had only to look at him to see that something terrible had happened to him some time. You saw it when his face was doing nothing: a queer, agonised look that made him strange to her while it lasted. It was more than suffering; it was almost as if he could be cruel, only he never was, he never could be. *People* were cruel, if you liked; they said his face put them off. Mildred could see what they meant. It might have put *her* off, perhaps, if she hadn't known what he had gone through. But the first time she had met him he had been pointed out to her as the man to whom just that appalling thing had happened. So far from putting her off, that was what had drawn her to him from the beginning, made her pity him first, then love him. Their engagement had come quick, in the third week of their acquaintance.

When she asked herself, "After all, what do I know about him," she had her answer, "I know *that.*" She felt that already she had entered into a mystical union with him through compassion. She *liked* the strangeness that kept other people away and left him to her altogether. He was more her own that way.

There was (Mildred Eve didn't deny it) his personal magic, the fascination of his almost abnormal beauty. His black, white, and blue. The intensely blue eyes under the straight black bars of the eyebrows, the perfect, pure, white face suddenly masked by the black moustache and small, black, pointed beard. And the rich vivid smile he had for her, the lighting up of the blue, the flash of white teeth in the black mask.

He had smiled then at her embarrassment as the awful word leaped out at him. He had taken it from her and turned the sharp edge of it.

"It would never do," he had said, "to spoil the *honeymoon.* You'd much better have my villa. Some day, quite soon, it'll be yours, too. You know I like anticipating things."

That was always the excuse he made for his generosities. He had said it again when he engaged her seat in the *train de luxe* from Paris and wouldn't let her pay for it. (She had wanted to travel third class.) He was only anticipating, he said.

He was seeing her off now at the Gare de Lyons, standing on the platform with a great sheaf of blush roses in his arms. She, on the high step of the railway carriage, stood above him, swinging in the open doorway. His face was on a level with her feet; they gleamed white through the fine black stockings. Suddenly he thrust his face forwards and kissed her feet. As the train moved he ran beside it and tossed the roses into her lap.

And then she sat in the hurrying train, holding the great sheaf of blush roses in her lap, and smiling at them as she dreamed. She was in the Riviera Express; the Riviera Express. Next week she would be in Roquebrune, at the Villa Désirée. She read the three letters woven into the edges of the grey cloth cushions: P.L.M.: Paris—Lyons—Mediterranée, Paris—Lyons—Mediterranée, over and over again. They sang themselves to the rhythm of the wheels; they wove their pattern into her dream. Every now and then, when the other passengers weren't looking, she lifted the roses to her face and kissed them.

She hardly knew how she dragged herself through the long dull week with her aunt at Cannes.

And now it was over and she was by herself at Roquebrune.

The steep narrow lane went past the Derings' house and up the face of the hill. It led up into a little olive wood, and above the wood she saw the garden terraces. The sunlight beat in and out of their golden yellow walls. Tier above tier, the blazing terraces rose, holding up their ranks of spindle-stemmed lemon and orange trees. On the topmost terrace the Villa Désirée stood white and hushed between two palms, two tall poles each topped by a head of dark-green, curving, sharp-pointed blades. A grey scrub of olive-trees straggled up the hill behind it and on each side.

Rolf and Martha Dering waited for her with Narcisse and Armandine on the steps of the verandah.

"Why on earth didn't you come to us?" they said.

"I didn't want to spoil your honeymoon."

"Honeymoon, what rot! We've got over *that* silliness. Anyhow, it's our third week of it."

They were detached and cool in their happiness.

She went in with them, led by Narcisse and Armandine. The caretakers, subservient to Mildred Eve and visibly inimical to the Derings, left them together in the salon. It was very bright and French and fragile and worn; all faded grey and old greenish gilt; the gilt chairs and settees carved like picture frames round the gilded cane. The hot light beat in through the long windows open to the terrace, drawing up a faint powdery smell from the old floor.

Rolf Dering stared at the room, sniffing, with fine nostrils in a sort of bleak disgust.

"You'd much better have come to us," he said.

"Oh, but—it's charming."

"Do you *think* so?" Martha said. She was looking at her intently.

Mildred saw that they expected her to feel something, she wasn't sure what, something that they felt. They were subtle and fastidious.

"It does look a little queer and—unlived in," she said, straining for the precise impression.

"I should say," said Martha, "it had been too much lived in, if you ask me."

"Oh no. That's only dust you smell. I think, perhaps, the windows haven't been open very long."

She resented this criticism of Louis's villa.

Armandine appeared at the doorway. Her little, slant, Chinesy eyes were screwed up and smiling. She wanted to know if Madame wouldn't like to go up and look at her room.

"We'll all go up and look at it," said Rolf.

They followed Armandine up the steep, slender, curling

staircase. A closed door faced them on the landing. Armandine opened it, and the hot golden light streamed out to them again.

The room was all golden white; it was like a great white tank filled with blond water where things shimmered, submerged in the stream; the white-painted chairs and dressing-table, the high white-painted bed, the pink-and-white striped ottoman at its foot; all vivid and still, yet quivering in the stillness, with the hot throb, throb of the light.

"Voilà, Madame," said Armandine.

They didn't answer. They stood, fixed in the room, held by the stillness, staring, all three of them, at the high white bed that rose up, enormous, with its piled mattresses and pillows, the long white counterpane hanging straight and steep, like a curtain, to the floor.

Rolf turned to Armandine.

"Why have you given Madame this room?"

Armandine shrugged her fat shoulders. Her small, Chinesy eyes blinked at him, slanting, inimical.

"Monsieur's orders, Monsieur. It is the best room in the house. It was Madame's room."

"I know. That's *why*——"

"But no, Monsieur. Nobody would dislike to sleep in Madame's room. The poor little thing, she was so pretty, so sweet, so young, Monsieur. Surely Madame will not dislike the room."

"Who *was*—Madame?"

"But, Monsieur's wife, Madame. Madame Carson. Poor Monsieur, it was so sad——"

"Rolf," said Mildred, "did he bring her here—on their honeymoon?"

"Yes."

"Yes, Madame. She died here. It was so sad. Is there anything I can do for Madame?"

"No, thank you, Armandine."

"Then I will get ready the tea."

She turned again in the doorway, crooning in her thick, Provençal voice. "*Madame* does not dislike her room?"

"No, Armandine. No. It's a beautiful room."

The door closed on Armandine. Martha opened it again to see whether she were listening on the landing. Then she broke out:

"Mildred—you know you loathe it. It's beastly. The whole place is beastly."

"You can't stay in it," said Rolf.

"Why not? Do you mean, because of Madame?"

Martha and Rolf were looking at each other, as if they were both asking what they should say. They said nothing.

"Oh, her poor little ghost won't hurt me, if that's what you mean."

"Nonsense," Martha said. "Of course it isn't."

"What is it, then?"

"It's so beastly lonely, Mildred," said Rolf.

"Not with Narcisse and Armandine."

"Well, I wouldn't sleep a night in the place," Martha said, "if there wasn't any other on the Riviera. I don't like the look of it."

Mildred went to the open lattice, turning her back on the high, rather frightening bed. Down there below the terraces she saw the grey flicker of the olive woods and, beyond them, the sea. Martha was wrong. The place was beautiful; it was adorable. She wasn't going to be afraid of poor little Madame. Louis had loved her. He loved the place. That was why he had lent it to her.

She turned. Rolf had gone down again. She was alone with Martha. Martha was saying something.

"Mildred—where's Mr. Carson?"

"In Paris. Why?"

"I thought he was coming here."

"So he is, later on."

"To the villa?"

"No. Of course not. To Cap Martin." She laughed. "So *that's* what you're thinking of, is it?"

She could understand her friend's fear of haunted houses, but not these previsions of impropriety.

Martha looked shy and ashamed.

"Yes," she said. "I suppose so."

"How horrid of you! You might have trusted me."

"I do trust you." Martha held her a minute with her clear loving eyes. "Are you sure you can trust *him*?"

"Trust him? Do *you* trust Rolf?"

"Ah—if it was like that, Mildred——"

"It *is* like that."

"You're really not afraid?"

"What is there to be afraid of? Poor little Madame?"

"I didn't mean Madame. I meant Monsieur."

"Oh—wait till you've seen him."

"Is he *very* beautiful?"

"Yes. But it isn't *that*, Martha. I can't tell you what it is."

They went downstairs, hand in hand, in the streaming light. Rolf waited for them on the verandah. They were taking Mildred back to dine with them.

"Won't you let me tell Armandine you're stopping the night?" he said.

"No, I won't. I don't want Armandine to think I'm frightened."

She meant she didn't want Louis to think she was frightened. Besides, she was not frightened.

"Well, if you find you don't like it, you must come to us," he said.

And they showed her the little spare-room next to theirs, with its camp-bed made up, the bedclothes turned back, all ready for her, any time of the night, in case she changed her mind. The front door was on the latch.

"You've only to open it, and creep in here and be safe," Rolf said.

II

Armandine—subservient and no longer inimical, now that the Derings were not there—Armandine had put the candle and matches on the night-table and the bell which, she said, would summon her if Madame wanted anything in the night. And she had left her.

As the door closed softly behind Armandine, Mildred drew in her breath with a light gasp. Her face in the looking-glass, between the tall lighted candles, showed its mouth half-open, and she was aware that her heart shook slightly in its beating. She was angry with the face in the glass with its foolish mouth gaping. She said to herself. Is it possible I'm frightened? It was not possible. Rolf and Martha had made her walk too fast up the hill, that was all. Her heart always did that when she walked too fast uphill, and she supposed that her mouth always gaped when it did it.

She clenched her teeth and let her heart choke her till it stopped shaking.

She was quiet now. But the test would come when she had blown out the candles and had to cross the room in the dark to the bed.

The flame bent backwards before the light puff she gave, and righted itself. She blew harder, twice, with a sense of spinning out the time. The flame writhed and went out. She extinguished the other candle at one breath, The red point of the wick pricked the darkness for a second and died, too, with a small crackling sound. At the far end of the room the high bed glimmered. She thought: Martha was right. The bed *is* awful.

She could feel her mouth set in a hard grin of defiance as she went to it, slowly, too proud to be frightened. And then suddenly, half-way, she thought about Madame.

The awful thing was, climbing into that high funeral bed that Madame had died in. Your back felt so undefended. But once she was safe between the bedclothes it would be all right. It would be all right so long as she didn't think about Madame. Very well, then, she wouldn't think about her. You could frighten yourself into anything by thinking.

Deliberately, by an intense effort of her will, she turned the sad image of Madame out of her mind and found herself thinking about Louis Carson.

This was Louis's house, the place he used to come to when he wanted to be happy. She made out that he had sent her there because he wanted to be happy in it again. She was there to drive away the unhappiness, the memory of poor little Madame. Or, perhaps, because the place was sacred to him; because they were both so sacred, she and the young dead bride who hadn't been his wife. Perhaps he didn't think about her as dead at all; he didn't want her to be driven away. The room she had died in was not awful to him. He had the faithfulness for which death doesn't exist. She wouldn't have loved him if he hadn't been faithful. You could be faithful and yet marry again.

She was convinced that whatever she was there for, it was for some beautiful reason. Anything that Louis did, anything he thought or felt or wanted, would be beautiful. She thought of Louis standing on the platform in the Paris station, his beautiful face looking up at her; its sudden darting forward to kiss her feet. She drifted again into her happy hypnotising dream, and was fast asleep before midnight.

She woke with a sense of intolerable compulsion, as if she were being dragged violently up out of her sleep. The room was grey in the twilight of the unrisen moon.

And she was not alone.

She knew that there was something there. Something that gave up the secret of the room and made it frightful and obscene. The greyness was frightful and obscene. It gathered itself together; it became the containing shell of the horror.

The thing that had waked her was there with her in the room.

For she knew she was awake. Apart from her supernatural certainty, one physical sense, detached from the horror, was alert. It heard the ticking of the clock on the chimney-piece, the hard sharp shirring of the palm-leaves outside, as the wind rubbed their knife-blades together. These sounds were witnesses to the fact that she was awake, and that therefore the thing that was going to happen would be real. At the first sight of the greyness she had shut her eyes again, afraid to look into the room, because she knew that what she would see there was real. But she had no more power over her eyelids than she had had over her sleep. They opened under the same intolerable compulsion. And the supernatural thing forced itself now on her sight.

It stood a little in front of her by the bedside. From the breasts downwards its body was unfinished, rudimentary, not quite born. The grey shell was still pregnant with its loathsome shapelessness. But the face—the face was perfect in absolute horror. And it was Louis Carson's face.

Between the black bars of the eyebrows and the black pointed beard she saw it, drawn back, distorted in an obscene agony, corrupt and malignant. The face and the body, flesh and yet not flesh, they were the essence made manifest of untold, unearthly abominations.

It came on to her, bending over her, peering at her, so close that the piled mattresses now hid the lower half of its body. And the frightful thing about it was that it was blind, parted from all controlling and absolving clarity, flesh and yet not flesh. It looked for her without seeing her; and she knew that, unless she could save herself that instant, it would find what it looked for. Even now, behind the barrier of the piled-up mattresses, the unfinished form defined and completed itself; she could feel it shake with the agitation of its birth.

Her heart staggered and stopped in her breast, as if her breast had been clamped down on to her backbone. She struggled against wave after wave of faintness; for the moment that she lost consciousness the appalling presence there would have its way with her. All her will rose up against it. She dragged herself upright in the bed, suddenly, and spoke to it:

"Louis! What are you doing there?"

At her cry it went, without moving; sucked back into the greyness that had borne it.

She thought: "It'll come back. It'll come back. Even if I don't see it I shall know it's in the room."

She knew what she would do. She would get up and go to the Derings. She longed for the open air, for Rolf and Martha, for the strong earth under her feet.

She lit the candle on the night-table and got up. She still felt that It was there, and that standing upon the floor she was more vulnerable, more exposed to it. Her terror was too extreme for her to stay and dress herself. She thrust her bare feet into her shoes, slipped her travelling coat over her nightgown and went downstairs and out through the house door, sliding back the bolts without a sound. She remembered that Rolf had left a lantern for her in the verandah, in case she should want it—as if they had known.

She lit the lantern and made her way down the villa garden, stumbling from terrace to terrace, through the olive wood and the steep lane to the Derings' house. Far down the hill she could see a light in the window of the spare room. The house door was on the latch. She went through and on into the lamp-lit room that waited for her.

She knew again what she would do. She would go away before Louis Carson could come to her. She would go away to-morrow, and never come back again. Rolf and Martha would bring her things down from the villa; he would take her into Italy in his car. She would get away from Louis Carson for ever. She would get away up through Italy.

III

Rolf had come back from the villa with her things and he had brought her a letter. It had been sent up that morning from Cap Martin.

It was from Louis Carson.

My darling Mildred,
You see I couldn't wait a fortnight without seeing you. I *had* to come. I'm here at the Cap Martin Hotel.

I'll be with you some time between half-past ten and eleven——

Below, at the bottom of the lane, Rolf's car waited. It was half-past ten. If they went now they would meet Carson coming up the lane. They must wait till he had passed the house and gone up through the olive wood.

Martha had brought hot coffee and rolls. They sat down at the other side of the table and looked at her with kind anxious eyes as she turned sideways, watching the lane.

"Rolf," she said suddenly, "do you know anything about Louis Carson?"

She could see them looking now at each other.

"Nothing. Only the things the people here say."

"What sort of things?"

"Don't tell her, Rolf."

"Yes. He *must* tell me. I've got to know."

She had no feeling left but horror, horror that nothing could intensify.

"There's not much. Except that he was always having women with him up there. Not particularly nice women. He seems," Rolf said, "to have been rather an appalling beast."

"Must have been," said Martha, "to have brought his poor little wife there, after——"

"Rolf, what did Mrs. Carson die of?"

"Don't ask *me*," he said.

But Martha answered: "She died of fright. She saw something. I told you the place was beastly."

Rolf shrugged his shoulders.

"Why, you said you felt it yourself. We both felt it."

"Because we knew about the beastly things he did there."

"*She* didn't know. I tell you, she saw something."

Mildred turned her white face to them.

"I saw it too."

"You?"

"What? What did you see?"

"Him. Louis Carson."

"He must be dead, then, if you saw his ghost."

"The ghosts of poor dead people don't kill you. It was what he *is*. All that beastliness in a face. A face."

She could hear them draw in their breath short and sharp. "Where?"

"There. In that room. Close by the bed. It was looking for me. I saw what *she* saw."

She could see them frown now, incredulous, forcing themselves to disbelieve. She could hear them talking, their voices beating off the horror.

"Oh, but she couldn't. He wasn't there."

"He heard her scream first."

"Yes. He was in the other room, you know."

"*It* wasn't. He can't keep it back."

"Keep it back?"

"No. He was waiting to go to her."

Her voice was dull and heavy with realisation. She felt herself struggling, helpless, against their stolidity, their unbelief.

"Look at that," she said. She pushed Carson's letter across to them.

"He was waiting to go to her," she repeated. "And—last night—he was waiting to come to me."

They stared at her, stupefied.

"Oh, can't you *see*?" she cried. "It didn't wait. It got there before him."

THE VOICE IN THE NIGHT

William Hope Hodgson

[1877–1918]

"Of rather uneven stylistic quality, but vast occasional power in its suggestion of lurking worlds and beings behind the ordinary surface of life, is the work of William Hope Hodgson, known today far less than it deserves to be. Despite a tendency toward conventional sentimental conceptions of the universe, and of man's relation to it and its fellows, Mr. Hodgson is perhaps second only to Algernon Blackwood in his serious treatment of unreality. Few can equal him in adumbrating the nearness of nameless forces and monstrous besieging entities through casual hints and insignificant details, or in conveying feelings of the spectral and the abnormal in connection with regions or buildings."

—H.P. Lovecraft

I T WAS A DARK, STARLESS NIGHT. We were becalmed in the Northern Pacific. Our exact position I do not know; for the sun had been hidden during the course of a weary, breathless week, by a thin haze which had seemed to float above us, about the height of our mastheads, at whiles descending and shrouding the surrounding sea.

With there being no wind, we had steadied the tiller, and I was the only man on deck. The crew, consisting of two men and a boy, were sleeping forrard in their den; while Will—my friend, and the master of our little craft—was aft in his bunk on the port side of the little cabin.

Suddenly, from out of the surrounding darkness, there came a hail:

"Schooner, ahoy!"

The cry was so unexpected that I gave no immediate answer, because of my surprise.

It came again—a voice curiously throaty and inhuman, calling from somewhere upon the dark sea away on our port broadside:

"Schooner, ahoy!"

"Hullo!" I sung out, having gathered my wits somewhat. "What are you? What do you want?"

"You need not be afraid," answered the queer voice, having probably noticed some trace of confusion in my tone. "I am only an old—man."

The pause sounded oddly; but it was only afterwards that it came back to me with any significance.

"Why don't you come alongside, then?" I queried somewhat snappishly; for I liked not his hinting at my having been a trifle shaken.

"I—I—can't. It wouldn't be safe. I—" The voice broke off, and there was silence.

"What do you mean?" I asked, growing more and more astonished. "Why not safe? Where are you?"

I listened for a moment; but there came no answer. And then, a sudden indefinite suspicion, of I knew not what, coming to me, I stepped swiftly to the binnacle, and took out the lighted lamp. At the same time, I knocked on the deck with my heel to waken Will. Then I was back at the side, throwing the yellow funnel of light out into the silent immensity beyond our rail. As I did so, I heard a slight, muffled cry, and then the sound of a splash, as though someone had dipped oars abruptly. Yet I cannot say that I saw anything with certainty; save, it seemed to me, that with the first flash of light, there had been something upon the waters, where now there was nothing.

"Hullo, there!" I called. "What foolery is this?"

But there came only indistinct sounds of a boat being pulled away into the night.

Then I heard Will's voice, from the direction of the after scuttle: "What's up, George?"

"Come here, Will!" I said.

"What is it?" he asked, coming across the deck.

I told him the queer thing which had happened. He put several questions; then, after a moment's silence, he raised his hands to his lips, and hailed:

"Boat, ahoy!"

From a long distance away, there came back to us a faint reply, and my companion repeated his call. Presently, after a short period of silence, there grew on our hearing the muffled sound of oars; at which Will hailed again.

This time there was a reply:

"Put away the light."

"I'm damned if I will," I muttered; but Will told me to do as the voice bade, and I shoved it down under the bulwarks.

"Come nearer," he said, and the oar-strokes continued. Then, when apparently some half-dozen fathoms distant, they again ceased.

"Come alongside," exclaimed Will. "There's nothing to be frightened of aboard here!"

"Promise that you will not show the light?"

"What's to do with you," I burst out, "that you're so infernally afraid of the light?"

"Because——" began the voice, and stopped short.

"Because what?" I asked, quickly.

Will put his hand on my shoulder.

"Shut up a minute, old man," he said, in a low voice. "Let me tackle him."

He leant more over the rail.

"See here, Mister," he said, "this is a pretty queer business, you coming upon us like this, right out in the middle of the blessed Pacific. How are we to know what sort of a hanky-panky trick you're up to? You say there's only one of you. How are we to know, unless we get a squint at you—eh? What's your objection to the light, anyway?"

As he finished, I heard the noise of the oars again, and then the voice came; but now from a greater distance, and sounding extremely hopeless and pathetic.

"I am sorry—sorry! I would not have troubled you, only I am hungry, and—so is she."

The voice died away, and the sound of the oars, dipping irregularly, was borne to us.

"Stop!" sung out Will. "I don't want to drive you away. Come back! We'll keep the light hidden, if you don't like it."

He turned to me:

"It's a damned queer rig, this; but I think there's nothing to be afraid of?"

There was a question in his tone, and I replied,

"No, I think the poor devil's been wrecked around here, and gone crazy."

The sound of the oars drew nearer.

"Shove that lamp back in the binnacle," said Will; then he leaned over the rail, and listened. I replaced the lamp, and came back to his side. The dipping of the oars ceased some dozen yards distant.

"Won't you come alongside now?" asked Will in an even voice. "I have had the lamp put back in the binnacle."

"I—I cannot," replied the voice. "I dare not come nearer. I dare not even pay you for the—the provisions."

"That's all right," said Will, and hesitated. "You're welcome to as much grub as you can take——" Again he hesitated.

"You are very good," exclaimed the voice. "May God, who understands everything, reward you——" It broke off huskily.

"The—the lady?" said Will abruptly. "Is she——"

"I have left her behind upon the island," came the voice.

"What island?" I cut in.

"I know not its name," returned the voice. "I would to God——!" it began, and checked itself as suddenly.

"Could we not send a boat for her?" asked Will at this point.

"No!" said the voice, with extraordinary emphasis. "My God! No!" There was a moment's pause; then it added, in a tone which seemed a merited reproach:

"It was because of our want I ventured—because her agony tortured me."

"I am a forgetful brute," exclaimed Will. "Just wait a minute, whoever you are, and I will bring you up something at once."

In a couple of minutes he was back again, and his arms were full of various edibles. He paused at the rail.

"Can't you come alongside for them?" he asked.

"No—I *dare not*," replied the voice, and it seemed to me that in its tones I detected a note of stifled craving—as though the owner hushed a mortal desire. It came to me then in a flash, that the poor old creature out there in the darkness, was *suffering* for actual need of that which Will held in his arms; and yet, because of some unintelligible dread, refraining from dashing to the side of our little schooner, and receiving it. And with the lightning-like conviction, there came the knowledge that the Invisible was not mad; but sanely facing some intolerable horror.

"Damn it, Will!" I said, full of many feelings, over which predominated a vast sympathy. "Get a box. We must float off the stuff to him in it."

This we did—propelling it away from the vessel, out into the darkness, by means of a boathook. In a minute, a slight cry from the Invisible came to us, and we knew that he had secured the box.

A little later, he called out a farewell to us, and so heartful a blessing, that I am sure we were the better for it. Then, without more ado, we heard the ply of oars across the darkness.

"Pretty soon off," remarked Will, with perhaps just a little sense of injury.

"Wait," I replied. "I think somehow he'll come back. He must have been badly needing that food."

"And the lady," said Will. For a moment he was silent; then he continued:

"It's the queerest thing ever I've tumbled across, since I've been fishing."

"Yes," I said, and fell to pondering.

And so the time slipped away—an hour, another, and still Will stayed with me; for the queer adventure had knocked all desire for sleep out of him.

The third hour was three parts through, when we heard again the sound of oars across the silent ocean.

"Listen!" said Will, a low note of excitement in his voice.

"He's coming, just as I thought," I muttered

The dipping of the oars grew nearer, and I noted that the strokes were firmer and longer. The food had been needed.

They came to a stop a little distance off the broadside, and the queer voice came again to us through the darkness:

"Schooner, ahoy!"

"That you?" asked Will.

"Yes," replied the voice. "I left you suddenly; but—but there was great need."

"The lady?" questioned Will.

"The—lady is grateful now on earth. She will be more grateful soon in—in heaven."

Will began to make some reply, in a puzzled voice; but became confused, and broke off short. I said nothing. I was wondering at the curious pauses, and, apart from my wonder, I was full of a great sympathy.

The voice continued:

"We—she and I, have talked, as we shared the result of God's tenderness and yours——"

Will interposed; but without coherence.

"I beg of you not to—to belittle your deed of Christian charity this night," said the voice. "Be sure that it has not escaped His notice."

It stopped, and there was a full minute's silence. Then it came again:

"We have spoken together upon that which—which has befallen us. We had thought to go out, without telling any, of the terror which has come into our—lives. She is with me in believing that to-night's happenings are under a special ruling, and that it is God's wish that we should tell to you all that we have suffered since—since——"

"Yes?" said Will, softly.

"Since the sinking of the *Albatross*."

"Ah!" I exclaimed, involuntarily. "She left Newcastle for 'Frisco some six months ago, and hasn't been heard of since."

"Yes," answered the voice. "But some few degrees to the north of the line she was caught in a terrible storm, and dismasted. When the day came, it was found that she was leaking badly, and, presently, it falling to a calm, the sailors took to the boats, leaving—leaving a young lady—my fiancée—and myself upon the wreck.

"We were below, gathering together a few of our belongings, when they left. They were entirely callous, through fear, and when we came up on the decks, we saw them only as small shapes afar off upon the horizon. Yet we did not despair, but set to work and constructed a small raft. Upon this we put such few matters as it would hold, including a quantity of water and some ship's biscuit. Then, the vessel being very deep in the water, we got ourselves on to the raft, and pushed off.

"It was later, when I observed that we seemed to be in the way of some tide or current, which bore us from the ship at an angle; so that in the course of three hours, by my watch, her hull became invisible to our sight, her broken masts remaining in view for a somewhat longer period. Then, towards evening, it grew misty, and so through the night. The next day we were still encompassed by the mist, the weather remaining quiet.

"For four days we drifted through this strange haze, until, on the evening of the fourth day, there grew upon our ears the murmur of breakers at a distance. Gradually it became plainer, and, somewhat after midnight, it appeared to sound upon either hand at no very great space. The raft was raised upon a swell several times, and then we were in smooth water, and the noise of the breakers was behind.

"When the morning came, we found that we were in a sort of great lagoon; but of this we noticed little at the time; for close before us, through the enshrouding mist, loomed the hull of a large sailing-vessel. With one accord, we fell upon our knees and thanked God; for we thought that here was an end to our perils. We had much to learn.

"The raft drew near to the ship, and we shouted to them, to take us aboard; but none answered. Presently, the raft touched against the side of the vessel, and, seeing a rope hanging downwards, I seized it and began to climb. Yet I had much ado to make my way up, because of a kind of grey, lichenous fungus, which had seized upon the rope, and which blotched the side of the ship, lividly.

"I reached the rail, and clambered over it, on to the deck. Here, I saw that the decks were covered, in great patches, with the grey masses, some of them rising into nodules several feet in height; but at the time, I thought less of this matter than of the possibility of there being people aboard the ship. I shouted; but none answered. Then I went to the door below the poop deck. I opened it, and peered in. There was a great smell of staleness, so that I knew in a moment that nothing living was within, and with the knowledge, I shut the door quickly; for I felt suddenly lonely.

"I went back to the side, where I had scrambled up. My—my sweetheart was still sitting quietly upon the raft. Seeing me look down, she called up to know whether there were any aboard the ship. I replied that the vessel had the appearance of having been long deserted; but that if she would wait a little, I would see whether there was anything in the shape of a ladder, by which she could ascend to the deck. Then we would make a search through the vessel together. A little later, on the opposite side of the decks, I found a rope side-ladder. This I carried across, and a minute afterwards, she was beside me.

"Together, we explored the cabins and apartments in the afterpart of the ship; but nowhere was there any sign of life. Here and there, within the cabins themselves, we came across odd patches of that queer fungus; but this, as my sweetheart said, could be cleansed away.

"In the end, having assured ourselves that the after portion of the vessel was empty, we picked our way to the bows, between the ugly grey nodules of that strange growth; and here we made a further search, which told us that there was indeed none aboard but ourselves.

"This being now beyond any doubt, we returned to the stern of the ship, and proceeded to make ourselves as comfortable as possible. Together, we cleared out and cleaned two of the cabins; and, after that, I made examination whether there was anything eatable in the ship. This I soon found was so, and thanked God in my heart for His goodness. In addition to this, I discovered the whereabouts of the freshwater pump, and having fixed it, I found the water drinkable, though somewhat unpleasant to the taste.

"For several days, we stayed aboard the ship, without attempting to get to the shore. We were busily engaged in making the place habitable. Yet even thus early, we became aware that our lot was even less to be desired than might have been imagined; for though, as a first step, we scraped away the odd patches of growth that studded the floors and walls of the cabins and saloon, yet they returned almost to their original size within the space of twenty-four hours, which not only discouraged us, but gave us a feeling of vague unease.

"Still, we would not admit ourselves beaten, so set to work afresh, and not only scraped away the fungus, but soaked the places where it had been, with carbolic, a can-full of which I had found in the pantry. Yet, by the end of the week, the growth had returned in full strength, and, in addition, it had spread to other places, as though our touching it had allowed germs from it to travel elsewhere.

"On the seventh morning, my sweetheart woke to find a small patch of it growing on her pillow, close to her face. At that, she came to me, so soon as she could get her garments upon her. I was in the galley at the time, lighting the fire for breakfast.

" 'Come here, John,' she said, and led me aft. When I saw the thing upon her pillow, I shuddered, and then and there we agreed to go right out of the ship, and see whether we could not fare to make ourselves more comfortable ashore.

"Hurriedly, we gathered together our few belongings, and even among these, I found that the fungus had been at work; for one of her shawls had a little lump of it growing near one edge. I threw the whole thing over the side, without saying anything to her.

"The raft was still alongside; but it was too clumsy to guide, and I lowered down a small boat that hung across the stern, and in this we made our way to the shore. Yet, as we drew near to it, I became gradually aware that here the vile fungus, which had driven us from the ship, was growing riot. In places it rose into horrible, fantastic mounds, which seemed almost to quiver, as with a quiet life, when the wind blew across them. Here and there, it took on the forms of vast fingers, and in others it just spread out flat and smooth and treacherous. Odd places, it appeared as grotesque stunted trees, seeming extraordinarily kinked and gnarled. The whole quaking vilely at times.

"At first, it seemed to us that there was no single portion of the surrounding shore which was not hidden beneath the masses of the hideous lichen; yet, in this, I found we were mistaken; for somewhat later, coasting along the shore at a little distance, we descried a smooth white patch of what appeared to be fine sand, and there we landed. It was not sand. What it was, I do not know. All that I have observed, is that upon it the fungus will not grow; while everywhere else, save where the sand-like earth wanders oddly path-wise, amid the grey desolation of the lichen, there is nothing but that loathsome greyness.

"It is difficult to make you understand how cheered we were to find one place that was absolutely free from the growth, and here we deposited our belongings. Then we went back to the ship for such things as it seemed to us we should need. Among other matters, I managed to bring ashore with me one of the ship's sails, with which I constructed two small tents, which, though exceedingly rough-shaped, served the purposes for which they were intended. In these we lived and stored our various necessities, and thus for a matter of some four weeks, all went smoothly and without particular unhappiness. Indeed, I may say with much of happiness—for—for we were together.

"It was on the thumb of her right hand that the growth first showed. It was only a small circular spot, much like a little grey mole. My God! how the fear leapt to my heart when she showed me the place. We cleansed it, between us, washing it with carbolic and water. In the morning of the following day, she showed her hand to me again. The grey warty thing had returned. For a little while, we looked at one another in silence. Then, still wordless, we started again to remove it. In the midst of the operation, she spoke suddenly.

" 'What's that on the side of your face, dear?' Her voice was sharp with anxiety. I put my hand up to feel.

" 'There! Under the hair by your ear. A little to the front a bit.' My finger rested upon the place, and then I knew.

" 'Let us get your thumb done first,' I said. And she submitted, only because she was afraid to touch me until it was cleansed. I finished washing and disinfecting her thumb, and then she turned to my face, After it was finished, we sat together and talked awhile of many things; for there had come into our lives sudden, very terrible thoughts. We were, all at once, afraid of something worse than death. We spoke of loading the boat with provisions and water, and making our way out on to the sea; yet we were helpless, for many causes, and—and the growth had attacked us already. We decided to stay. God would do with us what was His will. We would wait.

"A month, two months, three months passed, and the places grew somewhat, and there had come others. Yet we fought so strenuously with the fear, that its headway was but slow, comparatively speaking.

"Occasionally, we ventured off to the ship for such stores as we needed. There, we found that the fungus grew persistently. One of the nodules on the maindeck became soon as high as my head.

"We had now given up all thought or hope of leaving the island. We had realised that it would be unallowable to go among healthy humans, with the thing from which we were suffering.

"With this determination and knowledge in our minds, we

knew that we should have to husband our food and water; for we did not know, at that time, but that we should possibly live for many years.

"This reminds me that I have told you that I am an old man. Judged by years this is not so. But—but——"

He broke off; then continued somewhat abruptly:

"As I was saying, we knew that we should have to use care in the matter of food. But we had no idea then how little food there was left, of which to take care. It was a week later, that I made the discovery that all the other bread tanks—which I had supposed full—were empty, and that (beyond odd tins of vegetables and meat, and some other matters) we had nothing on which to depend, but the bread in the tank which I had already opened.

"After learning this, I bestirred myself to do what I could, and set to work at fishing in the lagoon; but with no success. At this, I was somewhat inclined to feel desperate, until the thought came to me to try outside the lagoon, in the open sea.

"Here, at times, I caught odd fish; but, so infrequently, that they proved of but little help in keeping us from the hunger which threatened. It seemed to me that our deaths were likely to come by hunger, and not by the growth of the thing which had seized upon our bodies.

"We were in this state of mind when the fourth month wore out. Then I made a very horrible discovery. One morning, a little before midday, I came off from the ship, with a portion of the biscuits which were left. In the mouth of her tent, I saw my sweetheart sitting, eating something.

" 'What is it, my dear?' I called out as I leapt ashore. Yet, on hearing my voice, she seemed confused, and, turning, slyly threw something towards the edge of the little clearing. It fell short, and, a vague suspicion having arisen within me, I walked across and picked it up. It was a piece of the grey fungus.

"As I went to her, with it in my hand, she turned deadly pale; then a rose red.

"I felt strangely dazed and frightened.

" 'My dear! My dear!' I said, and could say no more. Yet, at my words, she broke down and cried bitterly. Gradually, as she calmed, I got from her the news that she had tried it the preceding day, and—and liked it. I got her to promise on her knees not to touch it again, however great our hunger. After she had promised, she told me that the desire for it had come suddenly, and that, until the moment of desire, she had experienced nothing towards it, but the most extreme repulsion.

"Later in the day, feeling strangely restless, and much shaken with the thing which I had discovered, I made my way along one of the twisted paths—formed by the white, sand-like substance—which led among the fungoid growth. I had, once before, ventured along there; but not to any great distance. This time, being involved in perplexing thought, I went much further than hitherto.

"Suddenly, I was called to myself, by a queer hoarse sound on my left. Turning quickly, I saw that there was movement among an extraordinarily shaped mass of fungus, close to my elbow. It was swaying uneasily, as though it possessed life of its own. Abruptly, as I stared, the thought came to me that the thing had a grotesque resemblance to the figure of a distorted human creature. Even as the fancy flashed into my brain, there was a slight, sickening noise of tearing, and I saw that one of the branch-like arms was detaching itself from the surrounding grey masses, and coming towards me. The head of the thing—a shapeless grey ball, inclined in my direction. I stood stupidly, and the vile arm brushed across my face. I gave out a frightened cry, and ran back a few paces. There was a sweetish taste upon my lips, where the thing had touched me. I licked them, and was immediately filled with an inhuman desire. I turned and seized a mass of the fungus. Then more, and—more. I was insatiable. In the midst of devouring, the remembrance of the morning's discovery swept into my mazed brain. It was sent by God. I dashed the fragment I held to the ground. Then, utterly wretched and feeling a dreadful guiltiness, I made my way back to the little encampment.

"I think she knew, by some marvellous intuition which love must have given, so soon as she set eyes on me. Her quiet sympathy made it easier for me, and I told her of my sudden weakness; yet omitted to mention the extraordinary thing which had gone before. I desired to spare her all unnecessary terror.

"But, for myself, I had added an intolerable knowledge, to breed an incessant terror in my brain; for I doubted not but that I had seen the end of one of those men who had come to the island in the ship in the lagoon; and in that monstrous ending, I had seen our own.

"Thereafter, we kept from the abominable food, though the desire for it had entered into our blood. Yet, our drear punishment was upon us; for, day by day, with monstrous rapidity, the fungoid growth took hold of our poor bodies. Nothing we could do would check it materially, and so—and so—we who had been human, became—well, it matters less each day. Only—only we had been man and maid!

"And day by day, the fight is more dreadful, to withstand the hunger-lust for the terrible lichen.

"A week ago we ate the last of the biscuit, and since that time I have caught three fish. I was out here fishing tonight, when your schooner drifted upon me out of the mist. I hailed you. You know the rest, and may God, out of His great heart, bless you for your goodness to a—a couple of poor outcast souls."

There was the dip of an oar—another. Then the voice came again, and for the last time, sounding through the slight surrounding mist, ghostly and mournful.

"God bless you! Good-bye!"

"Good-bye," we shouted together, hoarsely, our hearts full of many emotions.

I glanced about me. I became aware that the dawn was upon us.

The sun flung a stray beam across the hidden sea; pierced the mist dully, and lit up the receding boat with a gloomy fire. Indistinctly, I saw something nodding between the oars. I thought of a sponge—a great, grey nodding sponge. The oars continued to ply. They were grey—as was the boat—and my eyes searched a moment vainly for the conjunction of hand and oar. My gaze flashed back to the—head. It nodded forward as the oars went backward for the stroke. Then the oars were dipped, the boat shot out of the patch of light, and the—the thing went nodding into the mist.

NOVEL OF THE WHITE POWDER

Arthur Machen

[1863–1947]

"Of living creators of cosmic fear raised to its most artistic pitch, few if any can hope to equal the versatile Arthur Machen, author of some dozen tales long and short, in which elements of hidden horror and brooding fright attain an almost incomparable substance and realistic acuteness.

"In the episodic novel of *The Three Imposters,* a work whose merit as a whole is somewhat marred by an imitation of the jaunty Stevenson manner, occur certain tales which perhaps represent the highwater mark of Machen's skill as a terror-weaver.

"In *The Three Imposters* is the *Novel of the White Powder,* which approaches the absolute culmination of loathsome fright. Francis Leicester, a young law student nervously worn out by seclusion and overwork, has a prescription filled by an old apothecary none too careful about the state of his drugs. The substance, it later turns out, is an unusual salt which time and varying temperature have accidentally changed to something very strange and terrible; nothing less, in short, than the mediaeval *vinum sabbati,* whose consumption at the horrible orgies of the Witches' Sabbath gave rise to shocking transformations and—if injudiciously used—to unutterable consequences."

—*H.P. Lovecraft*

Y NAME IS LEICESTER; my father, Major-General Wyn Leicester, a distinguished officer of artillery, succumbed five years ago to a complicated liver complaint acquired in the deadly climate of India. A year later my only brother, Francis, came home after a exceptionally brilliant career at the University, and settled down with the resolution of a hermit to master what has been well called the great legend of the law. He was a man who seemed to live in utter indifference to everything that is called pleasure; and though he was handsomer than most men, and could talk as merrily and wittily as if he were a mere vagabond, he avoided society, and shut himself up in a large room at the top of the house to make himself a lawyer. Ten hours a day of hard reading was at first his allotted portion; from the first light in the east to the late afternoon he remained shut up with his books, taking a hasty half-hour's lunch with me as if he grudged the wasting of the moments, and going out for a short walk when it began to grow dusk. I thought that such relentless application must be injurious, and tried to cajole him from the crabbed text-books, but his ardour seemed to grow rather than diminish, and his daily tale of hours increased. I spoke to him seriously, suggesting some occasional relaxation, if it were but an idle afternoon with a harmless novel; but he laughed, and said that he read about feudal tenures when he felt in need of amusement, and scoffed at the notions of theatres, or a month's fresh air. I confessed that he looked well, and seemed not to suffer from his labours, but I knew that such unnatural toil would take revenge at last, and I was not mistaken. A look of anxiety began to lurk about his eyes, and he seemed languid, and at last he avowed that he was no longer in perfect health; he was troubled, he said, with a sensation of dizziness, and awoke now and then of nights from fearful dreams, terrified and cold with icy sweats. "I am taking care of myself," he said, "so you must not trouble; I passed the whole of yesterday afternoon in idleness, leaning back in that comfortable chair you gave me, and scribbling nonsense on a sheet of paper. No, no; I will not overdo my work; I shall be well enough in a week or two, depend upon it."

Yet in spite of his assurances I could see that he grew no better, but rather worse; he would enter the drawing-room with a face all miserably wrinkled and despondent, and endeavour to look gaily when my eyes fell on him, and I thought such symptoms of evil omen, and was frightened sometimes at the nervous irritation of his movements, and at glances which I could not decipher. Much against his will, I prevailed on him to have medical advice, and with an ill grace he called in our old doctor.

Dr. Haberden cheered me after examination of his patient.

"There is nothing really much amiss," he said to me. "No doubt he reads too hard and eats hastily, and then goes back again to his books in too great a hurry, and the natural sequence is some digestive trouble and a little mischief in the nervous system. But I think—I do indeed, Miss Leicester—that we shall be able to set this all right. I have written him a prescription which ought to do great things. So you have no cause for anxiety."

My brother insisted on having the prescription made up by a chemist in the neighbourhood. It was an odd, oldfashioned shop, devoid of the studied coquetry and calculated glitter that make so gay a show on the counters and shelves of the modern apothecary; but Francis liked the old chemist, and believed in the scrupulous purity of his drugs. The medicine was sent in due course, and I saw that my brother took it regularly after lunch and dinner. It was an innocent-looking white powder, of which a little was dissolved in a glass of cold water; I stirred it in, and it seemed to disappear, leaving the water clear and colorless. At first Francis seemed to benefit greatly; the weariness vanished from his face, and he became more cheerful than he had ever been since the time when he left school; he talked gaily of reforming himself, and avowed to me that he had wasted his time.

"I have given too many hours to law," he said, laughing; "I think you have saved me in the nick of time. Come, I shall be Lord Chancellor yet, but I must not forget life. You and I will have a holiday together before long; we will go to Paris and enjoy ourselves, and keep away from the Bibliothèque Nationale."

I confessed myself delighted with the prospect.

"When shall we go?" I said. "I can start the day after to-morrow if you like."

"Ah! that is perhaps a little too soon; after all, I do not know London yet, and I suppose a man ought to give the pleasures of his own country the first choice. But we will go off together in a week or two, so try and furbish up your French. I only know law French myself, and I am afraid that wouldn't do."

We were just finishing dinner, and he quaffed off his medicine with a parade of carousal as if it had been wine from some choicest bin.

"Has it any particular taste?" I said.

"No; I should not know I was not drinking water," and he got up from his chair and began to pace up and down the room as if he were undecided as to what he should do next.

"Shall we have coffee in the drawing-room?" I said; "or would you like to smoke?"

"No, I think I will take a turn; it seems a pleasant evening. Look at the afterglow; why, it is as if a great city were burning in flames, and down there between the dark houses it is raining blood fast. Yes, I will go out; I may be in soon, but I shall take my key; so good-night, dear, if I don't see you again."

The door slammed behind him, and I saw him walk lightly down the street, swinging his malacca cane, and I felt grateful to Dr. Haberden for such an improvement.

I believe my brother came home very late that night, but he was in a merry mood the next morning.

"I walked on without thinking where I was going," he said, "enjoying the freshness of the air, and livened by the crowds as I reached more frequented quarters. And then I met an old college friend, Orford, in the press of the pavement, and then—well, we enjoyed ourselves, I have felt what it is to be young and a man; I find I have blood in my veins, as other men have. I made an appointment with Orford for to-night; there will be a little party of us at the restaurant. Yes; I shall enjoy myself for a week or two, and hear the chimes at midnight, and then we will go for our little trip together."

Such was the transmutation of my brother's character that in a few days he became a lover of pleasure, a careless and merry idler of western pavements, a hunter out of snug restaurants, and a fine critic of fantastic dancing; he grew fat before my eyes, and said no more of Paris, for he had clearly found his paradise in London. I rejoiced, and yet wondered a little; for there was, I thought, something in his gaiety that indefinitely displeased me, though I could not have defined my feeling. But by degrees there came a change; he returned still in the cold hours of the morning, but I heard no more about his pleasures, and one morning as we sat at breakfast together I looked suddenly into his eyes and saw a stranger before me.

"Oh, Francis!" I cried. "Oh, Francis, Francis, what have you done?" and rending sobs cut the words short. I went weeping out of the room; for though I knew nothing, yet I knew all, and by some odd play of thought I remembered the evening when he first went abroad, and the picture of the sunset sky glowed before me; the clouds like a city in burning flames, and the rain of blood. Yet I did battle with such thoughts, resolving that perhaps, after all, no great harm had been done, and in the evening at dinner I resolved to press him to fix a day for our holiday in Paris. We had talked easily enough, and my brother had just taken his medicine, which he continued all the while. I was about to begin my topic when the words forming in my mind vanished, and I wondered for a second what icy and intolerable weight oppressed my heart and suffocated me as with the unutterable horror of the coffin-lid nailed down on the living.

We had dined without candles; the room had slowly grown from twilight to gloom, and the walls and corners were indistinct in the shadow. But from where I sat I looked out into the street; and as I thought of what I would say to Francis, the sky began to flush and shine, as it had done on a well-remembered evening, and in the gap between two dark masses that were houses an awful pageantry of flame appeared—lurid whorls of writhed cloud, and utter depths burning, grey masses like the fume blown from a smoking city, and an evil glory blazing far above shot with tongues of more ardent fire, and below as if there were a deep pool of blood. I looked down to where my brother sat facing me, and the words were shaped on my lips, when I saw his hand resting on the table. Between the thumb and forefinger of the closed hand there was a mark, a small patch about the size of a six-pence, and somewhat of the colour of a bad bruise. Yet, by some sense I cannot define, I knew that what I saw was no bruise at all; oh! if human flesh could burn with flame, and if flame could be black as pitch, such was that before me. Without thought or fashioning of words grey horror shaped within me at the sight, and in an inner cell it was known to be a brand. For the moment the stained sky became dark as midnight, and when the light returned to me I was alone in the silent room, and soon after I heard my brother go out.

Late as it was, I put on my hat and went to Dr. Haberden, and in his great consulting room, ill lighted by a candle which the doctor brought in with him, with stammering lips, and a voice that would break in spite of my resolve, I told him all, from the day on which my brother began to take the medicine down to the dreadful thing I had seen scarcely half an hour before.

When I had done, the doctor looked at me for a minute with an expression of great pity on his face.

"My dear Miss Leicester," he said, "you have evidently been anxious about your brother; you have been worrying over him, I am sure. Come, now, is it not so?"

"I have certainly been anxious," I said. "For the last week or two I have not felt at ease."

"Quite so; you know, of course, what a queer thing the brain is?"

"I understand what you mean; but I was not deceived. I saw what I have told you with my own eyes."

"Yes, yes of course. But your eyes had been staring at that very curious sunset we had tonight. That is the only explanation. You will see it in the proper light to-morrow, I am sure. But, remember, I am always ready to give any help that is in my power; do not scruple to come to me, or to send for me if you are in any distress."

I went away but little comforted, all confusion and terror and sorrow, not knowing where to turn. When my brother and I met the next day, I looked quickly at him, and noticed, with a sickening at heart, that the right hand, the hand on which I had clearly seen the patch as of a black fire, was wrapped up with a handkerchief.

"What is the matter with your hand, Francis?" I said in a steady voice.

"Nothing of consequence. I cut a finger last night, and it bled rather awkwardly. So I did it up roughly to the best of my ability."

"I will do it neatly for you, if you like."

"No, thank you, dear; this will answer very well. Suppose we have breakfast; I am quite hungry."

We sat down and I watched him. He scarcely ate or drank at all, but tossed his meat to the dog when he thought my eyes were turned away; there was a look in his eyes that I had never yet seen, and the thought flashed across my mind that it was a look that was scarcely human. I was firmly convinced that awful and incredible as was the thing I had seen the night before, yet it was no illusion, no glamour of bewildered sense, and in the course of the evening I went again to the doctor's house.

He shook his head with an air puzzled and incredulous, and seemed to reflect for a few minutes.

"And you say he still keeps up the medicine? But why? As I understand, all the symptoms he complained of have disappeared long ago; why should he go on taking the stuff when he is quite well? And by the by, where did he get it made up? At Sayce's? I never send any one there; the old man is getting careless. Suppose you come with me to the chemist's; I should like to have some talk with him."

We walked together to the shop; old Sayce knew Dr. Haberden, and was quite ready to give any information.

"You have been sending that in to Mr. Leicester for some weeks, I think, on my prescription," said the doctor, giving the old man a pencilled scrap of paper.

The chemist put on his great spectacles with trembling uncertainty, and held up the paper with a shaking hand.

"Oh, yes," he said, "I have very little of it left; it is rather an uncommon drug, and I have had it in stock some time. I must get in some more, if Mr. Leicester goes on with it."

"Kindly let me have a look at the stuff," said Haberden, and the chemist gave him a glass bottle. He took out the stopper and smelt the contents, and looked strangely at the old man.

"Where did you get this?" he said, "and what is it? For one thing, Mr. Sayce, it is not what I prescribed. Yes, yes, I see the label is right enough, but I tell you this is not the drug."

"I have had it a long time," said the old man in feeble terror; "I got it from Burbage's in the usual way. It is not prescribed often, and I have had it on the shelf for some years. You see there is very little left."

"You had better give it to me," said Haberden. "I am afraid something wrong has happened."

We went out of the shop in silence, the doctor carrying the bottle neatly wrapped in paper under his arm.

"Dr. Haberden," I said, when we had walked a little way— "Dr. Haberden."

"Yes," he said, looking at me gloomily enough.

"I should like you to tell me what my brother has been taking twice a day for the last month or so."

"Frankly, Miss Leicester, I don't know. We will speak of this when we get to my house."

We walked on quickly without another word till we reached Dr. Haberden's. He asked me to sit down, and began pacing up and down the room, his face clouded over, as I could see, with no common fears.

"Well," he said at length, "this is all very strange; it is only natural that you should feel alarmed, and I must confess that my mind is far from easy. We will put aside, if you please, what you told me last night and this morning, but the fact remains that for the last few weeks Mr. Leicester has been impregnating his system with a drug which is completely unknown to me. I tell you, it is not what I ordered; and what the stuff in the bottle really is remains to be seen."

He undid the wrapper, and cautiously tilted a few grains of the white powder on to a piece of paper, and peered curiously at it.

"Yes," he said, "it is like the sulphate of quinine, as you say; it is flaky. But smell it."

He held the bottle to me, and I bent over it. It was a strange, sickly smell, vaporous and overpowering, like some strong anaesthetic.

"I shall have it analysed," said Haberden; "I have a friend who has devoted his whole life to chemistry as a science. Then we shall have something to go upon. No, no; say no more about that other matter; I cannot listen to that; and take my advice and think no more about it yourself."

That evening my brother did not go out as usual after dinner.

"I have had my fling," he said with a queer laugh, "and I must go back to my old ways. A little law will be quite a relaxation after so sharp a dose of pleasure," and he grinned to himself, and soon after went up to his room. His hand was still all bandaged.

Dr. Haberden called a few days later.

"I have no special news to give you," he said. "Chambers is out of town, so I know no more about that stuff than you do. But I should like to see Mr. Leicester, if he is in."

"He is in his room," I said; "I will tell him you are here."

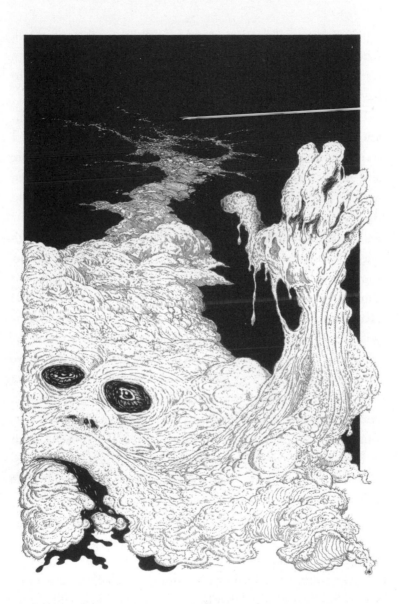

"No, no, I will go up to him; we will have a little quiet talk together. I dare say that we have made a good deal of fuss about a very little; for, after all, whatever the powder may be, it seems to have done him good."

The doctor went upstairs, and standing in the hall I heard his knock, and the opening and shutting of the door; and then I waited in the silent house for an hour, and the stillness grew more and more intense as the hands of the clock crept round. Then there sounded from above the noise of a door shut sharply, and the doctor was coming down the stairs. His footsteps crossed the hall, and there was a pause at the door; I drew a long, sick breath with difficulty, and saw my face white in a little mirror, and he came in and stood at the door. There was an unutterable horror shining in his eyes; he steadied himself by holding the back of a chair with one hand, his lower lip trembled like a horse's, and he gulped and stammered unintelligible sounds before he spoke.

"I have seen that man," he began in a dry whisper. "I have been sitting in his presence for the last hour. My God! And I am alive and in my senses! I, who have dealt with death all my life, and have dabbled with the melting ruins of the earthly tabernacle. But not this, oh! not this," and he covered his face with his hands as if to shut out the sight of something before him.

"Do not send for me again, Miss Leicester," he said with more composure. "I can do nothing in this house. Good-bye."

As I watched him totter down the steps; and along the pavement towards his house, it seemed to me that he had aged by ten years since the morning.

My brother remained in his room. He called out to me in a voice I hardly recognized that he was very busy, and would like his meals brought to his door and left there, and I gave the order to

the servants. From that day it seemed as if the arbitrary conception we call time had been annihilated for me; I lived in an ever-
present sense of horror, going through the routine of the house
mechanically, and only speaking a few necessary words to the servants. Now and then I went out and paced the streets for an hour
or two and came home again; but whether I were without or
within, my spirit delayed before the closed door of the upper
room, and, shuddering, waited for it to open. I have said that I
scarcely reckoned time; but I suppose it must have been a fortnight after Dr. Haberden's visit that I came home from my stroll
a little refreshed and lightened. The air was sweet and pleasant,
and the hazy form of green leaves, floating cloud-like in the
square, and the smell of blossoms, had charmed my senses, and I
felt happier and walked more briskly. As I delayed a moment at
the verge of the pavement, waiting for a van to pass by before
crossing over to the house, I happened to look up at the windows,
and instantly there was the rush and swirl of deep cold waters in
my ears, my heart leapt up and fell down, down as into a deep
hollow, and I was amazed with a dread and terror without form
or shape. I stretched out a hand blindly through the folds of thick
darkness, from the black and shadowy valley, and held myself
from falling, while the stones beneath my feet rocked and swayed
and tilted, and the sense of solid things seemed to sink away from
under me. I had glanced up at the window of my brother's study,
and at that moment the blind was drawn aside, and something
that had life stared out into the world. Nay, I cannot say I saw a
face or any human likeness; a living thing, two eyes of burning
flame glared at me, and they were in the midst of something as
formless as my fear, the symbol and presence of all evil and all
hideous corruption. I stood shuddering and quaking as with the

grip of ague, sick with unspeakable agonies of fear and loathing, and for five minutes I could not summon force or motion to my limbs. When I was within the door, I ran up the stairs to my brother's room and knocked.

"Francis, Francis," I cried, "for Heaven's sake, answer me. What is the horrible thing in your room? Cast it out, Francis; cast it from you."

I heard a noise as of feet shuffling slowly and awkwardly, and a choking, gurgling sound, as if some one was struggling to find utterance, and then the noise of a voice, broken and stifled, and words that I could scarcely understand.

"There is nothing here," the voice said. "Pray do not disturb me. I am not very well to-day."

I turned away, horrified, and yet helpless. I could do nothing, and I wondered why Francis had lied to me, for I had seen the appearance beyond the glass too plainly to be deceived, though it was but the sight of a moment. And I sat still, conscious that there had been something else, something I had seen in the first flash of terror, before those burning eyes had looked at me. Suddenly I remembered; as I lifted my face the blind was being drawn back, and I had had an instant's glance of the thing that was moving it, and in my recollection I knew that a hideous image was engraved forever on my brain. It was not a hand; there were no fingers that held the blind, but a black stump pushed it aside, the mouldering outline and the clumsy movement as of a beast's paw had glowed into my senses before the darkling waves of terror had overwhelmed me as I went down quick into the pit. My mind was aghast at the thought of this, and of the awful presence that dwelt with my brother in his room; I went to his door and cried to him again, but no answer came. That night one of the servants came up to me and told me in a whisper that for three days food had been regularly placed at the door and left untouched; the maid had knocked but had received no answer; she had heard the noise of shuffling feet that I had noticed. Day after day went by, and still my brother's meals were brought to his door and left untouched; and though I knocked and called again and again, I could get no answer. The servants began to talk to me; it appeared they were as alarmed as I; the cook said that when my brother first shut himself up in his room she used to hear him come out at night and go about the house; and once, she said, the hall door had opened and closed again, but for several nights she had heard no sound. The climax came at last; it was in the dusk of the evening, and I was sitting in the darkening dreary room when a terrible shriek jarred and rang harshly out of the silence, and I heard a frightened scurry of feet dashing down the stairs. I waited, and the servant-maid staggered into the room and faced me, white and trembling.

"Oh, Miss Helen!" she whispered; "oh! for the Lord's sake, Miss Helen, what has happened? Look at my hand, miss; look at that hand!"

I drew her to the window, and saw there was a black wet stain upon her hand.

"I do not understand you," I said. "Will you explain to me?"

"I was doing your room just now," she began. "I was turning down the bed-clothes, and all of a sudden there was something fell upon my hand, wet, and I looked up, and the ceiling was black and dripping on me."

I looked hard at her and bit my lip.

"Come with me," I said. "Bring your candle with you."

The room I slept in was beneath my brother's, and as I went in I felt I was trembling. I looked up at the ceiling, and saw a patch, all black and wet, and a dew of black drops upon it, and a pool of horrible liquor soaking into the white bed-clothes.

I ran upstairs and knocked loudly.

"Oh, Francis, Francis, my dear brother," I cried, "what has happened to you?"

And I listened. There was a sound of choking, and a noise like water bubbling and regurgitating, but nothing else, and I called louder, but no answer came.

In spite of what Dr. Haberden had said, I went to him; with tears streaming down my cheeks I told him all that had happened, and he listened to me with a face set hard and grim.

"For your father's sake," he said at last, "I will go with you, though I can do nothing."

We went out together; the streets were dark and silent, and heavy with heat and a drought of many weeks. I saw the doctor's face white under the gas-lamps, and when we reached the house his hand was shaking.

We did not hesitate, but went upstairs directly. I held the lamp, and he called out in a loud, determined voice—

"Mr. Leicester, do you hear me? I insist on seeing you. Answer me at once."

There was no answer, but we both heard that choking noise I have mentioned.

"Mr. Leicester, I am waiting for you. Open the door this instant, or I shall break it down." And he called a third time in a voice that rang and echoed from the walls—

"Mr. Leicester! For the last time I order you to open the door."

"Ah!" he said, after a pause of heavy silence, "we are wasting time here. Will you be so kind as to get me a poker, or something of the kind?"

I ran into a little room at the back where odd articles were kept, and found a heavy adze-like tool that I thought might serve the doctor's purpose.

"Very good," he said, "that will do, I dare say. I give you notice, Mr. Leicester," he cried loudly at the keyhole, "that I am now about to break into your room."

Then I heard the wrench of the adze, and the woodwork split and cracked under it; with a loud crash the door suddenly burst open, and for a moment we started back aghast at a fearful screaming cry, no human voice, but as the roar of a monster, that burst forth inarticulate and struck at us out of the darkness.

"Hold the lamp," said the doctor, and we went in and glanced quickly round the room.

"There it is," said Dr. Haberden, drawing a quick breath; "look, in that corner."

I looked, and a pang of horror seized my heart as with a white-hot iron. There upon the floor was a dark and putrid mass, seething with corruption and hideous rottenness, neither liquid nor solid, but melting and changing before our eyes, and bubbling with unctuous oily bubbles like boiling pitch. And out of the midst of it shone two burning points like eyes, and I saw a writhing and stirring as of limbs, and something moved and lifted up what might have been an arm. The doctor took a step forward, raised the iron bar and struck at the burning points; he drove in the weapon, and struck again and again in the fury of loathing.

A week or two later, when I had recovered to some extent from the terrible shock, Dr. Haberden came to see me.

"I have sold my practice," he began, "and tomorrow I am sailing on a long voyage. I do not know whether I shall ever return to England; in all probability I shall buy a little land in California, and settle there for the remainder of my life. I have brought you this packet, which you may open and read when you feel able to do so. It contains the report of Dr. Chambers on what I submitted to him. Good-bye, Miss Leicester, good-bye."

When he was gone I opened the envelope; I could not wait, and proceeded to read the papers within. Here is the manuscript, and if you will allow me, I will read you the astounding story it contains.

"My dear Haberden," the letter began, "I have delayed inexcusably in answering your questions as to the white substance you sent me. To tell you the truth, I have hesitated for some time as to what course I should adopt, for there is a bigotry and orthodox standard in physical science as in theology, and I knew that if I told you the truth I should offend rooted prejudices which I once held dear myself. However, I have determined to be plain with you, and first I must enter into a short personal explanation.

"You have known me, Haberden, for many years as a scientific man; you and I have often talked of our profession together, and discussed the hopeless gulf that opens before the feet of those who think to attain to truth by any means whatsoever except the beaten way of experiment and observation in the sphere of material things. I remember the scorn with which you have spoken to me of men of science who have dabbled a little in the unseen, and have timidly hinted that perhaps the senses are not, after all, the eternal, impenetrable bounds of all knowledge, the everlasting walls beyond which no human being has ever passed. We have laughed together heartily, and I think justly, at the occult follies of the day, disguised under various names—the mesmerisms, spiritualisms, materializations, theosophies, all the rabble rout of

imposture, with their machinery of poor tricks and feeble con-
juring, the true back-parlour of shabby London streets. Yet, in
spite of what I have said, I must confess to you that I am no mate-
rialist, taking the word of course in its usual signification. It is
now many years since I have convinced myself—convinced
myself, a sceptic, remember—that the old ironbound theory is
utterly and entirely false. Perhaps this confession will not wound
you so sharply as it would have done twenty years ago; for I think
you cannot have failed to notice that for some time hypotheses
have been advanced by men of pure science which are nothing less
than transcendental, and I suspect that most modern chemists
and biologists of repute would not hesitate to subscribe the
dictum of the old Schoolman, *Omnia exeunt in mysterium,* which
means, I take it, that every branch of human knowledge if traced
up to its source and final principles vanishes into mystery. I need
not trouble you now with a detailed account of the painful steps
which led me to my conclusions; a few simple experiments suggested a doubt as to my then standpoint, and a train of thought
that rose from circumstances comparatively trifling brought me
far; my old conception of the universe has been swept away, and
I stand in a world that seems as strange and awful to me as the
endless waves of the ocean seen for the first time, shining, from a
peak in Darien. Now I know that the walls of sense that seemed
so impenetrable, that seemed to loom up above the heavens and
to be founded below the depths, and to shut us in for evermore,
are no such everlasting impassable barriers as we fancied, but
thinnest and most airy veils that melt away before the seeker, and
dissolve as the early mist of the morning about the brooks. I know
that you never adopted the extreme materialistic position; you did
not go about trying to prove a universal negative, for your logical

sense withheld you from that crowning absurdity; but I am sure that you will find all that I am saying strange and repellent to your habits of thought. Yet, Haberden, what I tell you is the truth, nay, to adopt our common language, the sole and scientific truth, verified by experience; and the universe is verily more splendid and more awful than we used to dream. The whole universe, my friend, is a tremendous sacrament; a mystic, ineffable force and energy, veiled by an outward form of matter; and man, and the sun and the other stars, and the flower of the grass, and the crystal in the test-tube, are each and every one as spiritual, as material, and subject to an inner working.

"You will perhaps wonder, Haberden, whence all this tends; but I think a little thought will make it clear. You will understand that from such a standpoint the whole view of things is changed, and what we thought incredible and absurd may be possible enough. In short, we must look at legend and belief with other eyes, and be prepared to accept tales that had become mere fables. Indeed this is no such great demand. After all, modern science will concede as much, in a hypocritical manner; you must not, it is true, believe in witchcraft, but you may credit hypnotism; ghosts are out of date, but there is a good deal to be said for the theory of telepathy. Give superstition a Greek name, and believe in it, should almost be a proverb.

"So much for my personal explanation. You sent me, Haberden, a phial, stoppered and sealed, containing a small quantity of flaky white powder, obtained from a chemist who has been dispensing it to one of your patients. I am not surprised to hear that this powder refused to yield any results to your analysis. It is a substance which was known to a few many hundred years ago, but which I never expected to have submitted to me from the shop of a modern apothecary. There seems no reason to doubt the truth of the man's tale; he no doubt got, as he says, the rather uncommon salt you prescribed from the wholesale chemist's, and it has probably remained on his shelf for twenty years, or perhaps longer. Here what we call chance and coincidence begin to work; during all these years the salt in the bottle was exposed to certain recurring variations of temperature, variations probably ranging from 40° to 80°. And, as it happens, such changes, recurring year after year at irregular intervals, and with varying degrees of intensity and duration, have constituted a process, and a process so complicated and so delicate, that I question whether modern scientific apparatus directed with the utmost precision could produce the same result. The white powder you sent me is something very different from the drug you prescribed; it is the powder from which the wine of the Sabbath, the *Vinum Sabbati*, was prepared. No doubt you have read of the Witches' Sabbath, and have laughed at the tales which terrified our ancestors; the black cats, and the broomsticks, and dooms pronounced against some old woman's cow. Since I have known the truth I have often reflected that it is on the whole a happy thing that such burlesque as this is believed, for it serves to conceal much that it is better should not be known generally. However, if you care to read the appendix to Payne Knight's monograph, you will find that the true Sabbath was something very different, though the writer has very nicely refrained from printing all he knew. The secrets of the true Sabbath were the secrets of remote times surviving into the Middle Ages, secrets of an evil science which existed long before Aryan man entered Europe. Men and women, seduced from their homes on specious pretences, were met by beings well qualified to assume, as they did assume, the part of devils, and taken by their guides to some desolate and lonely place, known to the initiate by long tradition, and unknown to all else. Perhaps it was a cave in some bare and windswept hill, perhaps some inmost recess of a great forest, and there the Sabbath was held. There, in the blackest hour of night, the *Vinum Sabbati* was prepared, and this evil gruel was poured forth and offered to the neophytes, and they partook of an infernal sacrament; *sumentes calicem principis inferorum,* as an old author well expresses it. And suddenly, each one that had drunk found himself attended by a companion, a share of glamour and unearthly allurement, beckoning him apart, to share in joys more exquisite, more piercing than the thrill of any dream, to the consummation of the marriage of the Sabbath. It is hard to write of such things as these, and chiefly because that shape that allured with loveliness was no hallucination, but, awful as it is to express, the man himself. By the power of that Sabbath wine, a few grains of white powder thrown into a glass of water, the house of life was riven asunder and the human trinity dissolved, and the worm which never dies, that which lies sleeping within us all, was made tangible and an external thing, and clothed with a garment of flesh. And then, in the hour of midnight, the primal fall was repeated and re-presented, and the awful thing veiled in the mythos of the Tree in the Garden was done anew. Such was the *nuptioe Sabbati.*

"I prefer to say no more; you, Haberden, know as well as I do that the most trivial laws of life are not to be broken with impunity; and for so terrible an act as this, in which the very inmost place of the temple was broken open and denied, a terrible vengeance followed. What began with corruption ended also with corruption."

Underneath is the following in Dr. Haberden's writing:—

"The whole of the above is unfortunately strictly and entirely true. Your brother confessed all to me on that morning when I saw him in his room. My attention was first attracted to the bandaged hand, and I forced him to show it to me. What I saw made me, a medical man of many years' standing, grow sick with loathing, and the story I was forced to listen to was infinitely more frightful than I could have believed possible. It has tempted me to doubt the Eternal Goodness which can permit nature to offer such hideous possibilities; and if you had not with your own eyes seen the end, I should have said to you—disbelieve it all. I have not, I think, many more weeks to live, but you are young, and may forget all this.

JOSEPH HABERDEN, M.D."

In the course of two or three months I heard that Dr. Haberden had died at sea shortly after the ship left England.

Stephen Jones lives in London, England. He is the winner of three World Fantasy Awards, three Horror Writers Association Bram Stoker Awards and three International Horror Guild Awards, as well as being a Hugo Award nominee and a sixteen-times recipient of the British Fantasy Award. One of Britain's most acclaimed anthologists of horror and dark fantasy, he has more than eighty-five books to his credit, including *H.P. Lovecraft's Book of Horror, Shadows Over Innsmouth, Weird Shadows Over Innsmouth* and the annual *Mammoth Book of Best New Horror* series. You can visit his web site at www.herebedragons.co.uk/jones

Randy Broecker lives in Chicago, Illinois. Inspired by the pulp magazines and EC comics he read as a child, his artwork has appeared in books published by major imprints on both sides of the Atlantic, including *Weird Shadows Over Innsmouth* and *The Mammoth Book of Vampire Stories by Women*. He was Artist Guest of Honour at the 2002 World Horror Convention and is the author of the World Fantasy Award-nominated study *Fantasy of the 20th Century: An Illustrated History* from Collector's Press, which also formed part of a three-in-one omnibus entitled *Art of Imagination: 20th Century Visions of Science Fiction, Horror, and Fantasy*.